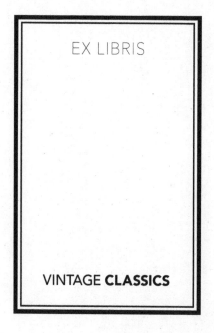

EX LIBRIS

VINTAGE CLASSICS

JOSÉ SARAMAGO

José Saramago is one of the most important international writers of the last hundred years. Born in Portugal in 1922, he was in his sixties when he came to prominence as a writer with the publication of *Baltasar & Blimunda*. A huge body of work followed, translated into almost fifty languages, and in 1998 he was awarded the Nobel Prize for Literature. Saramago died in June 2010.

Giovanni Pontiero, formerly Reader in Latin-American Literature at the University of Manchester, was, until his death in 1997, Saramago's regular English translator. His translation of *The Gospel According to Jesus Christ* was awarded the Teixeira-Gomes Prize for Portuguese translation. He was also the principal translator into English of the works of Clarice Lispector.

JOSÉ SARAMAGO

The Gospel According to Jesus Christ

TRANSLATED FROM THE PORTUGUESE BY
Giovanni Pontiero

VINTAGE

Vintage
20 Vauxhall Bridge Road,
London SW1V 2SA

Vintage Classics is part of the Penguin Random House group of companies
whose addresses can be found at global.penguinrandomhouse.com.

Penguin
Random House
UK

First published in Portuguese with the title *O Evangello segundo
Jesus Cristo* by Editorial Caminho, SARL, Lisbon 1991
First published in Great Britain by The Harvill Press in 1999
This edition reissued by Vintage in 2017

www.vintage-books.co.uk

A CIP catalogue record for this book is available from the British Library

ISBN 9781860466847

Printed and bound in Great Britain by Clays Ltd, Elcograf S.p.A.

Penguin Random House is committed to a sustainable future
for our business, our readers and our planet. This book is made
from Forest Stewardship Council® certified paper.

MIX
Paper from
responsible sources
FSC
www.fsc.org FSC® C018179

FOR PILAR

Forasmuch as many have taken in hand to set forth in order a declaration of those things which are most surely believed among us, even as they delivered them unto us, which from the beginning were eye-witnesses, and ministers of the word, it seemed good to me also, having had perfect understanding of all things from the very first, to write unto thee in order, most excellent Theophilus, that thou mightest know the certainty of those things, wherein thou hast been instructed.

LUKE, I, 1–4

Quod scripsi, scripsi.
What I have written, I have written.

PONTIUS PILATE

The sun appears in one of the upper corners of the rectangle, to the left of anyone looking at the picture. Representing the sun is a man's head which sends out rays of brilliant light and sinuous flames, like a wavering compass in search of the right direction, and this head has a tearful face, contorted by spasms of pain which refuse to abate. The gaping mouth sends up a cry we shall never hear, for none of these things is real, what we are contemplating is mere paper and ink, and nothing more. Beneath the sun we see a naked man tied to a tree trunk with a cloth tied round his loins to cover those parts we call private or the genital organs, and his feet are resting on a piece of wood set crosswise, to give him support, and to prevent his feet from slipping, they are held by two nails driven deeply into the wood. Judging from the anguished expression on the man's face, and from his eyes which are raised to heaven, this must be the Good Thief. His ringlets are another reassuring sign, for it is well known that this is how angels and archangels wear their hair, and so it would appear that the repentant criminal is already ascending to the world of heavenly creatures. Impossible to say whether the trunk is still a tree that has simply been arbitrarily transformed into an instrument of torture while continuing to draw nourishment from the soil through its roots, inasmuch as the lower part of the picture is covered by a man with a long beard. Richly attired in loose, flowing robes, he is looking upwards but not towards heaven. This solemn posture and sad countenance must surely belong to Joseph of Arimathaea, because the only other person who comes to mind, Simon of Cyrene, after being forced to help the condemned man to carry his cross, as was the practice when these executions took place, went about his own affairs, much more anxious about a business transaction which called for an urgent decision than about the sufferings of a miserable wretch about to be crucified. Now then, this Joseph of Arimathaea is that affluent and good-hearted man who donated a grave for the burial of the greatest criminal of all, but this act of generosity will be to no avail when the time comes to consider his beatification, let alone canonisation. All he has around his head is the turban he always wears outdoors, unlike this woman in the foreground of the picture whose hair hangs all the way down her back as she leans forward, enhanced by the supreme glory of a halo, and in her case edged with the finest embroidery. The kneeling woman must be Mary because, as we know, all the women gathered here have this name, with one exception, for she is also called Magdalene. Anyone viewing this picture, who is aware of the elementary facts of life, will swear at first sight that this is precisely the woman called Magdalene for only someone with her disreputable past would have dared to turn up at such a solemn occasion wearing a low-cut dress with a close-fitting bodice to emphasize her ample bosom, which inevitably attracts the lewd stares of passing men, putting their souls at grave risk, dragged to their perdition by that sinful flesh. Yet the expression on her face is one of sad contrition and her wilting body conveys nothing other than her sorrowing soul, which we cannot ignore, even if it is concealed by tempting flesh, for this woman could be completely naked, had the artist so chosen to portray her, and she would still be deserving of our respect and veneration. Mary Magdalene, if that is her name, is holding to her lips the hand of another woman who has collapsed on to the ground as if bereft of strength or mortally wounded. Her name is also Mary, second in order of appearance, but undoubtedly the most important Mary of all, if the central position she occupies in the lower part of the composition has any significance. Apart from her grieving expression and drooping hands, nothing can be seen of her body covered by the copious folds of her mantle and by her tunic tied at the waist by a coarsely woven cord. She is older than the other Mary, which is reason enough, although not the only one, why her halo should be much more elaborate, at least this is what one is entitled to conclude unless given more precise information about

2

the criteria of rank, privilege and seniority observed at that time. Bearing in mind, however, the considerable influence of this iconography exercised by one means or another, only some unlikely inhabitant from another planet, where no such drama has ever been enacted, could fail to recognize that this anguished woman is the widow of a carpenter called Joseph and the mother of numerous sons and daughters, although only one of her children, decreed by fate or whosoever governs it, was to achieve a little fame during his lifetime and a great deal more after his death. Reclining on her left side, Mary, the mother of Jesus, rests her forearm on the hip of another woman, also kneeling and also called Mary, and who might well be the real Mary Magdalene although we can neither see nor imagine the neckline of her tunic. Like the first woman in this trinity, she wears her long tresses hanging loose down her back, but to all appearances they are fair, unless it is only by chance that the penstrokes are different, more delicate, leaving empty spaces between the locks, thus allowing the engraver to lighten the overall tone of the woman's hair. We are not trying to prove that Mary Magdalene was, in fact, blonde, but simply conforming to the popular belief that women with blonde hair, whether it be natural or dyed, are the most effective instruments of sin and perdition. So Mary Magdalene who, as everyone knows, was as wicked a woman as ever lived, must have been blonde if we are to respect the firm opinion held, for better or worse, by half of mankind. However, it is not because this third Mary has fairer skin and hair than the first one that we are suggesting, notwithstanding the damning evidence of the other's low-cut dress and exposed bosom, that she is the Magdalene. The overwhelming evidence which confirms her identity is that this third Mary, who is distractedly supporting the limp arm of the mother of Jesus, is looking upwards and her enraptured gaze ascends with such power that it appears to elevate her entire being like a bright aureole capable of outshining the halo already encircling her head and of suppressing every thought and emotion. Only a woman who had loved as much as we believe Mary Magdalene to have loved could possibly have such an expression, conclusive proof that it is her and no other, and thus excluding the woman standing beside her. This is the fourth Mary, her hands half-raised in a gesture of piety, her expression vague, accompanied on this side of the engraving by a youth, barely adolescent, his knee bent languidly

3

as, with an affected and theatrical gesture of his right hand, he presents the four women playing out the poignant drama in the foreground. This is John, who looks so youthful, with his hair in ringlets and trembling lips. Like Joseph of Arimathaea, he also shuts out some of the background, his body concealing the foot of the tree trunk on the other side where no birds nest. All we see at the top is a second naked man hoisted into the air and bound and nailed to the wood like the first thief, but this one has smooth hair, his eyes lowered, perhaps still capable of seeing the ground below, his thin, emaciated face arousing our compassion, unlike the thief on the other side who, even in the final throes of torment, defiantly shows his face which was not always so pale, for thieving gave him a good living. Thin and smooth-haired, his head turned towards the earth that will devour him, condemned to both death and hell, this pathetic creature must be the Bad Thief, an upright man when all is said and done, who, free from divine and human laws, was honest enough not to pretend to believe that sudden repentance suffices to redeem a whole lifetime of evil or a mere moment of weakness. Above him, also weeping and wailing like the sun in front, we can see the moon in the guise of a woman with the most incongruous ring in one ear, an unprecedented liberty no artist or poet would ever be likely to emulate. Both sun and moon illuminate the Earth in equal measure, but the ambience of light is circular and shadowless causing everything on the distant horizon to stand out clearly, turrets and walls, a drawbridge crossing a moat where water glistens, Gothic arches, and on the crest of the furthest hill, the motionless sails of a windmill. Somewhat closer, because of the deceptive perspective, four horsemen with armour, lance and helmet, proudly parade their horses with admirable dexterity, but they appear to have come to the end of their display as they make farewell gestures to an invisible audience. The same impression of closing festivities is given by that foot-soldier who is on the point of going off, carrying something in his right hand which, seen from a distance, could be a cloth, perhaps even a mantle or tunic, while two more soldiers look annoyed and frustrated as if they had lost at gambling, although from afar it is difficult to make out the expressions on those minute faces. Hovering over these common soldiers and the walled city are four angels, two of them portrayed full length. They weep and mourn, with the exception of the angel who solemnly holds a goblet to the crucified man's right side in order to collect the very last drop of blood streaming from a lance wound. In this place known as Golgotha, many have met the same cruel fate and many others will follow them, but this naked man, nailed through his hands and feet to a cross, the son of Joseph and Mary, named Jesus, is the only condemned man whom posterity will honour by inscribing his initials in capitals, for all the others will soon be forgotten. So this is he whom Joseph of Arimathaea and Mary Magdalene are gazing upon, this is he who causes the Sun and Moon to weep, and who only a moment ago praised the Good Thief and despised the Bad Thief, because he failed to understand that there is no difference between the one and the other, or, if there is any difference, it is something else, for Good and Evil do not exist in themselves, each is simply the absence of the other. Shining above his head with a thousand rays brighter than those of the sun and moon put together, is a placard in Roman letters proclaiming him King of the Jews, surrounded by a wounding crown of thorns like that worn without their even knowing, or any visible sign of blood, by all those men who are not even allowed to be sovereign of their own bodies. Unlike the two thieves, Jesus has nowhere to rest his feet, the entire weight of his body would be supported by his hands nailed to the wood had he not enough life left in him to hold himself erect over his bent legs, that life which is nearing its end as the blood continues to spurt from the aforesaid wound. Between the two wedges which keep the cross upright and which have also been driven into a dark fissure in the ground, a gaping wound in the earth as irremediable as any human burial, there is a skull and also a shinbone and a shoulder blade, but what concerns us is the skull, for this is what Golgotha means, a skull, the two words do not appear to mean the same thing, but we would notice some difference if, instead of writing skull and Golgotha, we were to write golgotha and Skull. No one knows who put these human remains here or for what purpose, perhaps it was simply a sly and ominous warning to these poor wretches about the fate that awaits them before they turn to earth, dust and nothingness. But there are also some who claim that this is Adam's skull, risen from the murky depths of ancient geological strata, and because it can no longer return there, eternally condemned to confront nothing but earth, its only possible paradise and forever lost. Further back, in the same field where the horsemen

5

execute one last manoeuvre, a man is walking away but looking back in this direction. In his left hand he is carrying a bucket and in his right a staff. On the tip of the staff there ought to be a sponge, not easy to see from here, and the bucket, one can safely wager, contains water with vinegar. One day, and forever more, this man will be much maligned and accused of having given Jesus vinegar out of spite and contempt when he asked for water, but if truth be told, he offered him vinegar and water because at that time it was one of the best ways of quenching thirst. The man walks away, does not wait for the end, he has done all he could to assuage the mortal thirst of the three condemned men, and made no distinction between Jesus and the Thieves, for the simple reason that these are things of this Earth which will persist on Earth, and from these things the only possible history will be written.

Night is far from over. Hanging from a nail near the door, the oil lamp is burning, but the flickering flame, like a small, luminous almond, tremulous and unsteady, can barely impinge on the encroaching darkness which fills the house from top to bottom and penetrates the furthest corners where the shadows are so dense that they appear to form one solid mass. Joseph awoke with a fright, as if someone had roughly shaken him by the shoulder, but he must have been dreaming because he lives alone in this house with his wife who has not so much as stirred and is fast asleep. Not only is it unusual for him to wake in the middle of the night, but he rarely opens his eyes before daybreak when light begins to filter through the chink in the door, the grey, cold morning light. How often had he thought of repairing the door, what could be easier for a carpenter than to cover that chink with a piece of wood left over from some other job, but he had become so accustomed to seeing that vertical strip of light when he opened his eyes in the morning that he reached the absurd conclusion that without it he would be trapped forever in the shadows of sleep, in the darkness of his own body and in that of the world. That chink in the door was as much a part of the house as the walls and ceiling, as the oven and earthen floor. Whispering, to avoid disturbing his wife who was still asleep, he recited words of thanksgiving, words he recited each morning upon returning from the mysterious land of dreams, Thanks be to You, Almighty God, King of the Universe, Who has mercifully restored my soul to life. Perhaps because he had not fully regained the power of all five senses, unless at that time people were not yet aware of

7

some of them or, conversely, about to lose others which would serve little purpose nowadays, Joseph examined himself as if watching from a distance while his own body slowly came to be occupied by a soul gradually making its return, like trickling waters as they wend their way in rivulets and streams before penetrating the depths of the earth, feeding sap into stems and leaves. Looking at Mary as she lay sleeping beside him, Joseph began to realize just how laborious this return to wakefulness could be and a disturbing thought occurred to him, this wife of his, fast asleep, was really a body without a soul, for no soul is present in a body while it sleeps, otherwise there would be no sense in our thanking God each morning for having restored our soul as we awaken. Suddenly a voice within him asked, What thing or person inside us dreams what we dream, then he wondered, Are dreams perhaps the soul's memories of our body, and this seemed a feasible explanation. Mary stirred, could her soul have been near at hand, already here in the house, but in the end she did not awaken, no doubt in the midst of some troubled dream, and after giving a deep sigh, like a broken sob, she drew closer to her husband with a sensuousness she would never have dared indulge in while awake. Joseph pulled the thick, rough blanket over his shoulders and snuggled up close to Mary. He could feel her warmth, perfumed like a linen-chest filled with dried herbs, gradually penetrating the fibres of his tunic and merging with the heat of his own body. Then slowly closing his eyes, his thoughts suspended, and oblivious to his soul, he sank back into a deep sleep.

When he woke again, the cock was crowing. A dim, greyish light filtered through the chink in the door. Having waited patiently for the shadows of the night to disperse, time was preparing the way for yet another day to reach the world. For we no longer live in that fabulous age when the sun, to whom we owe so much, was generous to the point of halting its journey over Gibeon, thus giving Joshua ample time to overcome the five kings who were besieging the city. Joseph sat up on his mat, drew back the sheet, and at that moment the cock crowed for a second time, reminding him that there was another prayer of thanksgiving to be said, leaving aside any merits bestowed on the cock when the Creator distributed them among His creatures, Praise be to You, oh Lord, our God, King of the Universe, Who gave the cock the intelligence to distinguish between night and day, prayed Joseph, and the cock crowed for a third time. At the first sign of daybreak all the cocks in the neighbourhood would usually crow back to each other, but today they remained silent, as if their night had not yet ended or was just beginning. Joseph looked at his wife's face, puzzled by her deep slumber, for normally the slightest noise would awaken her as if she were a bird. Some mysterious power appeared to be hovering over Mary, pressing her down without completely immobilising her, for even in the shadows her body could be seen to tremble gently, like water rippling in the breeze. Could she be ill, he wondered, but he was distracted from this worrying thought by a sudden urge to urinate, and this, too, was unusual. He rarely felt any need to relieve himself at this early hour or with such urgency. Slipping quietly from under the sheet to avoid disturbing his wife, for it is written that a man should do everything possible to maintain his self-respect, he cautiously opened the creaking door and went out into the yard. At that hour of the morning everything seemed tinged in ashen hues. Joseph headed for a low shed where he tethered his donkey and there he relieved himself, listening with dreamy satisfaction to the explosive sound of his own urine as it spurted on to the hay scattered on the ground. The donkey turned its head, two huge eyes shining in the dark, then gave its furry ears a vigorous shake before sticking its nose back into the manger, foraging for any remains with thick, sensuous lips. Joseph fetched the large pitcher used for washing, tipped it sideways and let the water pour over his hands, then drying them on his tunic he praised God Who in His infinite wisdom had endowed mankind with the essential orifices and vessels in order to live, for if any one of them should fail to close or open as required, this would certainly result in death. Looking up at the sky, Joseph felt overwhelmed. The sun is slow in appearing and in the sky there is not even a hint of dawn's crimson tints, no shades of rose or cherry, nothing except clouds to be seen from where Joseph was standing, one vast roof of low clouds like tiny flattened balls of wool, all identical and in the same shade of violet which deepens and becomes luminous on the side where the sun breaks through, before becoming increasingly darker until merging with what remains of the night over on the other side. Joseph had never seen such a sky, although old men often spoke of portents in the skies which attested to the power of God, rainbows which covered one half of the celestial vault, towering ladders which one day connected heaven and earth, providential showers of manna from heaven, but never of this mysterious colour which might just as easily be the beginning or end of this world, floating and hovering over the Earth, a roof made up of thousands of tiny clouds which were almost touching each other, and scattered in all directions like the stones of the desert. Terror-stricken, he thought the world was coming to an end, and there he was, the only witness of God's final judgement, yes, the only one. Silence reigns in heaven and on earth, no sounds can be heard from the nearby houses, not so much as a human voice, a child weeping, the sound of a prayer or curse, a gust of wind, the bleating of a goat or the barking of a dog. Why are the cocks not crowing, he muttered to himself, and he repeated the question anxiously as if the crowing of cocks might bring one last hope of salvation. Then the sky began to change. Almost imperceptibly, pink tinges and streaks gradually crept into the violet on the lower side of this cloud formation, before it finally turned red and disappeared. There one minute, it was gone the next, and without any warning the sky exploded into a luminous wind, multiplied into shafts of gold that pierced the clouds which were no longer tiny but inflated and formidable, enormous barges hoisting blazing sails and plying a sky which had at last been liberated. Joseph's fears subsided, his eyes widened in astonishment and wonder, and with good reason, for he alone was witnessing this spectacle. In a loud voice he praised the Lord of all creation for the eternal majesty of those heavens whose ineffable splendours leave men struggling with simple words of gratitude, Thanks be to You, oh Lord, for this and that and the next thing. As he spoke, the tumult of life, whether summoned by his voice, or rushing through a door which had carelessly been left wide open, invaded the space which had previously belonged to silence, leaving it scarcely any room, the odd patch here and there, such as those tiny marshes which the murmuring forests engulf and hide from view. The sun came up and spread its light, a vision of almost unbearable beauty, two enormous hands sending into flight a shimmering bird of paradise which displayed its great peacock's tail with a thousand iridescent eyes, causing a nameless bird nearby to burst into song. Just then, a gust of wind hit Joseph in the face, caught his beard and tunic, eddied round him like a tiny whirlwind moving across the desert, unless he was imagining things and this was nothing more than blood rushing to his head, a shiver going up his spine like a tongue of fire, and betraying a quite different and more insistent urge.

As if moving inside a swirling column of air, Joseph went into the house and shut the door behind him, there he paused for a moment, waiting for his eyes to become accustomed to the shadows. The nearby lamp cast a faint glow and gave scarcely any light. Wide awake, Mary lay on her back, listening and staring into space as if waiting. Joseph furtively approached and slowly drew back the sheet. She averted her eyes, began tugging at the hem of her tunic and no sooner had she pulled it up as far as her navel than he was on top of her, his tunic hitched up to the waist. Meanwhile Mary had opened her legs, or they had opened by themselves as she dreamed, and remained open, perhaps because of this sudden lassitude or the mere premonition of a married woman who knows her duty. God, Who is omnipresent, was there, but pure spirit that He is, was unable to see how Joseph's skin came into contact with that of Mary, how his flesh penetrated hers as had been ordained, and perhaps He was not even there when the holy seed of Joseph spilled into the precious womb of Mary, both sacrosanct, being the fount and chalice of life. For in truth, there are things God himself does not understand, even though He created them. Out in the yard God could neither hear the anguished gasp which escaped Joseph's lips as he experienced an orgasm nor the gentle moan Mary was unable to repress. Joseph had rested on Mary's body for no more than a minute, perhaps even less. Pulling down her tunic and drawing up the sheet, she covered her face with the other arm. Joseph stood in the middle of the room, raised his hands and, looking up at the ceiling, gave the most dire thanksgiving of all which is reserved for men, I thank You, Almighty God, King of the Universe, for not having made me a woman. By then, God must have already abandoned the yard, for the walls did not shake or cave in, nor did the earth open up. All that could be heard was Mary saying for the first time, in that submissive voice one always expects from women, Thanks be to You, oh Lord, for having made me according to Your will. Now there is no difference between these words and those spoken to the angel Gabriel, for clearly anyone who could say, Behold the handmaiden of the Lord, do with me as You will, might just as easily have used those other words. Then the wife of the carpenter Joseph got up from her mat, rolled it up together with that of her husband, and folded the sheet they shared in common.

Joseph and Mary lived in a village called Nazareth, a place of little importance and with few inhabitants, in the region of Galilee, in a house no different from the others, like a lopsided cube made of bricks and clay, and as poor as poor could be. No striking examples of imaginative architecture were to be found here where the same uninteresting shape appeared everywhere. To economize on raw materials, the house had been built into a hillside which formed the rear wall and allowed easy access on to the flat roof serving as a terrace. As we know, Joseph was a carpenter by trade and fairly efficient, although he had neither the skill nor the talent for jobs which required fine workmanship. This criticism should not be taken too seriously for one needs time to gain experience and acquire certain skills, and we must not forget that Joseph is barely in his twenties and lives in a place with few resources and even fewer opportunities. However we must not measure a man's worth simply on the basis of his professional skills, it must be said that, for all his youth, this Joseph is one of the most honest and pious men to be found in Nazareth, assiduous in attending the synagogue, prompt in carrying out his duties, and while he may not have been endowed with any special powers of eloquence, he can sustain an argument and make astute observations, especially when given a chance to use some apt image or metaphor related to his work, such as the carpentry of the universe. Never having possessed, however, what one might call a truly creative imagination, he will not succeed during his brief life in coming up with a memorable parable to be handed down to posterity, let alone one of those brilliant conceits which are so clearly expressed that there is nothing more to say and yet which are so obscure and ambiguous that they intrigue scholars and intellectuals for years to come.

As for Mary's talents, these are even less apparent and no more than we might expect of a sixteen-year old girl who, although married, is still a vulnerable adolescent, a mere slip of a girl as it were, for even in those days people used such expressions. Notwithstanding her frail appearance, Mary works as hard as all the other women, carding, spinning and weaving cloth, baking the family bread each morning, fetching water from the well and then carrying it up the steep slope, a large pitcher supported on her head and another resting on her hip. Then in the late afternoon she sets off through the byways and woodlands of the Lord, gathering firewood and cutting stubble and filling an extra basket with cow's dung and the thistles and briers which thrive on the upper slopes of Nazareth, the best thing God could ever have invented for lighting a fire or braiding a crown. It would have been easier to load everything on to a donkey's back, were it not for the simple fact that Joseph needed the beast to carry his wood. Mary goes barefoot to the well, she goes barefoot into the fields, clad in well-worn clothes which are forever getting soiled and torn and which constantly need washing and mending, any new clothes or little extras are reserved for her husband, for women like Mary make do with very little. When attending the synagogue, she enters by the side door, as the law commands for women, and even if she should find herself there with thirty other women, with all the women of Nazareth, or the entire female population of Galilee, even so they are obliged to wait until at least ten men arrive for the service in which the women will only be passive participants. Unlike Joseph, her husband, Mary is neither upright nor pious, but she is not to blame for these moral blemishes, the fault lies with the language she speaks, if not with the men who invented it, because that language has no feminine form for the words upright and pious.

Now one fine day, four weeks after that unforgettable morning when the clouds in the sky mysteriously turned violet, Joseph happened to be at home. The sun was about to set and he was sitting on the floor, eating his food with his fingers, as was then the custom, while Mary stood there waiting for him to finish before having her own supper. Neither of them spoke for he had nothing to say and she was unable to express what was on her mind. Suddenly a beggar appeared at the yard gate, a somewhat rare occurrence in this village where people were poor, a fact unlikely to have escaped the begging fraternity which had a nose for places where there were rich pickings for the asking, and this was certainly not the case here. Nevertheless Mary ladled a good portion of the lentils with chopped onions and mashed chick-peas laid aside for her own supper into a bowl and took it out to the beggar who sat on the ground beyond the threshold. Mary did not need her husband's spoken permission, he merely nodded his approval for, as everyone knows, these were times when words were superfluous and a simple thumbs up or down was enough to condemn someone to death or grant a reprieve, as in the arenas of ancient Rome. Although quite different, this twilight, too, was spectacular with its myriad wisps of cloud scattered through the sky, rose-coloured, mother-of-pearl, salmon-pink, cherry, these are adjectives used here on Earth so that we may understand each other, for none of these colours, as far as we know, have names in heaven. The beggar must have gone without food for three days, and that is real hunger, to have scraped and licked his bowl clean so quickly, and back he comes to return the bowl and express his gratitude. Opening the door, Mary found the beggar standing there, but somehow looking so much broader and taller than before. So it must be true that there is a vast difference between having eaten and going hungry, for this man's face and eyes were glowing, his tattered clothes blowing about in some mysterious wind, blurring her vision so that those rags took on the appearance of rich garments, a sight to be seen to be believed. Mary stretched out her hands to receive the earthenware bowl which, because of some extraordinary optical illusion, perhaps due to the shimmering lights in the sky, was transformed into a vessel of the purest gold and, as the bowl passed from his hands into hers, the beggar proclaimed in resonant tones, for even the poor man's voice had changed, May the Lord bless you, good woman, and give you all the children your husband may desire, but may the same Lord protect you from my sad fate, for alas I have nowhere to rest my head in this wretched world. Mary held the bowl in cupped hands, one chalice resting on another, as if waiting for the beggar to fill it, which is precisely what he did. Without any warning he bent down and gathered a handful of earth and then, raising his arm, allowed it to trickle through his fingers while reciting in a low voice, Earth to earth, ashes to ashes, dust to dust, nothing begins without coming to an end, every beginning comes from some ending. Mary was puzzled and asked him, What does that mean, but the beggar simply replied, Good woman, you have a child in your womb and that is man's only destiny, to begin and to end, to end and begin, How did you know I'm with child, Even before there is any swelling, a child can be seen shining through its mother's eyes, If that is true, then my husband must already have seen his child in my eyes, Perhaps he's not looking at you when you look at him, Who are you who knows so much without hearing it from my own lips, I am an angel, but tell no one.

Just then his shining robes turned back to rags, the giant unexpectedly shrivelled up as if licked by a tongue of fire, and this wondrous transformation was enacted just in time, thanks be to God, for no sooner had the beggar quietly disappeared than Joseph emerged in the doorway, his suspicions aroused by whispering voices and Mary's prolonged absence. What else did the beggar want, he asked, and Mary, at a loss for words, could only repeat, From earth to earth, from ashes to ashes, from dust to dust, nothing begins without coming to an end, nothing ends without having a beginning. Was that what he said, Yes, and he also said that a father's child shines through its mother's eyes, Look at me, I'm looking, I can see a gleam in your eyes, said Joseph, and Mary told him, It must be your child. As the evening sky changed from blue to the sombre shades of night, the contents of the bowl began to glow with a dark radiance which transformed Mary's face, and her eyes seemed to belong to a much older woman. Are you pregnant, Joseph finally asked her, Yes, I am, replied Mary, Why didn't you tell me sooner, I meant to tell you today and was only waiting until you'd finished eating, And then the beggar turned up, That's right, What else did he have to say for he certainly took his time, That the Lord should give me all the children you might wish for, What have you got in that bowl to make it shine so, Nothing but earth, Soil is black, clay is green and sand is white, of these three sand alone glows in the sunlight, but it is night, Forgive me, I'm only a woman and cannot explain these things. You say he took some earth from the ground and dropped it into the bowl, at the same time uttering the words, Earth to earth, Yes, those very words.

Joseph went to open the gate, looked right and left. No sign of him, he's vanished, he told her, and feeling reassured, Mary retraced her steps to the house. She knew that the beggar, if he really was an angel, could only be seen if he so desired. She set the bowl down on the stone slab of the hearth, removed a live coal from the fire and lit the oil lamp, blowing until she raised a tiny flame. Looking bemused, Joseph returned indoors. He tried to disguise his suspicions and moved with the poise and solemnity of a patriarch which looked odd in someone so young. Furtively he examined the bowl filled with luminous earth, his ironic expression betraying his scepticism, but if he was trying to assert male superiority he was wasting his time, for Mary's eyes were lowered and her thoughts elsewhere. Using a tiny stick, Joseph poked at the earth, intrigued as he watched it darken when disturbed, only to regain its brilliance, sparkling light darting in all directions over the dull surface. There's some mystery here I cannot fathom, either the beggar brought this earth with him and you thought he gathered it here, or there is some magic at work, for who has ever seen luminous earth here in Nazareth. Mary remained silent. She was eating the remains of the lentils with onions and mashed chick-peas along with some bread dipped in oil. As she broke bread, she observed the Holy Law by giving thanks in the humble tones befitting a woman, Praise be to You, Adonai, Lord God and King of the Universe, Who can bring bread forth from the earth. She continued eating in silence while Joseph mused at length as if interpreting a verse from the Torah in the synagogue, or a phrase from the prophets, the words Mary had spoken, words he himself had used when breaking bread, and he tried to imagine what corn might grow and thrive from luminous earth, what bread it would produce and what light we would carry within were we to nourish ourselves on such bread. Are you sure the beggar scooped it up from the ground, he asked Mary a second time, and Mary answered, Yes, I'm quite sure. Perhaps it was shining all the time. No, I'm sure it wasn't shining on the ground. Such certainty would have allayed the worst fears of any man confronted with the sayings and doings of women in general and of his own wife in particular, but Joseph believed, like all men at that time and in this place, that the truly wise man is he who is on his guard against the wiles and deceptions of women. To converse little with women and pay them even less heed must be the motto of the prudent husband mindful of the wise advice of the words of the rabbi Josephat ben Yochanan, for at the hour of death each man must give account of any idle conversations he may have held with his wife. Joseph asked himself whether this conversation with Mary could be deemed necessary and having decided that it could, given the unusual nature of what had happened, he swore to himself that he would never forget the holy words of the rabbi, his namesake, for Josephat is the same as Joseph, rather than suffer remorse at the hour of death which, God willing, would be peaceful. Finally, after asking himself whether he should confide in the Elders of the synagogue about this curious affair of the mysterious beggar and the luminous earth, he decided that he must tell them in order to ease his conscience and keep the peace in his own home.

Mary finished eating. She took the bowls outside to wash them but, needless to say, not the one used by the beggar. There were now two lights in the house, that of the oil lamp struggling valiantly against the darkness of night and that luminous aura, flickering yet constant, like a sun which is slow in appearing. Seated on the floor, Mary was waiting for her husband to resume the conversation, but Joseph has nothing more to say to her as he mentally rehearses the speech he is to make tomorrow before the council of Elders. He finds it frustrating not to know precisely what transpired between his wife and the beggar, to know what else they might have said to each other, but he decides to question her no further since she is unlikely to divulge any more. He might as well believe the story she has already told him twice, because if she is lying, he will never know, but she will know and almost certainly be laughing at him, her mantle covering her face, just as Eve mocked Adam, but behind his back, for at that time people did not wear mantles. One thought led to another and Joseph soon convinced himself that the beggar had been sent by Satan. Aware that times had changed and that people were now more cautious, the great Tempter was no longer offering one of nature's fruits but holding out the promise of a different and luminous earth, counting once more on the credulity and weakness of women. Joseph's mind is in a turmoil, but he is pleased with himself and the conclusions he has reached. Unaware of her husband's tortuous thoughts about Satan's intrigues for which he holds her responsible, Mary, for her part, is troubled by this strange feeling of emptiness ever since telling her husband of her pregnancy. Not an inner emptiness, to be sure, for she knows perfectly well that from now on, and in the strict meaning of the word, her womb is full, but rather an outer emptiness as if the world from one moment to the next had receded and become remote. She recalls, but as if evoking some other life, that after supper and before unrolling the mats for the night, she always had some task in hand to while away the hours, but now she feels no inclination whatsoever to rise from where she is sitting on the floor, gazing at the light which is glowing back at her over the rim of the bowl, and awaiting the birth of her child. If truth be told, her thoughts were not all that clear, for thought, when all is said and done, as others and we ourselves have said before, is like a great ball of thread coiled around itself, loose in places, taut in others, and right here inside our head. It is impossible to know its full extent, one would have to unwind and then measure it but, however hard one tries, or pretends to try, this cannot be done without some assistance. One day, someone will have to come and tell us where one cuts the cord that ties man to his navel and links thought to its origin.

The following morning, after a restless night in which he was constantly disturbed by the same nightmare wherein he saw himself falling time and time again inside an enormous upturned bowl as if under a starry sky, Joseph went to the synagogue to seek the advice of the Elders. The story he had to tell was quite extraordinary, although he himself did not know just how extraordinary for, as we know, he had not been told the whole story. So were it not for the high esteem in which he was held by the veterans of Nazareth, he might have had to retrace his steps with his tail between his legs and with the reproachful words of Ecclesiasticus ringing in his ears: To trust a man hastily shows a shallow mind, and he, poor fellow, without the presence of mind to reply with words from the same Ecclesiasticus, apropos the dream which had haunted him all night long, What you see in a dream is nothing other than a reflection like that of a face in a mirror. Once he had finished telling his story, the Elders looked at each other and then at Joseph, and the oldest man there, translating the silent mistrust of the council into a direct question, asked, Is this the truth, the whole truth and nothing but the truth you have spoken, whereupon the carpenter replied, The truth, the whole truth and nothing but the truth, as God is my witness. The Elders then debated at length amongst themselves, while Joseph waited at a discreet distance until they finally summoned him and announced that, because of certain unresolved differences of opinion about how to proceed, they had decided to send three envoys to question Mary herself about these mysterious events in order to discover the identity of this beggar whom no one else had seen, to find out what he looked like, the exact words he had spoken, if anyone could remember seeing him beg for alms in Nazareth or could give any information whatsoever about this mysterious stranger. Joseph was secretly delighted because, although he would never admit it, he hated the idea of having to confront his wife alone. This habit of hers in recent days of keeping her eyes lowered was beginning to disconcert him. Modesty demanded such discretion, but there was also an unmistakable hint of provocation in this look of someone who knows more than she is prepared to disclose, and wants others to notice. In truth, in truth, I say unto you, the malice of women knows no limits, especially when they feign innocence.

And so the envoys depart, with Joseph leading the way, and they were called Abiathar, Dothan and Zacchaeus, names duly recorded here to ward off any lingering suspicion of historical inaccuracy in the minds of those who have acquired their version of these facts from other sources, perhaps more in accordance with tradition, but not necessarily more reliable. Having revealed the names and established the existence of the men who used them, any remaining doubts lose their force, not to mention their validity. Given the unusual sight of three Elders moving in solemn procession through the streets, their robes and beards caught in the breeze, local urchins soon gathered round them and began aping their movements as children will, jeering and shouting and chasing after the envoys all the way from the synagogue until they arrived at the house of Joseph, who was much put out by this boisterous parade which no one could fail to notice. Attracted by the noise, women began to appear in the doorways of the neighbouring houses and, sensing something amiss, they sent their children to find out what such a delegation was doing outside Mary's door. To no avail, because only the Elders were allowed to enter. The door was firmly closed behind them, and no woman of Nazareth, however inquisitive, was to discover to this day what took place in the house of Joseph the carpenter. Forced to invent something to satisfy their avid curiosity, they accused the beggar, whom they had never so much as set eyes on, of being a common thief, a great injustice, because the angel, but don't tell anyone that this is what he was, did not steal the food he ate and he even delivered a sacred pledge before taking his leave. And so while the two senior Elders continued to interrogate Mary, the youngest of the three, Zacchaeus, went around the immediate vicinity gathering any details people could remember about a beggar who looked like so, according to the description given by the carpenter's wife, but none of the neighbours could give him any information, No, Sir, no beggar passed this way yesterday and if he did, he didn't knock at my door, he must have been a thief passing through who, on finding someone at home, pretended to be a beggar and then disappeared in a hurry, the oldest ruse in the world.

Zacchaeus arrived back at Joseph's house without anything new to report about the beggar just as Mary was repeating for the third and fourth time the facts we already know. They were all inside the house, Mary standing there as if guilty of some crime, the bowl set on the ground, and inside it, constant as a throbbing heart, the mysterious earth, Joseph seated on one side, the Elders seated in front like a tribunal of judges. Dothan, the second of the three, said, It's not that we don't believe your story, but don't forget you're the only person to have seen this man, if he was a man, all your husband knows is that he heard his voice, and now Zacchaeus here tells me that none of your neighbours saw him. As God is my witness, I swear I'm telling the truth, The truth, perhaps, but is it the whole truth, I shall drink the water of the Lord and He will prove my innocence, The trial of bitter waters is for women suspected of infidelity but you couldn't have been unfaithful to your husband for he didn't give you enough time, Falsehood is said to be the same as infidelity, That's another kind of infidelity, My words are as true as the rest of me. Then Abiathar, the oldest of the three, told her, We shall question you no further, the Lord will reward you seven-fold for the truth you have spoken or punish you seven-fold should you have deceived us. He broke off and remained silent, then turning to Zacchaeus and Dothan, he asked them, What shall we do with this luminous earth which prudence demands should not remain here for this could be one of Satan's tricks. Dothan said, Let this earth return from whence it came, let it return to its former darkness.

Zacchaeus said, We know not who this beggar can be, or why he chose to be seen by Mary alone, or the meaning of this luminous earth in the bowl. Dothan proposed, Let's take it into the desert and scatter it there, far from the eyes of men, so that the wind may disperse it far and wide and the rain erase it. Zacchaeus said, If this earth is some divine gift then it must not be removed, if, on the other hand, it forbodes evil, then let those to whom it was given face the consequences. Abiathar asked, What do you suggest then, and Zacchaeus replied, That the bowl should be buried right here and covered up so that there is no contact with the natural earth, for a gift from God, even when buried, is never lost, and the power of evil is much diminished if hidden from sight. Abiathar asked, What do you say, Dothan, whereupon the latter replied, I agree with Zacchaeus, let's do as he says. Abiathar told Mary, Withdraw so that we may proceed, Where shall I go, she asked him, whereupon Joseph, somewhat agitated, interrupted, If we're to bury the bowl, let it be somewhere away from the house, for I shall never rest with a light buried underneath me. Abiathar reassured him, That can be done, then turning to Mary he told her, You will remain here. The men went out into the yard, Zacchaeus carrying the bowl. The sound of a spade could soon be heard digging as Joseph briskly set to work, and a few minutes later Mary recognised the voice of Abiathar, You can stop now, the hole is deep enough. Mary peered through the chink in the door, watched her husband cover the bowl with a curved potsherd and then lower it into the hole which was the length of his arm. Then getting up and grabbing his spade, he began filling in the hole, pressing the ground down firmly with his feet.

The men remained for some time in the yard conversing amongst themselves and gazing at the patch of fresh earth as if they had just buried some treasure and were trying to memorize the exact spot. But this was certainly not the topic of conversation because suddenly Zacchaeus could be heard saying aloud, in tones of playful reproach, Now then, Joseph, what kind of carpenter are you, when you can't even make a bed for your pregnant wife. The others laughed and Joseph joined in, rather than lose face by showing his annoyance. Mary saw them walk to the gate and now, seated on the stone slab by the hearth, she was looking round the room wondering where they could put a bed if Joseph should decide to make one. She tried not to think about the earthenware bowl or the luminous earth, or whether the beggar was really an angel or some practical joker. If a woman is promised a bed for her house, she must start thinking about the best place to put it.

Between the months of Tammuz and Ab, when grapes were gathered in the vineyards and the figs began ripening amidst the dark-green vine-leaves, certain events took place. Some were normal and commonplace, such as a man and woman coming together in the flesh, and after a while she tells him, I am carrying your child, others quite extraordinary, such as the first glimmerings of an annunciation being entrusted to a passing beggar whose only crime seems to have been that strange phenomenon of the luminous earth, now safe from any prying eyes, thanks to Joseph's mistrust and the prudence of the Elders. The dogdays are fast approaching, the fields are bare, nothing but stubble and parched soil. During the oppressive hours of day, Nazareth is a village submerged in silence and solitude. Only when night descends and the stars appear can one sense the presence of that landscape shrouded in darkness or hear the music of the heavenly planets as they glide past each other. After supper Joseph sat out in the yard on the right-hand side of the door to get some air. How he loved to feel the fresh evening breeze on his face and beard. Night had finally descended when Mary joined him, squatting on the ground like her husband but on the other side of the door, and there they remained in silence, listening to the sounds coming from the neighbouring houses, the bustle of domestic life which they, too, would experience once they had children. May God send us a boy, Joseph found himself praying throughout the day, while Mary, too, kept thinking, Let it be a boy, dear God, but she had other reasons for wanting a boy. Mary's belly was slow in growing bigger, weeks and months were to pass

25

before her condition became apparent, and since, out of modesty and discretion, she saw little of her neighbours, there was general surprise in the neighbourhood when she suddenly appeared looking as if she had turned into a balloon overnight. Perhaps the real reason for Mary's secrecy was her fear that someone might connect her pregnancy with the appearance of the mysterious beggar. Any such fears may strike us as being absurd, but in moments of weariness when her thoughts began to stray, Mary could not help asking how all this had come about. Tortured by foolish doubts and scruples, she could not help wondering who might be the real father of this child she was carrying in her womb. As everyone knows, when women are pregnant they are given to strange cravings and flights of fancy, some of them worse than those of Mary, which we shall not betray lest we tarnish the reputation of this mother-to-be.

Time passed, the weeks dragged on, the month of Elul, hot as a furnace, with the scorching winds from the southern deserts stifling the atmosphere, a season when dates and figs turn to trickling honey, the month of Tishri bringing the first rains of autumn to moisten the soil in time for tilling and sowing, and in the following month of Heshvan when olives are gathered and the days finally turn cooler, Joseph, incapable of making anything grander, decided to make a simple bed where Mary might at last find rest for her swollen and cumbersome womb. Heavy rains fell during the last days of Kislev and throughout almost the whole of Tebet, forcing Joseph to interrupt his work in the yard. He took advantage of any dry spells to assemble the larger pieces of wood, but for most of the time he had to work indoors in poor light and there he planed and polished the unfinished yokes, covering the floor all around him with shavings and sawdust which Mary would sweep up later and dispose of in the yard.

In the month of Shebat the almond trees blossomed, and the feast of Purim had already been celebrated in the month of Adar when Roman soldiers appeared in Nazareth, a familiar sight throughout Galilee as detachments went from village to city and from city to village, while others were despatched elsewhere in Herod's kingdom to inform the people that by order of Caesar Augustus, every family domiciled in the provinces governed by the consul Publius Sulpicius Quirinus must participate in a census, destined, like all the others, to bring the records up to date of all those liable to pay taxes to

Rome. Without exception, each family was ordered to register in their place of birth. Most of the people who had gathered in the square to hear the proclamation could readily ignore the imperial mandate, for as natives of Nazareth and settled here for generations, this was where they intended to register. But some families who had come from other parts of the kingdom, from Gaulanitis or Samaria, from Judaea, Peraea or Idumaea, from over here and over there, from far and wide, began making preparations for the long journey while complaining bitterly about the perversity and greed of Rome, and debated what would become of their crops since it was almost time to harvest the flax and barley. Those who had large families, with babes in arms or elderly parents and grandparents, unless they had enough transport of their own, wondered from whom they might borrow or hire donkeys at a reasonable price, especially if there was a long and arduous journey ahead which would require ample supplies of food, water-bags if they had to cross the desert, mats and mantles for sleeping, cooking utensils, and extra protection, for the cold, wet season was not yet over and they might find themselves spending nights out in the open.

Joseph only learned about the edict when the soldiers had already gone to carry their glad tidings elsewhere. His next-door neighbour, called Ananias, suddenly appeared in a great fluster to tell him what had happened. Fortunately for Ananias, he could register in Nazareth and, having decided not to celebrate Passover in Jerusalem this year because of the harvest, he would be spared both journeys. Ananias felt that it was only right that he should warn his neighbour, but with ever such a smug expression on his face as if he were bearing good news. Alas, even the best of people can be two-faced and we do not know this Ananias well enough to decide whether this is a momentary lapse from grace or if he has fallen under the influence of one of Satan's wicked angels with spare time on its hands. At first Joseph, who was hammering away at a plank of wood, did not hear Ananias calling him from the gate. Mary, whose hearing was keener, heard a voice call out Joseph, but it was her husband who was being summoned and who was she to tug at his sleeve and ask, Are you deaf, can't you hear someone calling you from the gate. Ananias called out even louder, the hammering stopped, and Joseph went to see what his neighbour wanted. Ananias was invited in, and after the customary greetings enquired in the voice of someone seeking reassurance, Where are you from, Joseph, and, taken unawares, Joseph told him, I'm from Bethlehem of Judaea, Isn't that near Jerusalem, Yes, quite near, And are you going there to celebrate the Passover, asked Ananias, and Joseph replied, No, I've decided not to go this year for my wife is expecting our child any day now, Oh, is that so, But why do you ask. Whereupon Ananias raised his arms to heaven and assuming a mournful expression wailed, Poor Joseph, the trouble that awaits you, all that unnecessary toiling and moiling, all this work waiting to be done here and you're expected to down tools and travel all that way, so help me God who sees and assists all things. Without questioning the reason for this sudden outburst, Joseph echoed his neighbour's pious sentiments, May God help me as well, to which Ananias without lowering his voice replied, Yes, with God all things are possible, He knows and sees all things, both in heaven and on earth, praise be to God for all eternity, but, forgive the irreverence, I'm not sure He can do much to help you this time because you're in the hands of Caesar. What are you trying to tell me, Only that soldiers have been here to proclaim that before the month of Nisan ends, all the families of Israel must go and register in their place of birth which in your case, dear Joseph, will mean quite a journey.

Before Joseph had time to react, Shua, the wife of Ananias, appeared and, going straight to Mary who was standing expectantly in the doorway, she began commiserating in the same tearful voice, Poor child, and so delicate, what is to become of you, about to give birth any day now and forced to make the journey to who knows where. To Bethlehem of Judaea, Shua's husband informed her, Good heavens, all that way, Shua exclaimed, and in all sincerity, for once on a pilgrimage to Jerusalem she had descended into nearby Bethlehem to pray at Rachel's tomb. Mary did not react and waited for her husband to speak first, but Joseph was furious that the grave news should not have come quietly and with measured words from his own lips, rather than have it blurted out in this tactless way by hysterical neighbours. To conceal his annoyance he put on a solemn expression and said, It's true that God doesn't always choose to wield the powers exercised by Caesar, but God has certain powers denied the Emperor. He paused as if anxious to savour the deep significance of the words he had just spoken, before announcing, We shall celebrate the Passover here in Nazareth and then set out for Bethlehem, and God willing, we shall be back in time for Mary to give birth at home unless God decides that our child should be born in the land of our ancestors. It might even be born on the road, murmured Shua, but Joseph overheard her and was quick to remind her, Many a child of Israel has been born on the road, and our child will be just one more. Ananias and his wife could only agree with these wise words. They had come to sympathise with these hapless neighbours who were being forced to make the long journey to Jerusalem, and to delight in their own solicitude, only to find themselves unceremoniously rebuffed. But Mary intervened and invited Shua indoors to ask her advice about some wool she had to card, and Joseph, anxious to make amends for his harsh words, said to Ananias, Good neighbour, could I ask you to look after my house while I'm away, for we shall be gone for at least a month, counting the time the journey takes, then the seven days of seclusion and more if, by any misfortune, the child should be a girl. Ananias reassured his neighbour that he would look after his property as if it were his own, and suddenly it occurred to him to ask Joseph, Would you care to honour me by celebrating the Passover with my family and friends since neither you nor your wife have any relatives here in Nazareth after the death of Mary's parents who were already so old when she was born that people are still asking themselves how Joachim could possibly have given Anne a daughter. Come now, Ananias, said Joseph, rebuking him playfully, have you forgotten how Abraham muttered into his beard in sheer disbelief when the Lord told him He would grant him offspring, and if Almighty God allowed a hundred-year-old man with a wife of ninety to conceive a child, why should my parents-in-law, Joachim and Anne, who were not as old as Abraham and Sarah, not do the same. Those were other times, Ananias replied, when God was ever present and not just in His works. Well-versed in matters of doctrine, Joseph retorted, God is time itself, neighbour Ananias, for God, time is indivisible. Ananias was left speechless for this was not the moment to bring up the same old argument about the powers, whether consubstantial or delegated, of God and Caesar. Despite this demonstration of practical theology, Joseph had not forgotten Ananias's sudden invitation to celebrate the Passover with him and his family. He did not wish, however, to appear too anxious to accept, even though he had already made up his mind for, as everyone knows, it is a sign of courtesy and good breeding to receive any favours graciously without being too effusive, otherwise the other party will think we were simply waiting to be asked. Joseph bided his time and, just as he was thanking Ananias for his thoughtful gesture, the women re-emerged from the house and Shùa was saying to Mary, You're a dab hand at carding, my girl, and Mary blushed on hearing herself being praised in front of Joseph.

One pleasant memory Mary would come to cherish of this auspicious Passover was not to have to help with the cooking or serve the men at table. The other women agreed she should be spared these chores in her condition, Don't tire yourself out, they warned her, or you'll do yourself some mischief, and they should know because most of them were mothers with young children. All she had to do was to attend to her husband who was sitting there on the floor with the other men. Stretching over with some difficulty, she filled his glass and replenished his plate with home-made delicacies, unleavened bread, stewed lamb, bitter herbs, and biscuits made from ground dried locusts, a tasty morsel much appreciated by Ananias, for these biscuits were something of a family tradition. Several guests declined, feeling ashamed of their ill-concealed disgust and painfully aware that they were unworthy of the edifying example of those prophets in the desert who made a virtue of necessity and ate locusts as if they were manna. As supper drew to an end, poor Mary was sitting apart, perspiration running down her face, her great belly resting on her haunches, and she was scarcely listening to the laughter, banter, stories and constant readings of the scriptures, feeling she might depart this world at any moment, her life suspended by the slender thread of one last, pure thought, random and unspoken. All she knew was that she was thinking without knowing what she was thinking or why she was thinking. She awoke with a start. In her drowsiness she had seen the beggar's face loom from some greater darkness, then his huge body covered in rags. The angel, if indeed he was an angel, had crept into her dream unannounced when he was furthest from her thoughts. Yet there he was, gazing at her intently. She sensed a hint of curiosity in his expression, but perhaps she was mistaken, it came and went in a flash, and Mary's heart was now fluttering like that of a nervous little bird. Difficult to say whether she had been startled or someone had whispered embarrassing phrases in her ear. The men and boys remained seated on the floor while the women, hot and flustered, rushed back and forth offering them second helpings, but they were already showing signs of having eaten their fill and the conversation became more animated as the wine began to take effect.

Without anyone noticing, Mary rose to her feet. Night had fallen. There was no moon in the clear sky, only the twinkling of stars which sent out a kind of echo, a muffled drone which was barely audible but which Joseph's wife could feel on her skin and in her bones. Almost impossible to explain, it was like a furtive voluptuous shiver which had not yet subsided. Mary crossed the yard and looked outside. She could see no one. The side-gate was closed, just as she had left it, but there was a vibration in the air as if someone had just gone running or flying past, leaving nothing more than a fleeting sign which would leave others baffled.

Three days later, after reassuring his customers that their jobs would be completed on his return, and after making his farewells in the synagogue and entrusting the care of his house and worldly possessions therein to his neighbour Ananias, Joseph the carpenter set out with his wife from Nazareth and headed for Bethlehem where they would register as decreed by Rome. If the news had not yet reached heaven, because of some delay in communication or some problem with simultaneous interpreting, the Lord God must have been surprised to see the landscape of Israel so radically altered, with hordes of people travelling in all directions, when normally during the first few days after the Passover people would be moving centrifugally, as it were, as they began the return journey from that earthly sun or luminous centre, otherwise known as Jerusalem. Force of habit, however fallible, and divine perspicacity, the latter absolute, will undoubtedly assist Him to recognize, even from on high, that these are pilgrims slowly making their way back to their towns and villages, but what about this bewildering maze as those obeying the profane orders of Caesar travel at random across more familiar routes. Another feasible explanation is that Caesar Augustus is unwittingly complying with the will of God, if it is true that in His divine wisdom he has ordained that Joseph and Mary should go to Bethlehem at this time. However arbitrary and irrelevant these theories may appear at first sight, they cannot be dismissed lightly, for they can help us to disprove the findings of those commentators who would have us imagine Joseph and Mary crossing the inhospitable desert all alone, without so much as a friendly face in

33

sight, and trusting solely in God's mercy and the protection of His angels. For no sooner have the couple reached the outskirts of Bethlehem than it becomes clear that they will not be on their own. Joseph and Mary meet up with two large families, a veritable clan of some twenty members, counting adults, grandparents and small children. It is true that they are not all travelling to Bethlehem, one of the families is only covering half the distance and will remain in a village near Ramah, the other will head south as far as Beersheba, but even if they should separate before reaching Bethlehem, because there is always the possibility that some travel faster, they will join up with other travellers on the road, not to mention those whom they will meet travelling in the opposite direction, probably on their way to register in Nazareth, the very place they have just left. The men walk ahead in one group, accompanied by all the boys who have reached the age of thirteen, while the women, girls and grand-mothers of all ages straggle behind accompanied by the younger boys. As they set off, the men in solemn chorus recited prayers suited to the occasion, while the women mumbled the words, all too aware that it is useless raising their voices if no one is likely to listen, even though they ask for nothing and are grateful for everything.

Amongst the women only Mary is in an advanced state of preg-nancy and such is the strain that, had providence not endowed donkeys with infinite patience and stamina to match, Mary would long since have given up and begged the others to abandon her at the roadside to await her hour, which we know is near, but who can say when or where, for this is not a race given to laying wagers or making predictions as to when or where Joseph's son will be born, and what a sensible religion to have prohibited gambling. Until that hour comes and for as long as this anxious period of waiting lasts, the pregnant woman will rely less on the distracted attentions of Joseph who is lost in conversation with the other men, than on the reliable support of the donkey who must be wondering, if beasts of burden are sensitive to such changes, why the whip has not been much in use, and most surprising of all, that it is no longer under pressure and allowed to go at its own relaxed pace and that of his species, for there are other donkeys making the journey. Travelling at their leisure, the women often lag behind, forcing the men who are way ahead of them to call a halt until the women get closer but not too close. The men prefer to give the impression that they have only paused for a rest because, if it is true that everyone may use the road, where cocks crow, hens must not squawk, at most they may cackle when they lay an egg, for such are the laws of nature that govern the world in which we live. And so Mary journeys on, swaying with the gentle rhythm of her mount, a queen among women, for she alone is allowed to ride, while the other donkeys carry pack-loads. To make things easier, she takes the three infants in the party on to her lap in turn, giving the other women some respite and at the same time preparing herself for motherhood.

On the first day of the journey, they soon tired and only covered a short distance. Their legs were unaccustomed to walking for hours on end, we must not forget the number of elderly people and small children making this journey. The former, after a long life, have sapped all their energies and can no longer pretend otherwise, the latter have still not learned how to conserve their increasing strength, and wear themselves out after a few hours of wild activity as if life were coming to an end and must be enjoyed to the full while it lasts. On reaching a large village called Jezreel, they stopped at the local caravanserai which they found in a state of chaos and uproar because of the heavy traffic, but, to tell the truth, there was more uproar than chaos in this madhouse for, as one's eyes and ears adjusted, some sense of order emerged from that multitude of people and animals swarming within the same four walls, like a startled anthill trying to find its bearings and come together again amidst so much dispersion. Despite the overcrowding, the three families had the good fortune to find shelter under an archway where the men would huddle together on one side and the women on the other as darkness fell and all the people and animals in the caravanserai settled down for the night. But first the women had to prepare some food and fill the water-skins at the well, while the men unloaded the donkeys and watered them after the camels had finished drinking. For in two great gulps a camel can empty the troughs which had to be refilled time and time again to slake their thirst. After watering and feeding the donkeys, the travellers finally sat down to eat, the men first for, as we know, women always take second place. How often we need to remind ourselves that Eve was created after Adam and taken from his rib, and will we ever learn that certain things can only be understood if we take the trouble to retrace their origins.

The men had already eaten and were back in their own corner, the women were finishing off the leftovers when Simeon, one of the most senior of the Elders, who was living in Bethlehem but obliged to register in Ramah, took advantage of the authority conferred by age and the wisdom believed to come thereof, by asking Joseph what he would do if Mary, although he did not mention her by name, should still be waiting to give birth when the last day of the census had passed. The question was clearly academic, if such a word is apt for the time and place, insofar as only the census officials, skilled in the finer points of Roman Law, could decide how to deal with a pregnant woman who turns up for registration and says, We've come to register, without anyone knowing whether she's carrying a boy or a girl, not to mention the likely possibility of twins nestling there, of the same or both sexes. Exemplary Jew as he believed himself to be, in both theory and practice, the carpenter would never dream of pointing out with simple western logic that it is not up to those who are simply obeying orders to compensate for any flaws in the law, and if Rome was incapable of foreseeing certain difficulties, then she was ill-served by her legislators and by interpreters of Holy Scripture. Once faced with this thorny problem, Joseph thought long and hard, searching in his mind for some subtle argument which would convince those gathered round the bonfire of his eloquence and natural flair for debate. After much reflection, the carpenter stopped staring at the flickering flames and raising his eyes he told them, If by the last day of the census my child has not yet been born, this will be a sign from God that He does not wish the Romans to know of the child's existence. Simeon replied, Such presumption, that you should claim to know what God does or does not wish. Joseph asked, Does God not see my ways and count all my steps, and these words, which we can find in the Book of Job, implied within the context of the discussion that before all present or absent Joseph was protesting his submission and humility in the eyes of the Lord, sentiments wholly opposed to the diabolical presumption of which Simeon accused him when he had tried to probe the inscrutable will of God. This is how the Elder must have interpreted his answer for he fell silent, waiting for Joseph to return to the attack, The days of each man's birth and death are put under seal and guarded by angels ever since the world began, and only the Lord, whensoever He may desire, can break the seal, first the one and then the other, often simultaneously, with His right and left hand, and there are times when He is so slow in breaking the seal of death that He seems almost to have forgotten the existence of certain living souls, Joseph paused for breath then, smiling mischievously he told Simeon, Let's hope this conversation doesn't remind the Lord of your existence. Those present laughed into their beards for the carpenter was not showing the respect due to an old man, however diminished the latter's judgement in his dotage. Tugging nervously at his sleeve, old Simeon made no attempt to conceal his annoyance as he told Joseph, Perhaps God was hasty in breaking the seal of your birth and you were born before your time, if this is the contempt and presumption with which you treat your elders who have seen more of life and gained more wisdom than you have. Whereupon Joseph replied, Listen, Simeon, you asked me what I would do if my child were still not born before the last day of the census, and I couldn't answer your question since I'm not familiar with Roman Law and I suspect neither are you. No, I'm not. Then I said, I know what you said, for you never tire of repeating yourself, It was you who started being offensive when you accused me of presuming to know God's will before it became manifest, so forgive me if I've hurt your pride, but you were the first to cause offence, and as my elder and better you ought to set an example. There was a quiet murmur of approval around the fire. The carpenter Joseph had clearly won the argument and the others waited to see how Simeon would react. Lacking in spirit and imagination, he peevishly told him, All you had to do was answer my question respectfully, and Joseph replied, Had I given you the answer you wanted, the foolishness of your question would have been clear for all to see, therefore you must admit, however much it rankles, that I showed the greater respect by providing you with an opportunity of debating something we'd all like to know, namely whether the Lord would ever wish to be able to conceal His people from the eyes of the enemy. Now you're speaking about God's people as if they were your unborn child, Don't put words into my mouth, Simeon, which I haven't spoken and am never likely to speak, and listen to what should be understood in one sense, and what should be understood in another. Simeon made no attempt to reply to this outburst. He got to his feet and took himself off into a corner along with the other men from his household, who felt obliged to accompany him because of ties of blood and kinship, although deeply disappointed in the patriarch's poor showing in this verbal exchange. The silence which followed the murmurings and whisperings of travellers settling down for the night, was broken once more by muffled conversations in the caravanserai, interrupted now and then by shrill cries, by the panting and snorting of animals, and intermittently by the horrendous bellowing of some camel on heat. Just then, the party from Nazareth, all discord forgotten, could be heard muttering in unison the last and longest of the prayers of thanksgiving offered up to the Lord at the end of the day, Praise be to You, oh God, King of the Universe, Who shuts our eyes without robbing them of light. Grant, oh Lord, that we may sleep in peace and awaken tomorrow to a happy and tranquil life, help us to obey Your commandments. Lead us not into temptation and deliver us from all evil. Lead us along the path of virtue and protect us from bad dreams, wicked thoughts and mortal sickness. Spare us visions of death. Within minutes, the more just, if not the more weary members of the party, were fast asleep, some of them snoring without spirituality. And soon the others joined them, the majority with nothing more than their tunics to cover them, for only the elderly and the very young, both delicate in their own way, enjoyed the warmth and protection of a coarse blanket or threadbare mantle. Deprived of wood, the fire began to die down, nothing but a few weak flames continuing to flicker over the last piece of firewood picked up on the road for this very purpose. Under the archway, the party from Nazareth slept soundly. Everyone except Mary. Unable to stretch out because of her swollen belly which could have been harbouring a giant, she reclined against some saddlebags in an effort to rest her aching loins. Like the others, she, too, had listened to Joseph arguing with old Simeon and rejoiced in her husband's victory, as befits any loyal wife no matter how harmless or innocent the conflict. But she could no longer remember what the argument was about, her recollections of the debate already submerged in the throbbing sensations in her body which came and went like the flow of the sea which she had never seen but heard others describe, the restless ebb and flow of waves as her child stirred in her womb. The strangest of sensations, as if that living creature inside her were trying to hoist her on to its shoulders. Only Mary lay there with her eyes wide open, shining in the shadows and still shining after the last flames had died away. No cause for wonder, for this happens to all mothers, and the wife of the carpenter Joseph was no exception, once the angel had appeared to her disguised as a beggar.

Even in the caravanserai there were cocks to greet the morning, but the travellers, merchants, drovers and cameleers had to make an early start and began preparing for the next stage of their journey before dawn. They loaded the animals with baggage and merchandise and made even more noise than on the previous evening. Once they have departed, the caravanserai will settle down to a few hours of peace and quiet, like a brown lizard stretched out in the sun. The only remaining guests are those who have decided to rest throughout the day, but by the evening another group of travellers will start arriving, some more bedraggled than others, but all of them weary, not that this has any effect on their vocal cords, for the moment they arrive they start shouting their heads off as if possessed by a thousand demons. Once back on the road, the party from Nazareth has inevitably grown bigger. Some ten more people have joined them, and anyone who imagines this place to be deserted is much mistaken, especially when the Feast of Passover and the census coincide.

No one needed to remind Joseph that it was up to him to make his peace with old Simeon, not because he was in the wrong but because he had been taught to respect his elders and especially those who were senile, poor men, and who were paying the price for long life by losing their minds and any influence they might have had over a younger generation. So Joseph went up to him and said in a submissive tone of voice, I've come to apologize for my insolence and presumption last night, I didn't mean to be disrespectful but you know what human nature is, one word leads to another, tempers are lost and caution goes to the wind. Without raising his eyes, Simeon heard him out in silence, then finally spoke, You're forgiven. Hoping for a conciliatory response to his friendly gesture from this stubborn old man, Joseph remained at his side for a fair stretch on the road. But Simeon, his eyes fixed on the dust at his feet, continued to ignore him, until Joseph in exasperation decided to give up. But at that very moment, seemingly roused from his thoughts, the old man detained him and, placing one hand on Joseph's shoulder, said, Wait a moment. Taken by surprise, Joseph turned round. Simeon had stopped and repeated, Wait. The others walked on, leaving the two men standing there in the middle of the road, a no-man's-land, situated between the group of men travelling ahead and the band of women coming behind which was gradually catching up on them. Above the latter's heads, Mary could be seen swaying with the rhythm of the donkey.

They had left the valley of Jezreel. Skirting great rocks, the road curved awkwardly up the first slope before penetrating the mountains of Samaria to the east, then along arid ridges before descending on the other side to the Jordan, where the burning plain stretched southwards and the desert of Judaea fired and scorched the ancient scars of a land promised to the chosen few but forever uncertain as to whom it should surrender. Wait, said Simeon, and the carpenter obeyed, suddenly feeling nervous and uneasy. The women were drawing nearer. Then the old man carried on walking, clutching Joseph by the sleeve, his strength appearing to fail him, and he confided, When I lay down to rest last night I had a vision, A vision, Yes, a vision, but no ordinary vision, for I could see the hidden meaning of words you yourself spoke, that if your child were still not born by the last day of the census, it would be because the Lord did not wish the Romans to learn of the child's existence and add its name to their list. Yes, that's what I said, but what did you see. I didn't see anything but suddenly felt that it would be better if the Romans were not to learn of your child's existence, that no one should be told of its whereabouts, and that if the child must be born into this world, at least let it live without torment or glory, like those men up there in front and those women bringing up the rear, that it should be as anonymous as the rest of us until the hour of death and forever thereafter. Humble carpenter as I am from Nazareth, what fate could my child possibly hope for other than the one you have just described. Alas, you are not the only one to dispose of your child's life, True, everything is in the hands of the Lord and He knows best. And so say I. But tell me about my child, what have you discovered, Nothing beyond those words you yourself spoke and which seemed to me to have another meaning, as if on seeing an egg for the very first time, I could sense the presence of a chick inside. God wills what He creates and created what He willed, my child is in His hands and there is nothing I can do. That is indeed true, but these are days when God still shares the child with its mother. But should it turn out to be a son, it will belong to me and to God. Or to God alone. All of us belong to God. Not quite all of us, some are divided between God and Satan. How can one tell. If the law had not silenced women for ever and a day, perhaps they could reveal what we need to know, for it was woman who invented that first sin from which all the rest originated. What do we need to know. Which part of woman's nature is demonic and which divine and the kind of humanity they possess. I don't understand, I thought you were referring to my child, No, I was not referring to your child, I was talking about women who generate creatures such as ourselves, and who may be responsible, perhaps unknowingly, for this duality in our nature, so base and yet so noble, so virtuous and yet so wicked, so tranquil and yet so troubled, so meek and yet so rebellious.

Joseph looked back. Mary was advancing on her donkey, with a young boy in front, sitting astride the saddle like a grown-up, and for one second Joseph thought he was looking at his own son, and seeing Mary for the first time, heading this group of women which had grown along the route. Simeon's strange words were still ringing in his ears, but he found it hard to accept that any woman could exercise so much power, especially this unassuming wife of his who had never shown any signs of being different from other women. Averting his gaze to look at the road ahead, he suddenly remembered the episode of the beggar and the luminous earth. He began shaking all over, his hair standing on end, his skin covered in goose-pimples, and matters got worse when he turned round again to take another look at Mary and saw as clearly as anything a tall stranger walking by her side, so tall that he stood head and shoulders above the women's heads, without a shadow of doubt this was the beggar whom he had missed seeing last time. Joseph took another look and there he was, an incongruous figure whose sinister presence among all those women defied any explanation. Joseph was about to ask Simeon to take a look in order to reassure himself that he was not imagining things, but the old man had moved on, he had spoken his mind and was now rejoining his male companions to resume his role as head of his clan, a role he cannot hope to play

41

for very much longer. Deprived of a witness, the carpenter took another look in his wife's direction. This time the beggar had vanished.

Heading south, they crossed the whole of Samaria at great speed, with one eye on the road, the other cautiously scanning their surroundings. They suspected some act of hostility, or rather of hatred by people living in these parts, the descendants of the ancient Assyrians renowned for their wicked deeds and heretical beliefs, who settled here during the reign of Shalmaneser, King of Nineveh, after the expulsion and dispersion of the Twelve Tribes. More pagan than Jewish, these people barely acknowledge the Five Books of Moses as sacred law, and dare to suggest that the place chosen by God for His Temple was not Jerusalem but Mount Gerizim which lies within their domain. The expedition from Galilee travelled at a brisk pace but could not avoid spending two nights out in the open in enemy territory, with guards and patrols for fear of ambush. The treachery of these villains knew no bounds and they were capable of refusing water even to someone of pure Hebrew stock who might be dying of thirst. But there were a few decent men amongst them. Such was the anxiety of the travellers during this stretch of the journey that, contrary to custom, the men divided into two groups, one in front of the women and children, and the other behind, to protect them from taunts and insults, or even worse. However, the inhabitants of Samaria must have been going through a peaceful phase because, apart from resentful looks and snide remarks, the party from Galilee met with no open aggression, there was no ambush, no gangs of robbers descended from the nearby hills or attacked them with stones.

Shortly before reaching Ramah, those who believed with greatest fervour or possessed a keener sense of smell, swore they were inhaling the sanctified odour of Jerusalem. Here old Simeon and his companions went their separate ways for, as we mentioned earlier, they had to register in a village in this region. Giving profuse thanks to God there in the middle of the road, the travellers made their farewells. The married women filled Mary's head with a thousand and one pieces of advice, the fruits of their experience, and then off they all went, some descending into the valley where they would soon recover after four days on foot, while others made for Ramah where they would seek shelter in the caravanserai for it would soon be dusk. On reaching Jerusalem, the rest of the group which had set out from Nazareth will go their separate ways, most of them heading for Beersheba which they should reach in two days, while the carpenter and his wife will remain in nearby Bethlehem. Amidst the confusion of embraces and farewells, Joseph called Simeon aside and, with all humility, asked him if he could remember anything more about his vision. I've already told you, it wasn't a vision. Whatever it might have been, I must know the destiny that awaits my child. If you don't even know your own destiny as you stand here before me asking questions, how can you expect to know the destiny of an unborn child. The eyes of the soul see further and, since yours have been opened by the Lord to certain manifestations reserved for the chosen, I thought you might have seen something where I can only see darkness. You may never live to discover your son's destiny and, who knows, perhaps you will meet your own fate very shortly, but no more questions, I beseech you, stop all this probing and live for the present. And with these words Simeon placed his right hand on Joseph's head, murmured a blessing no one could hear and rejoined his relatives and friends who were waiting for him. In single file they made their way down a sinuous path to the valley where Simeon's village nestled at the foot of the opposite slope, the houses almost merging with the boulders which stuck out of the ground like protruding bones. Joseph would never hear of him again other than to learn very much later that the old man had died before he could register.

After spending two nights under the stars, exposed to the cold on the barren plain, without as much as a camp-fire which might betray their whereabouts, the expedition from Nazareth decided to take refuge once more under the archways of a caravanserai. The women helped Mary to dismount from the donkey while trying to reassure her, Come, it'll soon be over, and the poor girl whispered back, I know, I can't have long to wait now, and what clearer proof than that great swollen belly. They made her as comfortable as possible in a quiet corner and set about preparing supper for it was getting late and the travellers planned to eat together. That night there were no conversations, prayers or stories around the fire, as if the nearby presence of Jerusalem demanded respectful silence, each man searching his heart and asking, Who is this person who resembles me yet whom I fail to recognize. This is not, in fact, what they actually said, for people do not start speaking to themselves just like that, nor was this consciously in their minds, but there can be no doubt that this silence, as we sit quietly staring into the flames of a camp-fire, can only be expressed with words like these which say everything. From where he was sitting, Joseph could see Mary in profile against the light of the fire. The reflection from its reddish glow softly lit up one side of her face, tracing out her features in chiaroscuro, and surprised that the thought should even cross his mind, he began to realize that Mary was an attractive woman, if one could say this of someone with such a childlike expression. Of course her body is swollen at present, but he can still see that agile and graceful figure she will soon regain once their child is born. These were the thoughts in Joseph's mind when, without any warning, as if his flesh were rebelling after all these months of enforced chastity, successive waves of desire incited by his imagination went surging through his blood and left him feeling dizzy. Mary called out in pain but he made no attempt to go to her assistance. As if someone had doused him in cold water, the sudden memory of the man whom he had momentarily caught sight of two days before walking beside his wife, soon dampened his ardour. The memory of that beggar had been haunting both of them ever since Mary discovered she was pregnant, for Joseph was no longer in any doubt that, even if the man had not reappeared until that day when he finally saw him with his own eyes, the mysterious stranger had never been far from Mary's thoughts throughout the nine months of her pregnancy. Joseph could not bring himself to ask his wife what kind of man he was or where he had gone when he suddenly vanished. The last thing he wanted was to hear her say in bewilderment, A man, what man, and were Joseph to insist, no doubt Mary

45

would have asked the other women to testify, Did any of you see a man in our group, and they would deny having seen him and shake their heads at any such suggestion, and one of them might even be bold enough to answer in jest, Any man who hangs around with women all the time is only after one thing. Joseph refused to believe that Mary was genuinely surprised and that she really had not seen the beggar, whether he be man or ghost. I saw him with my own eyes as he walked beside you, Joseph would insist, but Mary, who knew she was telling the truth, did not falter, As is written in holy law, a wife must always respect and obey her husband so, if you insist that you saw a beggar walking beside me, then I won't contradict you, but believe me, I didn't see him. It was the beggar all right, But how can you tell if you didn't catch sight of him the first time he appeared, It could only have been him, Much more likely to have been some traveller who was walking so slowly that we all overtook him, first the men, then the women, and he was probably alongside our group when you chanced to look back, Ah, so you agree he was there, Not at all, I'm simply trying as a dutiful wife to find some explanation that will satisfy you. Almost falling asleep, Joseph watches Mary through half-closed eyes in the hope that he will glean the truth from her expression, but Mary's face is now cast in shadow like the other side of the moon, her profile vaguely outlined against the waning light of the dying embers. Joseph nodded off, overcome by the sheer effort of trying to understand, taking with him, as he slept, the absurd idea that the beggar might be the image of his own son made man emerging from the future to tell him, This is what I'll look like one day, but you won't live to see it. Joseph slept with a resigned smile on his lips, but felt sad. He thought he could hear Mary saying, God forbid that I should be right in thinking that this beggar has nowhere to rest his head. For in truth I say unto you that many things in this world could be known before it is too late, if husbands and wives were only to confide in each other as husbands and wives.

Early next morning, most of the travellers who had spent the night in the caravanserai left for Jerusalem, but those on foot grouped together in such a manner that Joseph, without losing sight of his countrymen who were heading for Beersheba, accompanied his wife this time, walking alongside her as he had seen the beggar, or whatever he was, do on the previous day. But Joseph prefers not to think about the mysterious stranger. Deep down he is convinced that God bestowed a favour by allowing him to see his own son even before he is born, not wrapped in swaddling clothes to support his weak little bones, a tiny, unformed creature, smelly and vociferous, but a fully-grown man, taller than his father and most of the males of his race. Joseph is delighted to be taking his son's place, he is at once father and child, and this feeling is so strong that his real child, that unborn infant inside his mother's womb and heading for Jerusalem, suddenly becomes meaningless.

Jerusalem, Jerusalem, the pilgrims call out devoutly as the city looms into sight, suddenly rising before them like some apparition on the crest of the hill beyond the valley, a truly celestial city, the centre of the universe, and sparkling in all directions under the glare of the midday sun, a crystal crown which will turn to purest gold in the sunset and the colour of ivory by moonlight. Jerusalem, oh Jerusalem. The Temple appears at that very moment as if deposited there by God and the sudden breeze which caresses the faces, hair and clothes of the pilgrims and travellers could be some divine gesture for, looking carefully at the clouds in the sky, we shall see a huge hand withdrawing its fingers soiled with clay, its palm marked with the lines of life and death of every man and creature in this world, but the time has also come for us to trace the line of life and death of God himself. Trembling with emotion, the travellers raise their arms to heaven and raise their voices in thanksgiving, no longer in chorus, but each and every one of them lost in ecstasy, the more sober amongst them scarcely moving but looking heavenwards and praying with great fervour as if at that moment they were being allowed to speak to God on equal terms. The road slopes downwards and as the travellers begin descending into the valley and climbing up the next slope which will lead them to the city gates, the Temple appears to be towering higher and higher and, because of the perspective, screening the dreaded Antonia Fortress where, even from this distance, one can make out the shadowy forms of the Roman soldiers keeping a lookout from the terraces, and the intermittent gleam of their weapons. This is where the group from Nazareth must make its farewells, for Mary is exhausted and would never survive the bumpy ride downhill if she were to keep up this fast pace which accelerates into a headlong rush once the city walls loom into sight.

47

And so Joseph and Mary found themselves all alone on the road, she struggling to recover her strength, he rather impatient at the delay, now that they are so close to their destination. The sun beats down over the silence engulfing the travellers. Suddenly, a muffled scream escapes from Mary's lips. Nervously, Joseph asks her, Is the pain getting worse, and she can barely say, Yes. Just then an expression of disbelief creeps into her face, as though she has come up against something beyond her understanding. She certainly felt that pain in her body, but it seemed to belong to someone else, to whom then, to the child inside her womb. How could her body experience this pain which belonged to another, yet might well have been hers, rather like an echo which by some strange acoustical phenomenon can be heard with greater intensity than the sound that produced it in the first place. Scarcely wishing to know, Joseph cautiously asked her, Is the pain still as bad, and Mary was at a loss for an answer. She would be lying if she were to say no, and it would not be true if she were to say yes, and so she decides to say nothing but the pain is there all right and she can feel it, but it is so remote that she has the impression of watching her child suffer in her womb without being able to go to its assistance. No order has been given nor has Joseph used his whip, yet the donkey takes the steep slope leading to Jerusalem at a lively pace as if assured of a full manger and a nice long rest when it gets there. What the donkey does not know is that there is still some way to go before reaching Bethlehem, and once there it will discover that things are not as easy as they might seem. Of course it would be nice to proclaim, Veni, vidi, vici, like Julius Caesar at the height of his glory, only to be assassinated by his own son, whose only excuse was that he had been adopted. Conflicts between fathers and sons, the inheritance of guilt, the disavowal of kith and kin, the sacrifice of innocents, go back a long way in time and promise to be endless.

As they entered the city gates, Mary could no longer hold back her anguished cries, now as heart-rending as if a lance had pierced her. Only Joseph could hear them, such was the noise coming from the crowd, rather less from the animals, although between them they caused a deafening uproar reminiscent of a busy market-place. Joseph decided to take no chances, You're in no condition to go any further, let's try and find an inn nearby and tomorrow I'll go on to Bethlehem alone and explain that you're giving birth, you can always register later if it's really necessary, for I know nothing about Roman law, and who can tell, perhaps only the head of the family need register, especially in our situation. Mary reassured him, The pain has gone, and she was telling the truth, the stabbing pain which had caused her to cry out had become a mild throbbing, nagging but bearable, rather like wearing a hair-shirt. Joseph could not have been more relieved. To search for lodgings in Jerusalem with its maze of narrow streets was a daunting prospect especially in their present plight, with his wife in the throes of childbirth, and him as terrified as the next man at the thought of the responsibility although he would never admit it. He thought to himself that once they reached Bethlehem, which was not much bigger than Nazareth, things would certainly be easier, because it is well known that people are friendlier in smaller communities. Who cares whether Mary is simply not complaining, no longer in pain, or putting a brave face on things, for they are on their way and will shortly arrive at Bethlehem. The donkey receives a slap on its hind-quarters, which on closer inspection is not so much an incentive to try and go faster amidst all that traffic and indescribable confusion in which they find themselves, as an affectionate gesture expressing Joseph's relief. Merchants cram the narrow streets, people of every race and tongue jostle each other, but the streets clear almost miraculously whenever a patrol of Roman soldiers or a procession of camels appears in the distance, and the crowds disperse like the parting of the waters of the Red Sea. At a steady pace, the couple from Nazareth and their donkey gradually emerged from that seething and hysterical bazaar, frequented by ignorant and insensitive people to whom there would be no point in saying, See that man over there, that's Joseph and the woman who looks as if she is about to give birth at any minute is Mary, and they're on their way to register in Bethlehem. And if our kindness in trying to identify them goes unnoticed, it is simply because we live in a world where such names abound and where innumerable Josephs and Marys of every age and condition are to be found at every turn. And we must not forget that this is not the only couple called Joseph and Mary who are expecting a baby, who knows, perhaps two infants of the same sex and preferably male will be born at the same hour in these parts with only a road or a field of corn between them. The destinies that await these infants, however, will certainly be different even if, in one final attempt to add substance to the primitive astrologies of ancient times, we were to call both of them Yeshua, which is the same as Jesus. And lest we are accused of anticipating events by naming an unborn child, the fault lies with the carpenter who made up his mind some time ago that this is the name he would give his first son.

Leaving by the southern gate, the travellers took the road to Bethlehem, feeling somewhat relieved that they would soon reach their destination and be able to rest at long last after such a tiring journey. Mary's troubles, however, are not over yet; she, and she alone, still has to endure the trials of childbirth and who knows where and when. According to Holy Scripture, Bethlehem is the location of David's house and lineage from which Joseph claims descent, but with the passing of time, all his relations have died, or the carpenter has lost all contact, an unpromising situation which leads us to believe even before we get there that the couple will have great difficulty in finding lodgings. Arriving in Bethlehem, Joseph cannot knock on the first door he comes to and say, I'd like my child to be born here, and expect to be greeted with a welcoming smile from the affable mistress of the house, Come in, come in, Master Joseph, the water is boiling, the mat laid out on the floor, the swaddling clothes are ready, make yourself at home. Things might have been so in a Golden Age when the wolf, rather than devour the lamb, would feed on wild herbs. But this is an age of iron, cruel and unfeeling. The time for miracles has either passed or has not yet come, and besides, miracles, genuine miracles, whatever people say, are not such a good idea, if it means distorting logic and the very nature of things in order to prove them. Joseph feels tempted to linger rather than confront the problems which await him, but considering how much worse it would be were his child to be born by the roadside, he forces the donkey, poor beast, to go faster. Only the donkey knows how weary it feels, all God cares about are humans, and not all humans, for some of them live like donkeys or worse, and God makes no effort to come to their assistance. One of his fellow travellers told Joseph that there was a caravanserai in Bethlehem, a real stroke of luck which seemed to be the answer to his problem. But even a humble carpenter would find it embarrassing to see his pregnant wife exposed to the morbid curiosity and wagging tongues of drovers and cameleers in the caravanserai, for some of these fellows are as brutish as the beasts they handle, and their behaviour is much more contemptible, for as men they posses the divine gift of speech which animals are denied. Finally Joseph decides to seek the advice and guidance of the Elders of the synagogue, and wonders why he did not think of this sooner. Feeling somewhat relieved, Joseph wondered if he should ask Mary if the pains were still there, but in the end said nothing, for we must not forget that this whole process is unclean from the moment of impregnation until the moment of birth, that horrific female organ, vortex and abyss, the seat of all the world's evils, an inner labyrinth, blood, sweat, discharges, gushing waters, revolting afterbirth, dear God, how can You permit Your beloved children to be born from such impurity. How much better for You and us to have created them from light and transparency, yesterday, today and tomorrow, beginning, middle and end, and alike for everyone, without discrimination between aristocrats and commoners, between kings and carpenters, singling out with some ominous stigma those destined to remain forever unclean. Restrained by so many scruples, Joseph ended up by asking the question almost with indifference, seemingly preoccupied with more important matters and condescending to take an interest in the lower orders, How do you feel. The question was timely for Mary had just started to notice something different about the pain she was experiencing, an admirable phrase, if put in reverse order, for it would be more correct to say that the pain was finally experiencing her.

They had now been walking for more than an hour and Bethlehem could not be far away. To their surprise, after leaving Jerusalem they found the road deserted, for with Bethlehem so close to the city, one might have expected to find a continuous toing and froing of people and animals. At the point where the road divided, not far from Jerusalem, one road branching off to Beersheba, the other to Bethlehem, the world appeared to contract and fold over on itself. If one were to visualize the world as a person, it would be like watching someone cover his eyes with his mantle and listening to the travellers' footsteps, just as we listen to the song of birds nestling among the branches, and the same is true of us, for that is how we must appear to the birds hidden in the trees. Joseph, Mary and the donkey had crossed the desert, for the desert is not as we imagine, the desert is any unpopulated territory, not forgetting that we can find a barren desert amidst a great throng of people.

To the right stands the tomb of Rachel, the bride whom Jacob awaited for fourteen years. After seven years' service, he was wedded to Leah, but he had to wait another seven years before being allowed to marry his beloved Rachel, who would die in Bethlehem giving birth to a son whom Jacob named Benjamin which means son of my right hand, but whom Rachel, as she lay dying, rightly called Benoni, which means child of my sorrow, God forbid that this should be an omen. Houses now begin to appear, mud-coloured like those of Nazareth, but here in Bethlehem the colour is a mixture of yellow and grey, which turns paler in the sun. Mary is in a state of near collapse, her body slumping further forward over the saddlebags with each passing moment. Joseph has come to her assistance and she puts one arm around his shoulder to steady herself. What a pity there is no one here to witness this touching scene which is all too rare. And so they enter Bethlehem. Despite Mary's condition, Joseph enquired if there was a caravanserai nearby for he thought they might rest until the following morning. Mary was in great pain but still not showing any signs of being ready to give birth. But when they reached the caravanserai on the other side of the village which was squalid and rowdy, part bazaar and part stable, there was not a quiet corner to be found even though it was still early and most of the drovers and cameleers would only start arriving later. The couple turned back, Joseph left Mary beneath the shade of a fig tree in a tiny square surrounded by houses and went off to consult the Elders. There was no one in the synagogue apart from a caretaker who called out to an urchin playing nearby and told him to accompany the stranger to one of the Elders who might be able to help. Fortune, who protects the innocent whenever she remembers them, decreed that Joseph in this latest quest, should pass through the square where he had left his wife, and just in time to save Mary from the deadly shade of the fig tree which was slowly killing her, an unforgivable mistake for which they must share the blame, for fig trees abound in this land and they ought to have known better. So off they set once more like condemned souls in search of the Elder, but he had left for the countryside and was not expected home for some time. On hearing this, the carpenter summoned his courage and called out aloud, Is there anyone here who for the love of Almighty God will offer shelter to my dear wife who is about to give birth. All he asked was a quiet corner for they had brought their own mats. And could anyone tell him where to find a midwife in the village who would assist with the birth. Poor Joseph coloured with embarrassment as he heard himself blurt out these private worries and concerns. The female slave standing in the doorway went back inside to report to her mistress and after a while she reappeared to tell them that they could not stay here and must look for shelter elsewhere. There was not much chance of finding lodgings in the village and her mistress suggested that they should take refuge in one of the many caves on the nearby slopes. And what about a midwife, asked Joseph, whereupon the slave replied that if her mistress agreed and he was interested, she herself could help out, for she had been in service all her life and had assisted at many a birth. These are, indeed, cruel times when a pregnant woman comes knocking at our door and we deny her shelter in a corner of the yard and send her off to give birth in a cave, like the bears and wolves. However, something pricked our conscience and, getting up from where we were sitting, we went to the door to see for ourselves this husband and wife who so desperately needed a roof over their heads. The sad expression on that poor girl's face was enough to arouse our maternal instincts and we patiently explained why we could not possibly take them in, the house was already overcrowded with sons and daughters, grandchildren, sons and daughters-in-law. So as you can see, there simply isn't any room here but this slave will take you to a cave we use as a stable. There are no animals inside at present and you should be able to make yourselves comfortable. The young couple were most grateful for our generous offer and we withdrew, feeling we had done our best and that our conscience was clear.

With all this coming and going, walking and resting, enquiring and pleading, the deep blue sky has turned paler, and the sun will soon disappear behind that mountain. The slave Salome, for that is her name, leads the way. She is carrying some hot coals to make a fire, an earthenware pot to heat some water, and salt to rub down the new-born infant as a precaution against any infection. And since Mary has brought cloths and Joseph has a knife in his knapsack to cut the umbilical cord, unless Salome should prefer to use her teeth, everything is ready for the birth. A stable, when all is said and done, is as good as a house, and anyone who has enjoyed the pleasure of sleeping in a manger knows that it is almost as good as a cradle.

And the donkey is not likely to notice any difference, for straw is the same in heaven as on earth. They reached the cave around the third hour, when the hovering twilight was still shedding golden rays over the hills. If their progress was slow, it was not because of the distance but, now that Mary had a place to rest, she could at least abandon herself to her suffering. She pleaded with them to slow down, for whenever the donkey lost its footing on a stone she suffered the most agonizing pain. The waning light outside failed to penetrate the darkness inside the cave but with a handful of straw, some live coals, much puffing and blowing and some dry kindling wood, the slave soon had a fire blazing as bright as any dawn. Then she lit the oil lamp which was suspended from a rock jutting out of the wall, and after helping Mary to lie down, she went to fetch water from the nearby wells of Solomon. On returning, she found Joseph worried out of his mind and at a loss as to what he should do, but we must not be too hard on him for men are not expected to be able to cope in such a crisis, at most they can hold their wife's hand and hope that everything will be all right. Mary, however, is all alone. The world would fall apart if a Jewish man in those days had made any such encouraging gesture. The female slave came in, whispered a few words of comfort, then knelt down between Mary's legs, for a woman's legs should be kept apart whenever something goes in or comes out. Salome has lost count of the number of children she has helped to bring into the world and poor Mary's suffering is no different from that of any other woman, for as God warned Eve after she sinned, I will greatly multiply your suffering and your conception, in sorrow you will bring forth children, and after centuries of sorrow and suffering, God is not yet appeased and the agony goes on. Joseph is no longer present, not even at the entrance to the cave. He has fled rather than listen to Mary's cries of woe, but these cries haunt him as if the very earth were crying out. The noise is such that three shepherds who were passing with their flocks approached Joseph and asked him, What's going on, the earth seems to be crying out, and he told them, My wife is giving birth in yonder cave. They asked, Are we right in thinking you're a stranger to these parts, Yes, we've come from Nazareth in Galilee to register, and no sooner did we arrive than my wife started feeling worse and now she's in labour. The fading light made it difficult to see the faces of the four men, and soon their features will completely disappear, but their voices could still be heard. Have you any food, one of the shepherds enquired, A little, replied Joseph, and the same voice told him, Once the child is born, let me know and I'll bring you some sheep's milk, and then a second voice could be heard saying, And I'll give you some cheese. Then there was a prolonged silence before the third shepherd finally spoke. In a voice which also seemed to come from the bowels of the earth, he said, I'll bring you some bread.

The son of Joseph and Mary was born like any other child covered in his mother's blood, dripping with mucous membrane and suffering in silence. He cried because they made him cry, and he will cry for this one and only reason. Wrapped in swaddling-clothes he rests in the manger with the donkey standing nearby but unlikely to bite him because the animal is tethered and cannot move far. Salome is outside burying the afterbirth just as Joseph approaches. She waits until he has gone into the cave and lingers there inhaling the cool night breeze and feeling as exhausted as if she herself had just given birth, but this is something she can only imagine, never having had any children of her own.

Three men are coming down the slope. They are the shepherds. They enter the cave together. Mary is reclining and her eyes are closed. Seated on a stone, Joseph rests his arm on the edge of the manger and appears to be watching over his son. The first shepherd stepped forward and said, Here's some milk from my sheep which I drew with my own hands. Opening her eyes, Mary smiled. The second shepherd stepped forward and said in his turn, I myself churned the milk which made this cheese. Mary nodded and gave another smile. Then the third shepherd, whose massive frame seemed to fill the cave, stepped forward and, without so much as glancing at the new-born infant's parents, said, I have kneaded this bread with my own hands and baked it in the fire that burns beneath the earth. No sooner had he spoken than Mary recognized him.

Since the world began, for every person who is born another dies. The person now close to death is King Herod who, in addition to all imaginable evils, is suffering from a horrible itch which has almost driven him insane. He feels as if hundreds of thousands of ants were incessantly gnawing at his body with their tiny, savage jaws. Having tried to no avail all the balsams known to man, remedies from Egypt and India, the royal physicians scratched their heads in search of a cure, or to be more precise, were in grave danger of losing their heads as they frantically tried out ablutions and household potions, mixing with water or oil any herbs or powders reputed to do some good, however contradictory their effect. Foaming at the mouth as if bitten by a mad dog, beside himself with pain and fury, the king threatens to have all of them crucified unless they can relieve his afflictions which, as one might expect, go beyond the unbearable burning sensation on his skin and convulsions which often leave him exhausted and writhing on the floor, his eyes bulging from their sockets as those ants continue to multiply and wreak havoc beneath his robes. Worst of all is the gangrene which has set in during the last few days, and this mysterious affliction which has set tongues wagging in the palace, as worms begin to ravage the genital organs of his royal person and truly start devouring him alive. Herod's screams can be heard echoing throughout the halls and corridors of the palace, the eunuchs attending him are kept awake day and night, the slaves of lower rank flee in terror when they hear him approach. Dragging his body which stinks of rot, notwithstanding the perfumes lavishly sprinkled over his robes and rubbed into his dyed hair, Herod is only being kept alive by his own wrath. Carried around in a litter, surrounded by doctors and armed guards, he scours the palace from one end to another in search of traitors whom he imagines to be lurking everywhere, an obsession he has had for some time. Without any warning, he will suddenly point a finger perhaps at the chief eunuch whom he accuses of having too much influence or at some recalcitrant Pharisee who has criticized those who disobey the Law when they should be the first to respect it, there is no need to mention any names, and that finger is also pointed at his own sons, Alexander and Aristobulus, who were imprisoned and hastily sentenced to death by a tribunal of nobles convened for this purpose and no other, what choice did the poor King have when in a state of delirium he saw those wicked sons advancing upon him with bared swords, and, in the most terrifying nightmare of all, caught sight in a mirror of his own severed head. He has escaped that terrible end and can now quietly contemplate the corpses of those who, a moment before, were still heirs to the throne, his own sons found guilty of conspiracy, misconduct and arrogance, and strangled to death.

From the murky depths of his troubled mind comes another nightmare to disturb the sporadic moments of sleep to which he succumbs from sheer exhaustion. The prophet Micah comes to haunt him, that prophet who lived at the time of Isaiah and witnessed the terrible wars which the Assyrians waged in Samaria and Judaea. Micah appears before him, denouncing the rich and powerful as befits a prophet, especially in this accursed age. Covered in the dust of battle and wearing a blood-stained tunic, Micah storms into his dream amidst a deafening blast coming from some other world. With hands of lightning, he appears to be pushing open enormous bronze gates as he gives solemn warning, The Lord will come down from His holy Temple and tread upon the high places of the earth. He then threatens, Woe to them that devise iniquity, and work evil upon their beds, when the morning is light they practise it, because it is in the power of their hand, and denounce those who covet fields and homes, taking them both by violence, and stealing them away, so they oppress a man and his house, even a man and his heritage. After repeating these same words night after night, as if responding to some signal, Micah vanishes into thin air. What causes Herod, however, to wake up in a cold sweat is not so much the terror struck by those prophetic cries but the agonizing thought that his nightly visitor withdraws just as he is about to reveal something more. The prophet gets as far as raising his hand and parting his lips, only to disappear, leaving the King frustrated and filled with foreboding. Now as everyone knows, Herod is not likely to be intimidated by threats when he does not feel the slightest remorse for all those deaths he ordered. For this is the man who had the brother of Mariamne, whom he loved more than any other woman, burned alive, the man who ordered her grandfather to be strangled and finally, after accusing her of adultery, Mariamne herself. It is true that he later suffered some kind of brainstorm in which he called out for Mariamne as if she were still alive, but he recovered from this madness in time to discover that his mother-in-law, and not for the first time, was hatching a plot to remove him from power. In no time at all and to the misfortune of all concerned, this dangerous meddler was despatched to the pantheon of the family into which Herod had married. And so the King's three sons became heirs to the throne. Alexander and Aristobulus, whose sad end we have already mentioned, and Antipater who will soon meet a similar fate. But we must not forget, since there is more to life than tragedy and misfortune, that Herod had no fewer than ten comely wives to pamper him and arouse his lust although by now they could do little for him, and he even less for them. So the nightly apparition of an irate prophet intent on haunting the powerful King of Judaea and Samaria, of Peraea and Idumaea, of Galilee and Gaulanitis, of Trachanitis, Auranitis and Batanaea, and the mighty ruler of this vast domain, would make little impression were it not for that vague threat which suddenly interrupts the dream and leaves him in suspense, awaiting some new threat, but what and how and when.

Meanwhile, there in Bethlehem, right on the doorstep of Herod's palace as it were, Joseph and his family continued to live in the cave. They did not expect to remain there for long so there was little point in looking for a house, especially at a time when accommodation was scarce and the profitable practice of renting rooms had not yet been invented. On the eighth day Joseph took his first-born to the synagogue to be circumcised. Using a knife made of flint, the priest cut the wailing child's foreskin with admirable skill, and the fate of that foreskin would in itself be worthy of a novel from the moment it was cut away, a loop of pale skin, with scarcely any bleeding, until its glorious sanctification during the papacy of Paschal I, who reigned in the ninth century of Christianity. Anyone wishing to venerate that foreskin today need only visit the parish church of Calcata near Viterbo in Italy, where it is preserved in a reliquary for the spiritual benefit of the faithful and the amusement of prying atheists. Joseph announced that his son should be called Jesus, and this was the name inscribed in God's register after it had been added to the civil register of Caesar. Far from being resigned to this outrage inflicted on his person without any appreciable spiritual benefit in return, the infant howled all the way back to the cave where its mother, needless to say, was anxiously waiting, this being her first child. Poor little thing, poor little thing, she said soothingly and opening her tunic she began breast-feeding the child, first on the left teat, perhaps because closer to her heart. Jesus, although still unaware of his name because no more than a babe in arms, a mere chick, puppy or lambkin, Jesus, as we were saying, gave a deep sigh of contentment the moment he felt the gentle pressure of Mary's breast against his cheek and the moist warmth as her skin touched his. As the sweet taste of his mother's milk filled his mouth, the indignity of that circumcision, unbearably painful at the time, now became remote, dissipated into a vague sense of pleasure which surfaced and went on surfacing as if arrested at the threshold or impeded by a closed door or some prohibition. On growing up, he will forget these first sensations and find it difficult to believe he ever experienced them, something which happens to all of us, wherever we may have been born and whatever the destiny that awaits us. If we had the courage to ask Joseph such a question, and God forbid that we should commit any such indiscretion, he would tell us that a father's worries are rather more serious for he now faces the problem of feeding an extra mouth, an expression no less true or apt simply because a child is fed at its mother's breast. Indeed, Joseph has every reason to be worried. How are they to live until they can return to Nazareth. Mary is weak and in no condition to make the long journey and besides, she must wait until she is no longer unclean and remain in the blood of her purification for the next thirty-three days following her child's circumcision. The little money they brought from Nazareth has nearly all been spent and Joseph cannot work as a carpenter here without tools or the wherewithal to buy wood. At that time life was hard for the poor and God could not be expected to provide for everyone. From within the cave came a sudden whimper which soon stopped, a sign that Mary had changed the little Jesus over to her right teat, but that momentary frustration was enough to renew the pain where the child had been circumcised. Once having sucked to his satisfaction, Jesus will fall asleep in his mother's arms and scarcely open his eyes when she settles him gently in the manger as if entrusting him to an affectionate and faithful nurse. Seated at the entrance to the cave, Joseph is still trying to decide what to do. He knows that there is no work for him here in Bethlehem, not even as an apprentice, for when he made enquiries the answer was always the same. If I need any help I'll send for you, empty promises which do not fill a man's belly, although this race has been living off promises ever since it came into being.

Time and time again one has seen even in people not particularly given to reflection that the best way of finding a solution is to let one's thoughts drift while remaining alert until the right moment comes to pounce, like a tiger taking its prey by surprise. This was how the false promises of the master carpenters of Bethlehem led Joseph to think about God's true promises, and subsequently about the Temple of Jerusalem which was still under construction and where there must be some demand for labourers, not only bricklayers and stonemasons, but also for carpenters, even if only to square joists and plane boards, basic jobs which are well within Joseph's capabilities. The only drawback, assuming they give him a job, is the time it takes to reach the site, a good hour and a half's walk or more, going at a brisk pace because it is uphill all the way and there is no patron saint of hill-climbers to extend a helping hand, unless Joseph rides there, but that would mean finding a safe place to leave his donkey. This may be God's chosen land but there are still plenty of rogues around if we are to believe the dire warnings of the prophet Micah. Joseph was pondering these nagging problems when Mary emerged from the cave after feeding her child and settling him down to sleep. How is Jesus, his father asked, conscious of how foolish that question must sound but unable to suppress his pride as the father of a son who already had a name. The child is fine, replied Mary, for whom the name was of no importance. She would have been just as happy to call him her child for the rest of her life were it not for the fact that she would bear

61

more children, and to refer to all of them simply as her children would create as much confusion as in the Tower of Babel. Allowing the words to come out as if he were thinking aloud, which is one way of not showing too much confidence, Joseph said, I must find some way of earning a living while we are here but there's no suitable work to be got in Bethlehem. Mary said nothing, nor was she expected to speak, she was only there to listen and her husband had already made an enormous concession by taking her into his confidence. Joseph looked at the sun, trying to decide whether there was enough time for him to go and return. He went back into the cave to fetch his mantle and knapsack, and on reappearing told Mary, I'm off, trusting in God to find work for this honest artisan in His Tabernacle should He deem him worthy of such an honour. Joseph wrapped his mantle over his left shoulder, adjusted his knapsack and off he went without saying another word.

Truly all is not gloom. Although work on the Temple was making good progress, labourers were still being hired, especially if they could be paid low wages. Surprisingly, Joseph had no difficulty in passing the simple aptitude test set by the head carpenter, which should make us reflect whether our earlier disparaging comments about Joseph's professional skills might not have been unjustified. This latest recruit for the Temple site went off giving profuse thanks to God. Along the way he stopped a number of travellers and entreated them to join him in praising the Lord and they cheerfully obliged, for these people see one man's joy as something to be shared by everyone. We refer, of course, to those of humble condition. When he reached the spot where Rachel is buried, a thought occurred to Joseph which came from the heart rather than the mind, namely, that this woman who had been so anxious to have another child was to die at his hands, if you will pardon the expression, and before she could even get to know him. Without so much as a word or a glance, one body separates itself from another, as indifferent as the fruit that drops from the tree. Then an even sadder thought occurred to him, namely, that children should always die because of the fathers that begat them and the mothers who brought them into the world, and he took pity on his own son who was condemned to die although innocent. Filled with confusion and anguish as he stood there before the tomb of Jacob's beloved wife, carpenter Joseph's shoulders drooped and his head fell forward, his entire body breaking out in a cold sweat, and now there was no one passing on the road to whom he could turn for help. He realized that for the first time in his life he doubted whether the world had any meaning and, like someone who had lost all hope, he said in a loud voice, This is where I shall die. Perhaps in other circumstances and if spoken with the courage and conviction of those who commit suicide, these words, devoid of sorrow and weeping, would suffice to open the door by which we depart the land of the living. But most men are emotionally unstable and can be distracted by a cloud on high, by a spider weaving its web, a dog chasing a butterfly, a hen scratching the soil and clucking to its chicks, or by something as commonplace as a sudden itching on one's face which one scratches and then wonders, Now what was I thinking about. For this same reason Rachel's tomb reverted in a flash to being a small, whitewashed building, without windows and resembling a discarded dice, forgotten because not needed for the game under way, marks on the stone covering the entrance left by the sweaty and grimy hands of pilgrims who have been coming here since ancient times, and surrounded by olive trees which were perhaps already old when Jacob chose this spot for the poor mother's last resting place and felled as many trees as were necessary in order to clear the terrain. When all is said and done, we can confidently affirm that destiny exists and that each man's destiny is in the hands of others. Then Joseph moved on but not before saying a prayer suited to the time and place. He said, Praise be to You, oh Lord our God, and God of our forefathers. God of Abraham, God of Isaac, God of Jacob, great, almighty and wondrous God, praise be to You. On returning to the cave Joseph went to look at his little son asleep in the manger before even telling his wife that he had found work. He thought to himself, He'll die, he must die, and his heart grieved, but then he reflected that, according to the natural order of things, he himself would die first, and that his death and departure from the land of the living would bestow on his son a kind of finite eternity, a contradiction in terms, an eternity which allows one to go on for a little longer when those whom we know and love no longer exist.

Joseph had been careful not to mention to the head carpenter that he would only be staying for a few weeks, five at the most, allowing enough time to take his son to the Temple, to complete Mary's purification and pack their belongings. He had said nothing rather than be turned away, a detail which shows that the carpenter from Nazareth was not familiar with working conditions in his own country, no doubt because he rightly thought of himself as being his own master and took little interest in the rest of the working community which then consisted almost entirely of casual labour. He kept a careful count of the remaining days, twenty-four, twenty-three, twenty-two and, to avoid making any mistakes, he had improvised a calendar on one of the cave walls, nineteen, drawing so many lines which he then erased one at a time, sixteen, watched by an admiring Mary, fourteen, thirteen, who thanked the Lord for having given her, nine, eight, seven, six, such a clever husband who could turn his hand to anything. Joseph had told her, We'll leave after we've been to the Temple, for it's time I got back to my work in Nazareth where I have got customers waiting, and she discreetly suggested, rather than appear to be criticizing him, But surely we cannot leave without first thanking the woman who owns the cave and the slave who helped to deliver our child and who still calls every day to see how he's coming along. Joseph made no reply. He'd never admit to having overlooked such a common act of courtesy, although his first inclination had been to load the donkey before-hand, to tie it up during the ceremony and then set off at once for Nazareth without wasting any time on thanks and farewells. Mary was right, it would have been ill-mannered to go away without as much as a word of gratitude, but if truth, poor thing, were always to prevail, then Joseph would be obliged to confess that he was somewhat lacking in good manners. To be reminded of this omission caused him to sulk and become irritable with his wife, behaviour which usually served to ease his conscience and silence any remorse. So they would stay on for two or three days longer, make their farewells as was only fit and proper, and with all due respect and gratitude, so that they might finally depart leaving the inhabitants of Bethlehem with a favourable impression of this devout family from Galilee, well-mannered and dutiful and a notable exception, when one considers the low opinion in which people from Galilee are generally held by the inhabitants of Jerusalem and its environs.

The memorable day finally arrived when the child Jesus was carried to the Temple in his mother's arms, mounted on the patient donkey which had accompanied and assisted this family since the outset. Joseph leads the donkey by the halter, he is in a hurry to get there, anxious not to lose a whole day's work, even if their departure is imminent. Next day they were already on the road as dawn broke dispersing the last vestiges of night. Rachel's tomb was already some way behind. As they passed, the façade had taken on the fiery hue of a pomegranate, so different from its appearance at night when it became opaque, or that deathly pallor when the moon appears on high. After a time the infant Jesus woke up, but this time he was wide awake for he had scarcely opened his eyes when his mother wrapped him up for the journey, and he cried to be fed in that plaintive voice which is the only one he has so far. One day, like the rest of us, he will learn to speak with other voices, which will enable him to express other forms of hunger and experience other tears.

On the steep slopes not far from Jerusalem the family merged with the multitude of pilgrims and vendors who were flocking to the city, all seemingly intent upon arriving first, but cautiously slowing down and curbing their excitement when they came face to face with the Roman soldiers who were moving among the crowds in pairs, or with some detachment or other of Herod's mercenary troops which recruited every imaginable race, many Jews, as one might have expected, but also Idumaeans, Galatians, Thracians, Germans, Gauls, and even Babylonians, who were unrivalled as archers. A harmless carpenter who only handles peaceful weapons such as the plane, adze, mallet and hammer, or nails and bolts, Joseph becomes so perplexed with fear and revulsion when he runs into these loutish brutes that he can no longer behave naturally or disguise his true feelings. So he keeps his eyes lowered, and it is Mary, who has been shut away in that cave for weeks with no one to talk to apart from the female slave, it is Mary who takes a good look all around her, her dainty little chin held high with understandable pride, for she is carrying her first-born, a mere woman yet perfectly capable of giving children to God and her husband. She looks so radiant and happy that some fierce-looking Gauls, fair with great whiskers, their weapons at the ready, smile as the family passes, their cruel hearts no doubt softened by the appearance of this young mother with her first child. Smiling at this renewal of the world, they bare rotten teeth, but it's the thought that counts.

There is the Temple. Viewed at close quarters, from down below

65

where we are standing, the building gives one vertigo, a mountain of stones upon stones which no earthly power would seem capable of dressing, lifting, laying and fitting, yet there they are, joined together by their own weight, without any mortar, as if the entire world were simply a set of building blocks, and the uppermost cornices when seen from below appear to be grazing the sky, like another and quite different Tower of Babel which even God will be unable to save because it was doomed to the same destruction, confusion and bloodshed. Voices will ask, Why, a thousand times, believing there must be an answer, but they will eventually die away for it is better to remain silent. Joseph went off to tether the donkey in the caravanserai set aside for the animals. During Passover and other religious feasts the place gets so crowded that there is not enough room for a camel to shake the flies from its tail, but things are easier now that the last day of the census has passed and travellers have returned to their homes, and there is always a space to be found at this early hour. In the Court of the Gentiles, however, which was bordered by colonnades on all four sides with the temple precinct in the centre, there was already a large crowd of people, moneychangers, bird-catchers, merchants who were trading lambs and kids, pilgrims who always gathered here for one reason or another, and numerous foreigners curious to visit the famous Temple built by King Herod. But the Court was so extensive that anyone on the far side looked no bigger than a tiny insect. It was as though Herod's architects, seeing through God's eyes, had been determined to expose man's insignificance in the presence of Almighty God, especially if they happened to be Gentiles. As for the Jews, unless they have come for a leisurely stroll, their goal lies in the middle of the Court, here is the centre of their world, the navel of navels, the Holy of Holies. That is where the carpenter and his wife are heading, that is where Jesus is being carried once his father has purchased two turtle-doves from the steward of the Temple, if such a title is appropriate for someone who benefits from the monopoly of these religious transactions. The poor birds ignore the fate that awaits them, although the smell of flesh and singed feathers lingering in the air does not deceive anyone, not to mention the much stronger stench of blood and excrement as oxen are dragged away to be sacrificed and foul themselves in terror. Joseph cradles the doves in the palms of his calloused hands, and in their

66

innocence the poor birds peck with satisfaction at his fingers which he curves in the shape of a cage. It is as if they were trying to tell him, We are happy with our new master. Oblivious to everything around her, Mary only has eyes for her little son, and Joseph's skin is far too rough to feel or decipher the amorous nibbling of the two doves.

They enter by the Wooden Gate, one of thirteen entrances to the Temple. Like all the others, it has an inscription in Greek and Latin carved into the stonework which reads as follows, It is forbidden for any Gentile to cross this threshold and the balustrade surrounding the Temple. Trespassers will be sentenced to death. Joseph and Mary enter carrying Jesus between them, and at the right moment will make a safe exit, but the doves, as we know, must be killed according to the Law before Mary's purification can be acknowledged and ratified. Any ironic or irreverent disciple of Voltaire will find it difficult to resist making the obvious remark that things being what they are, it would appear that purity can only be maintained so long as there are innocent creatures to sacrifice in this world, whether they be turtle-doves, lambs or whatever. Joseph and Mary climb the fourteen steps to the platform of the Temple. Here is the Court of the Women, on the left the storehouse for the oil and wine used in the liturgy, on the right the Chamber of the Nazarites, priests who do not belong to the tribe of Levi and are forbidden to cut their hair, drink wine or go near a corpse. On the opposite side, to the left and right respectively of the door facing this one, are the chamber where the lepers who believe themselves to be cured wait for the priests to come and examine them, and the storehouse where the wood is kept and inspected daily because rotten and worm-eaten wood must not be thrown on to the altar fire. Mary has not much further to go. She still has to climb the fifteen semi-circular steps leading to the Nicanor Gate, also known as the Gate Beautiful, but there she will stop, for women are not permitted to enter the Court of the Israelites which lies beyond this Gate. At the entrance, the Levites receive those who have come to offer sacrifice, but the atmosphere is rather less pious unless piety at that time had another meaning. It is not just the smoke rising from the burning fat or the smell of fresh blood and incense, but also the shouting of the men, the howling, bleating and lowing of the animals awaiting their turn to be slaughtered, and the last raucous squawk of a bird once able to sing. Mary tells the Levite in attendance that she has come for purification and Joseph hands over the doves. For one brief second Mary places her hands over the birds, her only gesture before the Levite and her husband turn away and disappear through the Gate. Mary will not stir until Joseph returns, she simply draws aside so as not to obstruct the passage, and here she waits holding her son in her arms.

Within the Court of the Israelites there is a furnace and a slaughterhouse. On two large stone slabs larger animals such as oxen and calves are killed, also sheep, ewes and male and female goats. There are tall pillars alongside the tables where the carcasses are suspended from hooks set into the stonework, and here one can watch the frenzied activity as the butchers wield their knives, cleavers, axes and handsaws, the air filled with fumes rising from the wood and singed hides, from the vapours of blood and sweat. Anyone witnessing the scene would have to be a saint in order to understand how God could condone this appalling carnage if He is, as He claims, the Father of all men and beasts. Joseph has to wait outside the balustrade which separates the Court of the Israelites from that of Priests, but from where he is standing he can get a good view of the High Altar, four times higher than the tallest man, also of the Temple proper beyond, for the layout is like one of those Chinese boxes with each chamber leading into another. We see the building from afar and think to ourselves, Ah, The Temple, then we enter the Court of the Gentiles and once more think, Ah, The Temple, and now the carpenter Joseph, leaning on the balustrade, looks up and says, Ah, The Temple, and he is right, there is the wide front with its four columns set into the wall, the capitals festooned with laurel leaves in the Greek style, and the great gaping entrance which has no actual door, but to enter that Temple of Temples inhabited by God would be to defy all prohibitions, to pass through that Holy Place called Hereal, and finally enter Debir, which is the last chamber of all, the Holy of Holies, an awesome stone chamber as empty as the universe, windowless and dark as the tomb, and where the light of day has never or will ever penetrate, until the hour of its destruction when all the stones will be reduced to rubble. The more remote He is, the more godly He becomes, while Joseph is merely the father of a Jewish child among many, who is about to witness the sacrifice of two innocent doves, that is to say, the father rather than the son, for the latter, who is just as innocent, is in his mother's arms, perhaps thinking, if such a thing is possible at his age, that this is how the world must always be.

By the altar, which is made from massive slabs of stone untouched by any tools since hewn from the quarry and set up in this vast edifice, a barefooted priest wearing a linen tunic waits for the Levite to hand over the turtle-doves. He takes the first one, carries it to a corner of the altar and with a single blow knocks the head from its body. The blood spurts everywhere. The priest sprinkles blood over the lower part of the altar, and then places the decapitated bird on a dish to drain the rest of the blood. At the end of the day he will retrieve it, for the dead bird now belongs to him. The other turtle-dove has the honour of being completely sacrificed, which means it will be incinerated. The priest ascends the ramp leading to the top of the altar where the sacred fire is burning. On the right-hand edge of the altar, he beheads the bird, sprinkles its blood over the plinth adorned on each corner with sheeps' horns, and then plucks out the entrails. No one pays any attention to what is happening for this is a death of no consequence. Craning his neck, Joseph is trying to identify amidst all the smoke and smells, the smoke and smell of his own sacrifice when the priest, having poured salt over the bird's head and carcass, tosses the pieces into the fire. Joseph cannot be sure. Crackling amidst the billowing flames fuelled with fat, the limp, disembowelled carcass of the little dove would not even fill a cavity of one of God's teeth. And at the foot of the ramp three priests are already waiting. A calf topples to the ground, felled by a cleaver. My God, my God, how fragile You have made us and how vulnerable to death. Joseph has nothing more to accomplish there, he must withdraw, collect his wife and child and return home. Mary is pure once more, not in the strict sense of the word, for purity is something to which most human beings, and above all women, can scarcely hope to aspire. With time and a period of seclusion, her fluxes and humours have settled down, everything has returned to normal, the only difference being that there are now two doves fewer in the world and one more child who caused their death. The family left the Temple by the same gate they had entered, Joseph went to fetch the donkey, and stepping on a large stone Mary climbed on to the animal's back while Joseph held the child. This was not the first time, but perhaps the memory of that turtle-dove having its entrails plucked out now caused him to linger before handing Jesus back to his mother, as if convinced that no arms could protect his son better than his own. He accompanied his wife and child to the city gate before returning to the Temple site. He will also be here tomorrow to finish his week's work, and then, God willing, they'll be off to Nazareth with all haste.

The same night, the prophet Micah revealed what he had hitherto withheld. When King Herod, by now resigned to those tortured dreams, was waiting for the apparition to disappear after the usual ranting and raving, which no longer had much effect, the prophet's formidable shape suddenly grew bigger and he uttered words he had never spoken before, It was from you, Bethlehem, so insignificant amongst the families of Judah, that the future ruler of Israel has come. And at that moment the King awoke. Like the deepest chord of the harp, the prophet's words continued to resound throughout the room. Herod lay there with his eyes wide open, trying to fathom the ultimate meaning of that revelation, if there was any such meaning, so fully absorbed that he was scarcely aware of the ants gnawing under his skin and the worms rotting away his entrails. The prophecy was well-known to every Jew and revealed nothing he did not already know. Besides, he was never one to waste his time worrying about the sayings of the prophets. What was bothering him at this moment was a vague disquiet, a sense of agonizing alienation, as if the prophet's words had another meaning and that somewhere amongst those syllables and sounds there were some imminent and fearsome threat. He tried to rid himself of this obsession and get back to sleep, but his body resisted and ached to the marrow. Thinking offered some measure of protection. Staring up at the beams on the ceiling where the decoration appeared to vibrate by the light of odoriferous torches shielded by fire-screens, King Herod searched for an answer but could find none. He then summoned the chief eunuch from amongst those guarding his bedside and ordered him to fetch a priest at once from the Temple, bearing the Book of Micah.

This coming and going from Palace to Temple and from Temple to Palace went on for almost an hour. Dawn was already breaking when the priest entered the King's bed-chamber, Read, ordered Herod, and the priest began, The Word of the Lord as spoken to Micah of Maresheth in the days of Jotham, Ahaz and Hezekiah,

Kings of Judah. He continued reading until Herod told him, Read further on, and the priest, puzzled and bemused as to why he had been summoned, jumped ahead to another passage, Woe to those who plot evil and lay plans for wicked deeds as they lie abed, but at this point he stopped, horrified at this involuntary imprudence, became tongue-tied and, hoping Herod might forget what he had just said, he went on, In the end it will come to pass that the Lord's great mansion will rise above the hills. Further on, snarled Herod, impatient to get to the passage which interested him, and the priest finally got there, But it is from you, Bethlehem, so insignificant among the families of Judah, that the future ruler of Israel will come. Herod raised his hand, Repeat that passage, he insisted, and the priest obeyed. Once more, he ordered him, and the priest read it for a third time. That's enough, said the King after a prolonged silence, You may withdraw. All was now clear. The book announced a future birth, nothing else, while the ghost of Micah had come to warn him that this birth had already taken place. Your words, like those of all prophets, could not have been clearer, even when we interpret them badly. Herod thought and thought again, his expression becoming more and more grim and menacing. He then summoned the commander of the guards and gave him an order to be carried out forthwith. When the commander returned to report, Mission fulfilled, Herod gave another command to be carried out at daybreak, now only hours away. So we shall soon know what has been ordered, unlike the priest who was brutally assassinated by soldiers before reaching the Temple. There are many reasons for believing that this was the first of the two orders, so close are the likely cause and the necessary effect. As for the Book of Micah, it disappeared, and imagine what a loss that would have been, had there been only one copy.

A carpenter among carpenters, Joseph had finished eating his lunch and he and his companions still had some free time before the foremen gave the signal to get back to work. Joseph could sit around for a while, stretch out and take a nap or indulge in pleasant thoughts, imagine himself out on the open road, wandering the countryside amidst the hills of Samaria or, better still, looking down from a great height on the village of Nazareth which he sorely missed. His soul rejoiced as he told himself that this long separation would soon be over and he would be on his way with only the Morning Star in the sky, and singing praise to the Lord Who protects our homes and guides our footsteps. Startled, he opened his eyes, afraid that he might have dozed off and missed the foreman's signal, but he had only been daydreaming, his companions were still there, some chatting, others taking a nap, and the overseer's jovial mood suggested that he might decide to give his workers the day off without later going back on his word. The sun is overhead, sharp gusts of strong wind drive the smoke from the sacrificial fires in the opposite direction. In this ravine which looks on to the site where a hippodrome is under construction, not even the gabbling of the vendors in the Temple can be heard. The machine of time appears to have come to a standstill as if it, too, were awaiting a signal from the mighty overseer of universal space and time. Joseph suddenly became uneasy after feeling so happy only a moment ago. He looked all around him and saw the same familiar building site to which he had grown accustomed in recent weeks, slabs of stone and wooden planks, a thick layer of white dust everywhere and sawdust which never seemed to dry. Plunged into this unexpected gloom, he tried to find some explanation, only to conclude that it must be the natural reaction of someone who is obliged to leave his work unfinished, even if this particular job was not his responsibility and he had every reason for leaving. Rising to his feet, he tried to calculate how much time was left. The overseer did not so much as turn to look in his direction, therefore he decided to take one last look at the section of the building on which he had worked, to bid farewell as it were, to the timbers he had planed and the joists he had fitted, if they could possibly be identified, for where is the bee that can claim, This honey was made by me.

After taking a good look round, Joseph was heading back to the site when he paused for a moment to admire the city standing on the opposite slope, built up in stages, with stones burnt to the colour of bread. The overseer must have given the signal by now, but Joseph was in no hurry, he gazed at the city, waiting for who knows what. The minutes passed and nothing happened. Joseph was muttering to himself, Well, I suppose I might as well get back to work, when he heard voices on the path below the spot where he was standing and, leaning over the stone wall, he saw three soldiers. They must have been walking along the path and decided to stop for a rest, two of them were leaning on their lances and listening to the third man who looked older and was probably their officer, although it was not easy to tell the difference unless one was familiar with the various uniforms and understood the significance of the many insignia, stripes and braidings denoting rank. The words which Joseph could barely make out sounded like a question, such as, And when will that be, and one of the younger men answered in a clear voice, At the beginning of the third hour when everyone is indoors. Whereupon the other soldier asked, How many of us are being despatched, only to be told, I don't know yet but enough men to surround the village. Has an order been given to kill the lot. No, not all of them, only those under the age of three. It's difficult to tell the difference between two- and four-year-olds, And how many will that make, the second soldier wanted to know. According to the census, the officer told them, there must be around twenty-five. Joseph's eyes widened as if they could grasp this conversation more readily than his hearing and he was trembling from head to foot, for it was quite clear that these soldiers were talking

74

about killing people. People, what people, he asked himself, bewildered and distressed, No, no, they were not people, or rather, they were people, but children. Children under the age of three, the officer in charge said, or perhaps it was one of the junior soldiers, but where, where could this be, after all, Joseph could not very well lean over the wall and ask, Is there some war going on. Breaking out in a cold sweat, he could feel his legs shaking. He could hear one of the men say gravely but ill disguising his relief, How fortunate for us and our children that we don't live in Bethlehem. Does anyone know why they've chosen to kill the children of Bethlehem, one of the soldiers asked, No, the commander didn't tell me and I'll wager he doesn't know himself, the order came from the king, and that's all we need to know. Tracing a line on the ground with his lance, as if dividing and sharing out destiny, the other soldier said, Wretched are we who not only practise the evil which is ours by nature, but who must also serve as an instrument of evil for those who abuse their power. These words went unheard by Joseph who had stolen away from this vantage point, cautiously at first and then in one mad rush, like a startled goat, scattering pebbles in all directions as he went. And without Joseph's testimony we have every reason to doubt the authenticity of the soldier's philosophical statement, both in form and content, given the more than obvious contradiction between the aptness of those sentiments and the humble status of the person who expressed them.

Delirious, bumping into everything in sight, overturning fruit stalls and birdcages, even a moneychanger's table, and almost oblivious to the cries of fury coming from the vendors in the Temple, Joseph's only concern is that his child's life is in danger. He cannot imagine why anyone should want to do such a thing, his plight is desperate, he chose to father a child and someone else wants to take it from him, one desire is as valid as another, to do and undo, to tie and untie, to create and destroy. Suddenly he stops, realizes the risk he is running if he continues with this reckless flight, the Temple guards might appear and arrest him and he is surprised they have not already been alerted by the uproar. Then dissembling as best he could, like a louse taking refuge in the seams of a garment, he disappeared into the crowd and instantly became anonymous, the only difference being that he was walking a little faster, but this was scarcely noticed amidst the labyrinth of people. He knows he must not run until he reaches the city gate, but is distressed at the thought that the soldiers may already be on their way, ominously armed with lance, dagger and unprovoked hatred, if by any misfortune they should be travelling on horseback, he will never catch up with them and by the time he gets there his son will be dead, poor child, sweet little Jesus. At this moment of deepest anguish a foolish thought occurs to him, adding insult to injury, he remembers his wages, the week's wages he stands to lose, and such is the power of these vile material things that, without exactly coming to a halt, he slows down just long enough to ponder whether he might be able to rescue both his money and his child's life. Quick as a flash, this unworthy thought surfaced and disappeared without leaving any sense of remorse, that sentiment which often, but not often enough, proves to be our most reliable guardian angel.

Joseph finally leaves the city behind and there are no soldiers to be seen on the road for as far as the eye can reach, no crowds gathered as one might expect in the event of a military parade, but the most reassuring sight of all is that of children playing innocent games without any of that wild enthusiasm they display when flags, drums and bugles go marching past, or that time-honoured custom of tailing the parade. If any soldiers had passed this way there would be no boys in sight, for they would have escorted the detachment at least to the first bend in the road, and perhaps the odd one, his heart set on becoming a soldier one day, would have decided to accompany them on their mission and so discover the fate that awaits him, namely, to kill or be killed. Now Joseph can run as fast as he likes and he takes advantage of the slope, hampered only by his tunic which he hitches up over his knees. As in a dream, he has the agonizing sensation that his legs are incapable of keeping up with the impetus of the rest of his body, heart, head and eyes, hands eager to offer protection yet so painfully slow in their movements. Some people stop on the road and shake their heads disapprovingly at this undignified frenzy, for these people are well-known for their composure and noble bearing. The only justification for Joseph's extraordinary behaviour in their eyes is not that he is running to save his child's life, but that he is Galilean, an ill-mannered lot with no real breeding as has often been observed. He is already passing in front of Rachel's tomb, and that good woman could never have suspected that she would have so much cause to weep for her children, to cover the nearby hills with her cries and lamentations, to claw at her face, tear out her hair, and then beat her bare skull. Before approaching the first houses on the outskirts of Bethlehem, Joseph leaves the main road and travels cross-country, I am taking a short-cut, he would reply if we were to question this sudden diversion, which might be shorter but is certainly much less comfortable. Taking care not to encounter any labourers working in the fields and hiding behind boulders whenever he saw any shepherds in the vicinity, Joseph had to take a circuitous route before arriving at the cave where his wife is not expecting him at this hour, and his son is not expecting him at all because he is fast asleep. Halfway up the slope of the last hill, from where he can already see the dark chasm of the grotto, Joseph is assailed by a terrifying thought, suppose his wife has gone to the village taking the child with her, nothing more natural, knowing what women are, than for her to take advantage of being on her own in order to make a farewell visit to Salome and several families with whom she had become acquainted during recent weeks, leaving Joseph to thank the owners of the cave with all due formality. For an instant he saw himself running through the streets and knocking on every door, Is my wife here. It would be foolish to enquire anxiously. Is my son here, in case some woman, for example, carrying a child in her arms should ask, on perceiving his distress, Is there something wrong, No, nothing, he would reply, Nothing at all, it's just that we have to set off at first light and we still haven't packed our belongings. Seen from here, the village with its identical roof-terraces reminds Joseph of the building-site, stones scattered everywhere until the workers assemble them, one on top of another, in order to erect some watchtower, an obelisk to commemorate some victory, a wall for lamentations. A dog has barked in the distance, others have barked in response, but the warm evening silence continues to hover over the village like a forgotten blessing about to lose its effect, like a wisp of a cloud on the point of vanishing.

This pause was short-lived. In one last spurt the carpenter reached the entrance to the cave and called out, Mary, are you there. She called out in reply, and Joseph realized that his legs were shaking, probably after all that running, but also from the sheer relief of knowing his child was safe and well. Inside the cave Mary was chopping up vegetables for the evening meal, the child asleep in the manger. Worn out, Joseph collapsed on to the ground but was soon back on his feet, We must leave, we must get out of this place. Mary looked at him in dismay, Are we leaving, she asked him, Yes, this very minute, But you said, Be quiet and start packing while I harness the donkey. Aren't we going to eat first, No, we'll eat something on the way, But it will soon be dark and we might get lost, whereupon Joseph lost his temper, Be quiet, woman, I've already told you we're leaving, so do as I say. Tears sprang to Mary's eyes. This was the first time her husband had ever raised his voice to her, and without another word she began collecting their scant possessions. Be quick, be quick, he went on repeating as he saddled the donkey and tightened the straps and started cramming whatever came to hand into the baskets, while Mary looked on dumbfounded at this husband she barely recognized. They were ready to leave, all that remained to be done now was to damp down the fire with earth. Joseph signalled to his wife to wait until he took a look outside. The ashen shadows of twilight merged heaven and earth. The sun had not yet set, but the heavy mist, while sufficiently high not to blot out the surrounding fields, prevented the light from dispersing. Joseph listened attentively, took a few steps, his hair standing on end, a scream could suddenly be heard coming from the village, so shrill that it scarcely sounded human, its echoes resounding from hill to hill and followed by more screaming and wailing which could be heard everywhere. Those were no weeping angels lamenting human misfortunes, these were the voices of men and women maddened by grief beneath an empty sky. Slowly, afraid of being heard, Joseph stepped back inside the entrance to the cave and collided with Mary who had disregarded his warning. She was trembling from head to foot, What are those screams, she asked, but without replying he pushed her back inside and hastily began throwing earth on to the fire. What are those screams, Mary asked a second time, invisible in the darkness, and Joseph eventually replied, People are being put to death. He paused and then added in a whisper, Children, by order of Herod, his voice breaking into a dry sob, That's why I said we should leave. There was a muffled sound of clothing and hay being disturbed, Mary was lifting her child from the manger and pressing him to her bosom, Sweet little Jesus, who would want to harm you, her words drowned in tears, Be quiet, said Joseph, don't make a sound, perhaps the soldiers won't find

78

this place, they've been ordered to kill all the children in Bethlehem under the age of three. How did you find out, I overheard it in the Temple and that's why I came rushing back, So what do we do now, We're on the outskirts of the village, the soldiers aren't likely to look inside these caves, they've been ordered to carry out a house-to-house search, so let's hope no one reports us and we're spared. He took another cautious look outside, the screaming had stopped and nothing more could be heard except a wailing chorus which gradually subsided. The massacre of the innocents had ended. The sky was still overcast. Encroaching darkness and the mist overhead had erased Bethlehem from the horizon of those inhabiting heaven. Joseph warned Mary, Don't move from here, I'm going out on to the road to see if the soldiers have gone. Be careful, said Mary, forgetting that her husband was in no danger, only children under the age of three, unless someone else had gone out on to the road with the intention of betraying him, telling the soldiers, This is Joseph, the carpenter, whose child is not yet two years old, a little boy called Jesus, who could be the child mentioned in the prophesy, for we have never seen it written or been told that our children are destined for glory, and it is most unlikely, now that they are dead.

Inside the cave one could touch the darkness. Mary, who had always been afraid of the dark, was used to having some light in the house, either from the fire or an oil lamp, or both, and the feeling, all the more threatening now that she was hiding away here in the earth, that fingers of darkness might reach out and touch her lips, filled her with terror. She had no desire to disobey her husband or to expose her child to any danger by leaving the cave, but she was becoming more terrified by the minute. Mounting panic would soon breach the precarious defences of common sense, it was no good telling herself, If there was nothing in the cave before putting out the fire then why should there be anything now, although the thought gave her just enough courage to grope her way to the manger where she settled her child, and then, carefully creeping around until she found the spot where the fire had been, she poked the ashes with a piece of firewood until some embers appeared which had not been fully extinguished. Her fears vanished at once, mindful of the luminous earth as she watched that tremulous glow with criss-crossing flashes of light like a flaming torch darting over the ridge of a mountain. The image of the beggar surfaced only to disappear, pushed aside by the urgent need to create more light in that terrifying cave. Fumbling her way around, Mary went to the manger to fetch a handful of straw. Guided by the faint glow on the ground, she was back in an instant and soon had the oil lamp set up in a corner where it could cast a pale but reassuring light on the nearby walls without attracting the attention of anyone outside. Mary went to her child who carried on sleeping, indifferent to fears, worries or violent deaths. Taking him into her arms, she went and sat near the lamp and waited. Time passed, her child woke without fully opening his eyes and when she saw he was about to cry Mary acted on maternal instinct and, opening her tunic, brought the child's avid lips to her breast. Jesus was still feeding at his mother's breast when she heard footsteps. Mary's heart almost stopped beating. Could they be soldiers, but surely these were the footsteps of some-one on his own, and soldiers normally went around at least in pairs if they were carrying out a search so that the one could cover the other in the event of any surprise attack. It must be Joseph, she thought, and feared that he might scold her for having the lamp lit. The steps came closer, Joseph was already entering the cave, when suddenly a shiver went up Mary's spine, these were not Joseph's firm, heavy footsteps, perhaps some itinerant labourer was seeking shelter for the night, as had happened twice before, although Mary had not been afraid on those previous occasions, because it never occurred to her that anyone, however heartless and cruel, would harm a woman with a child in her arms. She forgot about those infants who had been slaughtered in Bethlehem, some perhaps in their mothers' arms, just as Jesus lies in hers, innocent babes still sucking the milk of life as swords pierced their tender flesh, but then those assassins were soldiers and not vagrants, that makes all the difference. No, it was not Joseph, it was not a soldier looking for some military exploit he would not have to share, or some casual labourer without work or shelter. Once more in the guise of a shepherd, it was the man who had appeared several times as a beggar and who had claimed to be an angel without revealing, however, whether he had come from heaven or hell. At first, Mary had thought it could not possibly be him, but she now realized it could not be anyone else.

The angel said, Peace be with you, wife of Joseph, and peace be with your child, how fortunate for both of you to have found shelter in this cave, otherwise one of you would already be broken and dead and the other broken although still alive. Mary told him, I heard cries for help. The angel told her, Yes, this time you only heard them, but one day those cries will be raised to heaven in your name, and even before then you will hear thousands of cries beside you. Mary told him, My husband has gone to the road to see if the soldiers have left, he must not find you here when he comes back. The angel said, Don't worry, I'll be away before he arrives, I only came to warn you that you'll not see me again for some time, all that was decreed in heaven has come to pass, these deaths were as inevitable as Joseph's crime, Mary asked, What crime, my husband hasn't committed any crime, he is an honest man. The angel told her, An honest man who has committed a crime. You've no idea how many honest men have committed crimes in the past, for their crimes are countless, and contrary to common belief, they're the only crimes which cannot be forgiven. Mary asked, What crime has my husband committed. The angel replied, Need I tell you, surely you don't want to share his guilt. Mary said, I swear I'm innocent. The angel told her, Swear if you must, but any oath taken before me is like a puff of wind which knows not where it's going. Mary pleaded, What crime have we committed. The angel replied, Herod's cruelty unsheathed those daggers, but your selfishness and coward-ice were the cords which bound the victims' hands and feet. Mary asked, What could I have done. The angel told her, You couldn't have done anything for you found out too late, but the carpenter could have done something, he could have warned the villagers that the soldiers were coming to kill their children when there was still time for parents to gather them up and escape, to hide in the wilder-ness, for example, or flee to Egypt to await Herod's death which is fast approaching. Mary said, Joseph didn't think. The angel retorted, No, he didn't think but that scarcely excuses him. Mary tearfully implored him, Angel that you are, forgive him. The angel replied, I'm not an angel who grants pardons. Mary pleaded, Forgive him. The angel was intransigent, I've already told you, there's no forgive-ness for this crime, Herod will be pardoned sooner than your hus-band, for it's easier to pardon a traitor than a renegade. Mary asked him, What are we to do. The angel told her, You will live and suffer like everyone else. Mary asked, And what about my son. The

81

angel said, A father's guilt falls on the heads of his children and the shadow of Joseph's guilt already darkens his son's forehead. Mary sighed, Wretched are we. Indeed, replied the angel, and there's nothing to be done. Mary lowered her head, pressed her child closer to her bosom as if protecting him from those promised evils, and when she turned round the angel had vanished. But this time there was no sound of footsteps. He must have flown away, Mary thought to herself. She got up and went to the entrance of the cave to see if there were any traces of the angel's flight in the sky or any sign of Joseph nearby. The mist had cleared, the first stars glittered like metal, and wailing voices could still be heard coming from the village. Just then a thought as presumptuous as spiritual pride itself blotted out the angel's dark forebodings and caused Mary's head to spin. Suppose her son's salvation had been a gesture on the part of God, for surely the child's escape from a cruel death must mean something when so many others who perished can do nothing except wait for a suitable opportunity to ask God himself, Why did you kill us, and be satisfied with whatever reply He might choose to give them. Mary's delirium soon passed and the thought occurred to her that she, too, could be nursing a dead child like all those other mothers in Bethlehem, and she shed floods of tears for her spiritual welfare and the salvation of her soul. She was still weeping when Joseph arrived. She heard him coming but did not stir, what did she care if he should rebuke her, Mary was now crying with the other women, all of them seated in a circle with their children on their laps and awaiting resurrection. Joseph saw that she was weeping, he understood and said nothing.

Inside the cave, Joseph did not appear to notice the burning oil lamp. A fine layer of ashes now covered the embers but in the centre there was still the faintest flicker of a flame struggling to survive. As he began unloading the donkey, Joseph reassured Mary, We're no longer in any danger, the soldiers have gone and we might as well spend the night here. We'll leave before dawn, avoid the main road and take a short-cut, and where there are no byways we'll find a path through somehow. Mary murmured, All those dead children, which provoked Joseph into asking brusquely, How do you know, have you counted them, and Mary continued, I even knew some of those children. You ought to be thanking God for having spared your own son, I will, And stop staring at me as if I'd committed some crime, I wasn't staring at you, Don't answer back in that accusing tone of voice, Very well, I won't say another word, Just as well. Joseph tethered the donkey to the manger where there was still some hay. It cannot be all that hungry and, in fact, has fared rather well, lots of fodder and plenty of fresh air, but the donkey is preparing itself for the arduous journey back with a full load. Mary put her child down and said, I'll get the fire going, What for, To prepare some supper, I don't want any fire in here to attract the attention of some passer-by, let's eat whatever there is that doesn't need to be cooked. And so they ate. The light from the lamp made the cave's four inhabitants look like ghosts, the donkey motionless as a statue, its nose buried in the straw but without actually eating, the child dozing, the man and woman satisfying their hunger with a few dry figs. Mary laid out the mats on the sandy ground, threw a cover over them and, as usual, waited for her husband to go to bed. First Joseph went to take another look at the night sky, all was peaceful in heaven and on earth, and no more cries or lamentations could be heard coming from the village. Rachel only had enough strength left to sigh and whimper inside the houses where doors and souls remained firmly closed. Stretched out on his mat, Joseph felt quite exhausted after all that worry and panic, and he could not even claim that his wild chase had helped to save his son's life. The soldiers had strictly obeyed their orders. To kill the children of Bethlehem, without taking any further initiative such as searching all the caves in the neighbourhood to ferret out any fugitives in hiding, or even entire families who were making their homes there. Normally Joseph did not mind if Mary only came to bed after he had fallen asleep, but on this occasion he could not bear to think of her watching him without pity as he lay sleeping. He told her, I do not want you waiting up, come to bed. Mary made no protest. After making sure, as usual, that the donkey was securely tethered, she lay down with a sigh on her mat, firmly closed her eyes and waited for sleep to come. In the middle of the night, Joseph had a dream. He was riding down a road leading into a village and the first houses were coming into view. He was wearing military uniform and fully armed with sword, lance and dagger, a soldier amongst soldiers. The commanding officer asked him, Where do you think you're going, carpenter, to which he replied, proud of being so well prepared for the mission entrusted to him, I'm off to

Bethlehem to kill my son, and as he said those words, he woke up with the most fearsome growl, his body twitching and writhing with fear. Mary asked him in alarm, What's the matter, what happened, as Joseph shaking from head to foot kept repeating, No, no, no. Suddenly, he broke down and sobbed bitterly. Mary got up, fetched the lamp and held it to his face, Are you ill, she asked him. Covering his face with his hands, he shouted, Take that lamp away at once, woman, and still sobbing aloud he went up to the manger to see if his child was safe. He's fine, Master Joseph, worry not, in fact, the child gives no trouble, good-natured, quiet, all he wants is to be fed and sleep, and here he rests as peaceful as could be, oblivious to the dreadful death he has miraculously escaped, just think, to be put to death by the father who gave him life, for if death is the fate that awaits all of us, there are other ways of dying. Terrified that the dream might come back, Joseph did not lie down again. Wrapped in his mantle, he sat by the entrance to the cave beneath an overhanging rock which formed a natural porch and the moon on high cast a black shadow over the opening which the faint glow of the oil lamp within could not dispel. Were Herod himself to have been carried past by his slaves, escorted by legions of barbarians thirsting for blood, he would have told them calmly, Don't bother searching this place, carry on, there's nothing here except stones and shadows, what we want is the tender flesh of new-born babes. The very thought of that dream was enough to make Joseph shiver. He wondered what it could possibly mean, for, as the heavens could testify, he had raced down that slope like a madman, a Via Dolorosa if ever there was one, He had scaled rocks and walls in his haste to rescue his child like a good father, yet in his dream he saw himself depicted as a wicked fiend intent upon murder. How wise the proverb which reminds us that there is no constancy in dreams. This must be the work of Satan, he decided, making a gesture to drive out evil spirits. The piercing trill of an invisible bird rent the air, perhaps some shepherd whistling, but surely not at this hour, when the flocks are asleep and only the dogs are keeping watch. But the night, calm and remote from all living creatures and things, betrayed that supreme indifference which we associate with the universe, or that other absolute indifference of emptiness that will remain, if there is such a thing as emptiness, once all has been fulfilled. The night ignored the meaning and rational order which appear to govern the world at those moments when we can still believe it was made to harbour us and our insanity. That terrifying dream began to seem unreal and absurd, dispelled by the night, the shining moon, and the presence of his child asleep in the manger. Joseph was awake and as much in command of himself and his thoughts as any man could be, thoughts which were now charitable and peaceful, yet just as capable of engendering monstrosities such as his gratitude to God because his beloved child had been spared, undoubtedly out of ignorance or neglect, by soldiers who had slaughtered so many innocents. The same night descends over carpenter Joseph and the mothers of the children of Bethlehem, forgetting their fathers and even Mary for a moment, since they do not figure here for some strange reason. The hours passed quietly, and at first light Joseph got up, went to load the donkey and, taking advantage of the last rays of moonlight before the sky turned clearer, the whole family, Jesus, Mary and Joseph, were soon on their way back to Galilee.

Stealing out of her master's house where two infants had been killed, the slave Salome rushed to the cave that same morning, convinced that the same sad fate must have befallen the child whom she had helped to bring into the world. She found the place deserted, nothing remained except footprints and the traces of a donkey's hooves, dying embers beneath the ashes . . . but no bloodstains. Gone, she said, little Jesus has escaped this first death.

Eight months had passed since that happy day when Joseph arrived in Nazareth with his family safe and sound, despite so many dangers, the donkey less so, for it was limping slightly on its right hoof, when the news broke that King Herod had died in Jericho, in one of his palaces where he had taken refuge to escape the rigours of a Jerusalem winter which spares neither the weak nor the infirm. There were also rumours that once robbed of its mighty monarch, the kingdom was to be divided between three of his sons who had survived the feuding and destruction, namely, Herod Philip, who would govern the territories lying east of Galilee, Herod Antipas, who would inherit Galilee and Peraea, and Archelaus, who would rule Judaea, Samaria and Idumaea. One of these days, some passing muleteer with a flair for narrating tales, both real and fictitious, will give the people of Nazareth a graphic description of Herod's funeral, which he will swear to have witnessed. The corpse was placed in a magnificent sarcophagus made of the purest gold and inlaid with precious stones, transported on a gilded carriage draped with cloth of purple and drawn by two white oxen. The corpse was also covered in cloth of purple, all that could be seen was a human form with a crown resting where the head should be. Behind followed the musicians playing their flutes and the professional mourners who could not avoid inhaling the overpowering stench, and as I stood there at the roadside even I felt squeamish, then came the King's guards on horseback, followed by foot-soldiers armed with lances, swords and daggers as if marching to war, an endless procession wending its awesome way like a serpent without any visible

87

head or tail. I watched those soldiers in horror, marching in procession behind a corpse but also to their own death, to that death which sooner or later comes knocking on every door. Time to leave, comes the order promptly to kings and vassals alike, making no distinction between the rotting corpse at the head of the procession or those in the rear choking on the dust of an entire army, for the moment still alive, but heading for a place where they will remain forever. Clearly this muleteer would be more at home as an Aristotelian scholar strolling beneath the Corinthian capitals of some academy rather than prodding donkeys along the roads of Israel, sleeping in smelly caravanserais or narrating tales to rustics such as these from Nazareth.

Among the crowd in the square in front of the synagogue was Joseph, who happened to be passing and had stopped to listen. He did not pay much attention to the descriptive details of the funeral procession and he soon lost interest once the poet began to strike an elegiac note, for bitter experience had made the carpenter much more sensitive to this particular chord on the harp. One only had to look at him and examine that face. One thing was his composure when he tried to conceal his youth by looking solemn and thoughtful, another was the expression of bitterness which has marked him with lines deeper than open scars. But what is really disturbing about Joseph's face are those eyes which look dull and expressionless except for a tiny gleam inflamed by insomnia. It is true that Joseph rarely gets any sleep. Sleep is that enemy he confronts each night as if fighting for his very life, and it is a battle he invariably loses, for even when he seems to be winning and falls asleep from sheer exhaustion, he no sooner closes his eyes than he sees a detachment of soldiers appearing from nowhere on the road, with Joseph himself riding in their midst, sometimes brandishing a sword above his head, and it is just at that moment, when fear begins to get the better of him, that the leader of the expedition asks him, Where do you think you're going, carpenter, and the poor man, who would rather not say, resists with whatever strength he has left. But the malignant spirits in that dream are too strong for him and they prise his mouth open with hands of steel, reducing him to tears and despair and forcing him to confess, I'm on my way to Bethlehem to kill my son. We will not ask Joseph if he remembers how many oxen pulled the carriage bearing Herod's corpse or whether they were white or dappled. As he heads for home, all he can think of are the closing phrases of the muleteer's tale, when he described how that multitude accompanying the procession, slaves, soldiers, royal guards, professional mourners, musicians, governors, princes, future kings, and all the rest of us, whosoever we might be, do nothing else in life except search for that place where we shall remain forever. If only it were true, mused Joseph, with the unmistakable bitterness of someone who had given up all hope. If only it were true, he repeated to himself, thinking of all those who never left their place of birth yet death went there to find them, which only goes to prove that fate is the only real certainty. It is so easy, dear God, we need only wait for everything in life to be fulfilled in order to be able to say, It was fate. Herod was destined to die in Jericho and be drawn on a carriage to the Fortress of Herodium, but death exempted the infants of Bethlehem from having to travel anywhere. And Joseph's journey, which in the beginning seemed to be part of some divine plan to save those holy innocents, turned out to be futile. The carpenter listened and said nothing, he ran off to rescue his own child and left the others to their dreadful fate, and never was there a truer expression. So now we know why Joseph cannot sleep, and when he does it is only to awaken in a state of agitation, confronted with a reality which does not allow him to forget his dream, so that even when awake he dreams that same dream which haunts his sleep night after night, and when asleep, even while trying desperately to avoid it, he knows he will encounter that dream time and time again, for it hovers on the threshold between sleep and wakefulness, and Joseph must confront it on entering and leaving. This confused state of affairs is best defined as remorse. Yet human experience and the practice of communication have shown throughout the ages that synthesis is merely an illusion, an invalidation of language, almost like having a speech defect, and not so much trying to say love without being able to get the word out, as having a tongue in one's head yet not able to achieve love.

Mary is pregnant again. No angel disguised as a beggar has come knocking at the door this time to announce the child's arrival, no sudden gust of wind has swept the heights of Nazareth, no luminous earth has been discovered in the ground. Mary told Joseph in the simplest words, I'm with child. She did not say to him, for example, Look into my eyes and see how our second child is shining there, and this time he did not reply, Don't think I hadn't noticed, I was waiting for you to tell me. He just listened and remained silent, and eventually said, Oh, is that so, and carried on planing a piece of wood with apparent indifference, but then we know that his thoughts are elsewhere. Mary also knows, ever since that night of torment when her husband blurted out the secret he had been keeping to himself, and she was not altogether surprised, she had been expecting something like this after the angel told her in the cave, You will have a thousand cries all around you. A good wife would have said to her husband, Leave well alone, what's done is done, and besides, your first and only duty was to rescue your own child. But Mary had changed and was no longer what one would normally refer to as a good wife, perhaps because she had heard the angel speak those grave words which apparently excluded no one, I'm not an angel who grants pardons. Had Mary been allowed to discuss these intimate matters with Joseph, who was so well versed in Holy Scripture, he could have pondered the nature of this angel who appeared from nowhere to announce that he did not grant pardons, a statement which seems superfluous since everyone knows that the power to forgive belongs to God alone. For an angel to say that he does not grant pardons is either meaningless or too meaningful by far. An angel of judgement perhaps, who might well exclaim, You expect me to forgive you, what a silly idea, I'm not here to forgive, I'm only here to punish. But angels, by definition, leaving aside those cherubim with flaming swords who were posted by the Lord to guard the path to the tree of life lest our first parents or we, their descendants, should try to return to steal the fruits, angels, as we were saying, are not vigilantes entrusted with the corrupt but socially essential enforcement of repression. Angels exist to make our lives easier, they protect us when we are about to fall down a well, help us to cross the bridge over the precipice, drag us to safety just as we are about to be crushed by a runaway chariot or a fast car without brakes. An angel worthy of the name could easily have spared Joseph all this torment, simply by appearing in a dream to the fathers of the children of Bethlehem in order to warn them, Fetch your wife and child and flee to Egypt and stay there until I tell you to return, for Herod means to slaughter your child. In this way all those children could have been saved, with Jesus hidden away in the cave with his parents, and the others on their way to

Egypt where they would remain until the same angel returned to tell them reassuringly, Arise, fetch your wife and child and go back to Israel, for those who tried to kill your children are dead. With this kind warning the angel would ensure that the children returned to the places from whence they came, and where they would eventually meet their death at the appointed hour, because angels, however powerful, have their limitations just like God, and cannot ward off death. After much thought, Joseph might reach the conclusion that the angel who appeared in the cave was some infernal creature, an agent of Satan disguised as a shepherd this time, and further proof of the weakness and gullibility of women, who can be led astray by a fallen angel. If Mary could speak, if she were less secretive and prepared to reveal the details of that strange annunciation, things would be different, and Joseph would use other arguments to support his theory and, most crucial of all, the fact that this so-called angel did not proclaim, I am an angel of the Lord, or, I came in the name of the Lord. He simply said, I am an angel, before adding cautiously, Keep this to yourself, as if afraid that anyone else should know. Some may argue that these minor details contribute nothing new to our understanding of this all too familiar story, but as far as this narrator is concerned, it is essential to know whether the angel came from heaven or hell when interpreting past and future events. Between angels of light and darkness there are differences not just of form but also of essence, substance and content, and while it is true that Whoever created the former also created the latter, He subsequently tried to correct His mistake.

Mary, like Joseph, but obviously for different reasons, often looks distracted, her expression becomes blank, her hands drop in the middle of some task, gestures are suddenly interrupted, she stares into the distance, not all that surprising for a woman in her condition, were it not for the thoughts which occupy her mind and which could be summed up with infinite variations in the following question, Why did the angel announce the birth of Jesus, yet say nothing of this second child. Mary looks at her first-born, crawling around on all fours as children do at that age, she studies him and tries to perceive some special trait, some mark or sign, a star on his forehead, a sixth finger on his hand, but all she sees is a child like any other, who slobbers, gets dirty, and cries, the only difference being that he is her son, whose hair is black like that of his parents, the irises in his eyes already losing that whitish tinge inaccurately described as milky-white, and taking on their natural colour, dark brown genetically inherited, which gradually becomes a sombre green as it moves away from the pupil, if one can so describe a chromatic quality, but these characteristics are scarcely unique and are only important when the child belongs to us or, as in this case, to Mary. Within weeks this child will be making his first attempts to stand up and walk, he will fall on to his hands countless times, stay there staring ahead, lifting his head with some difficulty as he hears his mother say, Come here, come here, my child. Then he will begin to feel the urge to speak, sounds will form in his throat and at first he will not know what to do with them, he will get them mixed up with sounds he already knows and makes, such as gurgling and crying, until he begins to realize they must be articulated in a different and more deliberate way, and he will move his lips like his father and mother until he succeeds in pronouncing his first word, perhaps da, or dada or daddy, or perhaps even mummy, but what we do know is that henceforth little Jesus will not have to poke the forefinger of his right hand into the palm of his left hand if his mother and her neighbours should ask him for the umpteenth time, Where does the hen lay her egg. This is just another of those indignities to which a human being is subjected, to be treated like a lapdog and trained to react to certain sounds, a tone of voice, a whistle or the crack of the whip. Now Jesus is capable of replying that the hen can lay the egg wherever she wishes so long as she does not lay it in the palm of his hand. Mary looks at her little son, sighs, downhearted that the angel is not likely to return. You won't see me again for a while, he told her, but if he were to appear now she would not be as intimidated as on previous occasions, she would ply the angel with questions until he gave her an answer. Already a mother and expecting her second child, Mary is no innocent lamb, she has learned to her cost what suffering, danger and worry mean, and with all that experience on her side she can easily tip the scales to her advantage. It would not be enough for the angel to reply, May the Lord never allow you to see your child as you see me now without anywhere to lay my head. Firstly, the angel would have to identify this Lord in whose name he claimed to speak, secondly, convince her that he was telling the truth when he said he had no place to lay his head, which seemed unlikely for an angel, unless he was only saying it in his rôle as a beggar, and thirdly, what future did those dark, threatening words he had uttered augur for her son, and finally, what was the mystery surrounding that luminous earth buried near the door, and where a strange plant had grown after their return from Bethlehem, nothing but stalk and leaves which they had given up pruning after trying in vain to pull it up by the roots, only to find it reappearing with even greater vigour. Two of the Elders of the synagogue, Zacchaeus and Dothan, had come to inspect the phenomenon, and although they knew little about botany, they were in agreement that the seed must have been transferred with the mysterious soil and had then sprouted at the right moment, for as Zacchaeus observed, Such is the law of the Lord of life. Once she had got used to this stubborn plant, Mary decided it added a festive touch at the entrance to the house, while Joseph continued to be suspicious and he moved his carpenter's bench to another part of the yard rather than have to look at the wretched thing. After trying to cut it back with an axe and saw, he poured boiling water over it and even scattered burning coals round the stalk, but superstition prevented him from taking a spade and digging up the bowl of luminous earth which had been the cause of so much trouble. This was how matters stood when their second child, whom they called James, was born.

Over the next few years there were not many changes in the family apart from the arrival of more children, including two daughters, while their parents lost the last traces of youth. In the case of Mary this was not surprising, for we know how childbearing, and she had borne so many children, gradually saps any freshness and beauty a woman may possess and causes her face and body to age and wither, suffice it to say that after James came Lisa, after Lisa came Joseph, after Joseph came Judas, after Judas came Simon, then Lydia, then Justus, then Samuel, and if any more came after them they perished without trace. Children are the delight and joy of their parents, as the saying goes, and Mary did her utmost to appear contented, but after carrying for months on end all those fruits who avidly consumed her strength, she often felt impatient and resentful, but in those days it would never have occurred to her to blame Joseph, let alone almighty God who governs the life and death of His creatures and assures us that even the very hairs of our head are numbered. Joseph had little understanding of the whys and

93

wherefores of begetting children, apart from the practical rudiments which reduced all enigmas to one plain fact, namely, that if a man and woman come together, in all probability he will impregnate the woman and after nine months, rarely after seven, a child is born. Released into the female womb, the male seed transmits, minute and invisible, the new being chosen by God to continue populating the world He has created. Sometimes, however, this fails to happen, and the fact that this transmission of the male seed into a female womb is essential but not always enough to generate a child, is further evidence of the impenetrable nature of God's designs. Allowing the seed to spill on to the ground, as in the case of the unfortunate Onan, whom the Lord punished with death when he refused to give his brother's widow children, rules out any possibility of the woman falling pregnant, but time and time again, as someone once said, the pitcher goes to the fountain until there is no more water and it comes back empty. For it has been proved that it was God who put Isaac into the little semen that Abraham was still capable of producing, and it was God who poured it into Sarah's womb, because frankly she was past conceiving children. Seen from a theogenetic angle, as it were, we may conclude without offending logic, which must preside over everything in this and every other world, that it was God himself who was forever inciting Joseph to have intercourse with Mary so that they might have lots of children and help Him quell the remorse which had been haunting Him ever since He permitted, or willed, without considering the consequences, the massacre of those innocent children of Bethlehem. But the strangest thing of all, and which goes to show that the designs of the Lord are not only inscrutable but also disconcerting, is that Joseph, in his subconscious, truly believed he was acting of his own accord and obeying God's will, as he made strenuous efforts to beget more and more children to compensate for all those killed by Herod's soldiers, so that the numbers would tally in the next census. God's remorse and that of Joseph were one and the same, and if people in those days were already familiar with the expression, God never sleeps, we now know that He never sleeps because He made a mistake for which no man would be forgiven. With every child begotten by Joseph, God raised His head a little higher, but He will never raise it fully, because twenty-seven infants were massacred in Bethlehem and Joseph did not live long enough to impregnate one woman with so many children, and Mary, worn out in body and soul, could never have withstood that number of pregnancies. The carpenter's house and yard were full of children and yet they might as well have been empty.

On reaching the age of five, Joseph's son started going to school. Each morning his mother took him to the synagogue and left him in charge of the steward who taught beginners, and it was there in the synagogue-cum-classroom that Jesus and the other little boys of Nazareth under the age of ten observed the wise man's precept, The child must be instructed in the Torah just as the ox is bred in the corral. The lesson ended at the sixth hour which we now refer to as midday. Mary would be waiting for her child and the poor woman was not allowed to ask him how he was coming along, even this simple right was denied her, for as the wise man's maxim categorically states, Better that the Law should go up in flames than be entrusted to women. Besides, if by any chance little Jesus had already been taught the true status of women in this world, including mothers, then he might have given her the wrong answer, the kind of answer that can reduce anyone to insignificance. Take Herod, for example, with all that wealth and power, yet if we were to see him now we would not even be able to say, He is dead and rotting, for he is nothing but mould, dust, bones and filthy rags. When Jesus arrived home, his father asked him, What did you learn today and, having been blessed with an excellent memory, Jesus repeated word for word and without a moment's hesitation, the lessons of the day. First they had been taught the letters of the alphabet, then the most important words and finally whole sentences and passages from the Torah which Joseph accompanied, beating out the rhythm with his right hand and slowly nodding his head. Standing aside, Mary looked on and learned things she was never allowed to ask, a clever ploy on the part of women and practised to perfection throughout the ages. Whenever forbidden to find out things for themselves they listen in and soon learn everything, even to the extent of knowing the difference between falsehood and truth, which is the height of wisdom. But what Mary did not understand, or understand sufficiently, was the mysterious bond between her husband and Jesus, although even a stranger would have noticed that look of tenderness and sadness on Joseph's face when he spoke to his first-born as if he were thinking to himself, This beloved son of mine is my sorrow.

95

All Mary knew was that Joseph's nightmares, like some scourge on his soul, refused to go away, and these nightly afflictions were now so frequent that they had become as much a habit as sleeping on the right side or waking up with thirst in the middle of the night. While Mary, as a good and dutiful wife, had not ceased to worry about her husband, the most important thing of all for her was to see her son alive and well, a sign that Joseph's crime had not been too serious otherwise the Lord would have punished him without mercy, as is His wont. Take the case of Job, broken and leprous, yet he had always been an honest, upright and God-fearing man, Job's misfortune was to have become the involuntary cause of a dispute between Satan and God himself, both of them clinging tenaciously to their own ideas and prerogatives. And then they are surprised that a man should despair and cry out, Perish the day I was born and the night in which I was conceived, let that day turn to darkness and be erased from the calendar, and that night become sterile and devoid of all happiness. It is true that God compensated Job by repaying him twice as much as He had taken, but what about all those other men in whose name no book has ever been written, men who have been deprived of everything and been given nothing in return, to whom everything was promised but never fulfilled. Yet life was peaceful in this carpenter's house, and however frugal their existence, there was always bread on the table and enough food to keep body and soul together. As for possessions, the only thing Joseph and Job had in common was the number of sons. Job had seven sons and three daughters, while Joseph had seven sons and two daughters, giving the carpenter the advantage of having put one woman less into the world. However, before God doubled his possessions, Job already owned seven thousand sheep, three thousand camels, five hundred yokes of oxen and five hundred donkeys, not counting the slaves of which he had many, whereas Joseph only has his donkey and nothing else. And there's no denying that it is one thing to feed two mouths, then a third, even if only indirectly during the first year, and quite another to find oneself saddled with a houseful of children who demand more and more food once they start growing. And since Joseph's earnings were not enough to hire an apprentice, it was only natural that he should make his children work, besides, this was his fatherly duty, for as the Talmud says, Just as a man must feed his children, he must also teach them to work, otherwise he will turn his own sons into good-for-nothings. And bearing in mind the precept of the rabbis that, The artisan must never think himself inferior to the greatest scholar, we can imagine how proudly Joseph began instructing his older sons one after another, as they came of age, first Jesus, then James, then Joseph, then Judas, in the secret skills of the carpenter's trade, ever mindful of the ancient proverb, A child's service is little, yet he is no little fool that despises it. When Joseph returned to work after the midday meal, his sons lent him a hand, a good example of domestic economy, and capable of producing a whole dynasty of carpenters for future generations, if God in His wisdom had not decreed otherwise.

As if the humiliation inflicted on the Hebrew race for more than seventy years were not enough to satisfy the shameless arrogance of the Empire, Rome decided, using the division of the former kingdom of Herod as a pretext, to update the previous census. This time, however, the men would not have to register in their place of origin, thus avoiding the damaging effect on agriculture and commerce and all the other upheavals we witnessed earlier, as in the case of Joseph and his family. The new decree ruled that the censors were to go from village to village, from town to town, and from city to city, where they would summon all the men, whatever their status, to the main square or some other suitable open-air venue, where their name, occupation and taxable wealth would be entered into the public records under the surveillance of the guards. Now it must be said that such procedures are not viewed with any favour in this part of the world, and this is nothing new, for Holy Scripture narrates the unfortunate decision of King David when he ordered Joab, the leader of his army, to carry out a census of Israel and Judah with the following words, Go through all the tribes of Israel from Dan to Beersheba and carry out a census of the people, and since a royal command was never questioned, Joab silenced his doubts, gathered together his army and set off to do the King's bidding. Nine months and twenty days later Joab returned to Jerusalem with the results of the census which had been carefully counted and verified. In Israel there were eight hundred thousand armed soldiers and five hundred thousand in Judah. Now we all know God does not like anyone usurping His authority, especially when it comes to His chosen people whom He will never allow to be ruled by any other lord or master, least of all by Rome, ruled as it is by false gods and men, firstly because such gods do not really exist, and secondly, because the sheer vanity of that pagan cult only serves to expose the falseness of its followers. But let us forget Rome for a moment and return to King David whose heart sank the moment the leader of his army began reading his report, but it was too late to feel remorseful and he confessed, I have committed a grave sin, but I beg you, Lord, forgive your humble servant's folly. And next morning, a prophet named Gad, who was, in a manner of speaking, the King's soothsayer and intermediary, with Almighty God, came to David as he was rising and told him, The Good Lord wishes to know whether you prefer three years of famine on earth, three months of persecution at the hands of your enemies, or three days of plague throughout the land. David did not enquire how many people would have to die in each case, he reckoned that in three days, even with plague, fewer people would die than in three years of war or famine. So he prayed, God willing, let there be plague. And God ordered plague and seventy thousand men died, not counting the women and children who had not been registered. The Lord finally agreed to quell the plague in exchange for an altar, but the dead were dead, either God had forgotten them or it was not convenient to have them resurrected, since we can safely assume that innumerable inheritances and divisions of property were already being debated and contested, because there is no reason why God's chosen people should disclaim worldly goods which rightfully belong to them, whether acquired by the sweat of their brow, in litigation, or as the spoils of war. The outcome is what matters.

But before passing judgement on human and divine actions, we must also bear in mind that God, who lost no time in making David pay dearly for his mistake, now appears to be unaware of the humiliation being inflicted by Rome on His chosen children and, more perplexing still, seems indifferent to this blatant lack of respect for His name and authority. Now, when something like this happens, that is to say, when it becomes clear that God is showing no sign of coming soon, man has no other choice than to take His place, to abandon his own house and restore order in this poor old world of ours which belongs to God. Now then, those censors, as we mentioned earlier, were strutting around with all the arrogance of those in power, backed up by a military escort, an expressive if somewhat misleading metaphor which simply means that the soldiers were there to protect them from insults and assault once people started to rebel in Galilee and Judaea. Putting their strength to the test, some protest, quietly at first, then in despair gradually become more aggressive and defiant, an artisan bangs on the censor's table and swears they will never get a name out of him, a merchant takes refuge in his tent with his entire family and threatens to smash up everything and tear off all his clothes, a farmer sets fire to the harvest and brings a basket of ashes saying, This is the money Israel will pay to those who offend her. These troublemakers were arrested immediately, thrown into prison, flogged and humiliated, but since human resistance has its limits, frail creatures that we are, their courage soon failed them, the artisan shamelessly revealed his most intimate secrets, the merchant was prepared to sacrifice several daughters in addition to paying his taxes, the farmer covered himself in ashes and offered himself as a slave. The few who resisted were put to death while others, who had long since learned that the good invader is also a dead one, took up arms and fled into the mountains. The arms in question were stones, slings, sticks, clubs and cudgels, a few bows and arrows, scarcely enough to start an intifada, and the odd sword or lance captured in rapid skirmishes, but unlikely to do them much good, accustomed as they were, since David's reign, to the primitive weapons of placid shepherds rather than those of trained warriors. However, whether a man be Jewish or not, he adapts more readily to war than to peace, especially if he can find a leader who shares his convictions. This insurrection against the Romans began when Joseph's first-born was about eleven years old, and it was led by a man called Judas who hailed from Galilee and was therefore known as Judas the Galilean or Judas of Galilee. This simple method of naming people was common at the time, as we can see from names such as Joseph of Arimathaea, Simon of Cyrene or the Cyrenian, Mary Magdalene or Mary from Magdala. And if Joseph's son had lived and prospered, he would most probably have been called Jesus of Nazareth or the Nazarene, or perhaps something even simpler. But this is mere conjecture and we must never forget that destiny is a casket like no other, open yet closed at the same time. We can look inside and see all that has happened, the past transformed into fulfilled destiny, but we have no way of seeing into the future, apart from the odd presentiment or intuition as in the case of this Gospel, which could not be written were it not for those prodigious signs forecasting a destiny perhaps greater than life itself. But coming back to what we were saying, Judas the Galilean had rebellion in his blood. His father, old Hezekiah, had participated in the popular revolts waged against Herod's presumed heirs after his death and before Rome could acknowledge the division of the kingdom and the authority of the new tetrarchs. These matters are beyond our understanding for, while we are all made from the same all too human substance, the same flesh, bones, blood, skin and laughter, tears and sweat, some of us become cowards and others heroes, some are aggressive and others pacifists. The same substance used to make a Joseph also made a Judas, and while the latter passed on to his sons this thirst for battle he had inherited from his own father, and sacrificed a peaceful existence in order to defend God's rights, the carpenter Joseph remained at home with his nine young children and their mother, confined to his work bench in order to eke out a living and provide food for his family. For no one can tell who will triumph tomorrow, some say God, others say nobody, one hypothesis is as good as the other because to speak of yesterday, today and tomorrow is simply to give different names to the same illusion.

But the men from the village of Nazareth, most of them youths, who went to join the guerrilla force of Judas the Galilean, nearly all disappeared without any warning, they simply vanished without trace from one minute to the next, their families sworn to secrecy, and this silence was so strictly observed that no one would have dreamed of asking, Where's Nathanael, I haven't seen him for days, if Nathanael no longer appeared at the synagogue or amongst the reapers in the fields, there was simply one man missing and the others carried on as if Nathanael had never existed, well not quite, for some know that Nathanael had been seen entering the village under cover of darkness and leaving again before dawn. The only indication of his arrival and departure was the smile on the face of Nathanael's wife. A smile can be most revealing, a woman can be standing motionless staring into space, at the horizon or simply the wall in front, and then she suddenly smiles, a slow, pensive smile, like an image coming to the surface and playing on restless waters, one would have to be blind to believe that Nathanael's wife had spent the night without her husband. And human nature is so perverse that some women, who were never without their husband at their side, began sighing as they tried to imagine those encounters, and they hovered round Nathanael's wife like bees around a flower heavy with pollen. Mary's situation was different, with nine children to care for and a husband who spent his nights tossing and turning in anguish and terror, often waking up the little ones and scaring them out of their wits. After a time they more or less got used to it, but the eldest boy, whose own dreams were disturbed by some mysterious presence, was forever waking up and in the beginning would ask his mother, What's wrong with Father, and she would brush the question aside, reassuring him, It's only a nightmare. She could not very well tell her son, Your father dreamt he was marching with Herod's soldiers along the road to Bethlehem. Which Herod. The father of the present king. Was that why he was groaning and shouting. Yes, that's right. I can't see how being the soldier of a king who's already dead can give one nightmares. Your father was never one of Herod's soldiers, he's been a carpenter all his working life. Then why does he have nightmares. People don't choose their dreams. Dreams choose people, not that I've ever heard it said, but it must be so. And what about all that groaning and moaning, Mother. That's because your father dreams he's on his way to kill you. Obviously Mary could never have brought herself to say those things or to reveal the cause of her husband's nightmare to Jesus who, like Abraham's son Isaac, was cast in the rôle of the victim who escaped, yet is inexorably condemned. One day, when he was helping his father to make a door, Jesus summoned his courage and questioned him. After a long pause and without raising his eyes, Joseph told him, My son, you are aware of your duties and obligations, carry them out and you will be justified in the eyes of God, but examine your conscience and ask yourself if there might not be other duties and obligations waiting to be fulfilled. Is this what you dream, Father. No, the fear that I might have neglected some duty or worse is the cause of my dreams. What do you mean by worse. I didn't think. And the dream itself. The dream is the thought that wasn't thought when it should have been, and now it haunts me night after night and I can't forget it. And what should you have thought. Not even you have any right to ask me all these questions, and I have no answer to give you. They were working in the shade in the yard, for it was summer and the sun was blazing. Jesus's brothers were playing nearby except for the youngest who was indoors being fed at his mother's breast. James had also been helping but he soon got tired and bored, little wonder, for the year between them made all the difference, Jesus will soon be old enough to make a more advanced study of religion now that he has finished his elementary schooling. In addition to further study of the Torah or written law, he is already being initiated in the oral law, which is much more difficult and complicated. This explains why even at such an early age he was able to conduct a serious conversation with his father, using words properly and debating with reflection and logic. Jesus is almost twelve, and on reaching manhood he will perhaps resume this interrupted conversation, if Joseph can find the courage to confide in his son and confess his guilt, that courage which failed Abraham when confronted by Isaac, but for the moment Joseph was content to acknowledge and praise the power of God. There can be no doubt that God's upright handwriting bears no resemblance to the crooked lines of men. Just think of Abraham, to whom the angel appeared and said at the last minute, Lay not your hand upon the child, and think of Joseph, who failed to seize the opportunity to save the children of Bethlehem when God sent an officer and three loquacious soldiers instead of an angel to warn him. But if Jesus goes on as well as he has started, perhaps he will get round to asking one day why God saved Isaac and did nothing to protect those poor children who were as innocent as Abraham's son, yet were shown no mercy before the throne of the Lord. And then Jesus will be able to say to Joseph, Father, you mustn't take all the blame, and deep down, who knows, he might dare to ask, When, oh Lord, will You come before mankind to acknowledge Your own mistakes.

While the carpenter, Joseph, and his son, Jesus, debated these important matters behind closed doors, the war against the Romans continued. It had been going on for more than two years, and now and then news of further casualties reached Nazareth. Ephraim was killed, then Abiezer, then Naphtali, then Eleazar, but no one could be certain where their corpses had been buried, between two stones on a mountain or at the bottom of some ravine, swept downstream by the current or lying beneath the futile shade of a tree. Unable to hold a funeral for those who had died, the villagers of Nazareth tried to ease their conscience by insisting, We neither caused nor witnessed this bloodshed. News also arrived of great victories. The Romans had been driven out of the nearby city of Sepphoris, also from vast regions of Judaea and Galilee where the enemy dared not venture, and even in Joseph's own village no Roman soldiers had been sighted for more than a year. Who knows, perhaps this is what prompted the carpenter's neighbour, the inquisitive and obliging Ananias, whom we have not mentioned for some time, to turn up in the yard one day and whisper in Joseph's ear, Follow me outside, and little wonder, because these houses are so tiny that it is impossible to have any privacy, everyone is crammed into one room by day and night, whatever the circumstances or occasion, so that when the Day of Judgement finally arrives, the Lord God should have no difficulty in recognizing his own. The request did not surprise Joseph, not even when Ananias furtively added, Let us go into the desert. Now, as we know, the desert is not simply that barren place, some vast expanse of sand or that sea of burning dunes we generally conjure up in our minds whenever we read or hear the word desert. As understood here, desert can also be found in the green land of Galilee, and the word means uncultivated fields where there are no signs of human habitation or labour. And such places cease to be a desert once humans arrive on the scene. But since there are only two men walking across this scrubland and Nazareth is still in sight as they head for three great boulders crowning the summit of the hill, there is no suggestion of the place being populated, and once the men have all gone this desert will revert to being desert. Ananias was sitting on the ground with Joseph at his side. There is the same age gap between them as there has always been but, while time passes for everyone, the consequences can be quite different. And so Ananias, who did not look his years when we first met him, now seems much older although the years have also left their mark on Joseph. Ananias is somewhat hesitant, the decisive manner with which he entered the carpenter's house soon changed once they were on the road and Joseph has to coax him to speak without appearing to pry. We've come a long way, he commented, giving Ananias his cue. This isn't something I could have discussed in your house or mine, explained Ananias, but now they can converse freely without any fear of being overheard in this remote place. You once asked me to look after your house during your absence, Ananias reminded him. Yes, replied Joseph, and I deeply appreciated your help, then Ananias continued, Now the time has come for me to ask you to look after my house while I'm gone. Are you taking your wife, No, I'm going alone, But surely if Shua is staying behind there's no need, She'll be going to stay with some relatives who live in a fishing village, Do you mean to tell me you're divorcing your wife, No, if I didn't divorce her when I found that she couldn't give me a son, why should I divorce her now, it's just that I shall be away for a while and I'd prefer Shua to stay with relatives. Will you be gone for long. I don't know, much depends on how long the war lasts. What does the war have to do with your absence, asked Joseph in surprise. I'm going off to look for Judas the Galilean. What do you want from him. To ask him if he'll allow me to join his army. I don't believe it, a peace-loving man like you, Ananias, getting involved in the war against the Romans, have you forgotten what happened to Ephraim and Abiezer, And also to Naphtali and Eleazar, Precisely, so listen to the voice of reason. No, you listen to me, Joseph, and to the voice which comes from my lips, I've now reached the age at which my own father died, and he achieved much more in life than this son of his who couldn't even beget children, I'm not as learned as you are or likely to become an Elder in the synagogue, all I have to look forward to is death, and I'm tied to a woman I don't even love. Then why not divorce her. Divorcing Shua is no problem, the real problem is how to divorce myself, and that's impossible. But how much fighting can you do at your age. Don't you worry, I'll go into battle as determined as if I were about to get a woman pregnant, I've never heard that expression before. Nor me, it came into my head this very minute. Very well, Ananias, you can rely on me to look after your house until you return. Should I not return and news reaches you that I've been killed, promise me you'll send for Shua so that she may claim my possessions. You have my promise. Let's get back now that my mind is at peace. At peace, when you're determined to go to war, I really don't understand you. Ah, Joseph, Joseph, for how many centuries shall we have to go on studying the Talmud before we begin to understand the simplest things. Why did we have to come all this way. I wanted to speak to you in the presence of witnesses. The only witnesses we need are Almighty God and this sky which covers us wherever we may be. And what about these stones. These stones are deaf and dumb and cannot bear witness. That may be so, but if you and I were to decide to give a false account of our conversation, these stones would accuse us and go on accusing us until they turned to dust and we to nothingness. Shall we go back. Yes, let's go. As they went, Ananias turned round several times to look at the stones until they finally disappeared behind a hillock, and just then Joseph asked him, Does Shua know, Yes, she knows, And what did she have to say, At first not a word, then she told me I should have abandoned her years ago and left her to her fate, Poor Shua, Once she's with relatives she'll soon forget me, and should I die in battle she'll forget me forever, forgetting is all too easy and that's life. They entered the village and when they arrived at the carpenter's house, which was the first of two houses on this side, Jesus, who was playing on the street with James and Judas, said his mother was with the neighbour next door. As the two men turned away, the voice of Judas could be heard announcing solemnly, I am Judas the Galilean, whereupon Ananias looked round and said with a smile to Joseph, Take a look, there goes my leader, but before the carpenter had time to reply the voice of Jesus could be heard saying, Then you don't belong here. Joseph felt a sword pierce his heart, as if those words were addressed to him, as if the game being played by his son was meant to convey another truth. Then he thought of the three boulders and tried, without knowing why, to envisage what life would be like if he were henceforth obliged to speak every word and perform every action in their presence, and suddenly remembering God, he felt stricken with terror. In Ananias' house they found Mary trying to console a distressed Shua, who dried her tears the moment the men arrived, not because Shua had stopped weeping but because women know from bitter experience when to suppress their tears. Hence the well-known saying, They're either laughing or weeping, but it simply is not true because they are still weeping quietly to themselves. Not that there was anything quiet about Shua's grief, and when Ananias departed she sobbed her heart out. One week later Shua's relatives came to fetch her. Mary accompanied her to the outskirts of the village where they embraced and said good-bye. Shua was no longer weeping, but her eyes would never be dry again. Nothing can ease her sorrow or extinguish the constant flame which scorches her tears before they surface and roll down her cheeks.

And so the months passed and news of the war continued to arrive, sometimes good, sometimes bad, but while the good news never went beyond vague allusions to victories which always turned out to be modest, the bad news now spoke of much bloodshed and heavy losses for the rebel army of Judas the Galilean. One day news came that Eldad had been killed when the Romans uncovered a guerrilla ambush, thus casting the spell on the sorcerer, and resulting in heavy casualties, but Eldad was the only recruit from Nazareth to have lost his life. And another day someone said that he had heard from a friend who had been told by someone else that Varus, the Roman governor of Syria, was on his way with two legions to put an end once and for all to this intolerable insurrection which had been dragging on for three years. The vagueness of this statement, Varus is on his way, and the lack of any precise details, spread panic amongst the people. They feared the dreaded insignia of war might appear at any moment heralding the arrival of a punitive force, bearing those initials which authorize and endorse military operations, SPQR, the Senate and People of Rome. Under this symbol and that flag, men go forth and kill each other, and the same thing could be said of those other well-known initials, INRI, Jesus of Nazareth, King of the Jews, but we must not anticipate events, for the dire consequences of Jesus's death will only emerge in the fullness of time. Everywhere there is much talk of imminent battles, while those with more faith in God predict that before the year is out the Romans will have been expelled from the Holy Land of Israel, but others, less confident, sadly shake their heads and foresee nothing but doom and destruction. And so it turned out. Following the news that Varus's legions were advancing, nothing happened for several weeks, allowing the rebels to intensify their attacks on the dispersed troops they were fighting, but the tactics behind this apparent inertia soon became clear when the sentries of Judas the Galilean reported that one of the legions was heading south in a circular movement, skirting the bank of the River Jordan, then turning right at Jericho in order to repeat the manoeuvre northwards, like a net being cast into the water and retrieved by an experienced hand, or throwing a lasso to capture everything in sight, while the other legion, carrying out a similar manoeuvre, headed southwards. The strategy could be described as a pincer movement, but it was more like two walls closing in simultaneously, knocking down those unable to escape and finally crushing them. Over hill and dale throughout Judaea and Galilee, the legions' advance was marked with crosses where Judas' men had been nailed by their wrists and feet. To hasten their deaths, their bones were broken with a hammer. The soldiers looted the villages and carried out house-to-house searches. No firm proof was needed in order to arrest suspects and condemn them to death. These unfortunate wretches, if you will pardon the irony, had the good fortune to be crucified near their homes so that relatives could remove the corpses once they were dead. And what a sad spectacle, as mourning mothers, widows, young brides and weeping orphans watched the bruised corpses being gently lowered from the cross, for there is nothing more distressing for the living than the shocking sight of an abandoned corpse. The crucified man was then carried to his grave to await the day of resurrection. But there were others, who had been wounded in combat either in the mountains or in some other lonely spot and were abandoned by the soldiers while still alive in the most absolute of all deserts, that of solitary death, and there they remained, slowly burnt by the sun, exposed to birds of prey and, after a time, stripped of flesh and bone, reduced to miserable remains without shape or form, repugnant to their very souls. Those questioning, not to say sceptical souls, enjoined on other occasions to oppose the facile acceptance of gospels such as these, will want to know how it was possible for the Romans to crucify such a large number of Jews, especially in these vast arid regions devoid of any trees, apart from the rare stunted bush where you can barely crucify a scarecrow. But they are forgetting that the Roman army has all the professional skills and organization of a modern army. A steady supply of wooden crosses has been maintained throughout the campaign, as witnessed by all these donkeys and mules following behind the troops, laden with the posts and crossbars which can readily be assembled on the spot, and then it is simply a question of nailing the condemned man's extended arms to the transom, hoisting the pole upright and then, after forcing him to draw in his legs sideways, securing his two feet, one placed on top of the other with a single long nail. Any executioner attached to the legion will tell you that this operation may sound complicated, but it is, in fact, much more difficult to explain than to carry out.

Those pessimists who predicted disaster were right. From north to south and south to north, men, women and children flee in panic before the advancing legions, some because they might be accused of having collaborated with the rebels, others simply in terror for, as we know, they are in danger of being arrested and put to death without being proved guilty. Now, one of these fugitives interrupted his retreat for a few moments to knock on Joseph's door with a message from his neighbour, Ananias, who had been severely wounded back in Sepphoris. Ananias wanted Joseph to know, The war is lost and there is no hope of escape, send for my wife and tell her to claim my possessions. Is that all he said, asked Joseph. Nothing more, replied the messenger. And why couldn't you have brought him here with you when you knew you had to pass this way, In his condition he would only have been a hindrance and I had to put my family's safety first. First, perhaps, but surely not to the exclusion of everyone else. What are you trying to say, after all, you yourself are surrounded by children and if you remain here that can only be because you're in no danger. There's no time to lose, be on your way and may God go with you, for without Him there is always danger. You sound like a man without faith for you should know the Lord is everywhere. Indeed, but He often ignores us, and don't speak to me about faith after abandoning my neighbour to his fate. Well then, why not go and rescue him yourself. That's exactly what I intend to do. This conversation took place in the middle of the afternoon. It was a fine, sunny day with a few white clouds drifting across the sky like unmanned barges. Joseph went to untie the donkey, called his wife and told her without further explanation, I'm off to Sepphoris to look for our neighbour Ananias who's been badly wounded and cannot make the journey on his own. Mary simply nodded in reply, but Jesus clung to his father and pleaded, Take me with you. Joseph looked at his son, placed his right hand on his head and told him, You stay here, I'll be back soon, travelling at a brisk pace I should be back before dawn, and he could be right, for as we know, the distance between Nazareth and Sepphoris cannot be much more than five miles, about the same distance as from Jerusalem to Bethlehem, further proof that the world is full of coincidences. Joseph did not mount the donkey because he wanted the animal to be fresh for the return journey, firm and steady on its feet and prepared to carry a sick man gently on its back, or to be precise, a wounded soldier, which is not quite the same thing. At the foot of the hill where almost a year before Ananias had told him of his decision to join the rebel army of Judas the Galilean, the carpenter looked up at the three enormous boulders on the summit which reminded him of the segments of a fruit. Perched on high, they appeared to be waiting for some reply from heaven and earth to the questions posed by all the creatures and things of this world even though they may not voice them, What am I, Why am I here, What other world awaits me, this one being what it is. Were Ananias to ask these questions, we could tell him that at least the boulders remain unscathed, notwithstanding the wind, rain and heat, and some twenty centuries hence they will probably still be here, and for twenty centuries after that, while the world changes all around them. To the first two questions, however, there is no reply. Throngs of fugitives were to be seen on the road, with that same look of terror on their faces as the messenger sent by Ananias. They looked at Joseph in amazement, and one man taking him by the arm, enquired, Where are you going, and the carpenter replied, To Sepphoris to rescue a friend, If you know what's good for you, you'll do no such thing, Why not, The Romans are approaching and there's no hope of defending the city, I must go, my neighbour is like a brother and there's no one else who can go and fetch him, Heed my advice, and with these words the wise counsellor went on his way, leaving Joseph standing there in the middle of the road, lost in thought, wondering whether his life was worth saving or whether he loathed and despised himself and, after giving the matter some thought, he decided he felt quite indifferent, like someone confronting a void which is neither near nor far, where there is nowhere to rest one's eyes, for who can focus on emptiness. Then it struck him that as a father he had a duty to protect his children, that he ought to return home rather than go chasing after a neighbour, and Ananias was no longer even that, for he had deserted his home and sent his wife away. But his children were safe, the Romans would do them no harm, committed as they were to pursuing rebels. Finally reaching this conclusion, Joseph heard himself say aloud, as if he were wrestling with his inner thoughts, And I'm not a rebel either. So without further ado he gave his animal a slap on its haunch, exclaimed, Giddy up, donkey, and continued on his way.

It was late evening when he arrived at Sepphoris. The extended shadows of houses and trees, which could be made out at first, gradually faded until they disappeared into the horizon like dark, cascading waters. There were few people on the streets of the city, no women or children, only weary men laying down their precarious weapons as they stretched out panting for breath, and it was difficult to tell whether they had been exhausted by combat or flight. Joseph asked one of these men, Are the Romans approaching. The man closed his eyes, slowly reopened them and said, They'll arrive by tomorrow, and then averting his gaze told Joseph, Get away from here, take your donkey and leave this place, But I'm searching for a friend who's been wounded, explained Joseph, If you were to count all those who have been wounded as your friends then you'd be the wealthiest man in the world, Where are the wounded, Here, there, everywhere, But is there some place in the city where they're being nursed, Yes, behind those houses you'll find a garrison where lots of wounded men have been given shelter, perhaps you'll find your friend there, but hurry, for more corpses are being carried out than men brought in alive. Joseph knew the place well, he had been here many times, both for reasons of work which was plentiful in a city as rich and prosperous as Sepphoris, and to attend certain minor religious feasts which scarcely justified the long and arduous journey to Jerusalem. Finding the storehouse was easy enough, all one had to do was to follow the terrible stench of blood and pus which hovered in the air. It was almost like a game of hide and seek, Hot, cold, hot, cold, it hurts, no, no, it doesn't, but now those pains were becoming unbearable. Joseph tethered the donkey to a long stake he found nearby and entered the storehouse which had been converted into one great dormitory. Between the mats on the floor there were tiny lamps which provided hardly any light, tiny, twinkling stars against a black sky, which helped to guide one's faltering footsteps. Joseph walked slowly between the rows of wounded men in search of Ananias. There were other strong odours in the air, the smell of oil and wine, used to heal wounds, the smell of sweat, excrement and urine, for some of these unfortunate men were unable to move and they tried in vain to prevent themselves from evacuating there and then what their bodies could no longer retain. He isn't here, Joseph thought to himself, as he reached the end of the row. He retraced his footsteps, walking more slowly this time and looking carefully to see if he could recognize him. Alas, they all looked alike, with their long beards, hollow cheeks, sunken eyes, and unwashed bodies covered in sweat. Some of the wounded followed him with an anxious expression, hoping that this able-bodied man had come for them, but that momentary glimmer in their eye soon disappeared and their long vigil for who knows whom or what continued. Joseph came to a sudden halt before an elderly man with white beard and hair, It's him, he thought, yet his appearance had somehow changed since he had passed this way the first time, his beard and hair had certainly been as white as snow, but now looked dirty while his eyebrows, which were still black, looked quite unnatural. The old man's eyes were closed and he was breathing heavily. In a low voice Joseph called out, Ananias, then moving closer he repeated the name aloud, and little by little, as if he were emerging from the depths of the earth, the old man's eyelids began to move and once his eyes were fully open there was no longer any doubt, this was definitely Ananias, the neighbour who had abandoned his home and wife to go and fight the Romans, and here he lies with atrocious abdominal wounds and stinking of rotting flesh. At first Ananias did not recognize Joseph, the poor light in this makeshift infirmary does not help and his eyesight is even poorer, but he recognizes him all right when the carpenter repeats his name in another tone of voice which almost betrays affection. The old man's eyes fill with tears and he says over and over again, It's you, it's you, what are you doing here, what have you come here for, and he tries to raise himself on one elbow and to stretch out his arm, but cannot find the strength, his body sags, his entire expression contorted with pain. I came to look for you, said the carpenter, my donkey is tethered outside and we can be back in Nazareth in no time at all. You shouldn't have come here, the Romans are expected to arrive any minute now, I can't move, I'm done for, and with trembling hands he opened his tunic. Beneath the rags soaked in wine and oil were two great, gaping wounds which gave off the most nauseating smell of putrefaction and made Joseph hold his breath and look away. The old man covered himself, his arms slumping to his sides as if the effort had been too much for him, Now you know why I can't leave this place, if you tried to move me my guts would spill out, You'll be all right with a bandage firmly round your belly and if we went slowly, insisted Joseph unconvincingly since it was obvious that even if he could get the old man on to the donkey's back, they would never make it to Nazareth. Ananias' eyes were closed again and without opening them he told Joseph, You must go back, I'm warning you, the Romans will be here soon, Don't worry, they won't attack at night, Go home, go home, muttered Ananias, and in reply Joseph said, Try to get some sleep.

Joseph watched over him all night long. Struggling to keep awake, he found himself wondering why he had come to this place, since there had never really been any deep friendship between Ananias and himself. There was a considerable difference in their ages and besides he had always had certain reservations about Ananias and his wife who could be prying and meddlesome even while doing one a favour and who always gave the impression of expecting to be recompensed on their terms. But he is my neighbour, Joseph thought to himself, and he could think of no better answer to silence his misgivings, he's my fellow creature, a man close to death and with his eyes already closed, not because he doesn't wish to look at me but because he wants to savour every minute of approaching death, and I can't abandon him now. He was sitting in the narrow space between the mat on which Ananias was lying and that of a young boy who couldn't have been much older than his son Jesus, the poor lad was moaning quietly and muttering to himself, his lips cracked with fever. Joseph held his hand to comfort him just as Ananias's hand began fumbling as if reaching for a weapon to defend himself, and there the three of them remained, Joseph alive and well between two men who were dying, one life between two deaths.

Meanwhile the tranquil night sky sent stars and planets into orbit and a shining white moon came floating through space from the other end of the world, shedding innocence over the whole of Galilee. It was only much later that Joseph emerged from the torpor to which he had reluctantly succumbed. He awoke with a sense of relief because this time he had not dreamed of the road to Bethlehem. On opening his eyes he saw that Ananias, whose eyes were also open, was dead. At the last moment he had been unable to withstand the vision of death and his hand was gripping Joseph's so firmly that he felt his bones were being crushed. To rid himself of this painful sensation, he released his other hand which was clasping that of the boy, and still in a state of semi-consciousness, he noticed the boy's fever had subsided. Joseph looked out through the open door, the moon had set and there was daylight, an indeterminate sky in shades of sepia. Human forms could be seen stirring in the storehouse, those wounded men who could get up unaided went outside to watch the sunrise. They might well have asked each other or even the sky itself, What will this new dawn bring. One day we shall learn not to raise useless questions but until that day comes let us take this opportunity to ask ourselves, What will this new dawn bring. Joseph thought to himself, I might as well go, I can do nothing more here, and there was a questioning note in those words which prompted him to think, I could take his corpse to Nazareth, and the idea seemed so obvious that he almost convinced himself this was why he had come, to find Ananias alive and carry him off dead. The boy asked for water. Joseph held an earthenware bowl to his lips, How do you feel, he asked him, Better, At least the fever seems to have passed, Let me see if I can stand up, said the boy, Be careful, replied Joseph, trying to restrain him, and then another idea suddenly occurred to him, all he could do for Ananias was to bury him in Nazareth, but the boy's life could still be saved if he were to rescue him from this mortuary, so that one fellow creature, in a manner of speaking, could be substituted for another. He no longer felt any compassion for Ananias, whose body was now an empty shell, his soul evermore remote each time he looked at him. The boy appeared to sense that something good might be about to happen to him and his eyes were shining, but before he could ask any questions Joseph had already gone to fetch the donkey. Blessed is the Lord Who puts such splendid ideas into the heads of mankind. But the donkey had vanished. All that remained was a bit of rope tied to the pole. The thief had wasted no time in trying to untie the knot and using a sharp knife had simply cut through it.

This latest misfortune drained the strength from Joseph's body. Like one of those felled calves he had watched being sacrificed in the Temple, he dropped to his knees and, covering his face with his hands, shed all the tears which had been welling up for the last thirteen years as he awaited the day when he might be able to forgive himself or face up to final condemnation. God does not forgive the sins He makes us commit. Joseph did not return to the storehouse for he realised that his actions had become forever meaningless, that the world itself was meaningless. The sun was about to rise, but why, oh Lord, were there thousands of tiny clouds scattered throughout the sky like stones in the desert. Anyone watching Joseph there, as he wiped away the tears with the sleeve of his tunic, would have thought he was mourning the death of some relative recovered with the other wounded men in the store-house, when, if truth be told, Joseph had just shed the last of his natural tears, the tears of life's sorrow. After wandering through the city for more than an hour, hoping to the last that he might still find the stolen animal, he was just about to give up the search and return to Nazareth, when he was arrested by Roman soldiers who had besieged Sepphoris. They asked him his name, I'm Joseph, the son of Heli, and then where he lived, In Nazareth, and where he was going, Back to Nazareth, and what brought him to Sepphoris, Someone told me a neighbour of mine was here, and who was this neighbour, Ananias, and had he found him, Yes, and where had he found him, In a storehouse with others, and what others might they be, Wounded men, and in which part of the city, Over in that direction. They took him to a square where a group of men were assembled, twelve or fifteen men sitting on the ground, some of them obviously wounded, and the soldiers ordered him, Join the others. Realizing that the men sitting there were rebels, he protested, I'm a carpenter and man of peace, and one of the rebels spoke up and said. We don't know this man, but the officer in charge of the prisoners refused to listen and, giving Joseph one mighty push, sent him flying to the ground where he ended up amongst the others. The only place you're going is to meet your death, the officer told

him. The double shock of this terrible misfortune and the fate awaiting him left Joseph stunned. But once he had regained his composure, he felt a great tranquillity, convinced that this was all a
nightmare which would soon pass and that there was no point in
tormenting himself over these threats for they would vanish the
moment he opened his eyes. Then he remembered that when he
dreamed of the road to Bethlehem he had also been certain of waking
up, and suddenly he began to tremble as the cruel certainty of his
fate finally dawned, I'm going to die, I'm going to die even though
I'm innocent. He felt a hand being placed on his shoulder, the hand
of the prisoner beside him, When the commanding officer arrives,
we'll explain you're not one of us and he'll order your release, And
what about the rest of you, The Romans have crucified every rebel
they've captured so far and they're not likely to treat us any better,
God will save you, But surely you're forgetting God saves souls
rather than bodies. The soldiers arrived with more prisoners, in
twos and threes, and then a large group of about twenty. The
inhabitants of Sepphoris had gathered in the square and there were
even women and children in the crowd. A restless murmur could
be heard but no one dared move without the permission of the
Roman soldiers who were still on the lookout for anyone who might
have assisted the rebels. After a while, another man was dragged
into the square and the soldiers who had captured him announced,
That's all for now, whereupon the officer in charge shouted, On
your feet you lot. The prisoners thought the commanding officer
of the cohort must be approaching and the man sitting beside Joseph
told him, Prepare yourself, what he meant was, Prepare yourself
for release, as if one needed to prepare oneself for freedom, but if
anyone arrived there, it was not the commanding officer nor did
anyone ever discover who it might have been, because the officer
in charge suddenly gave an order in Latin to the soldiers. Needless
to say, everything said so far by the Romans has been expressed in
Latin because it would have been unthinkable for the descendants
of the She Wolf to speak in barbarian tongues, they have interpreters
for this purpose, but since the conversation here was between the
soldiers themselves no translation was required. Obeying their
superior's orders, the soldiers quickly rounded up the prisoners,
Forward march, and the procession of condemned men with the
crowd trailing behind made its way out of the city. Forced to march

with the other prisoners, Joseph had nowhere to turn for mercy. He raised his arms to heaven and called out, Save me, I'm not one of them, help me, I'm innocent, whereupon a soldier arrived and prodded him from behind with the butt of his lance, almost knocking him to the ground. All was lost. In despair, he felt nothing but hatred for Ananias who was to blame for getting him into this predicament, but this feeling soon passed, giving way to a sense of emptiness. He thought to himself, There is nowhere else to go, but he was wrong, and he would soon be there. Strange as it may seem, the certainty of death calmed him. He looked around at his companions in misfortune who seemed quite composed, some were naturally downhearted, but others defiantly held their heads high. The majority of them were Pharisees. Then for the first time Joseph remembered his children, and for one fleeting moment even his wife, but all those faces and names were too much for his tired brain. In need of sleep and food, he felt weak and could scarcely concentrate, the only image to remain was that of Jesus, his first-born and his ultimate punishment. He recalled their conversation about his dream, and remembered telling Jesus, It just isn't possible for you to ask me all the questions, or for me to give you all the answers, but now the time for answering questions was over.

On a stretch of high ground which overlooked the city, forty thick posts had been erected in rows of eight, strong enough to take a man's weight. And at the foot of each post lay a transom, long enough to allow a man to extend his arms. At the sight of these instruments of torture, some of the prisoners tried to escape but, baring their swords, the soldiers drove them back. One of the rebels tried to impale himself on one of these weapons, but to no avail for he was dragged off at once to be crucified. Then the laborious task began of nailing the wrists of each condemned man to a cross-bar before hoisting them up on the upright posts. The screams and moans could be heard throughout the countryside and the people of Sepphoris wept before this sad spectacle which they were obliged to watch as a warning. One by one, the crosses went up with a man hanging from each of them, the legs drawn in as we saw before, who knows for what reason, perhaps an order from Rome intended to make the job easier and save on materials, because one does not need to know much about crucifixions in order to see that a cross made to the measurements of the average man would require more work, be heavier to carry and more awkward to handle, not to mention the one serious disadvantage for the victims, because the closer their feet to the ground, the easier it is to lower their corpses afterwards, without having to use ladders, thus allowing them to pass directly, as it were, from the arms of the cross into the arms of their relatives, if they have any, or of the appointed grave-diggers who will not just leave them lying there. As it happened, Joseph was the last to be crucified, and this meant he had to look on as, one by one, his thirty-nine unknown companions were tortured and put to death. When his turn finally came, he was resigned to his fate and no longer had the strength to go on protesting his innocence and he probably missed one last opportunity to save himself when the soldier doing the hammering said to the officer in charge, This is the man who protested he was innocent, the officer paused for a moment, giving Joseph just enough time to call out, I'm innocent, but instead he chose to remain silent. The officer looked up and probably decided the symmetry would be destroyed if the last cross were not to be erected and that forty made a nice round figure, he gave a signal, the nails were driven in, Joseph let out a scream and went on screaming, then they hoisted him up, his weight held by the nails piercing his wrists, and there were more cries of pain as a long nail was driven through his heels. Dear God, this is the man You created, blessed be Your holy name, since it is forbidden to curse You. Suddenly, as if someone had given a signal, panic gripped the inhabitants of Sepphoris, not because of the crucifixions they had just witnessed but at the sight of flames spreading rapidly throughout the city as fire destroyed the houses and public buildings, and even the trees in the inner courtyards. Indifferent to the fires being set alight by their comrades, four soldiers from the cohort moved between the rows of dying men, methodically breaking their shin bones with iron rods. All Sepphoris was burning wherever one looked, as the crucified men passed away, one after another. The carpenter, named Joseph, son of Heli, was a young man in his prime who had just turned thirty-three.

When this war ends, and it will not be long now, for as we can see it is already in its dying stages, there will be a final reckoning of those who lost their lives, so many here, so many there, some near, some further away, and if it is true that with the passing of time the number of those who were killed in ambushes or open warfare loses all importance and is soon forgotten, those crucified, who number around two thousand according to the most reliable statistics, will long be remembered by the people of Judaea and Galilee, even after further wars have broken out and more blood has been shed. Two thousand crucified men is a lot, but it would seem even more if we were to imagine them set out a mile apart all along a highway, or encircling, for example, the country that one day will be known as Portugal, and which has a periphery more or less this size. Between the river Jordan and the sea widows and orphans weep, an ancient custom, that is why they are widows and orphans, so that they may weep, and once their boys grow up and go to fight some new war, there will be more widows and orphans to take their places, and even if customs were to change in the meantime, if black should become the colour of mourning instead of white, or vice versa, if the women were to wear black mantillas, whereas before they tore their hair out, tears of grief, when they are sincere, never change.

So far, Mary is not weeping, but in her soul she has a presentiment of death, for her husband has not returned home and in Nazareth it is rumoured that Sepphoris has been burned down and that men have been crucified. Accompanied by her eldest son, Mary retraces the route taken by Joseph yesterday. Very likely, at some point or other, her feet will touch the footprints left by her husband's sandals, for this is not the rainy season and there is nothing but the gentlest breeze to disturb the soil. Joseph's footprints could be mistaken for the traces of some prehistoric animal which inhabited these parts in some bygone age. We say, Only yesterday, and we might as well say, A thousand years ago, for time is not a rope one can measure from knot to knot, time is a slanted and undulating surface which only memory can stir and bring closer. A group of villagers from Nazareth accompany Mary and Jesus, some moved by compassion, others simply curious, and there are some distant relatives of Ananias, but the latter will return home as doubtful as when they left, for since they have not found a corpse he could still be alive. It never occurred to them to go and search amidst the debris of the storehouse where they might have recognized his body amongst the charred remains. These Nazarenes had covered half the journey when they met a detachment of soldiers which had been sent to search their village, some turned back, concerned about what might happen to their property, for one can never predict what soldiers will do when they knock on a door and find there is no one at home. The officer in charge wanted to know why these villagers were on their way to Sepphoris, and they replied, We're off to see the fire, an explanation which the officer accepted because fires have had an irresistible attraction for mankind since the world began and there are even those who say fire is a kind of inner call, instinctive and reminiscent of the original fire, as if the ashes somehow retained what had been burned, thus justifying, according to this theory, that look of fascination on our faces as we watch the flames of a camp-fire or the flickering of a candle in a dark room. Were we humans as foolhardy or daring as those butterflies, moths and other winged insects, to throw ourselves all together on to the flames, then who knows, perhaps the blaze would be so fierce and the light so dazzling that God would open His eyes and be roused from His torpor, too late, of course, to recognize us, but in time to see the impending void once we had gone up in smoke. Although she had left behind a house full of children without anyone to look after them, Mary refused to turn back and she was fairly easy in her own mind because it is not every day that soldiers invade a village and set about slaughtering young children. Besides, these Romans are generally not only willing but even anxious to see these children grow up so long as they remain servile and pay their taxes on time. Mother and son are walking along the road by themselves while Ananias' relatives, some half-dozen of them, are so busy chatting that they start to trail behind. Mary and Jesus have nothing but words of anguish to exchange and so prefer to remain silent rather than distress each other, a strange silence hovers everywhere, no birds can be heard singing, the wind has died down, there is nothing but the sound of footsteps, and even this retreats, like an intruder who has entered an empty house in good faith. Sepphoris suddenly came into sight as they rounded the last bend in the road. Several houses were still burning, thin columns of smoke rose here and there, walls were blackened, trees scorched from top to bottom, the foliage intact but the colour of rust. And here on our right the rows of crosses.

Mary started running, but they were still some distance away and she had to slow down and catch her breath. After giving birth to all those children without respite, her heart is much weaker. Jesus, as a respectful son, would have preferred to accompany his mother and to remain at her side, now and later, so that they might share the same joys and sorrows, but she is walking so slowly and dragging her feet, At this rate, Mother, we'll never get there, she makes a gesture as if to say, You go on ahead and I'll catch up, and leaving the road, Jesus sprints across the fields to save time, Father, Father, he calls out, hoping that he will not be there, fearing that he has already found him. He has reached the first row, some of the crucified men are still hanging from their crosses while others have already been taken down and lie waiting on the ground. Few have any relatives to gather round them for most of those rebels have come from afar, they belong to a mixed contingent which made its last united assault, now finally dispersed, each man left to confront alone the ineffable solitude of death. Jesus does not see his father, his heart wishes to rejoice but his reason tells him, Wait, We haven't got to the end of the row but, in fact, the end is right here. Stretched out on the ground is the father he has been seeking, there is little blood, only those open wounds on his wrists and feet, You could be sleeping, Father, but no, you're not asleep, how could you possibly sleep with your legs all twisted in that position, how charitable of them to take you down from the cross, but there are so many corpses here that the good souls who looked after you had no time to straighten your broken bones. The boy called Jesus is kneeling beside his dead father and weeps, he cannot bring himself to touch the corpse, much as he would like to, but there comes a moment when grief overcomes his fear of death, and he embraces that inert body. Father, Father, he sobs aloud, and another cry accompanies his, What have they done to you, Joseph, it is the voice of Mary who has arrived at last, exhausted and sobbing her heart out, for when she saw her son come to a halt in the distance, she knew what to expect. Mary's tears overflow when she sees the pitiful state of her husband's legs. We really do not know what happens to life's sorrows after death, especially those last moments of suffering, it is possible that everything ends with death but we cannot be certain that the memory of suffering does not linger at least for several hours in this body we describe as dead, nor can we rule out the possibility that matter uses putrefaction as a last resort in order to rid itself of suffering. With a tenderness she would never have permitted herself to show while her husband was alive, Mary pulled down Joseph's tunic after trying to straighten his broken legs which gave him the grotesque appearance of a puppet coming apart. Without touching the body, Jesus helped his mother to pull the tunic down over those thin shin bones, perhaps the most vulnerable part of the human body and a painful reminder of our fragile state. Those broken shin bones left the feet hanging sideways and, attracted by the smell of blood, flies kept swarming round the wounds inflicted by the nail. Joseph's sandals had fallen to the ground beside that thick trunk of which he was the last fruit. Worn out and covered in dust, they would have lain there forgotten if Jesus had not salvaged them without thinking. As if obeying an order and unnoticed by Mary, he stretched out his arm and tucked them under his belt, the perfect symbolic gesture as Joseph's first-born claims his inheritance, for certain things begin as simply as this and even today people say, In my father's boots I also become a man, or, expressed in more radical terms, In my father's boots I am a man.

From a discreet distance Roman soldiers kept a lookout, ready to intervene should they see any disorderly behaviour amongst those mourning and preparing the dead for burial. But these people showed no signs of wanting to stir up trouble, and were doing nothing other than pray as they went from one corpse to another and this task took more than two hours. Rending their garments, they recited the prayers for the dead over each corpse, relatives on the left, others on the right, their voices interrupting the evening silence as they chanted the following verses, Lord, what is man that You are merciful of him, and the son of man that You should visit him, man is but a puff of wind, his days pass like a shadow, just as man exists and fails to see death, and saves his soul by escaping to the tomb, man born of woman is given little time and much disquiet, he buds like a flower and like a flower perishes, he disappears like a shadow and has no permanence, what is man that You are mindful of him, and the son of man that You should visit him. Yet after acknowledging man's fatal insignificance in the eyes of God, in tones so deep that they seemed to come from inner awareness rather than from the voice itself, the chorus soared in exaltation to proclaim before Almighty God our unsuspected worth, Do not forget, oh Lord, that You made man a little lower than the angels and have crowned him with glory and honour. When the mourners reached Joseph whom they failed to recognize and who was the last of the forty, they passed on quickly, but the carpenter took with him to the other world everything he needed, and their haste was justified because the law does not allow the crucified to remain unburied until the following day and the sun is already going down. Given his youth, Jesus was not obliged to rend his garments, he was exempt from this show of mourning, but his strong, clear voice could be heard above those of all the others when he intoned, Blessed be the Lord, our God, King of the Universe, who created you with justice, kept you alive with justice, nourished you with justice, Who with justice allowed you to know this world, and with justice will resurrect you, Blessed be the Lord, who resurrects the dead. Stretched out on the ground, perhaps Joseph, if he can still feel the pain of those nails, may also hear these words, and he must know what part God's justice played in his life, now that he can no longer expect anything more from either the one or the other. Having finished praying, they now had to bury their dead, but there were so many of them and with night fast approaching, it is impossible to find a fitting place for all of them, that is to say a real tomb covered with a stone, and as for wrapping the corpses in mortuary cloths or even a simple shroud, there is simply no hope. So they decided to dig a long trench to hold all of them, and this was not to be the first nor will it be the last time that corpses are buried on the spot just as they are. Jesus was also handed a spade and he set about digging vigorously alongside the grown-ups. Destiny in its wisdom decreed that Joseph should be buried in a grave dug by his own son, thus fulfilling the prophecy, The son of man will bury man, while he himself will remain unburied. However enigmatic these words may seem at first sight, they merely state the obvious, namely that the last man, by virtue of being last, will have no one to bury him. Now this will not be the case of the boy who has just buried his father, the world will not end with him and we shall be here for thousands and thousands of years in a constant succession of births and deaths, and if man has always been the implacable foe and executioner of man, all the more reason why he should go on being his own grave-digger.

The sun has already disappeared behind the mountain. Enormous dark clouds over the valley of Jordan move slowly westward, as if drawn by this fading light which tinges their upper edges crimson. It has suddenly become cooler and rain seems likely tonight although unusual for this time of the year. The soldiers have already withdrawn, taking advantage of the fading light to return to their encampment which is some distance away and where their comrades-in-arms have probably arrived already after carrying out a similar search in Nazareth. This is how a modern war should be fought, with the utmost co-ordination, not in the haphazard fashion of Judas the Galilean's rebel force, and the outcome is there for all to see, thirty-nine of his men crucified, the fortieth an innocent man who came with the best of intentions and met a miserable death. The people of Sepphoris will look for somewhere to spend the night amongst the ruins of their burnt-out city and at daybreak each family will salvage whatever possessions they can from their former homes, and then go off to make a new life for themselves elsewhere, for Sepphoris has not only been razed to the ground but Rome will make sure that the city is not rebuilt for some time. Mary and Jesus are two shadows in the midst of a dark forest consisting of nothing but tree trunks, the mother draws her son to her bosom, two frightened souls searching as one for courage, and the dead beneath the ground seemingly anxious to detain the living. Jesus suggested to his mother, Let's spend the night in the city, but Mary told him, We cannot, your brothers and sisters are all alone and they must be famished. They could scarcely see where they were treading. After much stumbling and tripping, they finally reached the road, stretching out in the dark like a parched river bed. No sooner had they left Sepphoris than it started raining, heavy drops to begin with which produced a gentle sound as they made contact with the thick dust on the ground. Then the rain became more insistent and oppressive, the dust soon turned to mud and Mary and her son had to remove their sandals to avoid losing them on the way. They walk in silence, the mother covering her son's head with her mantle, they have nothing to say to each other, perhaps they might even be vaguely thinking that Joseph is not dead after all, that on arriving home they will find him attending to the children as best he can and he will ask his wife, What on earth possessed you to go out without asking my permission, but the tears have welled up again in Mary's eyes, not only because of her sorrow and grief, but also because of this infinite weariness, this continuous and persistent rain, this grim darkness, all much too sad and black for any remaining hope that Joseph might still be alive. One day someone will tell this widow about the prodigy witnessed at the gates of Sepphoris when the tree trunks used to crucify the prisoners took root again and sprouted new leaves, and prodigy is the right word, firstly because the Romans were in the habit of taking the crosses away with them when they left, and secondly because it was impossible for tree trunks which had been chopped, top and bottom, to have any sap left or shoots capable of transforming thick, bloodstained posts into living trees. The credulous attributed this wonder to the blood of martyrs, the sceptics preferred to think it was the rain, but no one had ever heard of blood or rain reviving trees once they had been made into crosses and abandoned on mountain slopes or on the plains of the desert. What no one dared to suggest was that this had been willed by God, not only because His will, whatever it may be, is inscrutable, but also because no one could think of any good reason why the crucified of Sepphoris should be the beneficiaries of this singular manifestation of divine grace, which was really much more in keeping with that of pagan gods. These trees will survive here for a long time and the day will come when this episode will be forgotten and, since mankind always seeks an explanation for everything, whether it be true or false, tales and legends will be invented, more or less factual to begin with, then gradually move further and further away from the truth until everything becomes pure fantasy. Then a time will come when the trees finally die of old age or be cut down to make way for a road, a school, house, shopping centre or military fortress, the excavators will dig up the soil and unearth those skeletons buried there for two thousand years. Then the anthropologists will appear on the scene and an expert in anatomy will examine the remains in order to announce to a shocked world that there is conclusive evidence that men were crucified in those days with their legs bent at the knees. And unable to discredit these findings on scientific grounds, people will find them aesthetically deplorable.

When Mary and Jesus arrived home, drenched to the skin, covered in mud and shivering with cold, they found the children in better spirits than one might have expected, thanks to the resourcefulness of James and Lisa who were older than the others. When the night turned cold, they had remembered to light the fire, where they sat huddled up against each other and tried to forget the pangs of hunger. On hearing someone knocking outside, James went to open the door. The rain was bucketing down and as their mother and brother crossed the threshold the house seemed to become flooded. The children stared and realized their father would not be coming back when Jesus closed the door but they said nothing until James finally asked, Where is father. The ground slowly absorbed the water dripping from their wet clothes, the silence only interrupted by the sound of damp wood crackling in the hearth. The children went on staring at their mother. And James repeated the question, Where is father, Mary opened her mouth to speak, but that fatal word, like a hangman's noose, almost choked her, forcing Jesus to intervene, Father is dead, he told them and without knowing why, perhaps as incontrovertible evidence that Joseph was definitely dead, he took the wet sandals from his belt and showed them to his brothers, I've brought these back. The older children were already close to tears but the sight of those forlorn sandals was too much for all of them and the widow and her nine children were soon crying their hearts out. Not knowing which of them she should comfort, Mary sank to her knees in a state of exhaustion and the children gathered around her, like a cluster of grapes from the vine which did not need to be trampled in order to release the colourless blood of tears. Only Jesus had remained standing, clasping the sandals to his bosom, musing that one day he would wear them, even this very minute if he could summon enough courage. One by one the children stole away from their mother, the older children discreetly leaving her to grieve, the younger children following their example. Unable to share their mother's sorrow, they simply wept and in this respect young children are like the very old who cry for nothing, even when they no longer feel anything or because they are incapable of feeling anything. Mary remained kneeling there in the middle of the room, as if awaiting some decision or sentence. Starting to shiver, she became aware of her wet clothes, got to her feet, opened a chest and took out an old, patched tunic which had belonged to her late husband. Handing it to Jesus, she told him, Remove that wet tunic, put this on and go and sit by the fire. Then she summoned her two daughters Lisa and Lydia, and made them hold up a mat to form a screen while she also changed, before starting to prepare some supper with the few provisions left in the house. Wearing his father's tunic, Jesus sat by the fire. The tunic was too long for him at the hem and sleeves and in other circumstances his brothers would have mocked him for looking like a scarecrow but this was not the time for jesting, not only because they were in mourning, but also because of the air of superiority which emanated from the boy, who suddenly appeared to have grown in stature, and this impression became even stronger when slowly and deliberately he held his father's wet sandals in front of the fire, a gesture unlikely to serve any useful purpose since their owner had already departed this world. James, who was the second eldest, went and sat beside Jesus and asked him in a low voice, What happened to father, They crucified him with the other rebels, Jesus whispered back, But why, Who knows, there were forty men there and father was one of them, Perhaps he, too, was a rebel, Who are you talking about, Father, of course, Impossible, he was always here at home, working away at his bench, And what about the donkey, did you find it, Nowhere to be seen, alive or dead. Supper was ready and they all sat around the common bowl and ate what little food there was. By the time they had finished eating the younger children were already nodding off to sleep, no doubt still troubled in spirit, but their bodies in need of rest. The boys' mats had been laid out along the wall at the far end of the room, Mary told the two girls, You will sleep here beside me, one on either side to avoid any jealousy. Cold air came through the gap in the door but the house remained warm. There was still some heat coming from the fire, and huddling up against each other the children gradually fell into a deep sleep notwithstanding their sighs of sorrow. Holding back her tears, Mary persuaded them to go to sleep for she was anxious to lament her loss undisturbed, her eyes wide open as she contemplated the future without a husband and with nine mouths to feed. Without any warning the sorrow went from her soul and her body succumbed to fatigue and now they are all asleep.

In the middle of the night Mary was awakened by the sound of someone moaning. She thought she must have dreamt it, but she had not been dreaming, she heard it a second time and this time it was much louder. Taking care not to disturb her daughters, she sat up and looked around her, but the light from the oil lamp did not reach to the far end of the room, Which of them could it be, she wondered, but deep down she knew it was Jesus who was moaning. She got up quietly, went to fetch the lamp hanging from a nail on the door and raising it above her head to get more light, she examined the children one by one, Jesus is tossing and turning and muttering to himself as if he were having a nightmare, he must be dreaming about his father, a mere boy and yet he has already witnessed so much suffering, death, bloodshed and torture. Mary felt she ought to rouse him, interrupt this other form of agony, then changed her mind, she had no desire to know what her son had been dreaming, but even this thought slipped her mind when she noticed that Jesus was wearing his father's sandals. She found this so strange that it worried her, what a foolish idea, quite unjustified and so disrespectful, wearing his father's sandals on the very day of the poor man's death. Not knowing what to think, she returned to her mat. Perhaps because of those sandals and the tunic, her son was reliving in a dream his father's mortal adventure from the day he left home and had thus passed into the world of men, to which he already belonged by the law of God, but could now enter with greater confidence as the heir to Joseph's few possessions, a much-mended tunic and a pair of worn-out sandals, and his dreams, even if only to retrace his father's last steps on earth. It never occurred to Mary that he might be dreaming about something else.

Day broke with a clear sky. When the sun appeared it was warm and bright and there was no sign of further rain. Mary set out early with all her sons of school age, accompanied by Jesus who, as we mentioned earlier, has already finished his studies. She was on her way to the synagogue to inform the Elders of Joseph's death and the presumable circumstances which led to his crucifixion, cautiously adding that as many of the burial rites as possible had been duly observed, notwithstanding the haste and improvisation with which everything had to be done. Finding herself alone with Jesus as they headed for home, Mary thought this might be her opportunity to ask him why he had decided to wear his father's sandals, but something dissuaded her at the last moment. In all probability Jesus would have been at a loss to explain and have felt deeply embarrassed. And unlike the child who gets up in the middle of the night to steal food and is caught in the act, he could not very well make the excuse that he was feeling hungry unless he was speaking of some other kind of hunger unknown to us. Then another idea occurred to Mary. Now that her son was the head of the household, it seemed only right that as his mother and dependant she should show him respect and consideration and take a closer interest in the ominous dream that disturbed his nights, Were you dreaming about your father, she asked him, and Jesus pretended not to have heard, he turned his face away, but undeterred his mother repeated the question, Were you dreaming. She was taken aback when her son at first replied, Yes, and then almost immediately said, No, his expression clouding over as if he were seeing his dead father once more. They walked on in silence and when they arrived home Mary set about carding some wool, thinking to herself that she ought to exploit her skills and take on extra work to support her family. Meanwhile Jesus, after looking up at the sky to see if the good weather was likely to last, fetched his father's work bench from the shed, checked the jobs which still had to be finished and then examined the various tools. Mary was delighted to see her son taking his new responsibilities so seriously. When the younger boys returned from the synagogue and they all sat down to eat, only the most observant onlooker would have suspected that this family had just lost a husband and father and, apart from Jesus, whose dark, twitching eyebrows betrayed his anxiety, the others, including Mary, seemed tranquil and composed, for it is written, Make bitter weeping and make passionate wailing, and let your mourning be according to his desert for one day or two, lest evil be spoken of you, and so be confronted of your sorrow, for it is also written, Give not your heart unto sorrow, put it away remembering the last end, forget it not for there is no returning again, him you shall not profit, and will only hurt yourself. There will be a time to laugh and rejoice but not just yet as surely as one day follows another, one season another, and the best lesson of all comes from the Book of Ecclesiastes where it is written, There is nothing better for man in this world than that he should eat, drink and be merry even as he labours. For God gives to the man who is virtuous in His eyes wisdom and knowledge and joy. That same afternoon, Jesus and James went on to the terrace to repair the roof which had been leaking throughout the night, and in case anyone is wondering why this minor domestic problem was not mentioned earlier, let me remind them that the death of a human being, innocent or otherwise, should take priority over everything else.

Night returned and another day would soon dawn, the family supped as best it could and then settled down on their mats to sleep. Mary woke up with a start in the early hours, no, it was not Mary who was dreaming, but Jesus. It was heartbreaking to listen to his moaning and groaning which soon awakened the older children, but it would have taken much more to rouse the little ones who were enjoying the deep sleep of the innocent. Mary found her son tossing and turning on his mat, his arms raised as if he were fending off the blows of a sword or lance, but he gradually quietened down either because his would-be attackers had withdrawn or because his life was ebbing away. Jesus opened his eyes and wept in his mother's arms like a little child, for even grown men revert to being children when they are frightened or upset, they do not like to admit it, poor things, but there is nothing like a good cry to relieve one's sorrow. What's wrong, my son, what's troubling you, Mary asked in distress and Jesus could or would not answer. There was nothing childlike about those pursed lips, Tell me what you were dreaming about, insisted Mary, and trying to encourage him to speak she asked, Did you see your father, whereupon the boy shook his head, released his arms and fell back on to his mat. Try to get some sleep, he told her, and then turning to his brothers, It's nothing, go back to sleep, I'll be all right. Mary rejoined her daughters but lay awake until morning, half expecting Jesus's dream to come back at any moment. She wondered what this dream could be which caused him so much anguish, but nothing more happened. It never occurred to Mary that her son might also be lying there awake in order to avoid dreaming again, but what did cross her mind was this strange coincidence that Jesus, who had always slept peacefully, should have started having these nightmares immediately after his father's death, God forbid that it should be the same dream, she prayed inwardly. If her common sense was trying to reassure her that dreams are neither bequeathed nor inherited, she was much deceived because men do not need to confide their dreams to each other for fathers and sons to have the same dream at the same hour. Day finally dawned and the morning light streamed through the chink in the door. On opening her eyes, Mary noticed Jesus was no longer lying there on his mat, Where can he have gone, she asked herself. She got up and went to look outside. Jesus was sitting on a bed of straw in the shed, his head buried in his arms. Chilled by the cool morning air, and, unconsciously by the sight of her son's solitude, Mary went up to him, Are you feeling unwell, she asked. The boy raised his eyes, No, I'm not ill, Then what's ailing you, It's these dreams I keep having, Dreams, you say, No, the same dream for the last two nights, Did you dream of your father on the cross, No, I've already told you, I dream about my father but don't see him, You told me you weren't dreaming about him, That's because I don't see him, but I'm sure he is in my dream, And what is this dream that never stops tormenting you. Jesus did not reply immediately, he looked at his mother with a helpless expression, and Mary felt as if a finger had touched her heart, there was her son looking just like a little boy, with the wan expression of someone who had not slept, and the first signs of a beard which invited teasing affection, this was her first-born on whom she would rely for the rest of her life, Tell me everything, she pleaded, and Jesus finally spoke, I dream that I'm in a village which isn't Nazareth and that you are with me, but it's not you, because the woman who's my mother in the dream looks quite different, and there are other boys of my age, difficult to say how many, with women who could be their mothers, someone has assembled us in a square and we're waiting for soldiers who are coming to kill us, we can hear them on the road, they draw near but we can't see them. At this point I'm still not frightened, I know it's only a nightmare, then suddenly I feel sure father is coming with the soldiers, I turn to you for protection, uncertain whether you're really my mother, but you're no longer there, all the mothers have gone, leaving only us children, no longer boys but tiny babies, I'm lying on the ground and start to cry, and all the others are crying too, but I'm the only one whose father is accompanying the soldiers, we look at the opening into the square where we know they will enter but there's no sign of them, so we keep on waiting for them to appear but nothing happens and, to make matters worse, their footsteps can be heard getting closer, they're here, no, they're not, and then I see myself as I am now, trapped inside that infant and I struggle to get out, it's as if my hands and feet were tied, I call out to you, but you're not there, I call out to my father who's coming to kill me, and just at that moment I woke up both last night and the night before. As he spoke, Mary shuddered with horror and when the meaning of the dream dawned on her she lowered her eyes in anguish, her greatest fears were about to be confirmed, and for some inexplicable reason Jesus had inherited his father's dream, and although it was slightly different, it was as if father and son independently had the same dream at the same time. Still trembling with fear she heard her son ask, What was that dream father used to have every night, It was just a nightmare like any other. But what was it about, I've no idea, your father never told me, Come now, mother, don't hide the truth from your own son, It's best forgotten, How do you know what's good or bad for me, Show some respect for your mother, Of course I respect you, but why hide things which concern me, Don't oblige me to say any more, One day I asked father why he should be haunted by that dream, and he told me that I had no right to ask and that he had nothing to tell me. Well then, why not accept your father's words, I did accept them so long as he was alive, but now I'm in charge, I've inherited his tunic, a pair of sandals and a dream, and with these I can go out into the world but I must know more about the dream, Perhaps it won't come back. Staring into his mother's eyes, Jesus told her, I shall no longer insist on knowing so long as that dream doesn't come back, but if it does, swear to me you'll tell me everything, I swear it, replied Mary, giving way to her son's insistence and authority. From her anguished heart a silent plea went up to God, a prayer without words which might have sounded as follows, Oh Lord, send this dream to haunt my nights until the day I die, but I beseech You, spare my son, spare my son. Jesus warned her, Don't forget your promise, I won't forget, Mary assured him, inwardly repeating to herself, Spare my son, oh Lord, spare my son.

But her son was not spared. Night came, a black cock crowed at dawn, the dream returned and the head of the first horse appeared round the corner. Mary heard her son moan, but did not go to comfort him. Shaking with fear and covered in sweat, Jesus knew that his mother was lying there awake and listening. What will she have to tell me, he wondered, while Mary for her part thought, What am I going to say to him, and she desperately tried to think how she could get out of telling him everything. Next morning Mary was getting ready to take her sons to the synagogue when Jesus told her, I'm coming with you, then we can talk in the desert. Mary felt so nervous that she kept dropping things as she tried to prepare some food, but the wine of affliction had been served and now had to be drunk. Once the younger children had been taken to school, Mary and Jesus left the village, and there in the desert they sat beneath an olive tree where no one except God, should He chance to be around, could possibly overhear their conversation. For as we know, stones cannot speak, even if we strike them one against the other, and as for the earth below, that is where all words turn to silence. Jesus said, Now you must keep your promise, and Mary told him outright, Your father dreamt he was a soldier marching with other soldiers on their way to kill you, To kill me, Yes, to kill you, But that's my dream, I know, she told him, with a sigh of relief, That was easier than I imagined, she thought to herself before saying aloud, Now that you know, let's go back home, dreams are like clouds, they come and go, you only inherited this dream because you were so fond of your father, he didn't want to kill you nor could he ever have done such a thing, and even if the Lord Himself had ordered him to do so, an angel would have stayed his hand, as happened to Abraham when he was about to sacrifice his son Isaac. Don't speak of things you know nothing about, said Jesus bluntly, and Mary realized that the bitter wine would have to be drunk to the dregs. What I do know, my son, is that the Lord's will must be done, whatever that will may be, and if He should ordain one thing and something quite different later, there's nothing we can do. As she finished speaking, Mary crossed her hands on her lap and sat there waiting. Jesus asked her, Are you prepared to answer all my questions, Of course, she replied. When did father start having this dream, Many years ago, How many years, From the day you were born, Did he have that dream every night, Yes, I believe he did, after a while he didn't bother calling me, people get used to nightmares, Tell me, Mother, was I born in Bethlehem of Judaea, That's right, What happened when I was born that my father should dream he was going to kill me, It didn't happen when you were born, But you just said so, The dream started some weeks later, Later than what, Herod ordered that all infants under the age of three should be slaughtered, Why, I wish I knew, Did father know, If he did, he never told me, So how come Herod's soldiers missed me, We were living in a cave on the outskirts of the village, You mean the soldiers didn't kill me because they couldn't find me, Yes, Was father a soldier, Never, What did he do then, He worked on the site of the Temple, I don't understand, I'm trying to answer your questions, But if the soldiers didn't find me because we lived outside the village, if father wasn't a soldier and therefore not guilty, and had no idea why Herod wanted the infants killed, That's right, your father couldn't understand why Herod ordered the deaths of those children, And so, There's nothing more to tell, and unless you've any more questions to ask me, I've told you all I know, You're hiding something from me, Perhaps it's you who's blind. Jesus said nothing more, felt his authority evaporate like moisture drying up in the soil, while he sensed the presence of an unworthy thought unravelling in his mind, still wavering, but monstrous from the moment of its inception. He saw a flock of sheep crossing the slopes of the opposite hill, and both the shepherd and his sheep were the colour of earth, like earth moving over earth. Surprise crept into Mary's tense expression, that tall shepherd, that manner of walking, so many years later and just at this very moment, was this some omen, but then she stared hard and felt less certain, for now the shepherd looked just like any other villager from Nazareth as he led his tiny flock to pasture, the animals looking as rachitic as their owner. A thought suddenly came to Jesus, a thought which was struggling to get out if only he could bring himself to speak, until finally he blurted out nervously, Father knew those children were going to be slaughtered. It was not a question so there was no need for Mary to answer. How did he know, and this time it was a question. Your father was working on the Temple site in

Jerusalem when he overheard some soldiers discussing what they'd been sent to do, And then, He went running off to save you, And then, He decided there was no need for us to escape so long as we didn't leave the cave, And then, That was all, the soldiers carried out their orders and left, And then, Then we returned to Nazareth, And when did the dream start, It first started in the cave. Beside himself with grief, Jesus covered his face and cried out vehemently, Father murdered the children of Bethlehem, What are you saying, my son, they were slaughtered by Herod's soldiers, No, father was to blame, Joseph, son of Heli, was responsible for he knew those children were about to be killed and did nothing to warn their parents. Once these words had been spoken, any hope of consolation was lost forever. Jesus threw himself to the ground and wept. Those children were innocent, innocent, he said with bitterness, and how incredible that a simple boy of thirteen should have reacted so strongly when one thinks of how selfish children can be at that age and how indifferent most people are to the misfortunes of others. But people are not all alike, there are exceptions for better or for worse, and this is clearly one of the best, a young boy weeping his heart out because his father did wrong all those years ago, but he could also be weeping on his own account if, as it would appear, he loved this father who was twice guilty. Mary held out her hand and made to comfort him but Jesus drew away, Don't touch me, I feel deeply wounded. Jesus, my son, Don't call me your son, for you're also guilty. Such are the hasty judgements of adolescence, Mary, if truth be told, was as innocent as the slaughtered infants, and it is the men, as every woman knows, who make all the decisions, my husband arrived here and said, We're leaving, then changed his mind and without going into any details, told me, We're not going after all, and I even had to ask him, What is that screaming I can hear coming from outside. Mary made no attempt to defend herself. It would have been so easy to prove her innocence, but she thought of her crucified husband, he, too, had been killed although blameless, and she realized to her shame and sorrow that she now loved him even more than when he was alive, so she said nothing, for one person's guilt can be assumed by another. Mary simply said, Let's go home, we've nothing more to discuss here, and her son replied, You go, and leave me on my own. There were no tracks to be seen of shepherd or sheep, the desert was truly deserted and even the few scattered houses on the slope below looked like huge slabs of stones on some abandoned building-site, which were gradually sinking into the ground. When Mary disappeared from sight into the grey depths of the valley, Jesus fell to his knees and called out, his entire body burning as if he were sweating blood, Father, Father, why have You forsaken me, for this was how the poor boy felt, abandoned and desperate, lost in the infinite solitude of another wilderness, without father, mother, brother or sisters, and already pursuing a path of death. Concealed by his sheep, the shepherd sat watching him from afar.

Two days later, Jesus left home. During this time he had said very little and, unable to sleep, he had spent the nights awake. He could picture that horrendous massacre, the soldiers entering the houses and searching for cradles, their swords striking and stabbing those tender little bodies, their mothers in despair, their fathers roaring like chained bulls, and he also had a vision of himself inside a cave he had never seen before, and at such moments, as if great waves were slowly engulfing him, he inexplicably wished he were dead or, at least, no longer alive. One question which he had not mentioned to his mother bothered him, How many children had lost their lives, in his mind's eye there were so many of them, piled up on top of each other, like beheaded lambs thrown on to a heap and about to be cremated on a huge bonfire, and once reduced to ashes, they would go up to heaven in smoke. But since he did not raise the question when his mother had made those revelations, he felt that it would be in bad taste, if such an expression had been in use at the time, to go to his mother and say, By the way, Mother, I forgot to ask you the other day how many of those infants in Bethlehem passed on to a better life, whereupon she would reply, Ah, my son, try to put it out of your mind, There could not have been more than thirty and if they died then it was the will of the Lord, for He could have prevented that massacre had He so desired. But Jesus could not stop wondering, How many, he would look at his brothers and ask himself, How many, he wanted to know how many corpses were needed to balance the scales against his own salvation. On the morning of the second day, Jesus said to his mother, I can find no rest or peace of mind in this house, you stay here with my brothers, for I am going away. Mary raised her hands to heaven, horrified and close to tears, What are you saying, you, my eldest son, and ready to abandon your widowed mother, whoever heard of such a thing, what is the world coming to, how can you think of leaving your own home and family, what's to become of us without your support. James is only one year younger than me, he'll take my place and provide for all of you as I did after your husband died. My husband was your father, I don't want to talk about him, I have nothing more to say, give me your blessing for the journey but, with or without it, I'm off. And where are you going, my son, I'm not sure, perhaps Jerusalem, perhaps Bethlehem, to see the land where I was born. But no one knows you there, Probably just as well, but tell me, Mother, what do you think would happen if anyone were to recognize me, Be quiet, your brothers might hear you, One day they will also have to know the truth, But have you thought of the risk, travelling at a time like this, with Roman soldiers on all the roads searching for the rebels of Judas the Galilean, The Romans are no worse than the soldiers who served under the late Herod, and they're not likely to kill me with their swords or nail me to a cross, after all, I haven't done anything, I'm innocent. So was your father and look what happened to him, Your husband may have been wrongfully crucified but there was nothing innocent about his life. Jesus, my son, the devil's taken possession of your tongue, How do you know it isn't God, Don't take the name of the Lord in vain, Who can tell when the name of God is taken in vain, neither you, nor I, God alone can tell the difference and I doubt whether we'll ever understand His reasons, Listen, my son, where on earth have you picked up these ideas at your age, Who knows, perhaps men are born carrying the truth inside them but fail to speak it because they're not altogether certain it is the truth, You've decided then to leave us, Yes, Will you come back, I don't know, If this dream is troubling you, go by all means to Bethlehem, go to the Temple in Jerusalem and consult the teachers, they will advise you and put your mind at rest, then you can come back to your mother and brothers who need you, I can't promise to return, But how will you survive, your poor father didn't live long enough to teach you everything he knew, Don't worry, I'll work in the fields or tend sheep or persuade some fishermen to take me out to sea with them, Wouldn't you prefer to be a shepherd, Why, I don't know, a sudden feeling, that's all, We'll see what turns up, and now, Mother, I must be on my way, But you can't go like this, let me get you some food for the journey, we haven't much money, but something can be arranged, and take your father's knapsack which fortunately he left behind, I'll take the food but not the knapsack, It's the only one we have in the house, your father didn't have leprosy or some infectious disease, No, I cannot, One day you'll weep for your father and be sorry you didn't take it, I've already wept for him, You'll weep even more, and you won't be asking then what sins he committed. Jesus made no attempt to reply to these words. Unaware of the conversation between him and their mother, the older children gathered round Jesus and asked, Are you really going away, and James said, I wish I were going with you, for the boy dreamed of adventure, of travelling, of doing something challenging and different. You must stay here, Jesus told him, because someone has to look after our widowed mother, the word widowed involuntarily slipped out and he bit his lip trying to suppress it but what he couldn't suppress were his tears, the vivid memory of his father suddenly caught him unawares like a ray of dazzling light.

After the family had eaten together, Jesus departed. He bade his brothers farewell, one by one, embraced his tearful mother and told her, without knowing why, In one way or another I'll always return, and adjusting the knapsack over his shoulder he crossed the yard and opened the gate leading on to the street. There he stopped as if reflecting on what he was about to do, preparing to leave home and abandon his mother and brothers, how often we find ourselves on the point of crossing a threshold or taking a decision when further consideration makes us change our mind and turn back. The thought also occurred to Mary and her face lit up with jubilant surprise, but her joy was short-lived, because before turning back Jesus paused a while, laying down the knapsack as he stood there mulling over some nagging dilemma. Then Jesus passed between his brothers without so much as looking at them and went into the house. When he reappeared a few moments later he was carrying his father's sandals in his hand. In silence, his eyes lowered as if modesty or some hidden shame prevented him from looking anyone in the eye, he put the sandals into the knapsack and, without another word or gesture, walked off. Mary ran to the gate and her children followed, the older ones seemingly indifferent, no one waved good-bye because Jesus didn't look back even once. A neighbour who was passing and saw Jesus leave asked, Where's your son off to, Mary, and Mary replied, He's found work in Jerusalem and he'll be staying there for a while, a barefaced lie as we know, but this question of telling lies or the truth is complicated, better not to make any hasty moral judgements because if one waits long enough the truth becomes lies and lies become the truth. That night, as everyone in the house lay asleep except for Mary, who could not help wondering how and where her son might be at that hour, whether he was safe in some caravanserai, sheltering under a tree, huddled between the rocks of some dark ravine, or, God forbid, taken prisoner by the Romans. She heard the outside gate creaking and her heart leapt, It's Jesus coming back, she thought to herself, momentarily overcome with joy and confusion. What should I do, she wondered, reluctant to open the gate. To appear triumphant, to greet him with words such as, It didn't take you long to come back after giving your mother a sleepless night, would have been much too humiliating, better to keep calm and say nothing, pretend she was asleep, let him creep in quietly, and if he should stretch out on his mat without so much as saying I'm back, tomorrow I'll pretend to be surprised to find the prodigal son has returned. However brief his absence, her joy will be just as great, for absence, too, is a kind of death, the one important difference being that there is still some hope. But he's so slow in coming to the door, who knows, perhaps he changed his mind at the last moment, Mary cannot bear the suspense any longer, she can peep through the chink in the door without being seen and run back to her mat should her son decide to enter, and should he show signs of turning back she'll still be in time to stop him. Tip-toeing on bare feet, Mary went up to the door and peered out. The moon was bright and the ground in the yard shone like water. Moving slowly, a tall, dark figure advanced towards the door, and the moment Mary saw him she put her hands to her mouth to prevent herself from screaming. It was not her son. That gigantic figure was the beggar, covered in rags as when she first saw him, and now, as then, perhaps because of the moonlight, those rags were suddenly transformed into sumptuous robes which rustled in the strong breeze. Terror-stricken, Mary locked the door,

What can he want from me, she muttered with trembling lips, bewildered and apprehensive. The man, who had claimed to be an angel, moved to one side, was now right up against the door yet made no attempt to enter, Mary could hear him breathing and then the sound of something being ripped open, as if the earth were being split open to reveal an enormous abyss. Mary did not have to open the door or to ask who was there. The massive figure of the angel appeared again, for one fleeting moment his great shadow obstructing Mary's view, and then, without as much as glancing at the house, he moved away towards the gate, taking with him, roots and branch, the mysterious tree which had sprouted outside the door some thirteen years before, at the very spot where the bowl had been buried. Between the opening and closing of the gate, the angel changed back into a beggar and disappeared, whoever he was, behind the wall, dragging the fronded branches with him like a plumed serpent, this time in total silence. As if she had been dreaming or imagining things, Mary opened the door cautiously and looked out. The world was bright beneath a remote sky. Against the wall of the house there was a hole in the ground where the plant had been uprooted, and from there to the gate a trail of sparkling soil resembling the Milky Way, if such an expression existed in those days. It certainly was not the Road to Santiago, for the person who was to give the road its name was still a young boy living in Galilee, more or less the same age as Jesus, and God knows where those two were at that hour. Mary thought about her son but without any heartache, no harm could surely come to him under such a beautiful sky, serene and unfathomable, and this moon, like manna made from light, nourishing the earth's roots and sources. Her soul at peace, Mary crossed the yard and, fearlessly treading the stars on the ground, she went to open the gate. She looked outside, saw that the trail ended a short distance away, as if the iridescence of the leaves had been extinguished or, another flight of fancy on the part of this woman who can no longer make the excuse that she is pregnant, as if the beggar had reverted to being an angel and was finally making use of his wings to mark this special occasion. Mary pondered over these strange events and they seemed to her as simple and natural as contemplating her own hands under the moonlight. She then walked back to the house, lifted the oil lamp from the hook on the wall and went to take a closer look at the deep hole where the plant had been uprooted. At the bottom lay the empty bowl. She put her hand in and lifted it out, the same plain bowl she remembered with very little earth left inside and no longer shining, an ordinary household utensil restored to its proper function. From now on it will be used to serve milk, water or wine, according to one's taste and means, and how true that saying which reminds us that everyone has his hour and everything its time.

On the first night of his travels Jesus found shelter. Dusk was falling as he came within sight of a tiny hamlet just outside the city of Jenin and fate, which had predicted so much ill-fortune since the day he was born, relented on this occasion. The owners of the house where he sought shelter without much expectation turned out to be hospitable people who could never have forgiven themselves if they had left a boy of his age out in the open all night, especially at a time like this with so much fighting and violence everywhere, with men being crucified and innocent children hacked to death for no apparent reason. Jesus told his kind benefactors that he hailed from Nazareth and was on his way to Jerusalem, however he refrained from repeating the shameful lie he had heard his mother tell when she said he had gone off to do a job. He simply told them he was on his way to consult the teachers of the temple about a point of holy law which greatly concerned his family. The head of the household expressed his surprise that such an important mission should be entrusted to a mere boy, however advanced in his religious studies, and Jesus explained he was dealing with this matter as the eldest son, but made no mention of his father. He ate with the rest of the family and then settled down under the lean-to in the yard, which was the best they could offer any passing traveller. In the middle of the night the dream returned to haunt him although this time his father and the soldiers did not get quite so close and the horse's nose did not appear around the corner. Do not imagine, however, that the dream was any less terrifying. Let us put ourselves in Jesus's place, suppose we were to dream that the father who gave us life was pursuing us with drawn sword. Those asleep indoors were completely unaware of the drama being enacted in the yard. Jesus had learned to master his fear even while sleeping. When it became unbearable he would instinctively cover his mouth with his hand in one last attempt to stifle the terrible cries of anguish silently throbbing in his head. In the morning, he joined the family for breakfast, then thanked them for their hospitality with such courtesy and eloquence that the whole family, without exception, felt that they were momentarily sharing in the ineffable peace of the Lord, humble Samaritans though they were. Jesus said goodbye and departed, his benefactor's parting words ringing in his ears, Blessed be You, oh Lord our God, King of the Universe, who guides our footsteps, words which he himself repeated in kind, praising that same Lord, God and King, the provider of all our needs, as can be clearly seen from everyday experience, in accordance with that most just rule of direct proportion which decrees that more should be given to those who have more.

The rest of the journey before reaching Jerusalem was not so easy. In the first place, there are Samaritans and Samaritans, which means that even at that time one swallow was not enough to make a summer, one needed two, that is to say, two swallows rather than summers, provided there is a fertile male and female and they have offspring. No more doors opened when Jesus knocked and all our traveller could do was to find somewhere to sleep outdoors, once under a fig tree of the large, spreading variety which resemble a dirndl skirt, on another occasion by joining a caravan which, fortunately for Jesus, had to pitch tents in the open countryside because the nearby caravanserai was full. We say fortunately because in the meantime, while crossing some uninhabited mountains on his own, the poor boy had been attacked by two cowardly thieves who mercilessly robbed him of the little money he possessed, which meant Jesus had no hope of finding lodgings at any of the inns which were run for profit and where everything had to be paid for. Anyone witnessing that episode would have looked with pity on the poor boy, abandoned to his fate by those heartless rogues who went off laughing at his plight. He lay there in a lamentable state with nothing but the sky overhead and the surrounding mountains, the infinite universe stripped of any moral significance, and peopled with stars, thieves and executioners. You might try to argue that a boy of thirteen could never have had sufficient knowledge of science or philosophy or even enough experience of life for any such thoughts and that this boy in particular, notwithstanding his religious studies in the synagogue and his natural flair for debate, would be incapable of the words and deeds attributed to him. There is no lack of carpenters' sons in these parts, or of sons whose fathers have been crucified, but even supposing another man's son had been chosen, we are in no doubt that whosoever he might have been, he would have given us just as much food for thought as young Jesus. Firstly because it is well known that every man is a world unto himself, either through paths of transcendence or immanence, and secondly, because this land has always been different from any other, one need only consider how many people, both rich and poor, have travelled these parts preaching and prophesying, from Isaiah to Malachi, nobles, priests, shepherds, men from every conceivable walk of life, which teaches us to be cautious before jumping to any conclusions, the humble origins of a carpenter's son do not give us any right to make hasty judgements which could jeopardize his future. This boy who is on his way to Jerusalem at an age when most children do not venture outside the front door, may not be exactly a genius or luminary, but he deserves our respect. His soul, as he himself confessed, has been deeply wounded and since, given his reflective nature, the scars are unlikely to heal quickly, he has gone out into the world perhaps to multiply those wounds and combine them into one definitive sorrow. It may seem wholly inappropriate to put the complex theories of modern thinkers into the head of a Palestinian who lived so many years before Freud, Jung, Groddeck and Lacan appeared on the scene. But if you will pardon our presumption, this lapse is not all that foolish or outrageous if one considers that the scriptures from which Jews derive their spiritual nourishment consistently reveal that man, whatever the age in which he lives or may have lived, is the contemporary of all other men in matters of intellect. Adam and Eve were the only notable exceptions, not only because they were the first man and woman, but because they had no childhood. And while biology and psychology may be invoked to prove that the human mind as we know it today can be traced back to Cro-Magnon man, that debate is of no interest here insofar as Cro-Magnon man is not even mentioned in the Book of Genesis, which is all Jesus ever studied about the origins of the world.

Distracted by these reflections which are not entirely irrelevant to the essence of the gospel we have been explaining, to our shame we have forgotten to accompany Joseph's son on the final stages of his journey to Jerusalem where he is just arriving, penniless but safe, his feet badly blistered after the long journey, but as steadfast as when he left home three days before. He has been here before, so his excitement is no greater than one might expect from a devout man whose god has become or is about to become familiar. From this mountain known as Gethsemane or the Mount of Olives, one can get a view of Jerusalem's magnificent architecture, of the city's Temple, towers, palaces and houses, which give the impression of being within reach, but this depends on the degree of mystical fervour which can lead the faithful to confuse the limitations of the body with the infinite power of the universal spirit. The evening is drawing to a close and the sun is already setting over the distant sea, Jesus has begun his descent into the valley, wondering where he will spend the night, whether within or outside the city walls. On other occasions when he accompanied his parents during Passover, the family spent the night outside the city walls in a tent which had been thoughtfully provided by the civic and military authorities to receive pilgrims, all of them segregated, needless to say, the men with the men, the women with the women, and the children, too, divided according to sex. When Jesus reached the city walls the night air was already turning chilly. He arrived just as the gates were being closed, but even though the watchmen allowed him to enter and, as those great wooden crossbars slammed into position, Jesus might have started to feel remorse for some past error or to imagine himself caught in a trap, its iron teeth about to snap, a capsule of spittle ensnaring a fly. However, at the age of thirteen his sins cannot be all that many or serious; he is still not at an age to be killing or stealing or bearing false witness, of coveting his neighbour's wife, house or fields, his neighbour's male or female slave, his ass, his ox or any other goods that may belong to him, therefore this boy walks pure and undefiled even though he may already have lost his innocence, for no one can witness death without being affected. The roads become deserted at this hour as families gather for supper, and out on the roads there are only beggars and vagabonds. But they, too, will retreat into their own dens and hideaways, for any minute now Roman soldiers will be scouring the streets in search of malefactors who venture even into the capital of Herod Antipas' kingdom to commit every manner of crime and iniquity, notwithstanding the severe sentences which await them if they get caught, as we saw in Sepphoris. At the end of the road a night patrol carrying blazing torches marches past amidst the clanging of swords and shields and to the rhythm of their feet clad in military sandals. Hiding in a dark corner, the boy waited for the soldiers to disappear, then went to look for somewhere to sleep. As expected, he found the very place among the many building sites around the temple, a gap between two great stone slabs with another slab on top to form a roof. There he munched what remained of the hard, mouldy bread, along with some dry figs he found at the bottom of his knapsack. He felt thirsty but resigned himself to going without any water. Then, stretching out on his mat, he covered himself with the little mantle which he carried as part of his baggage and, curling up to protect himself from the cold which penetrated both sides of his precarious refuge, he managed to fall asleep. Being in Jerusalem did not prevent him from dreaming, but perhaps because he was close to God's holy presence his dream was merely a repetition of familiar scenes merging with the arrival of the patrol he had encountered earlier. He awoke just as the sun was rising. Wrapped in his mantle, he dragged himself out of that hole, cold as a tomb, and saw the houses of Jerusalem before him, low-lying houses made of stone, their walls tinged pale crimson by the morning light. Then, with great solemnity, coming as it did from the lips of someone who after all is still a boy, he offered up prayers of thanksgiving, Thanks be to You, oh Lord our God, King of the Universe, Who through the power of Your mercy restored my soul, fervent and loyal. There are certain moments in life which should be arrested and protected from time, and not simply be transmitted in a gospel or painting or, as in this modern age, in a photograph, film or video. How much more interesting it would be if the person who lived those moments or brought them to life were to remain forever visible to their descendants, so that those of us alive today could go to Jerusalem and see with our own eyes young Jesus, the son of Joseph, all wrapped up in his small threadbare mantle, see the houses of Jerusalem and give thanks to the Lord Who mercifully restored the boy's soul. Since his life is just beginning at the age of thirteen, one can assume there are brighter and sadder hours in store for him, moments of greater joy and despair, greater pleasure and grief, but this is the moment we ourselves would choose, while the city slumbers, the sun is at a standstill, the light intangible, a young boy looking wide-eyed at the houses, wrapped in a mantle, a knapsack at his feet, and the entire world, near or far, waiting in suspense. Alas, he has already moved, the instant has come and gone, time has carried us into the realms of memory, it was like this, no, it was not, and everything becomes what we choose to invent. Jesus is now walking through the narrow crowded streets, it is still too early to go to the temple, the doctors, as in all ages and places, only start appearing later. Jesus is no longer feeling cold but his stomach is rumbling, those two remaining figs only served to whet his appetite and Joseph's son is famished. Now he could be doing with the money those rogues stole from him, for city life is quite unlike that leisurely existence in the countryside where one goes around whistling and looking out for what may have been left behind by god-fearing labourers who carry out His commandments to the letter. When you are harvesting your fields and leave a sheaf behind, don't turn back to retrieve it, when you pick olives do not go back to collect any that may still be hanging on the branches, when you gather grapes from your vineyard, do not go rummaging for any you may have overlooked, leave them to be gathered by some stranger, orphan or widow, and always remember that you were once a slave in the land of Egypt. Now, because it is a large city, and despite God's decree that His earthly dwelling should be built there, these humanitarian precepts are not observed in Jerusalem so that for anyone arriving without either thirty or three pieces of silver in his pocket, the only solution is to beg and almost certainly be refused, or to steal and run the risk of being flogged and imprisoned or worse. This youth, however, is incapable of stealing and he is much too shy to beg. His mouth waters when he stares at the stacks of loaves, the pyramids of fruits, and cooked meats and vegetables set out on stalls all along the streets, and the sight of all that food after three days of fasting, if we discount the Samaritan's hospitality, almost makes him faint. It is true that he is heading for the Temple, but despite the claims of those mystics who believe in fasting, his body would be in a better condition to receive the word of the Lord if his mind were nourished with food. Fortunately, a Pharisee who happened to be passing noticed the boy's weak condition and took pity on him. Posterity will unjustly give the Pharisees the worst possible reputation, but at heart they were decent people, as this encounter clearly shows; Where are you from, asked the Pharisee, and Jesus replied, I'm from Nazareth of Galilee, Are you hungry, he asked and the boy lowered his eyes, there was no need to say anything for hunger was written on his face. Have you no family, Yes, but I'm travelling on my own, Did you run away, No, and it is true, he did not run away. We must not forget that his mother and brothers came to bid him an affectionate farewell at the gate, and the fact that he did not turn back even once did not mean that he had fled. The words we use are like that: to say Yes or No is the most straightforward answer of all, and, in principle, the most convincing, but the plain truth demands that we should start by giving a somewhat indecisive reply, Well no, not really, I didn't exactly run away, however, and at this point we would have to hear the story all over again. But, keep calm, it is unnecessary, firstly because the Pharisee, who will reappear in our gospel, does not need to hear it, and secondly, because we know the story better than anyone. Just think how little the main characters of this gospel know about each other, Jesus does not know everything about his mother and father, Mary does not know everything about her husband and son, and Joseph, who is dead, knows nothing about anything. Whereas we know everything that has been done, spoken and thought, whether by them or by others, although we have to act as if we, too, were in the dark, in that sense we are like the Pharisee who asked, Are you hungry, when Jesus's pinched, wan face spoke for itself, No need to ask, just give me something to eat. And that is exactly what that compassionate man did, he bought two loaves still hot from the oven and a bowl of milk and, without saying a word, handed them to Jesus, and as the bowl passed between them it so happened that a little milk spilled on to their hands, whereupon they both made the same gesture which must surely have come from the depths of time, simultaneously they lifted a wet hand to their lips to suck the milk, just like kissing bread when it has fallen on to the floor. What a pity these two were never to meet again once they had sealed such an admirable and symbolic pact. The Pharisee went about his affairs, but not before taking two coins from his pocket and saying, Take this money and return home, the world is much too big for someone like you. The carpenter's son stood there clutching the bowl and bread, no longer hungry or perhaps still hungry but incapable of feeling anything. He watched the Pharisee walk away and only then did he say Thank you, but in such a low voice that the Pharisee could not possibly have heard him, and if he had been expecting to be thanked then he must have thought to himself, What an ungrateful boy. Right there in the middle of the road Jesus suddenly regained his appetite. He lost no time in eating his bread and drinking his milk and then handed the empty bowl to the vendor who told him, The bowl is paid for, keep it, Is it the custom in Jerusalem to buy the bowl as well as the milk, No, but that's what the Pharisee wanted and you can never tell what's on a Pharisee's mind. So I can keep it, I've already told you, it's paid for. Jesus wrapped the bowl in his mantle and tucked it into his knapsack while thinking that he would have to handle it carefully from now on. These earthenware bowls are fragile and so easily broken, they are only made of a little clay on which fortune has precariously bestowed some consistency, and the same could be said of mankind. His body nourished and his spirits revived, Jesus set off in the direction of the Temple.

A large crowd had already gathered on the concourse facing the steep stairway leading up to the entrance. Ranged along the walls on either side were the tents of the pedlars and traders selling animals for sacrifice and, dispersed here and there, moneychangers at their stalls, groups of people engaged in conversation, gesticulating merchants, Roman soldiers on foot and on horseback who were keeping a watchful eye, litters carried by slaves, camels and donkeys laden with baggage and frenzied shouting everywhere, interrupted by the feeble bleating of lambs and goats, some carried in people's arms or on their backs like tired children, others dragged by a rope round their necks, and all of them destined to perish by sword or fire. Jesus passed the bathhouse used for purification, climbed the steps and, without stopping, crossed the Court of the Gentiles. He entered the Court of the Women through the door between the Chamber of the Holy Oils and the Hall of the Nazarites and there he found what he was looking for, the assembly of elders and scribes who traditionally gathered to discuss holy law, answer questions and offer advice. They stood around in groups, and the boy joined the smallest of them just as a man was raising his hand to ask a question. The scribe invited him to speak and the man asked, Can you tell me if we should accept, word for word, the commandments given by the Lord to Moses on Mount Sinai when He promised peace on earth and told us no one would disturb our sleep, when He announced that He would banish dangerous animals from our midst, that the sword would not pass through our land, and that if our enemies were to pursue us they would fall under our sword, for as the Lord himself said, Five of you will pursue a hundred men, a hundred of you ten thousand, and your enemies will fall before your sword. The scribe eyed his interrogator suspiciously and, thinking that he might be a rebel in disguise sent by Judas the Galilean to stir up trouble with wicked insinuations about the Temple's passive resistance to Roman domination, he replied brusquely, Those words were spoken by the Lord when our fore-fathers were in the desert and being persecuted by the Egyptians. The man raised his hand a second time and asked another question, Are we to understand then, that the Lord's words on Mount Sinai were only meaningful so long as our forefathers were still searching for the promised land, If that's how you choose to interpret them, then you're not a good Israelite, the word of the Lord must prevail in every age, past, present and future, for those words were in the Lord's mind before He uttered them and there they remained even after he had spoken. But it was you yourself who said what you're forbidding me to think, And what do you think, That the Lord consents that our swords should not be raised against this military force which is oppressing us, that a hundred of our men don't have the courage to face up to five of theirs, that ten thousand Jews are forced to cower before a hundred Romans, Let me remind you that you're in the Temple of the Lord and not on some battlefield, The Lord is the God of legions, True, but don't forget that God imposed His conditions, What conditions, The Lord said, So long as you observe my laws and keep my commandments, But what are these laws and commandments we're ignoring, that we should have to accept Roman domination as just and necessary, and punishment for our sins. The Lord must know, Yes, the Lord must know, and how often man sins without knowing, but would you care to explain why the Lord should make use of the Roman army to punish us instead of confronting His chosen people and punishing us himself, The Lord knows His intentions and chooses His own means, So you're trying to tell me that the Lord wants the Romans to govern Israel, Yes, Well, if that is so, then surely the rebels fighting the Romans are also opposing the Lord and His holy will, You're jump-ing to the wrong conclusion, And you, Scribe, are contradicting yourself, God's will may be not-to-will and that not-to-will be His will, So, only the will of man is genuine yet of no importance in the eyes of God, That's right, So man is free, Yes, free so that he might be punished. A murmur went up amongst bystanders, some stared at the person who had asked the questions, no doubt pertinent in the light of the texts but politically inopportune. They looked at him accusingly as if he were the culprit who should answer for the sins of all Israel, the sceptical somewhat reassured by the victory scored by the scribe, who acknowledged their praise and applause with a complacent smile. Exuding self-confidence, the scribe looked around him and asked if there were any further questions, like a gladiator who, after despatching a weak opponent, demands a more challenging match in order to gain greater glory. Another hand went up and a different question was raised, The Lord spoke to Moses and told him, The stranger in your midst shall be treated as one of your own and you will love him as you love yourselves, for you were strangers in the lands of Egypt, as the Lord himself told Moses. But before the man could finish speaking, the scribe, still flushed from his previous victory, interrupted him in a sarcastic tone of voice, I hope you're not about to ask me why we don't treat the Romans as our compatriots since they, too, are foreigners, No, what I want to ask is whether the Romans would treat us as their compatriots if both sides were to spend less time arguing about the differences between our laws and gods, So you've also come here to anger the Lord with blasphemous interpretations of His holy word, scoffed the scribe, On the contrary, all I'm asking is whether you truly believe that we are obeying the holy words of the Lord, when those people are not so much strangers to the land in which we live as to the religion we profess, To which strangers are you referring, To some in our own day and age, to many in the past, and probably to many more in years to come, I've no time to waste on enigmas and parables, so try to make yourself clear, When we arrived from Egypt there were other nations living in the land we call Israel, whom we had to fight, and in those days we were the foreigners and the Lord ordered us to slaughter and exterminate those who opposed His will, The land was promised to us but had to be conquered, we didn't buy the land nor was it offered to us, And now we find ourselves living under foreign domination, we have lost the land we had made our own, The image of Israel lives forever in the spirit of the Lord, so that wheresoever His people may be, whether united or dispersed, there terrestrial Israel will be, Which presumably means that wherever we Jews may find ourselves the others will always be the foreigners, Certainly in the eyes of the Lord, But the stranger who lives amongst us, according to the word of the Lord, will be our compatriot and we must love him as we love ourselves for we, too, were once strangers in Egypt, That's what the Lord said, Now in that case, surely the foreigners we're expected to love must be those who, even while living amongst us, are not so powerful that they can oppose us, as at present under the Romans. Yes, I'd agree, Then tell me, do you believe that if we were one day to become powerful, the Lord would permit us to oppress those foreigners whom He Himself commanded us to love, All Israel can do is to obey the will of the Lord and, since the children of Israel are His chosen people, The Lord wills only what is good for them, Even if it means not loving those we should, Yes, if so willed. Willed by whom, the Lord or Israel, By both, for they are one and the same, You will not violate the stranger's rights, said the Lord, When that stranger has any rights and we acknowledge them, replied the scribe. Once again, those present murmured their approval, causing the scribe's eyes to gleam like those of a champion wrestler, discus thrower, gladiator, or charioteer. Jesus put up his hand. No one present found it strange that a boy of his age should come forward to question a scribe or doctor of the Temple, the young have always been plagued by doubt ever since the time of Cain and Abel, they tend to ask questions to which adults react with a condescending smile and a pat on the shoulder, When you grow up, young man, you'll stop worrying about such matters, while the more understanding will say, When I was your age I also thought the same. Some of those present moved away and others were preparing to do so, to the obvious annoyance of the scribe seeing his hitherto attentive audience about to disperse, but Jesus's question caused some to turn back and listen, What I want to discuss is guilt, You mean your own guilt, No, guilt in general, but also the guilt a man may feel without having sinned himself, Explain yourself more clearly, The Lord said that parents will not die for their children or children for their parents, and that each man will be sentenced for his own crimes, True, but you ought to know that this was a precept for those ancient times when an entire family, however innocent, paid for the crime of any one of its members, But if the word of the Lord is forever and there is no apparent end to guilt, and as you yourself have just said, man is free so that he might be punished, then one has a right to believe that the father's guilt, even after he's been punished, doesn't cease to exist but is passed on to his children, just as all of us who are alive today have inherited the guilt of Adam and Eve, our first parents. I'm amazed that a boy of your age and humble circumstances should know so much about the scriptures and be able to debate these matters with such ease, I only know what I've been taught, Where are you from, From Nazareth of Galilee, I thought as much from your manner of speaking, Please answer my question, We may assume that the gravest sin of Adam and Eve when they disobeyed the Lord wasn't so much their having eaten the fruit from the tree of knowledge of good and evil, as the inevitable consequences, because their sin prevented the Lord from carrying out the plan He had in mind when He created first man and then woman. Whereupon the second bystander to ask a question challenged the scribe with another gem of sophistry which the carpenter's son would never have had the courage to voice in public. Do you mean to say that every human act, such as that of disobedience in Paradise or whatever, is likely to interfere with God's will which might well be compared to an island in the middle of the ocean surrounded and assailed by the turbulent waves of human wills. Not exactly, the scribe replied cautiously, the will of the Lord is not simply content to prevail over all things, His will makes everything what it is, But you yourself said that it is because of Adam's disobedience that we do not know the plan God had conceived for him, That's what our reason tells us, but the will of God, the Creator and Ruler of the universe, embraces all possible wills, His own as well as that of every man born into this world, If this were so, intervened Jesus with a sudden flash of inspiration, each man would be a part of God, Probably, but even if all men were to be united as one, that part would be a mere grain of sand in the infinite desert which is God. Looking much less complacent, the scribe is sitting on the ground surrounded by onlookers who watch him with mixed feelings of awe and fear, as if they were in the presence of a magician who had unwittingly conjured up powers greater than his own. With drooping shoulders and doleful expression, his hands resting warily on his knees, his entire body seemed to be pleading that he be left alone with his anguish. People in the group started rising to their feet, some made their way to the Court of the Israelites, some to join other groups still engaged in discussion. Jesus said, You didn't answer my question. The scribe sat up slowly, stared at him like someone coming out of a trance and then after a long, tense silence, replied, Guilt is a wolf that eats its cub after having devoured its father, The wolf of which you speak has already devoured my father, Then it will soon be your turn, And what about you, have you ever been devoured, Not only devoured, but also spewed up.

Jesus rose to his feet and left. Heading for the gate through which he had entered, he paused and looked back. The column of smoke coming from the sacrificial fires was rising into the heavens where it dispersed and vanished, as if sucked in by God's mighty lungs. It was mid-morning, more and more people were arriving, and inside the Temple sat a man, broken and shattered by the sense of emptiness, and waiting to regain his composure, so that he might be able to reply calmly to anyone who should turn up wanting to know if the pillar of salt which Lot's wife turned into was made of rock salt or sea salt, or if Noah got drunk on white or red wine. Already outside the Temple, Jesus asked the way to Bethlehem, his second destination. He lost his way twice amidst the confusion of streets and people before he found the gate through which he had passed whilst inside his mother's womb thirteen years earlier, almost ready to enter the world. Do not imagine, however, that this is in Jesus's mind, for as we all know, manifestations of the obvious clip the wings of the restless bird of imagination. To take but one example, if any reader of this gospel were to look at a photograph of his pregnant mother when she was carrying him, could he possibly imagine himself inside that womb. Jesus descends in the direction of Bethlehem, now he can reflect on the scribe's answers not just to his own questions but also to those raised by others. What worries him, however, is the uncomfortable feeling that all those questions were ultimately one question, and that the reply given in each case answered all their questions, especially the last one which summed up all the rest, the insatiable hunger of the wolf for guilt which is forever gnawing, devouring and spewing up. Thanks to the unreliable nature of memory we very often do not know, or know while trying to forget, what caused or provoked feelings of guilt, or speaking metaphorically like the scribe, the lair from which the wolf set forth to pursue us. But Jesus knows and that is where he is heading. He does not have any idea what he'll do when he gets there, but just to be on his way is as good as going around announcing to all and sundry, I'm here, and waiting for someone to turn up and ask him, What do you want, punishment, pardon or oblivion. Like his father and mother before him, he stopped before Rachel's tomb to pray. Then, feeling his heart beat faster and faster, he resumed his journey. The first houses of Bethlehem were within sight, this was the main road into the village from which his homicidal father and the soldiers erupted in his dream night after night. In daylight, it scarcely seems the place for such horrors, even the tranquil white clouds drifting across the sky are like benevolent gestures from God and the very earth appears to be slumbering beneath the sun, as if bidding us, Let's leave things as they are, there's nothing to be gained from raking over the past, and, before a woman with a child in her arms appears at a window asking, Who are you looking for, better to turn back, erase our footprints, and pray that the perpetual motion of the sieve of time may quickly obliterate with impenetrable dust even the faintest memory of these events. Too late. There comes a moment when the fly is just about to brush past the web and still has time to escape, but should it so much as touch the web and find its wing immobilised, then the slightest movement will suffice to trap and paralyse it, forever lost, however much the spider may despise its latest victim. For Jesus, that moment has passed. In the middle of a square with a spreading fig tree stands a tiny square building and one does not have to look twice to realize it is a tomb. Jesus approached, walked round it slowly, paused to read the faded inscriptions on one side, and this was enough to satisfy him that he had found what he was looking for. A woman crossed the square leading a five-year-old child by the hand. She stopped, looking inquisitively at the stranger and asked him, Where do you come from, and, trying to justify her question, added, You're not from these parts, No, I'm from Nazareth in Galilee, Have you relatives here, No, I was visiting Jerusalem and it seemed a good opportunity to take a look at Bethlehem, Are you passing through, Yes, I'll head back to Jerusalem later this afternoon once it starts getting cooler. Lifting the child on to her left arm, the woman said, May the Lord go with you, then made as if to withdraw, but Jesus detained her asking, Whose tomb is this. The woman pressed the child to her bosom as if anxious to protect it from some threat, and replied, Twenty-five little boys who died many years ago are buried here, How many did you say, Twenty-five, I mean how many years ago, Oh, probably about fourteen, So many, I think that's about right, those children would be about your age if they were still alive today, Yes, of course, but what about the little boys, Oh, one of them was my brother, You have a brother buried here, Yes, And this child in your arms, is he your son, He's my first-born, Why did they only kill the little boys, No one knows, I was only seven at the time, But you must surely have heard your parents and the other adults talking about it, There was no need, I myself saw some of them being killed, Your brother as well, Yes, even my brother, And who killed them, Some of the King's soldiers appeared searching for little boys up to the age of three and they killed all of them, Yet you don't know why, No one has found out to this day, And after Herod died, did anyone try to pursue the matter or go to the Temple to ask the priests to investigate, I really don't know, If the soldiers had been Romans, one might have understood it, but to have our own King ordering his people to be slaughtered, mere babes, seems very strange unless there was some reason, The will of kings is beyond our understanding, may the Lord go with you and protect you, It's a long time since I was three, At the hour of death men go back to being children, replied the woman before departing. Once alone, Jesus knelt on the ground beside the boulder covering the entrance to the tomb, took the last piece of stale bread from his knapsack, rubbed it into crumbs between his palms and sprinkled them all along the entrance as if making an offering to the invisible mouths of the innocents buried there. No sooner had he finished than another woman appeared from around the nearby corner, but this one was very old and bent and walked with the aid of a stick. No longer capable of seeing things clearly, she had caught a vague glimpse of the boy's gesture. She stopped, watched him attentively, saw him get to his feet and bow his head as if he were praying for the repose of the souls of those unfortunate infants, and although customary, we will refrain from adding the word eternal, for our imagination failed us on the one and only occasion when we tried to envisage eternal rest. Jesus ended his prayer and looked around him, blank walls, closed doors, nothing except that old woman standing there, dressed in a slave's tunic and leaning on her stick, the living image of that third part of the sphinx's famous enigma about the animal that walks on four feet in the morning, two at midday and three in the evening, It is man replied the ever so astute Oedipus, who was forgetting that some do not even get as far as midday, and that in Bethlehem alone, twenty-five infants disappeared at one fell swoop. The old woman drew closer, hobbling at a snail's pace and now she is standing before Jesus, she twists her neck to get a better look at him and asks, Are you looking for someone. The boy did not answer immediately, in fact he was not searching for people, those he has met so far are all dead, buried close by, and not even what one could call people, mere infants still in nappies and with a dummy in their mouths, whimpering and with running noses, yet death suddenly struck and turned them into an enormous presence which cannot be stored in any ossuary or reliquary, corpses which come out of their graves each night, if there is any justice, to show their mortal wounds, those gaping holes opened at sword-point allowing life to escape, No, replied Jesus, I'm not looking for anyone. The old woman made no attempt to leave, she seemed to be waiting for him to continue, and this caused Jesus to confide unintentionally, I was born in this village, in a cave, and was curious to see the place. The old woman stepped back unsteadily and strained her eyes to get a better look, her voice trembling as she asked him, What is your name, where do you come from, who are your parents. No one need feel obliged to answer a slave, but the elderly, however lowly their condition, deserve our respect, we must never forget that they have not much time left for asking questions and it would be cruel in the extreme just to ignore them, after all we might come up with the very answer they have been waiting for. My name is Jesus and I come from Nazareth of Galilee, the boy told her, and he seems to have been saying nothing else since he left home. The old woman stepped forward again, And your parents, what are their names, My father's name was Joseph, my mother is called Mary, How old are you, I'm almost fourteen. The woman looked around her as if searching for somewhere to sit, but a square in Bethlehem of Judaea is not the same as a garden in São Paulo de Alcântara, with its park benches and pleasant view of the castle, here we have to sit on the dusty ground, at best on some doorstep, or, if there's a tomb, on the stone beside the entrance for the repose and respite of the living who come there to mourn their loved ones, or perhaps also for the ghosts who leave their graves to shed any remaining tears, as in the case of Rachel, buried in the tomb nearby where it is written, Here lies Rachel who weeps for her children and seeks no consolation for they no longer exist, and one does not need to be as shrewd as Oedipus to see that this place befits the circumstances, and Rachel's sorrow, the cause of all her grief. The old woman lowered herself on to the stone with some effort and the boy made as if to go to her assistance, but too late, half-hearted gestures are never made in time. I know you, the old woman told him, You must be mistaken, replied Jesus, I've never been here before and I've never seen you in Nazareth, The first hands to touch you were not those of your mother but mine, How come, old woman, My name is Salome, and I was the midwife who delivered you into the world. Acting on impulse, which only goes to prove the sincerity of gestures if made spontaneously, Jesus fell to his knees at the old woman's feet, instinctively wavering between his desire to know once and for all and the need to show his gratitude to this woman who, just by being present at his birth, had brought him out of a limbo without memory in order to release him into a world which would mean nothing without it. My mother never mentioned you, said Jesus, There was no need, your parents turned up on my master's doorstep and I offered to help since I had some experience as a midwife. Was that at the time when the innocents were massacred, That's right, you were fortunate they didn't find you, Because we lived in a cave, It was either that or because you'd already left, I never found out for when I went to see what had happened to you the cave was empty. Do you remember my father, Yes, I remember him well, at that time he was in his prime, a fine figure of a man, and honest, He's dead, Poor man, he didn't last long, but if you're his heir what are you doing here for I suppose your mother is still alive, I came to see the place where I was born, also to find out more about the children who were slaughtered here, God alone knows why they had to die, the angel of death, disguised as Herod's soldiers, descended into Bethlehem and condemned them to death, So you believe it was God's will, I'm only an old slave, but all my life I've heard people say that everything that happens in this world, even suffering and death, can only happen by the will of God, So it is written. I can understand that God may decide I must die any day now, but these were innocent little children, Your death will be decided by God in His own good time, but it was a man who ordered that these children should be killed. So when all is said and done, the hand of God can do precious little, when it cannot even come between the sword and those condemned to die, You mustn't offend the Lord, good woman, An ignorant old woman like me isn't likely to cause any offence, This very day in the Temple I heard it said that every human action, however insignificant, interferes with the will of God, and that man is only free in order to be punished, My punishment doesn't come from being free, it comes from being a slave, the old woman told him. Jesus fell silent. He had scarcely heard Salome's words because it suddenly dawned on him that man is a mere toy in the hands of God and forever subject to His will, no matter whether he imagines himself to be obeying or disobeying Him in all things.

The sun was going down, and the fig tree's evil shadow lengthened and came closer. Jesus moved a little further back and called out to the old woman. Salome raised her head with some effort, What do you want, she asked him, Take me to the cave where I was born, or at least tell me how to get there if it's too far for you to walk. I'm not very steady on my feet but you won't find it unless I show you, Is it far from here, No, but there are lots of caves around and they all look alike, Let's go then, As you wish, she replied. Anyone who happened to be watching that day when Salome and the unknown boy passed by, must have asked themselves where those two could have met. But they were never to know because the old slave revealed nothing until the day she died, and Jesus was nevermore to return to the land of his birth. Next morning Salome went to the cave where she had left the boy. No sign of him. Deep down she was relieved not to find him. For even if he had still been there, they would have had nothing more to say to each other.

Much has been said about life's coincidences but little or nothing about the daily encounters which nearly always guide and determine life, although, in defence of this partial perception of vital contingencies, one could argue that an encounter, strictly speaking, is a coincidence, although obviously it does not follow that all coincidences have to be encounters. Throughout this gospel there have been many coincidences, and if we look carefully at the so-called life of Jesus, especially after he left home, we can see that there has been no lack of encounters either. Leaving aside his unfortunate adventure with the thieves, since it is too early to predict what the consequences might be in the near and distant future, Jesus's first journey on his own has resulted in many encounters, such as the providential appearance of the philanthropic Pharisee, thanks to whom the fortunate boy not only satisfied his hunger, but by eating in haste reached the Temple in time to listen to the questions and answers which prepared the ground, as it were, for his question about guilt and remorse, a question which has brought him all the way from Nazareth. When critics discuss the rules of effective narration, they insist that decisive encounters, in fiction as in life, should be interspersed and criss-crossed with countless others of no real importance, so that the hero of the story does not find himself transformed into a singular human being to whom nothing ordinary ever happens. They also claim this is the narrative process which best serves the ever desirable effect of verisimilitude, for if the episode imagined and described is not and is never likely to become or supplant factual reality, then there must be at least some similitude. Not as in the present narrative, in which the reader's credence has clearly been put to the test, Jesus taking himself to Bethlehem where he no sooner arrives than he comes face to face with Salome who assisted at his birth, as if that other encounter with the woman carrying a child in her arms, whom we deliberately planted there to fill in the story with her remonstrations, had not been licence enough. However, the most incredible part of our story has still to come, once the slave Salome has accompanied Jesus to the cave and leaves him there at his request, Leave me alone between these dark walls so that I may hear my first cry in this deep silence if echoes can last that long. These were the words the woman thought she heard and so they are recorded here, at the risk of once more offending verisimilitude, but then we can always blame the unreliable testimony of a senile old woman. Unsteady on her feet, Salome hobbled off, moving cautiously, one step at a time and leaning heavily on her staff which she gripped with both hands. Now it would have been a nice gesture on the boy's part to help this poor, suffering creature to return home, but such is youth, selfish and thoughtless, and there is nothing to suggest that Jesus was any different from other boys of his age.

He is sitting on a stone, and on another stone beside him rests an oil lamp casting its dim light over the cave's rough walls, on the dark heap of coals where there was once a fire, over his limp hands and pensive face, This is where I was born, he thought to himself, I once slept in that manger, my father and mother once sat on this very stone where I'm sitting now, this is where we took refuge as Herod's soldiers searched the village and slaughtered infants. But try as hard as I might, I shall never succeed in hearing that cry of life I gave at birth, or the cries of those dying children and the parents who watched them die, there is nothing but silence in this cave where a beginning and an end came together. As I learned in the Temple, parents pay for the sins they've committed, their children for those sins they might one day commit, but if life is a sentence and death just punishment, then there was never a more innocent community than that of Bethlehem, infants who died in all innocence, parents who had done no wrong, nor a more guilty man than my father who remained silent when he should have spoken, and now me, whose life was saved so that I might learn of the crime which saved my life, and even if I were to commit no other offence, this will suffice to kill me. Amidst the shadows of the cave Jesus got to his feet as if anxious to escape, but after taking a few faltering steps his legs suddenly gave way, and he put his hands to his eyes to catch his tears, poor boy, writhing in the dust as if he were in agony, tormented by remorse for a crime he had not committed, yet cruelly condemned to feel guilty for the rest of his life. This flood of bitter tears will leave its mark for ever in Jesus's eyes, a dull glimmer of sadness and despair as if he had just stopped crying. Time passed, the sun outside began to set, the earth's shadows lengthened, the prelude to that great shadow which descends from the heavens at dusk. The encroaching darkness penetrated the cave where shadows were already threatening to extinguish the lamp's tiny flame, the oil is clearly running out and this is what it will be like when the sun finally disappears, when men will say to each other, We're losing our sight, unaware that their eyes are no longer of any use to them. Jesus is now asleep, overcome by the merciful exhaustion of recent days, his father's horrible death, the inherited nightmare, his mother's resignation, and then the tiring journey to Jerusalem, the daunting vision of the Temple, the discouraging words uttered by the scribe, the descent into Bethlehem, the fateful encounter with Salome who appeared from the depths of time to reveal once and for all the circumstances of his birth, therefore it is not surprising that his weary body should have lowered his spirits, he appeared to be resting both in body and soul, but his spirit is already stirring and in his dream rouses his body so that they may go together to Bethlehem and there, in the middle of the main square, confess their atrocious crime. By means of the physical instrument of voice, his spirit will declare, I am he who brought death to your children, judge me, condemn this body I bring before you, this body of which I am both heart and soul, so that you may abuse and torture it, for as is well known, only by mortifying and sacrificing the flesh can we hope to gain absolution and the rewards of the spirit. In his dream Jesus can see the mothers of Bethlehem bearing tiny corpses, only one of those infants is alive and its mother is that woman who appeared to Jesus with a child in her arms, and it is she who replies, Unless you can restore their lives, be silent, for who needs words in the presence of death. In self-abasement, his soul withdrew into itself like a tunic folded three times, before surrendering his defenceless body to the mercy of the mothers of Bethlehem, but Jesus was never to know that his body would be spared because just as the woman with the child in her arms was about to tell him, You're not to blame, you may go, a flash of lightning filled the cave and woke him with a start, Where am I, was the first thought that came into his head, and struggling to his feet from the dusty ground and with tears in his eyes, he saw a giant of a man towering over him with his head aflame, but then he realized that he was mistaken, the man was holding a torch in his right hand which was almost touching the ceiling of the cave. The head was a little lower down and so huge it could have been taken for that of Goliath, however there was nothing aggressive about the face with its gratified expression of someone who had been searching and found what he was looking for. Jesus rose to his feet and backed against the wall of the cave, from where he could get a better look at the giant who was not so big after all, perhaps a span taller than the tallest man of Nazareth. These optical illusions, without which there can be neither prodigies nor miracles, were discovered ages ago, and the only reason why that same Goliath did not become a basketball player is because he was born before his time. And who are you, the man asked him, but Jesus saw he was only trying to make conversation. Resting his torch on a jutting piece of rock, he stood the two sticks he was carrying with him against the wall, one with great knots smoothed down by constant use, the other still covered in bark and recently cut from some tree. Then, seating himself on the largest stone, he began pulling the vast mantle he was wearing down over his shoulders. I'm Jesus of Nazareth, the boy replied. What are you doing here if you're from Nazareth, Although I'm from Nazareth, I was born here in this cave and I've come to see the place where I was born, Where you were born, my lad, was in your mother's belly and you'll never be able to creep back in there. Unaccustomed to such crude language, the man's words made Jesus blush and he could think of nothing to say. Have you run away from home, the man asked him. The boy hesitated as if searching in his heart to see if his departure could be described as running away before answering, Yes. Did you quarrel with your parents, My father's dead, Oh, was all the man said, but Jesus had a strange feeling that the man was already aware of this and all the rest and that he knew what had been said and remained to be said. You didn't answer my question, the man insisted, What question, Did you quarrel with your parents, Mind your own business, Don't be rude to me, boy, unless you want a good thrashing, and not even God will hear your cries for help in this place. God is eye, ear and tongue, He sees and hears everything, and it's only because He chooses not to, that He doesn't say everything, What does a boy of your age know about God, What I learned in the synagogue, You never heard anyone in the synagogue say that God is an eye, an ear and a tongue, I myself decided that if this were not so then God would not be God, And why do you think that God has an eye and an ear and not two eyes and two ears like the rest of us, So that the one eye cannot deceive the other, or the one ear the other, and as for the tongue there is no problem because we only have one tongue. The tongue of man is also two-sided and serves both truth and falsehood, God cannot lie, Who's to prevent Him, God himself, otherwise He'd deny himself, Have you ever seen Him, Seen who, Seen God, Some have seen Him and announced His coming. The man stared at the boy in silence as if looking for some familiar trait, then said, True, some have believed they've seen Him. He paused, then continued with a mischievous smile, You still haven't answered my question, What question, Did you quarrel with your parents. I left home because I wanted to see the world, You've mastered the art of lying, my boy, but I know perfectly well who you are, you were born to a simple carpenter called Joseph and a wool-carder called Mary, How do you know, I found out one day and have remembered ever since, I don't understand, I'm a shepherd and I've spent nearly all my life breeding and caring for my sheep and goats and I happened to be in these parts when the soldiers came to slaughter the children of Bethlehem, so as you can see, I've known you since the day you were born. Jesus looked at the man nervously and asked, What is your name, My sheep don't know me by any name, But I'm not one of your sheep, Who knows, Tell me what you're called, If you must insist on giving me a name, call me Pastor, that'll be enough to summon me if you should ever need me, Will you take me with you to help with the flock, I was waiting for you to ask, Well then, Yes, you may join the flock. The man got to his feet, lifted his torch and went outside. Jesus followed. It was darkest night and the moon had still not risen. Gathered near the entrance to the cave, the sheep and goats stood around in silence, except for the faint jingling of bells from time to time. Patiently they awaited the outcome of the conversation between the shepherd and his latest helpmate. The man raised the torch exposing the black heads of the goats and the whitish snouts of the sheep, some scraggy with sparse hairs, others plump with woolly coats, and told him, This is my flock, take care not to lose even one of these animals. Seated at the entrance to the cave beneath the flickering light of the torch, Jesus and the shepherd ate cheese and stale bread from the knapsacks. Then the shepherd went inside and returned with the new stick which was still covered in bark. He lit a fire and deftly turning the wood amidst the flames he slowly scorched the bark until it began to peel off in long strips and then he roughly smoothed down the knots. Allowing the stick to cool, he then plunged it back into the fire, but turning it briskly this time to avoid burning the wood, darkening and strengthening the surface until it took on the appearance of seasoned wood. Handing the stick to Jesus once it was ready, he told him, Here's your shepherd's crook, strong and straight, and as good as a third arm. Although his hands were anything but delicate, Jesus dropped the stick with a howl. How could the shepherd hold anything so hot, Jesus asked himself without finding an explanation. When the moon finally appeared, they went into the cave to get some sleep. Some sheep and goats followed and lay down beside them. At first light, the shepherd shook Jesus, Time to get up, the flock has to be fed, from now on you'll take them out to pasture, as important a job as you're ever likely to be entrusted with. Moving as fast as their tiny steps allowed, the flock moved on, the shepherd walking in front, his helpmate at the rear. The cool, transparent dawn seemed to be in no hurry to make the sun appear, envious of that splendour heralding a world reborn. Hours later, an old woman, walking along slowly with the aid of a stick, emerged from amongst the houses of Bethlehem and entered the cave. It came as no surprise to find that Jesus was no longer there, and probably they would have had nothing more to say to each other. Amidst the eternal shadows inside the cave a tiny flame continued to shine now that the shepherd had filled the lamp with oil.

Four years hence, Jesus will meet God. This unexpected revelation, which is probably premature according to the rules of effective narration mentioned earlier, is simply intended to prepare the reader for some everyday scenes from pastoral life which will add little of substance to the main thread of our story, thus excusing any reader who might be tempted to jump ahead. Nevertheless, four years are four years, especially at an age when there are so many physical and mental changes in a youth, when his body grows so fast, the first signs of a beard, a swarthy complexion becoming even darker, the voice turning as deep and harsh as a stone rolling down a mountain slope and that faraway look as if day-dreaming, always reprehensible especially when one has a duty to be vigilant, like those sentinels in barracks, castles and encampments, or, before we stray from our story, like this shepherd boy who has been warned to keep a watchful eye on his master's goats and sheep. Although, if truth be told, we do not really know who that master is. Tending sheep, at this time and in these parts, is work for a servant or slave, obliged, under pain of punishment, to give a regular account of milk, cheese and wool, not to mention the number of animals, which should always be on the increase so that neighbours might see that the eyes of the Lord are looking down with indulgence on the pious owner of such abundant possessions, who, if he wishes to conform to the rules of this world, must have greater trust in the Lord's benevolence than in the genetic strength of the mating rams in his flock. Yet how strange that Pastor, as he asked to be called, does not seem to have any master over him, for during the next four years no one will come to the desert to collect the wool, milk or cheese, nor will Pastor leave the flock in order to give account of his duties. All would be well if Pastor were the owner, in the normal acceptance of the word, of these goats and sheep. But it is hard to believe that the real owner would allow such an incredible amount of wool to be lost, only shear his sheep in order to prevent them suffocating from the heat, or only use the milk, if at all, to make the day's supply of cheese and then barter the rest in exchange for figs, dates and bread, and, mystery of mysteries, never sell lambs and kids from his flock, not even during Passover, when they are much in demand and fetch such high prices. Little wonder, therefore, that the flock continues to grow bigger, as if obeying, with the persistence and enthusiasm of those who feel their life-span is guaranteed that famous mandate given by the Lord, Who may have been unconvinced of the efficacy of sweet, natural instincts, Go forth and multiply. In this unusual and wayward flock the animals tend to die of old age and Pastor himself serenely lends a hand by killing off those animals who can no longer keep up with the others because of disease or old age. The first time this happened after he had started working with Pastor, Jesus protested at such wanton cruelty, but the shepherd simply said, Either I kill them as I've always done, or I leave them abandoned to die alone in this wilderness, or I hold up the flock, wait for the old and sick to die and risk letting the healthy animals starve to death for lack of pasture. So tell me, what you would do if you were in my shoes and had power of life and death over your flock. Jesus did not know what to say and changed the subject by asking, Since you don't sell the wool, have more milk and cheese than we need in order to live, and you never take the lambs and kids to market, why do you allow this flock to get bigger and bigger. One of these days your goats and sheep will cover every hill in sight and there will be no land left for pasture. Pastor told him, The flock was here and somebody had to look after the animals and protect them from thieves, and that person happened to be me, What do you mean by here, Here, there, everywhere, So are you asking me to believe that this flock has always been here, More or less, Did you buy the first sheep and goat, No, Who then, I simply found them, I don't know if anyone bought them, but there was already a flock by the time I got here, Were they given to you, No one gave them to me, I found them, and they found me, So you're the owner. No, I'm not the owner, nothing in this world belongs to me, Because everything belongs to the Lord as you ought to know, True, How long have you been a shepherd, I was a shepherd before you were born, How many years, Difficult to say, perhaps if we multiplied your age by fifty, Only the Patriarchs before the Great Flood lived that long and no one nowadays can hope to reach their age, No need to tell me, Well if you agree, yet insist on saying you've lived all this time, don't expect me to believe you're human, I don't. Now if Jesus, who was as skilled in the art of interrogation as any disciple of Socrates, had asked, What are you then, since you aren't man, Pastor would most probably have answered nonchalantly, I'm an angel, but don't tell anyone. This often happens, we refrain from asking questions because we are unprepared or simply too afraid to hear the answers. And when we summon the courage to raise them, no answers are forthcoming, just as Jesus will one day refuse to answer when asked, What is truth. A question which remains unanswered to this day.

Whatever he may be, Jesus knows without having to ask that his mysterious companion is not an angel of the Lord because the angels of the Lord forever sing His glories, unlike men who only praise Him under obligation and on statutory occasions, although it is worth pointing out that angels have greater reason for singing these glories since they live in intimacy, as it were, with the Lord in His heavenly kingdom. What really surprised Jesus from the outset was that when they left the cave at first light, Pastor, unlike Jesus, did not praise the Lord for all the usual blessings, such as having restored man's soul and having endowed the cock with intelligence, and when forced to disappear behind a rock to relieve himself, he gave no thanks to the Lord for all the providential orifices and vessels that help the human body to function and without which we would be in a sorry state. Pastor looked at heaven and earth as one does on getting out of bed, muttered something about the fine day ahead and, putting two fingers to his lips, gave a shrill whistle which brought the entire flock to its feet as one. And that was all. Jesus thought he might have forgotten, always possible when one's mind is on other matters, such as how to teach this boy, accustomed to the easy life of a carpenter, the first rudiments of tending sheep and goats. Now as we know, in a normal situation amongst ordinary people, Jesus would not have had to wait long in order to discover the extent of his master's piety, since Jews in those days gave thanks to the Lord some thirty times each day and on the slightest pretext, as we have often seen throughout this Gospel, without needing any further proof. But the day passed and Pastor showed no signs of offering prayers of thanksgiving, dusk fell and they settled down to sleep out in the open and not even the majesty of God's sky above touched the shepherd's heart or brought so much as a word of praise or gratitude to his lips, after all, it might have been raining and it was not, which to all intents and purposes, both human and divine, was a clear sign that the Lord was watching over His creatures. Next morning, after they had eaten and his master was preparing to inspect the flock to make sure they were all there and that some restless goat had not decided to wander off in the vicinity, Jesus announced in a firm voice, I'm leaving. Pastor stopped, looked at him without altering his expression, and simply said, Have a good journey, there's no need to tell me since you're not my slave and there is no legal contract between us, you can leave whenever you choose, But don't you want to know why I'm leaving, I'm not all that curious, Well I'll tell you just the same, I'm leaving because I've no desire to work with someone who doesn't fulfil his obligations to the Lord, What obligations, The simplest obligations, such as offering up prayers of thanksgiving. Pastor said nothing, his eyes half smiling, then finally he spoke, I'm not a Jew and therefore have no such obligations to fulfil. Deeply shocked, Jesus backed away. That the land of Israel should be swarming with foreigners and worshippers of false gods, he knew all too well, but this was the first time he had actually slept beside such a person or shared his bread and milk. And as if holding a sword and shield before him, he exclaimed, The Lord alone is God. Pastor's smile faded and his mouth became twisted and embittered, Certainly if God exists He must be only one Lord, but it would be preferable if He were two, then there would be a god for the wolf and one for the sheep, one for the victim and one for the assassin, a god for the condemned man and one for the executioner, God is one, whole and indivisible, exclaimed Jesus, almost weeping with pious indignation, whereupon Pastor retorted, I don't know how God can live, but he got no further before Jesus with all the authority of a teacher in the synagogue interrupted him, God does not live, God exists, These fine distinctions escape me, but I'll tell you this, I wouldn't like to be a god who guides the hand of the assassin clutching a dagger while presenting the throat that is about to be cut, You offend God with these irreverent thoughts, You overestimate my worth, Remember God never sleeps and one day He'll punish you, Just as well He doesn't sleep so that He can avoid the nightmares of remorse, Why speak to me of the nightmares of remorse, Because we're discussing your god, And which god do you serve, Like my sheep, I have no god, But sheep, at least, produce lambs for the altars of the Lord, And I can assure you that their mothers would howl like wolves if they were to know. Jesus turned pale and could think of no reply. All was silent as the flock attentively gathered round them. The sun had already risen, its light casting a crimson glow on the fleecy coats of the sheep and the horns of the rams. Jesus said, I'm off, but showed no signs of moving. Leaning on his crook, as relaxed as if he had all the time in the world at his disposal, Pastor waited. At last Jesus took a few steps, opening a path through the sheep, then suddenly stopped and asked, What do you know about remorse and nightmares, That you are your father's heir. Those words were too much for Jesus. His legs buckled at the knees and the knapsack slipped from his shoulder, whereupon either by chance or necessity his father's sandals fell out and he could hear the noise of the Pharisee's bowl shattering into smithereens. Jesus began weeping like a lost child, but Pastor made no attempt to comfort him and merely said from where he was standing, You must never forget that I've known about you since the day you were born and now you'd better decide whether you're going or staying, First, tell me who you are. The time has not yet come for you to know, And when will I know, If you stay you'll regret not having gone away, and if you go, you'll regret not having stayed, But if I should go away, I shall never know who you are, You're mistaken, your hour will come and when it does I shall be there to tell you, and that's enough conversation for now, the flock can't remain here all day waiting for you to make up your mind. Jesus gathered up the broken pieces of the bowl, looked at them as if he couldn't bear to part with them, but for no good reason since two days ago at this hour he had not yet met the Pharisee. Besides, this was only to be expected, earthenware bowls break so easily. He scattered the pieces on the ground as if he were sowing seeds, and at that moment Pastor said, You will have another bowl, but the next one won't break while you're alive. Jesus didn't hear him, he had Joseph's sandals in his hand and was trying to decide if he should wear them. Not all that long ago they would have been much too big for him, but time, as we know, can be deceptive, Jesus felt as if he had been carrying his father's sandals around in his knapsack for ages and he would have been very surprised to find they were still too big for him. He slipped them on and, without knowing why he did so, packed his own. Pastor said, Once feet have grown they don't shrink again, and you won't have any offspring to inherit your tunic, mantle and sandals, but Jesus did not discard them, their weight helped to keep the almost empty knapsack on his shoulder. There was no need to give Pastor the answer he wanted, Jesus took his place behind the flock, his feelings divided between an indefinable sense of terror as if his soul were in peril, and another, even more indefinable sense of sombre fascination. I must find out who you are, murmured Jesus, choking on the dust raised by the flock as he chased after a sheep that was lagging behind, and this, he believed, was his real motive for finally deciding to stay with the mysterious shepherd.

This was the first day. No more was said about matters of faith and blasphemy, about life, death and inheritance, but Jesus, who had started to observe Pastor's every attitude and gesture, noticed that each time he offered up prayers of thanksgiving to the Lord, the shepherd would get down and place the palms of his hands on the ground, lowering his head and shutting his eyes, without uttering a word. One day, when he was still a little boy, Jesus had heard some elderly travellers who were passing through Nazareth relate that deep down in the world there existed vast caverns where one could find cities, fields, rivers, forests and deserts, just like those on the surface of the world, and that this underworld, a perfect image and likeness of the one we live in, was created by the Devil after God threw him down from the heavens as a punishment for his rebellion. And since the Devil, whom God had initially befriended and looked on with favour, causing people even in this world to comment that there had never been so close a friendship, since the Devil had witnessed the birth of Adam and Eve and learned how it was done, he then repeated the process and created man and woman for himself in his underworld, but with the one difference that, unlike God, he forbade them nothing, which explains why there has never been such a thing as original sin in the Devil's world. One of the old men even dared to suggest, And since there was no original sin, there was no other kind of sin either. After the old men had been sent on their way with the help of some persuasive stones thrown by outraged Nazarites, who soon realized what these irreverent old fools were getting at with their insidious remarks, there was a sudden tremor, nothing serious, a mere sign of confirmation coming from the bowels of the earth, which made young Jesus think, capable as he was of linking cause and effect even as a boy. And now, watching Pastor kneeling before him with his head lowered and palms resting lightly on the ground so as to be able to feel every grain of sand, each tiny pebble and shoot sprouting on the surface, Jesus was reminded of that old story and at certain moments was convinced this man must inhabit the hidden world created by the Devil in the image and likeness of the visible world. What is he doing here, Jesus asked himself, but dared not probe any further. When Pastor eventually got to his feet, he asked him,

What are you doing, I want to be sure the earth is still beneath me, Surely you can tell with your feet, My feet don't perceive anything, only my hands can tell me, when you adore your God, you don't raise your feet to Him but your hands, even though you could raise other parts of your body, even what's between your legs, unless you happen to be a eunuch. Overcome with shame and horror, Jesus turned the colour of beetroot. Do not offend the God Whom you do not know, he told him severely on recovering his composure, but Pastor insisted, Who created your body, It was God, of course, Just as it looks now, Yes, And did the Devil play any part in creating your body, None whatsoever, man's body is God's creation, So all the parts of your body are the same in the eyes of God, Obviously. So God isn't likely to disown what you've got between your legs, for example, No, I suppose not, but then the Lord created Adam, yet expelled him from Paradise even though he was His creation, Just give me a straight answer, boy, and stop talking like a teacher in the synagogue, You're trying to force me into giving the answers you want, but I could tell you, if necessary, all the circumstances in which man, because the Lord so ordained, must not under pain of contamination and death, expose his own or another's nakedness which proves that certain parts of the body are in themselves sinful, No more sinful than the mouth when it utters falsehood and slander, that same mouth with which you praise your Lord before uttering falsehood and after spreading slander, That's enough, I don't want to hear another word, You must hear me out if only to answer my question, What question, Can God disown what you have between your legs as something not of His making, just answer yes or no, No, He can't, Why not, Because the Lord cannot undo what He previously willed, Slowly nodding his head Pastor said, In other words, your God is the only warder of a prison where the only captive is your God. The final echo of these momentous words was still ringing in Jesus's ears when Pastor, trying unsuccessfully to sound natural, went on to say, You must choose a sheep, What did you say, asked Jesus in bewilderment, I told you to choose a sheep, unless you prefer a goat. Whatever for, Because you'll need it unless you really are a eunuch. When these words sank in, the boy felt stunned, but worst of all, was the onslaught of horrendous sensuality once he had suppressed his embarrassment and revulsion. Covering his face with both hands, he said in a hoarse voice, This is the word of the Lord, If a man should copulate with an animal he will be punished with death and the animal be slaughtered, and the Lord has also said, Cursed is the man who sins with an animal whatever its species, Did your Lord say all these things, Yes, and now leave me alone, abominable creature, for you are not God's creature but belong to the Devil. Pastor listened impassively, waiting for Jesus's tirade to have its full effect, whatever it might be, a sudden apparition, leprosy, the sudden demise of body and soul. But nothing happened. Wind came playing between the stones, raised a cloud of dust which swept across the wilderness, and then nothing, silence, the universe quietly watching men and animals, perhaps waiting to see what meaning they could find, recognize or attribute to those words, burning itself up in this vigil, and the primordial fire already reduced to ashes, while any reply is slow, in coming. Suddenly Pastor raised his arms and called out in a commanding voice to his flock, Listen, listen, my sheep, hear what this learned boy has come to teach us, God has forbidden that anyone should copulate with you, so worry not, but as for shearing you, neglecting you, slaughtering you, and eating you, all these things are permitted, because for this you were created by God's law and are sustained by His Providence. Giving three long whistles and waving his crook over his head, he called out, Be off, be off with you, whereupon the flock started heading for the spot where the column of dust had disappeared. Jesus just stood there watching until the tall figure of Pastor almost vanished from sight and the resigned rumps of the animals merged with the colour of the earth. I'm not going with him, Jesus had said, but he went. He adjusted the knapsack on his shoulder, tightened the straps of the sandals which had belonged to his father and followed the flock at a distance. He caught up with them at nightfall, and emerging from the shadows into the light of the camp-fire, announced, I'm here.

After time comes time is a well-known saying and to the point, yet not as obvious as it may seem to someone who is satisfied with the approximate meaning of words, whether taken separately or together, because everything depends on how something is said and this varies according to the mood of the person speaking. It is not the same thing when the words are expressed by someone whose life is going badly and who is hoping for better times, or utters them as a threat, promising vengeance at some future date. And the most extreme case would be that of someone who, without any strong or objective reasons for complaining about his health and well-being, sadly sighs, After time comes time, just because he is a pessimist by nature and given to foreseeing the worst. It would not be entirely plausible for Jesus to be going around saying these words at his age, whatever his meaning or tone of voice, but for us, yes, because like God, we know everything about time past and still to come, so we can say, mutter or whisper those words as we watch Jesus go about his tasks as a shepherd boy, crossing the hills of Judah, or when the time comes, descending into the valley of Jordan. And not just because we are writing about Jesus, but because every human being is constantly confronted with things good and bad, one thing coming after another, time following time. Since this gospel was never meant to dismiss what others have written about Jesus or to challenge their account of events by contradicting their every statement, and since Jesus is clearly the hero of our story, it would be all too easy for us to go up to him and predict his future, tell him what a wonderful life lies ahead, about those miracles he will perform to provide food or restore health, and one which will even overcome death, but it would scarcely be wise, because young Jesus, notwithstanding his aptitude for religious studies and his knowledge of patriarchs and prophets, enjoys the healthy scepticism one associates with youth and would send us away with a flea in our ear. Naturally, he will change his ideas once he meets God, but it is much too soon for this momentous encounter and before then Jesus will have to go up and down many a mountain slope, milk many a goat and sheep, help to make cheese, go and barter wares in the villages. He will also slaughter animals which are diseased or have outlived their use, and he will mourn their loss. But the one thing he will never do, so fret not, all you sensitive souls, is to engage in the horrid vice insinuated by Pastor, of copulating with a goat or a sheep or both, in order to relieve and satisfy the corrupt flesh inhabited by his pure soul. But this is neither the time nor place to ponder how often the soul, in order to be able to boast of a clean body has burdened itself with sadness, envy and impurity.

Although these initial exchanges on ethical and theological questions were to remain unsolved, Pastor and Jesus got along well enough with each other, the shepherd patiently teaching him how to tend the flock, the boy listening attentively as if it were a matter of life and death. Jesus learned how to send his crook whirling through the air to land on the rump of some animal which in a moment of distraction or daring had strayed from the flock, but this was a painful apprenticeship, because one day, while he was still struggling to master the technique, he threw the stick too low and accidentally hit the tender neck of a new-born kid with full force, killing the poor creature outright. Such accidents may befall anyone, even an experienced and skilful shepherd, but poor Jesus who is already burdened with so many sorrows, froze with horror as he lifted the little kid, which was still warm, into his arms. There was nothing to be done. Even the mother goat, after sniffing her offspring for a moment, moved away and carried on grazing, pawing at the tufts of grass which she pulled at with quick movements of her head, bringing to mind that well-known refrain, A bleating goat won't chew much grass, which is another way of saying, You can't cry and eat at the same time. Pastor came to see what had happened, Tough luck, no need for you to feel guilty, But I killed the poor little creature, Jesus said mournfully. So you did, but if he'd been an ugly and smelly old billy goat you wouldn't have felt much pity, put him on the ground and let me deal with this while you go and attend to that sheep over there which looks as if she's just about to give birth. What are you going to do with the kid, Skin it, of course, unless you expect me to work a miracle and bring it back to life. I swear I'll never touch that meat, Eating the animal we kill is our only way of showing respect, what is wrong is to eat what others have been forced to kill, I refuse to eat it, Please yourself, there will be all the more for me. Pastor drew a knife from his belt, looked at Jesus and said, Sooner or later this is something else you'll have to learn, to study the entrails of these animals who were created to serve and feed us. Jesus looked away and turned to go but Pastor, who had paused with knife in hand, went on to say, Slaves exist to serve us, so perhaps we should open them up to see if they carry slaves inside, or open up some monarch to see if he has another monarch in his belly, and I'll bet if we were to meet the Devil and he allowed us to open him up, we might be surprised to find God jumping out. As we said before, Pastor was still capable of provoking Jesus with these outrageous remarks. Jesus gradually learned that the best way to deal with Pastor's irreverence was to ignore him and say nothing. After all, Pastor might have gone even further and suggested that on opening up God one might find the Devil inside. Jesus went off in search of the sheep that was about to give birth, here at least there were no surprises awaiting him, a lamb just like any other would appear, in the true image and likeness of its mother, who in turn was identical to her sisters, for the one thing we can expect from these creatures is an unchallenged continuity of the species. The sheep had already given birth. Lying on the ground, the new-born lamb seemed to be all legs as its mother tried to help it to get to its feet, gently nudging it with her nose, but the poor, dazed creature could do nothing except cock its head as if trying to find the best angle of vision to take in this strange new world. Jesus helped to hold it steady on its feet, his hands sticky with the afterbirth from the sheep's womb, but he did not mind for one gets used to these things when in constant contact with animals, and this lamb is arriving at the right moment, so pretty with its curly coat, its pink little mouth already searching avidly for milk from those teats it is seeing for the first time and could never have imagined from inside its mother's womb. Frankly, no one has any grounds for complaining about God when we discover so many useful things from the moment we are born. Within sight, Pastor was stretching the kid's pelt on a wooden frame in the form of a star, the skinned carcass already inside his knapsack and wrapped in a cloth. He will salt it later when the flock settles down for the night, except for the piece Pastor intends to have for his supper, since Jesus is adamant he will never touch the meat of an animal he unintentionally killed. According to the religion he observes and the traditions he respects, these scruples on the part of Jesus are in conflict with the slaughter of all those other innocent animals sacrificed daily on the altars of the Lord, especially in Jerusalem where the victims are counted in hecatombs. Given the time and place, Jesus's attitude seems very odd, but perhaps it is really a question of susceptibilities, as it were, for we must not forget Joseph's tragic death and Jesus's recent discovery of the appalling massacre which took place in Bethlehem almost fifteen years ago, enough to disturb any young mind, not to mention those terrifying nightmares which we have not mentioned lately, although they still trouble him and refuse to go away. When he can no longer bear the thought that Joseph is coming to kill him, Jesus's cries even wake the flock in the middle of the night, whereupon Pastor gives him a gentle shake, What's this, what's going on, he asks, and roused from his nightmare Jesus falls into the shepherd's arms as if he were his unfortunate father. Soon after joining Pastor, Jesus confided in him, concealing however the root causes of this agonizing vision which haunted him night and day. Pastor told him, Save your breath, I know everything, even what you're trying to hide from me. This was about the time Jesus rebuked Pastor for his lack of faith and wicked conduct, especially, if you'll forgive me labouring the point, when it came to sexual matters. But Jesus realized that he had no one in the world other than the family he had abandoned and almost forgotten, except for his mother who had given him life although he often wished she had not, and after his mother only his sister Lisa, something he could not explain, but then memory is like that and has its own reasons for remembering or forgetting. These things being what they are, Jesus gradually began to enjoy Pastor's company, and it is easy to imagine his relief at not having to live alone with his remorse, to have someone at his side who understands, not having to pretend to forgive what cannot be forgiven, even if he had the

182

power to do so, someone who will treat him properly, exercising kindness and severity in accordance with that part of him which preserved its innocence even while hemmed in by guilt. We felt this needed explaining, so that the reader might find it easier to understand and accept that Jesus, so different in character and outlook from his ill-bred master, should decide to stay with him until his prophesied encounter with God, which promises to be momentous because God is not likely to appear to a simple mortal for no good reason.

Before then, however, those circumstances and coincidences, which we discussed at length, will dictate that Jesus should meet his mother and some of his brothers in Jerusalem during this Passover which he thought he would be celebrating for the first time without his family. That Jesus should want to celebrate the Passover in Jerusalem might have surprised and angered Pastor since they were in the hills and the flock needed all their attention. Besides, Pastor was not a Jew and had no other god to honour, so he might well have held out and refused Jesus permission, telling him, Oh no, you don't, you'll stay right here where you're needed, I'm the one who gives the orders and there's work to be done. Now it has to be said that none of this happened, Pastor simply asked him, Will you be coming back, although from the tone of his voice he seemed to be certain that Jesus would return, and indeed, the boy replied without a moment's hesitation yet nonetheless surprised that the words should come out so spontaneously, Yes, I'll be back. Then pick yourself a clean lamb, Jesus, and take it to be sacrificed, since you Jews attach so much importance to these customs and practices. Pastor was putting him to the test and simply wanted to see if Jesus was capable of leading to its death a lamb from that flock which they had worked so hard to maintain and protect. No one warned Jesus, no tiny, invisible angel quietly approached to whisper in his ear, Be careful, it's a trap, don't trust him, this fellow is capable of anything. His gentle nature provided him with a good answer, or perhaps it was the memory of the dead kid and the new-born lamb. I want no lamb from this flock, he said, Why not, I refuse to lead an animal which I myself reared to its death, Please yourself, but I hope you realize that you'll have to get a lamb from some other flock, I suppose so, since lambs don't fall from heaven, When are you thinking of leaving, Early tomorrow morning, Will you be coming back, Yes, I'll be back. They said no more on the subject, although it was difficult to see how Jesus would find enough money to buy a paschal-lamb when he can barely scrape a living. Not given to vices which cost money, one may presume he still has the few coins he received from the Pharisee almost a year ago, but they don't amount to much and, as we said before, at this time of the year the prices of livestock in general and especially of lambs rise out of all proportion so that one really has to put one's trust in God. Despite all the misfortunes which have befallen him, one is tempted to say that a lucky star is guiding and protecting this boy, but it would be somewhat feeble-minded of this or any other evangelist to believe that celestial bodies so remote from our planet should have any decisive effect on a human being's existence, however much the devout Magi may have invoked, studied and compared these stars. For, if what we are told is true, they must have travelled these parts some years ago, only to see what they saw and go away again. What we are simply trying to say with this long-winded speech is that our Jesus must somehow find a way of presenting himself worthily in the Temple with his little lamb, thus fulfilling what is expected of him. For he has proved himself to be a good Jew even in difficult situations such as these tense confrontations with Pastor.

About this time the flock was enjoying the rich pastures of the valley of Aijalon situated between the cities of Gezer and Emmaus. In Emmaus, Jesus tried to earn enough money to buy the much-needed lamb but he soon became aware that, after a year of tending sheep and goats, he no longer had the aptitude for any other kind of work, not even for carpentry where he had made no progress for lack of practice. So he took the road which goes up from Emmaus to Jerusalem, wondering what he should do, he had no money to buy the lamb, stealing was out of the question, and it would be more miracle than luck if he were to find a stray lamb on the road to Emmaus. There are plenty of lambs around, some with a rope around their necks trailing their owners, others fortunate enough to be carried in loving arms. Imagining themselves to be on an outing, these innocent creatures are excited and nervous, they are curious about everything, and because they cannot ask questions, they use their eyes in the hope of making sense of a world made of words. Jesus sat on a stone by the roadside to think of a solution to the material problem which is preventing him from fulfilling his spiritual duty, if only another Pharisee were to appear suddenly, or even the same one who probably gives alms daily, and to ask him, Are you in need of a lamb, just as he had previously asked him, Are you hungry. On that first occasion Jesus did not have to beg in order to receive, now without any real hope of being given anything he will be forced to beg. He already has his hand stretched out, a gesture so eloquent that it dispenses with all explanations, and so expressive that we nearly always avert our eyes rather than be confronted with some unsightly wound or distressing obscenity. A few coins were dropped into Jesus's palm by less distracted travellers, but so few that at this rate the road from Emmaus will never bring him to the gates of Jerusalem. Having added up whatever money he already had and what he has just collected, there isn't enough to buy even half a lamb for, as everyone knows, the Lord does not accept anything on His altars unless it is perfect and whole, and He refuses animals that are blind, crippled, mutilated, diseased or contaminated. So you can imagine the scandal in the Temple if we were to present ourselves at the sacrificial altar with the hindquarters of an animal, and, if by any misfortune the testicles might have been trampled, crushed, broken or cut, that, too, would lead to its exclusion. No one remembers to ask this boy why he needs the money, but wait, an elderly man with a long, white beard has just approached Jesus while his family pause in the middle of the road, respectfully waiting for the patriarch to rejoin them. Jesus thought he was about to receive another coin, but he was mistaken. The old man asked him, Who are you, and the boy stood up to answer him, I'm Jesus of Nazareth, Have you no family, Yes, I have, Then why are you not with them, I came to work as a shepherd in Judaea, this was a deceitful way of telling the truth or putting the truth at the service of a falsehood. The old man looked at him with a quizzical expression and finally asked, Why are you begging for alms if you have a trade, I'm earning my keep but cannot raise enough money to buy a lamb for Passover, So that's why you're begging, Yes, whereupon the patriarch ordered one of the men in his group, Give this boy a lamb, we can buy another when we arrive at the Temple. There were six lambs tied to the same rope, the man untied the last of them and handed it to the old man who told Jesus, Here's your lamb so that you, too, may offer sacrifice to the Lord this Passover, and without waiting to be thanked, he went to rejoin his family who received him with smiles and acclaim. Before Jesus could thank him, the old man was gone and suddenly the road was mysteriously empty, between one bend and the next there was only Jesus and the lamb who had finally found each other on the road to Emmaus, thanks to the generosity of an elderly Jew. Jesus is clutching the end of the cord, the animal looked up at his new master and started to bleat me-e-e-e in that nervous, tremulous way young lambs do before being sacrificed to placate the gods. That bleating which Jesus had heard thousands of times since becoming a shepherd's helpmate, touched Jesus's heart to the quick and he felt as if his limbs were dissolving with grief. There he was as never before, with this absolute power over the life and death of another creature, this immaculate white lamb deprived of will or desire, its trusting little face anxiously looking up at him, showing its pink tongue whenever it bleated, pink flesh beneath its soft hairs, pink inside its ears, pink nails on its feet just like humans, and which will not be allowed to harden and become known as hooves. Jesus stroked the lamb's head, it responded by craning its neck and rubbing the palm of his hand with its moist nose, sending a shiver up his spine. The spell broke as suddenly as it began. At the end of the road over towards Emmaus other pilgrims appeared in a swarm of fluttering tunics, knapsacks and staffs, with more lambs and prayers of thanksgiving to the Lord. Jesus lifted his lamb into his arms and started walking.

He had not been back to Jerusalem since that day long ago when he had come here out of necessity to discover the burden of sorrow and remorse in life, whether shared like an inheritance or kept entirely to oneself like death. The crowd swarming the streets resembled a brown, muddy river about to flood the concourse before the steps of the Temple. Holding the lamb in his arms, Jesus watched the crowds file past, some coming, others going, some carrying animals to be sacrificed, others returning without them, looking joyful and calling out, Alleluia, Hosannah, Amen, or saying none of those things because inappropriate for the occasion, as inappropriate as going around shouting, Hallelujah or Hip hip hurrah, although there is not really all that much difference between these expressions, we use them with the utmost enthusiasm until, with the passing of time and by dint of repetition, we finally ask ourselves,

What does this expression really mean, only to find there is no answer. The endless column of smoke spiralling above the Temple indicated to everyone for miles around that all those who had gone there to offer sacrifice were direct and legitimate descendants of Abel, that son of Adam and Eve who in his time had offered the first-born of his flock and their fat to the Lord which were favourably received, while his brother Cain who had nothing to offer other than the simple fruits of nature, saw that the Lord for some inexplicable reason averted his eyes without so much as looking at him. If this was Cain's motive for killing Abel, then we can put our minds at rest, for these men here are not likely to kill each other, they all offer the same sacrifice, and how that fat spits and those carcasses sizzle while God in the sublime heavens inhales with satisfaction the odours from all that carnage. Jesus pressed his lamb to his breast, unable to fathom why God cannot be appeased with a shellful of milk being poured over His altar, that sap of existence which passes from one being to another, or with a handful of wheat, the basic substance of immortal bread. Jesus will soon have to part with the old man's admirable gift. His for such a short time, the poor little lamb will not live to see the sun set this day, time to mount the stairs of the Temple, to deliver it to the knife and sacrificial fire, as if no longer worthy of existence or being punished by the eternal guardian of myths and fables for having drunk from the waters of life. Then Jesus, as if suddenly enlightened, decides in defiance of the law of the synagogue and the word of God that this lamb will not die, that what he had received to deliver to the altar will continue to live, and that having come to Jerusalem to offer sacrifice, he will leave Jerusalem a greater sinner than when he arrived. As if his previous offences were not enough, he was now committing this one, too, but the day will arrive when he will have to pay for all his sins because God never forgets. For a moment, fear of punishment made him hesitate, but suddenly in his mind's eye, he momentarily saw the horrifying vision of a vast sea of blood, the blood of the countless lambs and other animals sacrificed since the creation of mankind, for that is why men have been put on this earth, to adore and offer sacrifice. These thoughts were so disturbing that he imagined he saw the steps of the Temple awash with red, blood streaming down the steps, and he could see himself standing in a pool of blood and raising the lifeless body of his beheaded lamb to heaven. Deep in thought, Jesus seemed to be trapped inside a sphere of silence, but suddenly the sphere exploded, shattered into pieces and once more he was plunged into that clamour of invocations and blessings, pleas, cries, chanting and the pitiful bleating of lambs, until silenced in an instant by three low blasts from the shofar, the long, spiralled horn of a ram transformed into a trumpet. Covering the lamb with his knapsack as if defending it from some imminent threat, Jesus ran from the concourse and disappeared into a labyrinth of narrow alleyways without worrying where he might end up. When he finally paused for breath, he was already on the outskirts, having left the city by the northern gate, known as that of Ramah, the same gate he had passed through on arriving from Nazareth. He sat beneath an olive tree at the side of the road and took the lamb out of his knapsack, no one would have found it strange to see him sitting there, they would simply have thought, He has probably travelled a long way and is recovering his strength before taking his lamb to the Temple, so endearing, and we would not know whether the person thinking this was referring to the lamb or to Jesus. We find both of them endearing, but if we had to make a choice, the golden apple would almost certainly go to the lamb, on the one condition that it does not grow any bigger. Jesus is lying on his back and holding the end of the cord to prevent the lamb from escaping, but this precaution is unnecessary for the poor creature's strength is hanging by a thread, not just because of its tender age but also because of all the excitement, the constant toing and froing, fetching and carrying, not to mention the poor rations it was given this morning, for it is considered to be neither fitting nor decent for any creature, lamb or martyr, to die with a full belly. Stretched out on the ground, Jesus gradually recovers and starts breathing normally again. He can see the sky between the branches of the olive tree swaying gently in the wind, the sun's rays filtering through gaps in the foliage and playing on his face, it must be about the sixth hour, the sun directly overhead reduces the shadows and who would ever think that night will gradually come to extinguish this dazzling light. Some people pass on the road, others follow behind and when Jesus takes a good look at the second group he gets such a shock that his first instinct is to escape, but how can he, for coming towards him are his own mother accompanied by some of his brothers, the older sons James, Joseph and Judas, and

Lisa, too, but then she is a girl and should be mentioned separately rather than listed according to age, which would rank her between James and Joseph. They still have not seen him. Jesus goes down on to the road to meet them, once more carrying his lamb in his arms, but one suspects this is only to make sure his arms are full. The first to notice him is James who waves before turning to their mother in great excitement and now Mary is looking, they start walking faster and Jesus, too, feels obliged to hasten towards them but he cannot run with the lamb in his arms. We are taking so long over this that readers might get the impression we do not want them to meet, but this is not so, maternal, fraternal and filial love should give them wings, but there are reservations and certain constraints, we know how they separated, we do not know what effect all these months apart without news of each other might have had. If one keeps on walking, one eventually arrives, and there they are, face to face, Jesus says, Your blessing, mother, and his mother says, May the Lord bless you, my son. They embraced, then it was his brothers' turn, then finally Lisa's, followed by an awkward silence, all of them at a loss for words, Mary was not going to say to her son, Such a surprise, what on earth are you doing here, or Jesus say to his mother, I never expected to find you here, what brings you to the city, the lamb in his arms and the one they have brought speak for themselves, this is the Passover of the Lord, the difference being that one lamb is going to die and the other has already been saved. We've been waiting for ages to hear from you, Mary said at length, bursting into tears. Her eldest son stood before her, so tall, so grown up, with the beginnings of a beard and the weather-beaten complexion of someone who has spent his days out in the open, exposed to the sun, wind and dust of the desert. Don't cry, mother, I have work, I'm now a shepherd. A shepherd, Yes, a shepherd, But I was hoping you'd follow in your father's footsteps and take up the trade he taught you, Well, as things turned out, I became a shepherd and that's what I am, When are you coming back home, I don't know, one day I suppose, At least accompany your mother and brothers to the Temple, Mother, I'm not going to the Temple, Whyever not, you've got your lamb there. This lamb isn't going to the Temple either, Is there something wrong with it, No, nothing whatsoever, but I'm determined this lamb will die a natural death when the time comes, My son, I don't understand, You don't have to understand, if I save this lamb it's so that someone may save me, Then why not come with your family, I was just about to leave, Where to, Back to the flock where I belong, Where did you leave it, At present it's in the valley of Aijalon, Where is this valley of Aijalon, Over on the other side, What other side, On the other side of Bethlehem. Mary stepped back and turned quite pale, how she had aged although barely thirty, Why do you mention Bethlehem, she asked, Because that's where I met the shepherd who is my master, Who is this man, and before Jesus had time to reply, she said to the others, You go on ahead and wait for me at the entrance, Then taking Jesus by the hand, she led him to the side of the road, Who is this man, she asked him a second time, I don't know, Jesus answered, Doesn't he have a name, If he has, he's never told me, I simply call him Pastor and that's all. What does he look like, He's a big fellow, And where did you meet him, In the cave where I was born, Who took you there, A slave called Salome who told me she had helped to deliver me at birth, And this man, What about him, What did he say to you, Nothing you don't already know. Mary slumped to the ground as if some heavy hand were pushing her, That man is a demon, How do you know, did he tell you so. No, the first time I saw him he told me he was an angel and asked me not to say a word to anyone, When did you see him, The day your father learned I was pregnant, he turned up at our door disguised as a beggar and told me he was an angel, Did you ever see him again, On the road when your father and I travelled to Bethlehem for the census, then in the cave where you were born, and the night after you left home he walked into the yard, I mistook him for you and, peering through the gap in the door, I watched him uprooting the plant in the yard, don't you remember that bush which grew at the very spot where the bowl of luminous earth was buried, What bowl, what earth. You were never told, but the beggar gave it to me before he went away, and when he handed me back the bowl after he had finished eating, there was luminous earth inside, For earth to shine like that he really must have been an angel, At first I believed so, but the devil, too, has magical powers. Jesus had sat down beside his mother and left the lamb to roam at will. Yes, I've become aware that when they are both in agreement, it's almost impossible to tell the difference between an angel of the Lord and an angel of Satan, he told her. Stay with us, don't go back to that man, do this for your mother's sake. No, I promised to return and I intend to keep my word, People only make promises to the devil in order to deceive him, This man, who I'm sure isn't a man, but an angel or demon, has been haunting me since the day I was born and I want to know why, Jesus, my son, come to the Temple with your mother and brothers, by taking this lamb to the altar you'll fulfil your obligation and the lamb its destiny, and there you can ask the Lord to deliver you from the powers of Satan and all evil thoughts, This lamb will die when the time comes, But this is its day for dying, Mother, the lambs you gave birth to must die, but you must not will them to die before their time, Lambs are not men and even less so when those men are sons, When the Lord ordered Abraham to kill his son Isaac, no distinction was made then, My son, I'm a simple woman, I have no answer to give you, but I beseech you, give up these evil thoughts, Mother, thoughts are but passing shadows, neither good nor bad in themselves, actions alone count, Praised be the Lord Who blessed this poor, ignorant woman with such a wise son, yet I cannot believe this is the wisdom of God, One can also learn from the Devil, And I fear you're in his power, If his power saved this lamb, then something has been gained in this world today. Mary made no attempt to reply. They saw James approaching from the city gate. Mary got to her feet, I've found my son only to lose him again, she said, whereupon Jesus replied, If you haven't already lost him, you're not likely to lose him now. He put his hand into the knapsack and drew out the money he had been given as alms, This is all I've got, You've worked all those months for so little, I work to earn my keep, You must be very fond of that master of yours to be satisfied with so little, The Lord is my shepherd, Don't offend God, living as you do with a demon, Who knows, Mother, who knows, he could be an angel serving another God who reigns in another heaven, The Lord said, I am the Lord and you will worship no other god, Amen, responded Jesus. He gathered the lamb into his arms and said, I can see James coming, farewell, Mother, and Mary said, One would think you had more affection for that lamb of yours than for your own family. Right now I do, replied Jesus. Choking with grief and indignation, Mary turned away and ran to meet her other son. She never looked back.

Once outside the city walls, Jesus took another route across the fields before beginning the long descent into the Valley of Aijalon. He stopped at a village and bought food with the money his mother had refused to accept, some bread and figs, some milk for himself and the lamb, sheep's milk, and if there was any difference, it wasn't noticeable and, at least in this case, it's possible to accept that one mother is as good as another. Should anyone be surprised to hear of Jesus spending money on a lamb which by rights should now be dead, we could reply that this boy once owned two lambs, one was sacrificed and lives on in the glory of the Lord, while this other one was rejected by the Lord himself because it had a torn ear, Take a look, But there's nothing wrong with its ear, they would say, whereupon Jesus would reply, Well in that case I'll tear it myself, and lifting the lamb on to his shoulder, he went on his way. He caught sight of the flock as the evening light began to wane, all the more rapidly now that the sky had become overcast with dark, low clouds. The tension in the atmosphere forecast thunderstorms and this was confirmed when a flash of lightning rent the sky just as Jesus sighted the flock. There was no rain. This was one of those dry thunderstorms, all the more terrifying because they make one feel so vulnerable, without that screen of rain and wind, as it were, to shield and protect us in this naked battle between a thundering sky which tears itself apart and an earth which trembles and cowers helplessly beneath the onslaught of blows. A hundred paces away from Jesus, another blinding flash split an olive tree which immediately caught fire and blazed like a flaming torch. A loud burst of thunder shuddered across the entire sky as if ripping it open from end to end, and the impact knocked Jesus to the ground, leaving him senseless. Two more flashes of lightning struck, one here, another there, like two decisive words, until little by little the peals of thunder became more remote and finally died away into a gentle murmur, an intimate dialogue between heaven and earth. Having survived the storm unscathed and got over its fright, the lamb came up to Jesus and put its mouth to his lips, there was no sniffing, the merest contact was all that was needed, and who are we to question it. Jesus opened his eyes, saw the lamb standing there, then that livid sky, like a black hand suppressing any remaining light. The olive tree was still burning. Jesus's bones ached when he tried to move, but at least he still felt in control of his body, if this can be said of something so fragile that it only takes a blast of thunder to knock it to the ground. He sat up with some effort and, more by touch than sight, reassured himself that he was neither burnt nor paralysed, none of his bones were broken, and apart from a loud buzzing in his head which seemed as never-ending as the droning of a trumpet, he was alive and well. He drew the lamb towards him and finding words he did not know he possessed, he said, Don't be afraid, He only wanted to show you that you could have been dead by now if He had so willed, and to assure me that it was not me who saved your life, but Him. One last peal of thunder slowly rent the air like a sigh, while down below the white patch formed by the flock was like a beckoning oasis. Struggling to overcome his weakness, Jesus began descending the slope. Kept on a lead simply as a precaution, the lamb trotted at his side like a little dog. Behind them, the olive tree continued to burn. And the light it projected into the waning twilight allowed Jesus to see the tall figure of Pastor rise before him like an apparition wrapped in a mantle which trailed forever and holding his crook which might have touched the clouds were he to raise it. Pastor told him, I was expecting that thunderstorm, I'm the one who should have expected it, replied Jesus. Where did you get that lamb, I didn't have enough money to buy a lamb for Passover, so I stood by the roadside and begged for alms, then an old man appeared and gave me this lamb, Then why didn't you offer it in sacrifice, I couldn't, I just couldn't bring myself to do it. Pastor smiled, Now I'm beginning to understand, He waited for you, He allowed you to come to the flock in peace, in order to show His might before my eyes. Jesus did not reply, he had more or less said the same thing to the lamb, but having just arrived he had no desire to get involved in any discussion about God's motives and actions. So what are you going to do with your lamb, Nothing, I brought it here so that it might join the flock, All the white lambs look alike, tomorrow you won't even recognize it amongst the others, My lamb knows me, The day will come when it will start to forget you, besides the lamb will soon get tired of always having to come back and look for you, better to brand it or cut a piece off its ear, Poor little beast, What's the difference, after all, they branded you when they cut your foreskin so that people would know to whom you belong, It's not the same thing, It shouldn't be, but it is. As they were speaking, Pastor had gathered some wood and was now busily trying to light a fire with some flint. Jesus told him, It would be easier to go and fetch a branch from the burning olive tree, whereupon Pastor replied, One should always leave the heavenly fire to burn out by itself. The trunk of the olive tree was now one great ember shining in the darkness, the wind causing sparks to fly and sending incandescent strips of bark and burning twigs into the air where they soon burned out. The sky remained heavy and strangely oppressive. Pastor and Jesus ate together as usual which led Pastor to comment ironically, This year you're not partaking of the paschal-lamb. Jesus listened and said nothing, but deep down he felt uneasy, from now onwards he would have to face the awkward contradiction between eating lambs and refusing to slaughter them. So what's to be done, asked Pastor, before adding, Is the lamb to be branded or not, I couldn't do it, insisted Jesus, Give it to me then and I'll cope. With a firm, quick flick of the knife Pastor removed the tip of one of its ears, then holding it up, he asked, What shall I do with this, bury it or throw it away. Without thinking, Jesus replied, Give it to me, and dropped it into the fire. That's exactly how they disposed of your foreskin, said Pastor. Blood dripped from the lamb's ear in a slow, pale trickle which would soon run dry. The smoke from the flames gave off the intoxicating smell of charred young flesh. And so at the end of a long day in which much time had been wasted on childish and presumptuous gestures of defiance, the Lord finally received what was due to Him, perhaps because of those intimidating blasts of thunder and flashes of lightning which must inevitably have made a sufficiently deep impression to persuade these stubborn shepherds to show obedience. The earth quickly swallowed up the last drop of the lamb's blood for it would have been a great shame to lose the most precious drop of all from this much disputed sacrifice.

Transformed by time into an ordinary sheep which could only be distinguished from the others by the missing tip on one ear, this very same animal came to lose itself three years later in the wild countryside south of Jericho which borders on the desert. In so large a flock, one sheep more or less may not seem to make much difference, but we must not forget that this flock is not like any other, even its shepherds have nothing in common with others we have seen or heard about, so we must not be surprised if Pastor, looking from a hilltop, noticed that an animal was missing without having to count them. He called Jesus and told him, Your sheep is missing from the flock, go and look for it, and since Jesus himself did not ask Pastor, How do you know the sheep is mine, we will also refrain from asking Jesus. What really matters now is to see where Jesus, who is unfamiliar with this region where few have ventured, will head for on this broad horizon. Coming from the fertile land of Jericho where they decided not to linger for they much preferred to wander at their leisure rather than be trapped amongst people, it was much more likely that a person or sheep, especially if intent on getting lost, should choose places where the sheer effort of searching for food would not disturb their precious solitude. By this logic, it was clear that Jesus's sheep had deliberately lagged behind the others and was probably even now grazing on the fertile banks of the Jordan within sight of Jericho, for greater safety. Logic, however, is not everything in this life. Often what is foreseeable, simply because it is the most feasible outcome of a sequence of events, or because predetermined for some inexplicable reason, finally turns up in the most unlikely place and circumstances. If this is so, then our Jesus must find his lost sheep not in those rich pastures back there, but in the scorched and arid desert ahead of him. And no one need argue that the sheep would never have strayed off to die of hunger and thirst, firstly, because no one knows what really goes on inside a sheep's head, and secondly, because one must bear in mind what we have just said about the erratic nature of the foreseeable. And so we find Jesus already making his way into the desert. Pastor betrayed no surprise at his decision, in fact, said nothing and gave his tacit approval with a slow and solemn nod of the head which, strangely enough, could also have been mistaken for a farewell wave.

The desert in these parts is not one of those vast tracks of sand with which we are all familiar. Here the desert is more like a great sea of parched, rugged sand-dunes, straddling each other and creating an inextricable labyrinth of valleys. A few rare plants barely survive at the foot of these slopes, plants consisting of nothing but thorns and thistles which a goat might be able to chew, but which are likely to tear the sensitive chops of a sheep at the slightest contact. This desert is much more intimidating than one formed by smooth sands or shifting dunes in a state of constant transformation. Here every hill announces the hidden threat awaiting us on the next hill and when we arrive there in fear and trepidation, we can feel at once the same threat behind us. In this desert our cries would raise no echo, all we should hear in reply would be the hills themselves calling out, or the voice of that mysterious, unknown force concealed there. Carrying nothing except his crook and knapsack, Jesus went into the desert. He had not gone far, had barely crossed the threshold of the world, when he suddenly became aware that his father's old sandals were falling apart beneath his feet. They had been made to last with constant patching, often in extremis, but Jesus's mending skills could no longer save sandals which had walked so many roads and pounded so much sweat into the dust. As if obeying some mandate, the last of the fibres disintegrated, the patches came apart, the laces broke in several places and in no time at all Jesus was walking practically barefoot. The boy Jesus, as we have got used to calling him, although being Jewish and eighteen years of age, is more adult than adolescent, suddenly remembered the sandals he had been carrying all this time in his knapsack for the sake of old times and he foolishly thought they might still fit. Pastor was right when he warned him, Once feet grow they no longer shrink, and Jesus could scarcely believe he could once slip his feet into these tiny sandals. He confronted the desert in his bare feet, like Adam after being expelled from Paradise and, like Adam, he hesitated before taking that first painful step over the tortured earth that was beckoning him, But then, without asking himself why he was doing it, perhaps simply in memory of Adam, he dropped his knapsack and crook, and, lifting his tunic by the hem, he pulled it right over his head and stood there as naked as Adam himself. Here where he is standing, Pastor cannot see him, no inquisitive lamb has followed him, only birds venturing beyond this frontier can catch a glimpse of him from the sky, and the insects on the ground, such as ants, the odd centipede, a scorpion which in panic lifts its tail with its poisonous sting. These tiny creatures cannot remember ever having seen a naked man in these parts before and have no idea what he is trying to prove. If they were to ask Jesus, Why have you taken off your clothes, perhaps he would tell them, One must walk into the desert naked, a reply beyond the understanding of Myriapods and Arachnids, or of insects belonging to the Hemiptera order. Naked, we ask ourselves, with all those thorns to graze bare skin and get entangled with pubic hair, naked, with all those sharp thistles and that rough sand, naked under that scorching sun which can make a man blind and dizzy, naked, in order to find that lost sheep of ours which we branded with our own mark. The desert opens up to receive Jesus, then closes behind him, as if cutting off any path of retreat. Silence echoes in his ears like the noise from one of those dead, empty shells which are washed ashore where they absorb the vast sound of the waves until found by some passer-by who brings them slowly to his ear, listens and says, The wilderness. Jesus's feet are bleeding. the sun pushes back the clouds and stabs him in the back, thorns prick his legs like clawing nails, thistles scratch him. Sheep, where are you, he calls out, and the hills pass on his words, Where are you, where are you. This in itself would be the perfect echo, but the prolonged, faraway sound of the shell imposes itself, murmuring God, Gooooood, Gooooood. Then as if the hills had suddenly been swept away, Jesus emerged from the labyrinth of valleys into a flat and sandy arena with the sheep right in the centre. He ran towards it as fast as he could with his blistered feet, but a voice restrained him, Wait. Slowly spiralling upwards like a column of smoke, a cloud twice as tall as any man appeared before him. The voice was coming from this cloud. Who is speaking, Jesus asked in terror, already anticipating the reply. The voice answered, I am the Lord, and Jesus knew why he had felt obliged to strip off his clothes on the edge of the desert. You brought me here, what do You want with me, For the moment nothing, but the day will come when I shall want everything, What is everything, Your life. You are the Lord, and forever taking from us the life You gave us, There is no other solution, I cannot allow the world to become overcrowded, Why should You want my life, You will know when the time comes, I have merely come to warn you to prepare your body and soul because the destiny that awaits you is one of great, good fortune, My Lord, I do not understand what You mean nor what You want with me, I shall give you power and glory, What power, what glory, You will find out when the time comes to summon you once more, And when will that be, Don't be impatient, live your life as best you can, My Lord, I stand here before You, You have brought me here naked, I beg You, give me this day what You would give me tomorrow, Who told you I am about to give you anything, You promised, An exchange, nothing more than an exchange, My life in exchange for what, For power, And for glory, as I recall, but until I know more about this power, until You tell me what it is, over whom and in whose eyes, that promise will have come much too soon, You will find Me again when you are ready, but My signs will accompany you henceforth, Lord, tell me, Be quiet, ask no more questions, the hour will come, not a second sooner or later, and then you will know what I want with you, To hear You, Lord, is to obey, but I have one more question to ask you, Stop plying Me with questions, Please, Lord, I must, Very well then, speak, Can I bring my sheep, Oh, so that's what's bothering you, Yes, that's all, may I, No, Why not, Because you must offer it in sacrifice to Me in order to seal our covenant, You mean this sheep, Yes, Let me choose another from the flock, I'll be right back, You heard Me, I want this one, But, Lord, can't you see, its ear has been clipped, You're mistaken, take a good look, the ear is perfect, It isn't possible, I am the Lord and with the Lord all things are possible, But this is my sheep, Once again you're mistaken, the lamb was Mine and you stole it from Me, now you'll recompense Me with the sheep, Your will be done, for You rule the universe, and I am Your servant, Then offer this sheep in sacrifice or there will be no covenant, Take pity on me, Lord, I stand here naked and have neither cleaver nor knife, said Jesus, hoping that he might still be able to save the sheep's life, but God told him, I would not be God if I were unable to solve the problem on your behalf, take this. No sooner had He finished speaking, than a brand-new cleaver lay at Jesus's feet. Now be off with you, said God, for I have work to do and can't stay here chatting all day long. Holding the cleaver by the handle, Jesus advanced on the sheep. It raised its head and scarcely recognized him, never having seen Jesus naked before, and as everyone knows, these animals do not have a strong sense of smell. Are you crying, God asked him. The cleaver went up, took aim and came down as swiftly as an executioner's axe or the guillotine which had not yet been invented. The sheep did not so much as whimper. All one could hear was, Aha, as God gave a deep sigh of satisfaction. Jesus asked Him, May I go now, You may, and don't forget, from now on you are tied to Me in flesh and blood, How should I take my leave of You, It really doesn't matter, for Me there is neither front nor back, but it's customary to back away from Me, bowing as you go, Tell me, Lord, What a tiresome fellow you are, what's bothering you now, The shepherd who owns the flock, What shepherd, My master, What about him, Is he an angel or a demon, He's someone I know, But tell me, is he an angel or a demon, I've already told you, for God there is no front or back, goodbye for now. The column of smoke was gone and the sheep had vanished, all that remained were drops of blood and they were trying to hide in the soil.

When Jesus got back, Pastor stared at him and asked, Where's the sheep, and he explained, I met God, I didn't ask you if you'd met God, I asked if you'd found the sheep, I offered it in sacrifice, Whatever for, Because God was there and I had no choice. With the tip of his crook, Pastor drew a line on the ground, deep as a furrow, insurmountable as a wall of fire, then told him, You've learned nothing, be gone with you.

How can I go anywhere with my feet in this state, thought Jesus as he watched Pastor move over to the other side of the flock. God, Who had so efficiently disposed of the sheep, had not favoured poor Jesus with some divine spittle from that cloud so that he might use it to anoint and heal the sores on his feet oozing blood which glistened on the stones. Pastor is not going to help him. After uttering those threatening words, he withdrew, fully expecting his orders to be carried out and with no intention of watching Jesus prepare to leave, let alone bid him farewell. Crawling along with some difficulty on his hands and knees, Jesus reached the shelter where they stored the tools for handling the sheep, the receptacles for the milk, the cheese-presses and the sheepskins and goatskins they cured before trading them for anything they might need, a tunic, a mantle, provisions of every kind. Jesus thought no one would object if he were to make himself a pair of sandals or boots from the skins to protect his feet, with thongs made from strips of goatskin which were less hairy and therefore more pliable. On adjusting them, he was uncertain whether the wool should be on the inside or outside and ended up using it as padding because of the wretched state of his feet. The situation could really become awkward if the hairs were to stick to the sores, but having already decided to travel along the banks of the Jordan, he need only plunge his sandalled feet into the water and the congealed blood will soon dissolve. The sheer weight of those clumsy boots, for that is what they look like, once soaked in water, will soon separate the padding from the scabs of his feet without disturbing those protective and providential crusts which are gradually forming. The colour of the blood seeping from the sores confirmed to his surprise that they were not yet infected. On the slow journey northwards Jesus stopped twice and sat on the river-bank, plunging his feet into the cool water which was as good as medicine. It grieved him to have been sent away in that manner, after having met God, an unprecedented event in the fullest sense of the word, for to the best of his knowledge, there was not a single man in all Israel who could boast of having seen God and survived. It is true that he had not exactly seen Him, but if a cloud appears in the desert in the form of a column of smoke and says, I am the Lord, and then holds a conversation that is not only logical and sensible, but so compelling that it could only be divine, then to have even the slightest doubt would be offensive. The reply He gave when questioned about Pastor proved without a shadow of doubt that this was indeed the Lord, His dismissive attitude betraying contempt as well as a certain intimacy reinforced by His refusal to say whether Pastor was an angel or a demon. But the most interesting thing was that Pastor's words, cruel and seemingly divorced from the main issue, did nothing other than confirm the supernatural character of this encounter, I didn't ask you if you met God, as if to say, That much I knew already, as if the news were no surprise, and he had known beforehand. What was clear, however, was that Pastor still blamed him for the sheep's death, for those final words could have had no other meaning, You've learnt nothing, begone with you, before ostentatiously moving over to the other side of the flock, where he continued to ignore him until he had disappeared from sight. Now then, on one of these occasions when Jesus allowed his mind to ponder what the Lord might want from him when they met again, Pastor's words suddenly came back to him as loudly and clearly as if he were standing right there beside him, You've learnt nothing, and at that moment the feeling of loss, privation and solitude was so overwhelming that he felt quite alone, sitting here by himself on the bank of the Jordan, watching his feet in the transparent river and from one of his heels the fine thread of blood trickling and suspended in the water, suddenly that blood and those feet no longer belonged to him, it was his father who had come there, limping on pierced heels, to find relief in the cool waters of the River Jordan, and he repeated what Pastor had said, You must start all over again, for you've learnt nothing. As if he were lifting a long, heavy chain made of iron from the ground, Jesus recalled his life so far, link by link, the mysterious annunciation of his conception, the luminous earth, his birth in the cave, the massacred innocents of Bethlehem, his father's crucifixion, these nightmares he had inherited, the flight from home, the debate in the Temple, the revelations of Salome, the appearance of the shepherd, his experiences with the flock, the rescued lamb, the desert, the dead sheep, God. And as if this last word were too much for his mind to encompass, he concentrated on one obsessive question, why should a lamb rescued from death finally die as a sheep, an absurd question if ever there was one, but which would make more sense if rephrased as follows, No salvation suffices, yet condemnation is final. This is the last link in the chain, to be sitting here on the bank of the River Jordan, listening to the mournful song of a woman who cannot be seen from here, hidden amongst the rushes, perhaps washing clothes, perhaps bathing, and Jesus is trying to understand how all these things are connected, the living lamb which became a dead sheep, his feet bleeding with his father's blood, and the woman who is singing, naked, lying on her back in the water, firm breasts rising above the surface, dark pubic hairs ruffled by the breeze, for while it is true that Jesus has never seen a naked woman before, if a man just by departing from a simple column of smoke can predict what it will be like to be with God when the time comes, then why should he not be able to visualize a naked woman in every detail, assuming that she is naked, merely by listening to the song she is singing even though the words may not be addressed to him. Joseph is no longer here, he has returned to the common grave in Sepphoris, of Pastor not so much as the tip of his shepherd's crook is to be seen, and God, if He is everywhere, as people say, has not chosen a column of smoke to reveal himself. Perhaps He is in that current, in that very same water where the woman is bathing. Jesus's body gave a signal, something between his legs began to swell and, as with all humans and animals, the blood rushed to the same spot, causing his sores to dry up at once. Lord, this body has such strength, but Jesus made no attempt to go in search of the woman, and his hands resisted the violent temptations of the flesh, You are no one unless you love yourself, you will never reach God until you get close to your own body. No one knows who spoke those words, but God could not have spoken them for they are not beads from His rosary, Pastor might well have uttered them were he not so far away, so perhaps, in the end, they were the words of the song the woman was singing. Just then he thought, how I wish I could go there and ask her to explain, but the singing had stopped, perhaps swept away by the current, or perhaps the woman had simply stepped out of the water to dry herself and get dressed, thus silencing her body. Jesus slipped on his wet sandals and rose to his feet, dripping water everywhere like a sponge. The woman will get a good laugh if she passes this way and sees him wearing this grotesque footwear, but she will soon stop mocking him once her eyes begin to take in the shape of Jesus's body beneath his tunic, and stare at length into those eyes saddened by past and present sorrows and now looking anxious for a quite different reason. With few or no words, she will remove her clothes once more and offer to do what one might expect in such cases, she will take off his sandals with the utmost care and tend those sores, kissing each foot and then covering them with her own damp hair as if protecting an egg or cocoon. No sign of anyone coming along the road, Jesus looks around him, sighs, looks for somewhere to hide and heads there, but he comes to a sudden halt, remembering in time that the Lord punished Onan with death for having spilt his seed on the ground. Now, were Jesus to have given a somewhat more analytical twist to this classical episode, as was his wont, and had he not been deterred by the Lord's intransigence for two reasons, the first being that he had no sister-in-law with whom by law he should provide heirs for a deceased brother, and the second and perhaps more compelling reason being that the Lord, according to what He told him in the desert, had some firm plans for his future which were yet to be revealed, he would have found it neither feasible nor logical to forget the promises made and risk losing everything just because an uncontrolled hand had dared to stray where it should not. For the Lord knows our corporal needs which are not simply confined to food and drink, insofar as there are other forms of abstention which are just as hard to endure. These and similar reflections which should have encouraged Jesus to follow his natural inclinations and search out some quiet spot to satisfy his urge, ended up by having quite the opposite effect, they distracted him from what was on his mind and confused him so much that he soon lost any desire to yield to wicked temptation.

Resigned to his own virtue, Jesus lifted the knapsack on to his shoulder, took up his staff and went on his way.

On the first day of this journey along the banks of the Jordan, Jesus, who, after four years of solitude, had got used to a lonely existence, kept clear of inhabited places. But as he approached the Lake of Gennesaret it became increasingly difficult to avoid passing through villages especially since they were surrounded by cultivated fields which barred his way not to mention the suspicions his rough appearance aroused amongst the labourers. And so Jesus decided to go out into the world and was pleasantly surprised at what he saw there, all that really bothered him was the noise which he had almost forgotten. In the first village he entered, a group of rowdy urchins roared with laughter at the sight of his sandals, no bad thing in the end, because Jesus had enough money to buy some new ones. We must not forget that he has not touched any of the money he is carrying with him since being given two coins by the Pharisee and to have lived for four years with few needs and no expenses has proved to be the greatest fortune one could have wished from the Lord. Now after buying the sandals, he is left with two coins of little value but poverty does not worry him, very soon now he will arrive at his destination, Nazareth, the home where he is certain to return, for on the day he left, and he feels as if he had been away forever, he had said, One way or another I shall always return. He travels at a relaxed pace, following the thousand bends in the road along the Jordan, for his feet were really in no fit state to be making such a journey, though the main reason for his slow progress was his inner conviction that he would make it, as if thinking to himself, I'm almost there, but deep down something else was slowing him down, a vague premonition which might be expressed in these words, The more quickly I get there the sooner I must return. Following the shore of the lake in a northerly direction, he is already on the latitude of Nazareth, and should he decide to make straight for home, all he would have to do is to turn towards the setting sun, but he lingers by the waters of the lake, blue, extensive, tranquil. He loves sitting on the shore, watching the fishermen cast their nets, as a little boy he had often come to these parts with his parents, but he had never paused to observe the labours of these men who smell of fish as if they themselves inhabited the sea. As he went along, Jesus earned enough money to eat by doing whatever jobs he knew, which was nothing, or could do, which was not much, pulling a boat ashore or pushing it into the water, giving a hand to drag in a full net, and on seeing how hungry he looked the fishermen would offer him a handful of fish as payment. In the beginning Jesus felt shy and would go off to roast and eat them on his own, but after several days the fishermen invited him to join them. On the third and last day Jesus went out on the lake with two brothers, Simon and Andrew, who were both older than him and already in their thirties. Once they were out in the open water Jesus, who knew nothing about fishing and laughed at his own awkwardness, tried at the insistence of his new-found friends to cast the net with that broad gesture which, seen from a distance, resembles a blessing or challenge, but without success, and once he almost fell into the water. Simon and Andrew went into fits of laughter, well aware that Jesus only knew how to handle goats and sheep, and Simon said, Life would be much easier for us if this flock could be gathered and led, to which Jesus replied, At least they don't go astray or get lost, they are all here in the basin of the lake, escaping or falling into the net day after day. The day's catch had been disappointing, the bottom of the boat was almost empty and Andrew said, Brother, let's turn back, we're not likely to catch any more fish today. Simon agreed, You're right, brother, let's go. He slipped the oars into the rowlocks and was about to start rowing towards the bank when Jesus, not because of any inspiration or special insight, but simply as a gesture of gratitude, however inexplicable, suggested they should make three last attempts, Who knows, perhaps this maritime flock, led by its shepherd, has moved over to our side. Simon laughed. That's another good thing about sheep, they're visible, and turning to Andrew, told him, Cast the net over there, nothing ventured, nothing gained, whereupon Andrew threw the net and it came back full. The two fishermen gasped in amazement, but their alarm turned to wonder when the net was cast for a second and third time and came back full on both occasions. From a sea which had earlier seemed so devoid of fish, suddenly they came pouring forth like water from a fountain, fish such as had never been seen before, gleaming torrents of gills, backs and fins which left one dazed. Simon and Andrew asked Jesus how he had known that the fish would gather there from one minute to the next and Jesus assured them he had not known and was acting on impulse when he suggested trying just once more before giving up. The two brothers had no reason to doubt his words, pure chance can work such miracles, but Jesus was trembling inside and in the silence of his soul asked, Who can be responsible for this. Simon said, Give us a hand to grade them, and this is the moment to explain that it was not from the Sea of Galilee that the ecumenical proverb originated which says, Everything that falls into the net is fish, here different criteria prevail, the net may have caught fish, but on this point, the law, as elsewhere, is quite unambiguous, Behold what you may eat of the various aquatic species, you may eat anything which has fins and scales in the waters, seas and rivers, but everything in the seas and rivers which has neither fins nor scales, whether they be creatures that breed or live under water, you will shun and abhor for all time, you will refrain from eating the flesh of everything in the water which has neither fins nor scales and treat them as abominable. And so the condemned fish with smooth skins, those which cannot be served at the table of the people of the Lord, were returned to the sea, many of them were already so accustomed to this that they no longer worried when caught in the nets, for they knew they would soon be back in the water without any danger of being suffocated. With their fish mentality, they believed themselves to be beneficiaries of some special favour from the Creator, perhaps even of some special love, which brought them after a while to consider themselves superior to the other fish trapped on the boats, which must have committed many grievous sins beneath those dark waters for God to allow them to perish so mercilessly.

When they finally reached the river-bank, taking every precaution not to sink, for the waters of the lake came level with the edge of the boat as if about to swallow it up, the people on the shore were dumbfounded. They could not understand how this had come about, knowing that the other fishermen had returned with their boats empty, but by tacit and mutual agreement the three fortunate men revealed nothing of the circumstances which brought about their prodigious catch. Simon and Andrew were reluctant to see their reputation as fishermen diminished in public, Jesus, on the other hand, had no desire to find himself in demand as a decoy by other crews, which, it must be said, would only be just and fair if we are to abolish once and for all the discrimination between children and stepchildren which has caused so much harm in this world.

This thought led Jesus to announce that same night that he would depart the next day for Nazareth where his family were expecting him, after four years of continuous trials and tribulations which could only have been sent by Satan. This decision saddened Simon and Andrew who regretted losing the best look-out ever commemorated in the annals of Gennesaret. Two other fishermen also lamented his decision, these were James and John, the sons of Zebedee, two rather simple lads whom people used to ask in jest, Who is the father of the sons of Zebedee, throwing both of them into a state of confusion, and the fact that they obviously knew the answer since they themselves were his sons, did not spare them sudden bewilderment and anguish. They regretted Jesus's departure, not only because it meant no more prodigious catches, but being younger men, John was even younger than Jesus, they had hoped to form a crew which could compete with those of an older generation. Their simple nature had nothing to do with being stupid or mentally retarded, they simply went through life as if their thoughts were elsewhere, so that they were always being caught unawares whenever anyone asked them the name of the father of the sons of Zebedee, and puzzled by the merriment that broke out when they replied in triumph, Zebedee, of course. John decided to try and dissuade him, he went up to Jesus and said, Stay with us, our boat is bigger than Simon's and we can catch more fish, whereupon Jesus, wise and compassionate, replied, The measure of the Lord is not that of men, but the measure of His justice. At a loss for words, John went off looking despondent and the evening passed without any further approaches from interested parties. Next day, Jesus bade farewell to the first friends he had ever made and with his knapsack replenished, he turned his back on the lake of Gennesaret where, unless he was mistaken, God had given him a sign, and set off for the mountains leading to Nazareth. Fate decreed, however, that on passing through the town of Magdala, a troublesome sore on his foot should open up and it looked as if it would never stop bleeding. Fate also decreed that this unfortunate situation should arise just at the edge of Magdala and directly in front of a house standing on its own away from the other houses as if ostracized or reluctant to get any closer. When the blood began to show no signs of stopping, Jesus called out, Anyone at home, and suddenly a woman appeared in the doorway as if expecting to be called, although judging from the scant surprise on her face, we might have been led to believe that she was quite accustomed to people walking into the house without knocking which, on careful reflection, ought not to be the case, for this woman is a prostitute and the respect she owes her profession demands that she should close her front door when she receives a client. Jesus, who was sitting on the ground and pressing the open sore, looked up as the woman approached, Help me, he said, and taking hold of her outstretched hand he struggled to his feet and took a few faltering steps, You're in no fit state to be walking, she told him, come inside and let me bathe your foot. Jesus said neither yes nor no, the woman's perfume was so overpowering that the pain vanished as if by magic, and with one arm around the woman's shoulder while another arm went around his waist, which obviously could not be his, he could feel turmoil surging through his entire body, or to be more precise, through all his senses. For it was in his senses, at least in one of them which is neither that of seeing or smelling or tasting or touching, although all of these played some part, that he felt it most, God help him. The woman assisted him into the yard, locked the gate and made him sit down. Wait here, she told him. She went indoors and returned with an earthenware basin and a white cloth. Filling the basin with water she wet the cloth, and kneeling at Jesus's feet and resting the injured foot in the palm of her left hand she washed it gently, removing the dirt and softening the broken scab which spurted out blood and disgusting yellow pus. The woman told him, It will take more than water to heal these sores, and Jesus said, All I ask is that you should bandage my foot so that I might reach Nazareth. He was on the point of saying, My mother will treat it, but corrected himself in time for he did not wish to give the impression of being a mother's boy who only has to stub his toe on a stone, and he is crying to be comforted and nursed, It's nothing, child, look it's better already. It's a long way from here to Nazareth, the woman told him, but if that's what you want, let me rub in a little ointment. She went back into the house and seemed to be taking longer to come back this time. Jesus looked around him in surprise for he had never seen such a clean and tidy yard. He suspects the woman is a prostitute, not because he is particularly good at guessing people's professions at first sight, besides, not all that long ago he himself would have been identified as a shepherd by the stench of goat, yet now everyone would say, He's a fisherman. He got rid of one bad smell only to replace it with another. The woman reeks of perfume, but Jesus, who may be innocent, has learned the facts of life by watching the mating habits of goats and rams, and he has enough common sense to know that just because a woman uses perfume does not necessarily mean that she is a whore. After all, a prostitute ought to smell of the men she frequents, just as the goatherd smells of goat and the fisherman of fish, but who knows, perhaps these women perfume themselves so much precisely because they want to conceal, disguise, or even forget the very odour of a man's body. The woman reappeared with a small jar and she was smiling as if someone indoors had told her something amusing. Jesus saw her approach but unless his eyes were deceiving him, she was walking very slowly, as sometimes happens in dreams, her tunic flowing and revealing the curves of her body as she advanced, her hips swaying, her black tresses hanging loose over her shoulders and tossing like ears of corn in the wind. Her tunic was unmistakably that of a whore, her body that of a dancer, her laughter that of a woman of easy virtue. Deeply perturbed, Jesus searched his memory for some apt maxims by his famous namesake, Jesus the son of Sirach, and his memory obliged, discreetly whispering in his ear, Stay away from loose women lest you fall into their snares, Have nothing to do with female dancers lest you succumb to their charms, and finally, Do not fall into the hands of prostitutes lest you lose your soul and all your possessions, and Jesus's soul might well be in danger now that he has come to manhood, but as for his possessions, they are in no danger for, as we know, he does not possess anything. So he will be quite safe when the moment comes to fix a price and the woman enquires, How much money have you got. And Jesus was prepared and showed no surprise when the woman asked him his name as she rubbed ointment into the sores on his foot which was resting on her lap. I'm called Jesus, he replied without adding, from Nazareth, for he had said so beforehand, just as the woman who lived here was clearly from Magdala, and when he asked her name, she simply replied, Mary. Having carefully examined and dressed his injured foot, Mary Magdalene tied the bandage with a firm knot. That should do, she said, How can I thank you, asked Jesus, and for the first time his eyes met hers, black, bright as coals, and like water running over water, veiled

with a hint of sensuality which Jesus found irresistible. The woman
did not reply at once, she stared back at him as if weighing him up,
convinced the poor boy had no money, and at length she said to
him, Remember me, that's all I ask, and Jesus assured her, I shall
never forget your kindness, and then, summoning his courage, Nor
shall I forget you, Why do you say that, she asked smiling, Because
you're beautiful, You should have seen me in my youth, I find you
beautiful as you are. Her smile faded, vanished, Do you know who
I am, what I do, how I earn my living, I do, You only had to look
at me and you knew everything, I know nothing, Not even that I'm
a prostitute, That I know, That I go to bed with men for money,
Yes, Then as I said, you know everything about me, That's all I
know. The woman sat down beside him, gently stroked his hand,
touched his mouth with the tips of her fingers, If you really want
to please me, spend the day here with me, Impossible, Why, I have
no money to pay you, That's no surprise, Please don't mock me,
You may not believe me, but I'd sooner mock a man with a full
purse, It's not simply a question of money, What is it then, Jesus
fell silent and turned his face away. She made no attempt to help
him, she could have asked, Are you a virgin, but said nothing and
waited. The silence was so deep and intense that only their hearts
could be heard beating, his louder and faster, hers restless and
agitated. Jesus said, Your tresses remind me of a flock of goats
descending the mountain slopes of Gilead. The woman smiled and
remained silent. Then Jesus said, Your eyes are like the pools of
Heshbon by the Gate of Bath-Rabim. The woman gave another
smile yet continued to say nothing. Then Jesus slowly turned to
look at her and said, I have never been with a woman. Mary held
his hands, This is how everyone has to begin, men who have never
known a woman, women who have never known a man, until the
day comes for the one who knows to teach the other, for the one
who knows nothing to learn, Do you want to teach me, So that
you may thank me a second time, In this way, I shall never stop
thanking you, And I shall never stop teaching you. Mary got to her
feet, went to lock the yard gate, but only after hanging something
on the outside, a sign to any clients who might come looking for
her that she had closed her window because the hour had come to
sing, Awake, north wind, and come, you south, blow upon my
garden, that the spices thereof may flow out, let my beloved come

into his garden, and eat his pleasant fruits. Then together, Jesus's hand resting once more on the shoulder of Mary, this whore from Magdala who dressed his sores and is about to receive him in her bed, they went indoors into the welcome shade of a clean, fresh room. Her bed is no primitive mat stretched out on the floor with a coarse sheet on top, such as Jesus remembered from his parents' house, this was a real bed as once described elsewhere, I have adorned my bed with covers and embroidered sheets made of Egyptian linen, I have perfumed my couch with myrrh, aloes and cinnamon. Mary Magdalene led Jesus to the hearth with its floor of brick tiles, where she insisted on removing his tunic and washing him herself, stroking his body with her fingertips and kissing him softly on the chest and thighs, first on one side then the other. This delicate contact with hands and lips caused Jesus to shiver, to feel those nails lightly grazing his skin brought him out in gooseflesh, Don't be frightened, Mary Magdalene whispered. She dried him and led him to the bed, Lie down, I'll be with you in a moment. She drew a curtain, once more the sound of splashing water then a pause, the smell of perfume in the air, and Mary reappeared completely naked. Lying there as she had left him, Jesus, too, was naked. He thought to himself, this must be right and to cover the body she herself had stripped might have given offence. Mary lingered by the side of the bed, gazed on him with an expression at once passionate and tender, and told him, You are so handsome but to be perfect you must close your eyes. Jesus hesitantly opened his eyes, then closed them, and in a daze opened them again, and at that moment he understood the real meaning of King Solomon's words, The joints of your thighs are like jewels, your navel is like a round goblet filled with scented wine, your belly is like a heap of wheat set about with lilies, your breasts are like two young roes that are the twins of a gazelle, but he understood them much better and for evermore when Mary lay down beside him and taking his hands into hers drew them to her and guided them slowly over her entire body, her hair, face, neck, shoulders, breasts which he gently squeezed, her belly, navel, pubic hairs where he lingered, twining and untwining them with his fingers, then the curve of her smooth thighs and as she moved his hands, she kept on repeating in a low whisper, Come, discover my body. Jesus looked at his hands clasped in Mary's, wishing he could have them free to explore every part of her body, but she went on holding and guiding them, as she repeated over and over again, Come, discover my body, discover my body. Jesus was breathing fast, but for one moment he thought he was going to suffocate when her hands, the left one on his forehead, the right one on his ankles began caressing him slowly until they met in the middle where they paused for a second before slowly repeating the same movement all over again. You've learnt nothing, begone with you, Pastor had told him, and who knows, perhaps he had meant to say that he had not learnt to protect life. Now Mary Magdalene had instructed him, Discover my body, and she said it again, but in another way by changing one word, Discover your body, and there it was, tense, taut, roused and Mary Magdalene, naked and magnificent, was on top of him and saying, Relax, there is nothing to worry about, don't move, leave this to me, then he felt part of his body, this organ here, vanishing inside her body, a ring of fire encircling him, coming and going, a tremor passed through him, like a wriggling fish slipping free with a shout, impossible, surely not, after all, fish do not shout, it was him, yes, it was Jesus himself who was crying out at the same time as Mary slumped over his body with a moan and absorbed his cry with her lips, with an eager and anxious kiss which sent a second, interminable shudder through his body.

For the rest of that day, no one came to knock on Mary Magdalene's door. For the rest of that day Mary Magdalene served and instructed the youth from Nazareth who, without knowing whether she was good or bad, had come to ask her if she could relieve his pain and heal the sores which, unknown to her, had started with that other encounter, when Jesus met God in the desert. God had told Jesus, Henceforth, you will be mine in blood, the Devil, if that is who he was, had spurned him, You've learnt nothing, be gone with you, and Mary Magdalene, the perspiration running down her breasts, her loose tresses appearing to give off smoke, her lips swollen, her eyes like dark pools, said, You won't stay with me because of what I've taught you, but sleep here tonight. And Jesus, on top of her, replied, What you're teaching me is no prison, but freedom. They slept together but not only that night. When they woke up, it was already morning and after their bodies sought and found each other once more, Mary examined the sore on Jesus's foot, It's looking much better, but you should wait a while before

213

journeying home, walking can only make it worse, not to mention all that dust, I can't stay any longer and as you yourself have said, my foot is much better, Of course you can stay, it's a question of wanting to, and as for the gate in the yard, that will stay locked for as long as we please, What about your life here, Right now, my life is you, But why, Let me reply with the words of King Solomon, My beloved put his hand through the hole in the door and my heart trembled, But how can I be your beloved if you don't know me, if I am simply someone who came to ask your help and on whom you took pity, pity on my misfortune and ignorance, That's why I love you, because I've helped and instructed you, but you will never be able to love me, for you have neither instructed nor helped me, But you are not in pain, You will find my wound if you look carefully, What wound might that be, This open door through which others have entered but not my beloved, You said that I'm your beloved, That is why the door closed behind you as you entered, There's nothing I can teach you, only what I've learnt from you, Then teach me, too, so that I may know what it is like to learn from you, We cannot live together, You mean you cannot live with a whore, Yes, While you remain with me, I shall no longer be a whore, I stopped being a prostitute the moment you came into this house and it is up to you whether or not I go on living as a prostitute, You're asking too much, Nothing that you cannot give me for one or two days, or for as long as it takes your foot to heal, so that my wound may open up once more. It took me eighteen years to get here, A few days more won't make much difference, you're still young, So are you, Older than you, younger than your mother, Do you know my mother, No, Then why did you mention her, Because I'm too young to have a son of your age, How stupid of me, No, you're not stupid, simply innocent, But I'm no longer innocent, Just because you've been with a woman, No, I had already lost my innocence before going to bed with you, Tell me about yourself, but not just yet, for the moment all I want is to feel your left hand on my head and your right hand embracing me.

Jesus spent a week in Mary Magdalene's house, sufficient time for new skin to form beneath the scabs. The yard door continued to remain firmly closed. Several men, driven by lust or wounded pride, knocked impatiently at the gate, deliberately ignoring the sign meant to keep them away. They were curious to see this fellow who was taking so long, and one joker called over the wall, Either he isn't up to it or he has no idea what to do, open the gate, Mary, and I'll show him how it's done, and Mary Magdalene went out into the yard to warn him, Whoever you are, and however much you may boast, your days of sexual prowess are over, so be off with you, Damned whore, That's just where you're wrong for you won't find a woman anywhere more blessed than me. Whether it was because of this incident or because fate so decreed, no one else came knocking at the gate, but most likely any man living in Magdala or passing through who had heard of Mary's curse would want to avoid the risk of being condemned to impotency, for it is generally believed that prostitutes, especially those with know-how and experience, are not only capable of exciting a man's sexual urges, but also of deflating his pride and killing any desire. And so Mary and Jesus were left in peace for eight days, during which time the lessons given and received became but one discourse comprising gestures, discoveries, surprises, murmurings, inventions, like the pieces of a mosaic which are nothing if taken one by one yet become everything when assembled and put into their proper place. On several occasions, Mary Magdalene tried to persuade her beloved to talk about himself, but Jesus would change the subject and break into phrases such as, I am come into my garden, my sister, my spouse, I have gathered my myrrh with my spice, I have eaten my honeycomb with my honey, I have drunk my wine with my milk, phrases which he recited with passion before indulging in the poetic act itself, in truth, in truth, I say to you, dear Jesus, this is no way to hold a conversation. Until one day Jesus decided to tell Mary about his father who was a carpenter and his mother who carded wool, about his six brothers and two sisters and how, as was the custom, he had started to learn his father's trade before going off to be a shepherd for four years, and now he was returning home. He also mentioned the few days he had spent at sea with some fishermen without mastering their skills. Then one evening when they were eating out in the yard Jesus took Mary Magdalene into his confidence, and from time to time they would look up to watch the rapid flight of swallows as they passed overhead with strident cries. Judging from their silence, they appeared to have nothing more to say to each other, the man had confessed all to the woman, but as if disappointed, she asked him, Is that all, and nodding,

215

he assured her, Yes, that's all. The silence deepened, the circling swallows hovered elsewhere, and Jesus said, My father was crucified four years ago in Sepphoris, his name was Joseph, Am I right in thinking you're his eldest son, Yes, I'm the eldest, Then I don't understand, surely you ought to be looking after your family, We quarrelled, but don't ask me any more, No more about your family then, but what about your time as a shepherd, tell me about that, There's nothing to tell, every day the same thing, goats, sheep, kids, lambs and milk, lots of milk, milk everywhere, Did you enjoy being a shepherd, Yes, I did, Then why did you leave, I got restless, began missing my family, felt homesick, Homesick, what is that, Sadness at being so far away, You're lying, Why do you think I'm lying, Because I can see fear and remorse in your eyes. Jesus did not reply. He got up, took a stroll round the yard, then stopped in front of Mary, One day if we should meet again, perhaps I'll tell you the rest so long as you promise not to tell anyone, Why not tell me now, Never fear, I'll tell you when we meet again, You're hoping that by then I shall have given up prostitution, you still don't trust me and think I might sell your secrets for money or pass them on to the first man who turns up, just for amusement, or in exchange for a more glorious night of love than those you and I have shared, No, that's not the reason for my silence, Well let me assure you that Mary Magdalene, prostitute or not, will be at your side whenever you should need her, Who am I to deserve all this, Don't you know who you are. That night the same old nightmare returned, which had been much more bearable recently, a vague feeling of anguish which now and then disturbed his sleep. But this night, perhaps because it was the last night Jesus slept in that bed, perhaps because he had mentioned Sepphoris and the men crucified there, the nightmare, like a huge cobra awakening from hibernation, slowly began to uncoil in twists and turns and raise its hideous head, and Jesus woke up with a start, crying out in terror, his body covered in a cold sweat. What's wrong, what's happening, Mary asked him in alarm, I was dreaming, I was only dreaming, he said evasively, Tell me, and those simple words were said with so much love and tenderness that Jesus could not hold back his tears, and after much weeping he revealed what he had hoped to withhold, I am forever dreaming that my father is coming to kill me, But your father is dead and you're still alive, In my dream I'm still a child back in Bethlehem of Judaea and my father is coming to kill me, Why in Bethlehem, Because that's where I was born, Perhaps you think your father didn't want you to be born and that is why you have this dream, You don't know what happened, No I don't, Children in Bethlehem died because of my father, Did he kill them, He killed them because he made no attempt to save them, although it wasn't his hand which drew the dagger, And in your dream, are you one of those children, I have died a thousand deaths, Poor man, poor Jesus, That was why I left home, I'm beginning to understand, You think you understand, What more is there to know, What I cannot reveal just yet, You mean what you will tell me if we meet again, That's right. Resting his hand on Mary's shoulder, Jesus fell asleep, his cheek on her breast. Mary remained awake throughout the night. Her heart was aching for it would soon be morning and time to separate, but her soul was at peace. For she knew that this man in her arms was the man for whom she had been waiting all her life, the man who belonged to her and to whom she belonged, his body chaste, hers defiled and contaminated, but their world is just beginning, they have been together for eight days but only tonight has their union been confirmed and eight days is nothing when compared with a whole future, for this Jesus who has come into my life is so young, and here am I, Mary Magdalene, in bed with a man, as so often in the past, but this time deeply in love and ageless.

They spent the morning preparing for the journey. One would have thought young Jesus was travelling to the end of the world when in fact there are no more than fifteen miles to cover, a distance any healthy man could walk between noon and dusk, notwithstanding the rough road from Magdala to Nazareth with its precipitous slopes and rocky terrain. Take care, Mary warned him, you might run into rebel forces still fighting the Romans, After all this time, asked Jesus, You haven't lived here, this is Galilee, But I'm a native of Galilee and they're not likely to do me any harm, You can't be Galilean if you were born in Bethlehem of Judaea, My parents conceived me in Nazareth, and to be honest, I wasn't even born in Bethlehem, I was born in a cave inside the earth, and now I feel as if I've been reborn here in Magdala. Mothered by a whore, You're no whore in my eyes, said Jesus vehemently. Alas, that's the life I've led. These words were followed by a long silence, Mary waiting for Jesus to speak, Jesus trying to fight off his disquiet. Finally he asked her, Do you intend to remove that object you hung on the gate to discourage any man from entering. Mary Magdalene looked at him with a serious expression, then smiled mischievously, I couldn't possibly have two men in the house at the same time, What are you trying to say, Simply that you are leaving but will still be here. She paused, then added, The sign hanging on the gate will remain there, People will think you're with some man, And they'll be right for I shall be with you, Are you telling me no man will ever pass through that gate again, That's right, for this woman whom they call Mary Magdalene stopped being a prostitute the moment you walked into this house, But how will you earn your living. Only the lilies in the fields thrive without working or spinning. Jesus took her hands into his and told her, Nazareth isn't far from Magdala, one of these days I shall return. If you should come looking for me, you'll find me here, My desire is to find you always, You will find me even after death, You mean I shall die before you, Since I'm older than you are, I'll almost certainly die first, but if you should die before me, I shall go on living just so that you may find me. And if you should die first, Blessed be the woman who brought you into the world during my lifetime. With these words, Mary served Jesus some food, and he did not have to tell her, Sit with me, for since their first day together behind locked doors, this man and woman divided and multiplied between them feelings and gestures, spaces and sensations without paying too much attention to rules, norms or laws. They certainly would not know what to say if we were to ask them how they would behave without the protection of these four walls where they have been free for some days to forge a world in the simple image and likeness of man and woman. A world which is more hers than his, let it be said in passing, but since they are both so confident about meeting again, we need only have the patience to wait for the time and place when, side by side, they will confront the outside world where people are already asking themselves anxiously, What's going on in there, and they are not referring to familiar antics in the bedroom. After they had eaten, Mary helped Jesus into his sandals and told him, You must leave if you're to reach Nazareth before nightfall, Farewell, said Jesus, and taking up his knapsack and staff, he went out into the yard. The sky was covered with clouds as if lined with unwashed wool, and the Lord could not be finding it easy to keep a watchful eye on His sheep from on high. Jesus and Mary Magdalene embraced at length before exchanging a farewell kiss, which did not take quite so long, and little wonder, for this was scarcely the custom at that time.

The sun had just set when Jesus arrived back in Nazareth, four long years, give or take a week, since the day he fled from there, still a mere child, driven by desperation to go out into the world in search of someone who might help him to understand the first unbearable truth about his existence. Four years, however long, may not be enough to heal one's sorrow, but usually help to bring some relief. He had asked questions in the Temple, retraced mountain paths with the Devil's flock, met God, and slept with Mary Magdalene. On reaching Nazareth, he no longer appears to be suffering except for those tears in his eyes we mentioned earlier, but which on reflection could also be the delayed effect of smoke from the sacrifices, or sudden rapture in his soul on looking down on that horizon from elevated pastures, or the fear of someone all alone in the desert who has heard a voice say, I am the Lord, or even more likely, being more recent, yearning and desire for the woman he left only a few hours ago, I have comforted myself with raisins, I have strengthened myself with apples, for I am swooning with love. Jesus might have recited these sweet words to his mother and brothers, but he paused on the threshold to ask himself, Who are my mother and brothers, not that he does not know, the question is do they know who he is, he who asked questions in the Temple, who gazed on the horizon, who met God, who has experienced carnal love and discovered his manhood. Before this same door once stood a beggar who claimed to be an angel, and who could easily have burst into the house with a great commotion of ruffled wings, if he really was an angel, yet preferred to knock and beg for alms like any pauper.

The door is only on the latch. Jesus will not need to call as he did down in Magdala, he will calmly walk into his own home, the sores on his feet completely healed, but then, sores that bleed and fester are much quicker to heal. There was no need to knock but he did. He had heard voices over the wall, recognized that of his mother coming from further away, but could not summon the courage simply to push the door open and announce, I'm here, like someone who knows his presence is welcome and wishes to give everyone a pleasant surprise. The door was opened by a little girl about eight or nine years old, who did not recognize the visitor, and the voice of blood and kinship did not come to his assistance by saying, This is your brother Jesus, don't you remember him. It was Jesus himself who said, despite the four years which had passed since they had last seen each other and the fading light, You must be Lydia, and she answered, Yes, amazed that a complete stranger should know her name, but the spell was broken when he said, I'm your brother Jesus, may I come in. In the yard under the lean-to adjoining the house, he could see shadowy figures whom he assumed to be his brothers, now they were looking in the direction of the door and two of them, the oldest boys, James and Joseph, approached. They had not heard Jesus's words, but they could spare themselves the trouble of identifying the visitor for Lydia was already calling out excitedly, It's Jesus, it's our brother, whereupon the shadows stirred and Mary appeared in the doorway, accompanied by Lisa, the other daughter, who was almost as tall as her mother, and both of them called out with one voice, My son, My brother, and the next moment they were all embracing him in joyful reunion there in the middle of the yard, always a happy event, especially when it is the eldest son who is returning to his loved ones. Jesus greeted his mother, then each of his brothers and was given a warm welcome by all of them, Brother Jesus, how good to see you again, Brother Jesus, we thought you had forgotten us, but no one had the courage to say, Brother Jesus, you don't look any richer. They moved indoors and sat down to the meal his mother had been preparing when he knocked at the door. One might almost say to Jesus coming from where he does, indulging his sinful flesh and keeping bad company, one could almost say with the brutal frankness of simple people who suddenly see their share of food get smaller, When it's time to eat, the devil always brings an extra mouth to feed. No one present dared put the thought into words and it would have been awkward if they had, after all, one extra mouth scarcely makes much difference when there are already nine mouths to feed. And besides, the new arrival has more right to be there than any of them. During supper, the younger children were curious to know about his adventures, while the three older children and Mary noted at once there had been no change in his occupation since their meeting in Jerusalem, especially since the smell of fish had long since disappeared and the wind had swept away the sensuous aromas of Mary Magdalene, not to mention all the sweat and dust acquired along the road, unless, of course, one chanced to take a close sniff at Jesus's tunic, but if his own family did not take that liberty then why should we. Jesus told them how he had tended one of the largest flocks ever seen, and how he had recently been out to sea helping fishermen to land the most extraordinary catches of fish, and that he had also experienced the most wonderful adventure any man could ever imagine or hope for, but he would tell them about it some other time and then only some of them. On saying this, the younger children pleaded, Tell us, please tell us, when Judas, the middle brother, asked him in all innocence, Did you earn a lot of money while you were away, whereupon Jesus replied, Not so much as three coins, or two, or even one, nothing, and seeing the look of disbelief on their faces, he emptied his knapsack without further ado. And truly, he had little to show for his labours, his only belongings a metal knife which was worn and bent, a bit of string, a chunk of bread as hard as a rock, two pairs of sandals reduced to tatters, the remnants of an old tunic. This once belonged to your father, said Mary, stroking the tunic, then the larger pair of sandals, she told him, These, too, were his. The others lowered their heads in memory of their dead father, and Jesus was putting everything back into the knapsack when he suddenly noticed that there was a great, heavy knot in the hem of the tunic. The blood rushed to his face, it could only be money, money which he had denied possessing and which must have been put there by Mary Magdalene, and therefore not earned by the sweat of one's brow as dignity demands, but with false moans and groans and dubious perspiration. His mother and brothers stared at that tell-tale knot, then, as if acting to plan, stared at him. Uncertain as to whether he should try and conceal the proof of his deception or bluff his way out without being able to offer a satisfactory explanation, Jesus opted for the more difficult expedient. He untied the knot and revealed the treasure, twenty coins the likes of which had never been seen in this house, and said, I had no idea this money was here. Their silent rebuke passed through the air like a torrid desert wind, how shameful, the eldest son and caught out telling such a lie. Jesus searched in his heart and could not bring himself to be annoyed with Mary Magdalene. He felt nothing but deep gratitude for her generosity, for this touching gesture on her part of giving him money she knew he would have been ashamed to accept openly, for it is one thing to have said, Your left hand is under my head and your right hand embraces me, and another not to think that other left and right hands have embraced you, without wishing to know if you ever longed for somewhere to rest your head. Now it is Jesus who is staring at his family, defying them to doubt his word, I had no idea this money was there, undoubtedly true, but not quite the whole truth, and silently daring them to ask him the question to which there is no answer, If you didn't know you had this money, how do you account for it being here now. He cannot tell them, A prostitute with whom I've spent the last eight days put the coins here, money received from the men she slept with before I turned up. Scattered on the soiled, threadbare tunic of the man who was crucified four years ago and whose remains were shamefully dumped in a common grave, the twenty coins shine like the luminous earth which one night struck terror in this same household, but no Elders will come from the synagogue this time to say, The coins must be buried, just as no one here will ask, Where have they come from, in the hope that the reply will not oblige us to give them up against our will. Jesus gathers the money into the palms of his hands and says once more, I didn't know I had these coins, as if giving his family one last chance, and then, glancing at his mother, said, It is not the Devil's money. His brothers shuddered in horror, but Mary replied without showing any anger, Nor did it come from God. Jesus playfully tossed the coins into the air, once, twice, and said as naturally as if he were announcing he would get back to his carpenter's bench next day, Mother, we'll discuss God in the morning, then turning to his brothers James and Joseph, he added, I also have something to say to you, and this was no deferential gesture on the part of Jesus, for both brothers have already come of age according to their religion and are therefore entitled to be taken into his confidence. But James felt that, given the importance of this particular matter, something ought to be said beforehand about the reasons for this promised conversation, for no brother, however senior, can expect to appear unannounced and say, We must have a discussion about God. So, with an ingratiating smile, he told Jesus, If, as you say, you travelled these hills and dales for four years as a shepherd, there couldn't have been much time left to attend the synagogue and acquire so much knowledge that no sooner do you arrive back home than you want to talk to us about the Lord. Jesus sensed the hostility beneath those bland words and replied, Ah, James, how little you understand God if you fail to see that we don't have to go in search of Him if He has decided to come to us, Am I right in thinking you're referring to yourself, Save your questions until tomorrow when I shall tell you all I have to say. James was muttering to himself, no doubt making some sour comment about those who presume to know everything. Turning to Jesus with a weary expression on her face, Mary said, You can tell us tomorrow, or the day after tomorrow or whenever you like, but for the time being tell us what you intend to do with this money, for we are in dire straits, Don't you want to know where it came from, You said you didn't know, That's the truth, but I've been thinking hard and I can guess how it got there, If the money doesn't taint your hands then it won't taint ours, Is that all you have to say about this money, Yes, Then let's spend it, as is only right, on the upkeep of the house. There was a general murmur of approval, even James seemed satisfied with this decision, and Mary said, If you don't mind, we'll put some of the money aside for your sister's dowry. You didn't say anything about Lisa getting married, Yes, in the spring, Tell me how much you need, That depends on how much these coins are worth. Jesus smiled and said, I'm afraid I don't know how much they are worth, only their value. He laughed, amused by his own words and the entire family looked at him in bewilderment. Only Lisa lowered her eyes, she is fifteen, still innocent and has all the mysterious intuitions of adolescence. Amongst those present, she most of all is troubled about this money. No one cares to ask, To whom does it belong, where has it come from, and how was it earned. Jesus handed a coin to his mother and said, You can change it tomorrow, then we'll know how much it's worth, Someone is sure to ask me where it came from, and think that anyone who possesses such a coin is certain to have others hidden away, Simply tell them that your son Jesus has returned from his travels and that there is no greater fortune than the return of a prodigal son.

That night Jesus dreamt of his father. He had settled down to sleep in the lean-to out in the yard rather than be with all the others indoors. He could not bear the idea of sleeping in the same room as everyone else, ten persons trying unsuccessfully to get a little privacy, no longer like a flock of little lambs but growing fast, all legs and arms and far from comfortable in these cramped conditions. Before falling asleep, Jesus thought about Mary Magdalene and everything they had done together, and though these thoughts roused him to such a pitch that he had to get up twice and take a stroll around the yard to cool his blood, when sleep finally came he slept as peacefully as any small child, as if his body were floating slowly downstream with the current while he watched branches and clouds pass overhead, and the comings and goings of a silent bird. No sooner had Jesus's dream begun than he imagined he felt a slight jolt, as if his body had brushed against another. He thought it was Mary Magdalene and smiled, and still smiling turned his head in her direction, but the body drifting past, carried by the same current, beneath the same sky and branches, and the fluttering of the same silent bird, was that of his father. That familiar cry of terror began forming in his throat but stopped there, this was not his usual dream, he was no longer an infant in a public square in Bethlehem awaiting death with other children, there was no sound of footsteps, no neighing of horses or the clanking and scraping of weapons, nothing except the gentle murmur of water, the two bodies forming a raft, as father and son were carried along by the same river. At that moment, all the fear went out of Jesus. Suddenly overcome with feelings of rapture and exultation, he called out, Father, in his dream, Father, he repeated awakening, but now with tears in his eyes, realizing he was all alone. He tried to revive his dream, to repeat it all over again, in order to feel that sudden jolt once more, and to discover his father floating alongside him so that they might drift together on these waters to the end of time. That night he did not succeed, but his former dream never came back, from now on he will experience elation instead of fear, companionship instead of solitude, promised life instead of deferred death. Now let the wise men of the Holy Scriptures explain, if they can, the meaning of Jesus's dream, the significance of this river and current, of the overhanging branches, the drifting clouds, and the silent bird, all of which made it possible for father and son to be united even though the guilt of the one cannot be pardoned or the sorrow of the other relieved.

The following day Jesus offered to help James with some woodwork but it soon became clear that good intentions were no substitute for the skills he lacked and had never fully acquired even by the time his father died. To meet his customers' needs, James became a reliable carpenter, and even young Joseph, who was not yet fourteen, already knew enough about the job to be able to teach his eldest brother, had any such disrespect for seniority been allowed within the strict family hierarchy. James laughed at Jesus's clumsiness and told him, Whoever turned you into a shepherd has led you astray, light-hearted words of gentle irony which no one would have suspected of concealing some deeper meaning or ambivalence, but which caused Jesus to rise abruptly from the workbench and Mary to rebuke her second son, telling him, Speak not of perdition, lest you summon Satan and bring evil into our home. Taken aback, James protested, But I summoned no one, Mother, all I said was, We know what you said, interrupted Jesus, Mother and I heard what you said, it was Mother who linked the word shepherd with perdition in your head, not you, and you don't know why, but she does, I warned you, Mary said forcefully, You warned me when the evil had already been done, if it was evil, for when I look at myself I cannot see it, replied Jesus, whereupon Mary told him, There are none so blind as those who will not see. These words annoyed Jesus and he said reproachfully, Be quiet, Mother, if your son's eyes saw evil, they saw it after you, but these same eyes which strike you as being blind, have also seen things you've never seen nor are likely to see. Her son's authority and harshness of tone, not to mention the strange words he spoke, were enough to make Mary yield, but her reply conveyed one final warning, Forgive me, I didn't mean to offend you, may the Lord always protect the light in your eyes and soul. James looked at his mother, then at his brother, saw there was some conflict, but could not imagine what might have caused it, clearly something from the past, for his brother had not been back long enough for any further discord. Jesus made for the

227

house but on reaching the door turned and said to his mother, Send the children out to play, I must talk to you in private along with James and Joseph. The others left, and the house which had been so crowded until a moment ago suddenly seemed empty. There were four people left sitting on the floor, Mary between James and Joseph, with Jesus facing them. A long silence followed, as if by common consent they were giving the others time to get far enough away where not even the faintest echo of a cry would reach them. Jesus finally spoke, pronouncing his words carefully, I have seen God. The first visible reaction on the faces of his mother and brothers was one of awe, followed by a look of disbelief, and between the one and the other there was a hint of cynical mistrust in James's expression, of wonder in that of Joseph, of resigned bitterness in that of Mary. All three remained silent, and Jesus said for a second time, I have seen God. If a moment of silence, as the popular saying goes, marks the passing of an angel, here they were still passing, Jesus had said all there was to say, his family were at a loss for words, and soon they will rise to their feet and each go about their affairs wondering if this had all been a dream, difficult though it is to believe. Yet if given enough time, silence has the surprising power of making people speak. Unable to control his impatience any longer, James asked a question, the most innocent question of all, pure and gratuitous rhetoric, Are you sure. Jesus did not reply, simply looked at James as God had probably looked at him from within the cloud, and for the third time said, I have seen God. Mary, who had no questions to ask, told him, You must have imagined it, whereupon Jesus replied, Mother, things imagined do not speak but God spoke to me. Having recovered his composure, James decided this must be some kind of madness, a brother of his speaking to God, how ridiculous, Well who knows, perhaps it was God Who put the money in your knapsack, he said, smiling ironically. Jesus reddened but replied coldly, Everything comes to us from the Lord, He is forever finding and opening up paths to reach us, and although this money may not have come from Him, it came through Him. And what did the Lord say to you, where did you see Him, and were you asleep or keeping watch, I was in the desert looking for a stray sheep when He called out to me, Are you allowed to tell us what He said, That one day He will ask for my life, All lives belong to the Lord, That's what I told Him, And what did He say, That in exchange for the life I must give Him, I shall have power and glory, You will have power and glory after you die, asked Mary, unable to believe her ears, Yes, Mother, What power and glory can be given to someone after death, I don't know, Were you dreaming, I was awake and looking for my sheep in the desert, And when is the Lord going to ask you for your life, I don't know, but He told me we would meet again when I was ready. James looked at his brother in dismay and could no longer contain his suspicions, The sun in the desert has affected your brain, you've been suffering from sunstroke, and Mary suddenly interrupted to ask, And what about the sheep, what happened to the sheep, The Lord ordered me to sacrifice it to seal our covenant. These words provoked James, who protested, You're offending the Lord, the Lord made a covenant with His people and He's not likely to make one with an ordinary man like you, the son of a carpenter, a shepherd, and who knows what else. Mary appeared to be carefully following some thread of thought as if afraid of seeing it break before her very eyes, but by persevering, she found the question she had to ask, What sheep was that, The lamb I had with me when we met in Jerusalem at the Gate of Ramah. In the end, what I tried to keep from the Lord the Lord took from me, And God, what did God look like when you saw Him, Like a cloud, Open or closed, asked James, A column of smoke, You're mad, Brother, If I'm mad, God is to blame, You're under Satan's power, said Mary, shouting rather than speaking, It wasn't Satan I met in the desert, it was the Lord, and if it's true that I'm under Satan's power, then the Lord has so ordained. You've been in the clutches of Satan since the day you were born, You ought to know, Yes, I know all right, you chose to live with the Devil for four long years rather than with God, And after spending four years with the Devil, I met God, You're telling the most awful lies, I'm the son you brought into the world, either believe in me or renounce me, I believe in you, but not in what you say. Jesus got to his feet, raised his eyes to heaven and said, When the Lord's promise has been fulfilled, you will be obliged to believe what people will say of me. He went to fetch his knapsack and staff and put on his sandals. On reaching the door, he divided the money into two parts and said, This is Lisa's dowry when she marries, and arranging the coins side by side on the ground, he added, The rest will be returned where it came from, and perhaps also be used as a dowry. He turned towards the door, was about to leave without saying goodbye, when Mary remarked, I noticed you no longer carry a bowl in your knapsack, I had one but it broke, There are four bowls over there, choose one and take it with you. Jesus hesitated, preferring to leave empty-handed, but he went to the hearth where the four bowls were standing stacked one on top of the other. Choose one, Mary said a second time. Jesus looked and made his choice, I'll take this one which has seen better days, You've chosen the right one for you, said Mary, Why do you say that, It's the colour of the black earth, it neither disintegrates nor perishes. Jesus put the bowl into his knapsack, tapped his staff on the ground, Tell me once more that you don't believe me, We don't believe you, said his mother, and now less than ever because you chose the Devil's symbol, What symbol are you talking about, That bowl. At that very moment, Pastor's words came back to Jesus from the depths of memory, You will have another bowl which will not break so long as you are alive. A rope seemed to have been extended its full length, ending up in a circle and tied with a knot. Jesus was leaving home for the second time, but on this occasion he did not say, One way or another I shall always come back. As he turned his back on Nazareth and began descending the first mountain slope, an even sadder thought crossed his mind, Suppose Mary Magdalene were not to believe him either.

This man who carries God's promise with him, has nowhere else to go except to the house of a prostitute. He cannot return to his flock, Begone with you, were Pastor's last words to him, nor can he return home, We don't believe you, his family told him, and his steps begin to falter, he is afraid to move, nervous of arriving. It is as if he were back in the middle of the desert, Who am I, but the mountains and valleys refuse to answer, not even the heavens which ought to know everything. If he were to return home now and repeat the question, his mother would say to him, You're my son but I don't believe you, so the time has come for Jesus to sit on this stone which has been reserved for him since the world began, to sit there shedding tears of misery and solitude. Who knows, perhaps the Lord will appear to him once more, even if only in the form of smoke and cloud, all He has to say to him is, Come on, man, there's no need for all this weeping and wailing, what's the matter with you, we all have our bad moments, and there's one important thing I should have mentioned earlier, everything is relative in life, and every misfortune becomes bearable when compared with something worse, so dry your tears and behave like a man, you've already made your peace with your father, what more do you want, and as for this friction with your mother, I'll deal with that when the time comes, what didn't please Me much was your affair with Mary Magdalene, a common whore, but then you're still young and might as well enjoy life while you can, the one thing doesn't rule out the other, there's a time for eating and a time for fasting, a time for sinning and a time for being afraid, a time for living and a time for dying. Jesus wiped his tears on the back of his hand, blew his nose, using who knows as what, and to be frank there was no point in spending the whole day there, the desert is what it is, it surrounds and encircles us, in some way protects us, but when it comes to giving, it gives us nothing, simply looks on, and when the sun suddenly clouds over so that we find ourselves thinking, The sky is reflecting our sorrow, we are being foolish because the sky is quite impartial and neither rejoices in our happiness nor is cast down by our grief. People are heading in this direction on their way to Nazareth, and Jesus does not wish to make a fool of himself, a grown man with a beard and crying like a child to attract attention. From time to time a few travellers pass each other on the road, some going up, others coming down, greeting each other effusively, but only after they are certain of their mutual goodwill, for when one speaks of bandits in these parts, they are of two types. There are those who hold up travellers like the insolent rogues who robbed Jesus some five years ago, when the poor fellow was on his way to Jerusalem to find solace for his woes. Then there are those worthy rebels who certainly do not make a habit of travelling the main roads, but who sometimes appear in disguise to spy on the movements of Roman troops before setting up the next ambush, or turn up without any disguise to strip any wealthy travellers collaborating with the Romans of their silver, gold and other valuables, and even their well-armed bodyguards are powerless to spare them this outrage. It was only natural that the eighteen-year-old Jesus should yearn for adventure as he gazed on those lofty mountains with their ravines and caves where the followers of Judas the Galilean continued to take refuge. Then he began to wonder what he would do if a band of rebels were to appear from nowhere and invite him to join them, exchanging the amenities of peace, however desirable, for the glory of victory and power, for it is written that one day the Lord will bring forth a Messiah, an envoy who will deliver His people once and for all from present oppressions and give them strength for future hostilities. A flurry of mad hope and irresistible pride blows, like a sign from the Spirit, on Jesus's forehead, and this carpenter's son for one spellbinding moment sees himself as captain, leader and supreme commander, with raised sword, his very presence striking awe and horror in the Roman legions, who throw themselves over precipices like pigs possessed by demons, so much for senatus populusque romanus. Alas, Jesus suddenly remembered that he has been promised power and glory, but only after his death, so he might as well enjoy life and if he has to go to war, let it be on one condition, that in the event of a truce he will be allowed to leave the lines and go and spend a few days with Mary Magdalene, unless they allow one female companion for each soldier, for anything more would lead to promiscuity and Mary Magdalene has already said she has given that up. Let us hope so, for Jesus feels his strength redoubled at the very thought of the woman who cured his painful wound, which she replaced with the intolerable wound of desire. And here is the problem, how is he to face that locked gate with the sign up unless absolutely certain that he will find on the other side the person he thinks he left behind, a woman who waits for him alone in body and soul, for Mary Magdalene will not accept the one without the other. Evening is drawing to a close, the houses of Magdala can be seen in the distance huddled together like a flock. Mary's house, like the sheep that wandered off, cannot be sighted from here, amidst the great boulders which skirt the road, bend after bend. Now and again, Jesus remembered that sheep he had to kill in order to seal in blood the covenant imposed by the Lord and his soul, now free of battles and triumphs, became excited at the idea of searching once more for his sheep, not to kill it or lead it back to the flock, but so that together they might climb up to fresh pastures which are still to be found if we look carefully enough in this vast and much travelled world, and if we look even closer into those impenetrable gorges, sheep that we are. Jesus stopped in front of the door and discreetly confirmed it was locked on the inside. The sign is still hanging there, Mary Magdalene is not receiving anyone. Jesus would only have to call out, to say, It's me, in order to hear her joyfully sing, This is the voice of my beloved, behold him who has come leaping over mountains and jumping over hills, there he waits on the other side of this wall, behind this door, and it is true, but Jesus would rather knock on the door, once, twice, without uttering a word, waiting for someone to open, Who's there, what do you want, a voice asked from within. Jesus foolishly decided to disguise his voice and pretend to be an eager client with money to spend, using words such as, Open up, flower, you won't regret it for I'll pay and service you well, and if the tone of voice sounded false, his words were true enough when he said, I'm Jesus of Nazareth. Mary Magdalene was slow in opening the door because the voice did not quite match the words, besides she thought it unlikely that Jesus could be back so soon, when he had promised her, One of these days, I'll come and visit you, after all, Nazareth isn't far from Magdala. People often say these things just to please the listener, and one day could mean three months but never tomorrow. Mary Magdalene opens the door, throws herself into Jesus's arms, cannot believe her good fortune. In her excitement, she foolishly imagines that he has come back because the sore on his foot has re-opened, and with this in mind, she leads him indoors, sits him down and fetches the lamp, Your foot, show me your foot, but Jesus tells her, My foot has healed up, can't you see. Mary Magdalene could have replied, No, I can't, which was true, for her eyes were filled with tears. She had to put her lips to the sole of his foot which was covered in dust, to untie with great care the thongs attaching the sandal to his ankle, to stroke with her fingertips the new skin which had formed in order to verify that the ointment had done its work, while secretly acknowledging that love had played some part in this cure.

During supper, Mary Magdalene asked no questions, she simply wanted to know, and this, needless to say, was not a question, if he had had a good journey, or encountered any evils on the road, small talk and nothing more. Once they had finished eating, there was prolonged silence for it was not her turn to speak. Jesus stared at her as if weighing up his strength against that of the sea from a high rock, not because he was afraid of any man-eating animals or dangerous reefs beneath the smooth surface, but simply putting his courage to the test. He has known this woman for a week, sufficient time and experience to know whether she will receive him with open arms yet he is afraid of having to reveal, now the moment has come, what has just been spurned by those of his own flesh and blood, who should also have been with him in spirit. Jesus hesitates, tries to find words to express what he has to say but all that comes out is a phrase to gain time, not to say lose it, Weren't you surprised to see me back so soon, I started waiting for you the moment you left and never counted the hours between your leaving and returning, nor should I have counted them had you stayed away for ten years. Jesus smiled, shrugged his shoulders, he should have known there was no point in pretending or being evasive with this woman. They were sitting on the ground facing each other with a lamp in the middle and the leftovers from their supper. Jesus took a piece of bread, broke it in two and, giving a piece to Mary said, Let this be the bread of life, let us eat it so that we may believe and never doubt, whatever we may say and learn here, So be it, said Mary Magdalene. Jesus ate his bread, waited for her to finish hers, and said for the fourth time, I have seen God. Mary Magdalene's expression did not change, she simply fidgeted, her hands crossed on her lap, and asked him, Was this what you had to tell me if we should meet again, Yes, as well as all the other things that have happened to me since I left home four years ago, I feel they are all somehow linked to each other, although I cannot explain how or why, I am your lips and ears, replied Mary Magdalene, whatever you may say you will be saying it to yourself, for I am simply she who is inside you. Now Jesus can begin to speak, for they have both partaken of the bread of truth, and there are few such hours in life. Night turned to dawn, the flame in the lamp died twice only to revive, Jesus's entire history as we know it was narrated there, even including certain details we scarcely considered worthwhile and countless thoughts which have escaped us, not because Jesus tried to conceal them but simply because this Evangelist could not be everywhere at the same time. As Jesus began narrating in a weary voice what happened after he returned home, grief caused him to waver, just as dark foreboding had made him pause before knocking at the door. Breaking her silence for the first time, Mary Magdalene asked him in the tone of voice of someone who already knows the answer, Your mother didn't believe in you, That's right, replied Jesus. And so you've come back to your other home, Yes, If only I could lie to you and tell you that I don't believe you, Why, So that you would do what you've just done once more, go from here as you left your own home, and I, not believing you, would not have to follow you, That doesn't answer my question, True, it's not a reply, Well then, were I not to believe in you, I would not have to share the dreadful fate that awaits you, How do you know a dreadful fate awaits me, I know nothing about God except that His preferences must be as terrifying as His aversions, Whatever put that strange idea into your head, You have to be a woman to know what it means to live with God's contempt and now you'll have to be more than a man to live and die as one of His elect, Are you trying to scare me, Let me tell you about my dream, one night a little boy appeared to me from nowhere and told me God is horrible, and with those words he disappeared, I have no idea who that child could have been, from where he came or to whom he belonged, It's only a dream, You of all people speaking of dreams in that way, And then what happened, Then I turned to prostitution, But you've given that up, But not in the dream, not even after I met you, Tell me again what the child said, God is horrible. Jesus saw the desert, the dead sheep, the blood on the sand, heard the column of smoke sighing with satisfaction and said, Could be, could be, but it's one thing to hear that said in a dream and another to experience it in real life. God forbid that you should ever come to experience it, Each one of us has to fulfil his destiny, And you've been given the first solemn warning about yours. Studded with stars, the heavenly dome turns slowly over Magdala and the wide world. Somewhere in the infinite which He occupies, God advances and withdraws the pawns of the other games He plays, but too soon to worry about this one, all He need do for the present is to allow things to follow their natural course, apart from the odd adjustment with the tip of his little finger to make sure some stray thought or action does not interfere with the constant harmony of destinies. Hence His lack of interest in the rest of the conversation between Jesus and Mary Magdalene, And now what are you going to do, she asks him, You said you would accompany me wherever I might go, I said I would be with you wherever you might be, What's the difference, None at all, but you can stay here as long as you like if you don't mind living with me in what was once a house of sin. Jesus paused, reflected at length and finally said, I shall find some work in Magdala and we can live together as husband

and wife, You are promising too much, I'm quite content just to sit here at your feet.

Jesus found no work, but met with what he could have expected, jeers, ridicule, insults, which was scarcely surprising, for here was a mere youth living with the notorious Mary Magdalene, It won't be long before we see him sitting at the front door waiting his turn like all her other clients. He tolerated their jibes and insults for several weeks but finally Jesus said to Mary, I must get away from this place, But where can we go, Somewhere by the sea. They left before dawn and the inhabitants of Magdala arrived too late to be able to salvage anything from the flames.

Some months later on a cold and rainy winter night, an angel quietly entered the house of Mary of Nazareth without disturbing anyone. Mary herself only noticed the visitor's arrival because the angel spoke to her as follows, You must know, Mary, that the Lord mixed His seed with that of Joseph on the morning you conceived for the first time, and it was the Lord's seed rather than that of your husband, however legitimate, which engendered your son, Jesus. Fortunately the essence of this revelation did not escape Mary despite the angel's obscure speech, and, much surprised, she asked him, So Jesus is my son and the son of the Lord, Woman, what are you saying, show some respect for rank and precedence, what you must say is the son of the Lord and of me, Of the Lord and of you, No, of the Lord and of you, You're confusing me, just answer my question, is Jesus our son, You mean to say the Lord's son because you only served to bear the child, So the Lord didn't choose me, Don't be absurd, the Lord was merely passing as anyone watching would have seen from the colour of the sky, when His eye caught you and Joseph, a fine, healthy couple, and then, if you can still remember how God's will was made manifest, He ordained that Jesus should be born nine months later. Is there any real proof that it was the Lord's seed which engendered my first-born, Well, it's a delicate matter, and what you're demanding is nothing less than a paternity test which in these mixed unions, no matter how many analyses, tests, and globule counts one carries out, can never give conclusive results. And there was me thinking the Lord had chosen me for His bride that morning, and now you tell me it was pure chance and that He could just as easily have chosen someone else, Well let me tell you, I wish you hadn't descended into Nazareth to leave me in this state of uncertainty, besides, surely any son of the Lord, even with me as a mother, would have stood out at birth and on growing up would have had the same bearing, appearance and manner of speaking as the Lord himself, and though people say a mother's love is blind, my son Jesus looks ordinary enough to me. That's your first mistake, Mary, to think I only came here to discuss some sexual episode in the Lord's past life, and your second mistake is to think that the beauty and eloquence of mankind resembles that of the Lord, when I can vouch as someone close to Him, that the Lord's way of doing things is always the opposite of what humans imagine, and strictly between ourselves, I'm convinced the Lord couldn't live in any other way, and the word most frequently on his lips is not yes, but no, But surely it's the Devil who's supposed to be the spirit of denial, No, my child, the Devil only denies himself, and until you learn to tell the difference, you'll never know to whom you belong, I belong to the Lord, So, you belong to the Lord, do you, well there's your third and greatest mistake, not to have believed in your son, You mean in Jesus, Yes, in Jesus, for none of the others saw God or are ever likely to see Him, Tell me, angel of the Lord, is it really true that my son Jesus saw God, Yes, like a child finding his first nest he came running to show you, and you, cautious and mistrusting, told him it couldn't be true, that if there was any nest it was hollow, if there were any eggs they were empty, and if there were no eggs a snake had devoured them. Forgive me, angel of the Lord, for having doubted, Now I cannot be sure whether you are talking to me or to your son, To him, to you, to both, what can I do to make amends for the harm done, Listen to your maternal heart, Then I should go and find him, tell him that I believe in him, ask him to forgive me and to return home, where the Lord will summon him when the time comes, I honestly don't know whether you will reach him in time, there is no one more sensitive than an adolescent, you risk being insulted and having the door slammed in your face, If such a thing should happen, that demon who bewitched and led him astray is to blame, and I cannot understand how the Lord, as a father, could have consented to such liberties and given the rascal so much freedom, To which demon are you referring, To the shepherd my son accompanied for four years and

238

whose flock he tended for no good reason. Oh, that shepherd, Do you know him, We went to school together, And does the Lord permit that such a demon should thrive and prosper, The harmony of the universe demands it, but the Lord will always have the last word, only we don't know when He will say it, but you'll see, one of these days we shall wake up and find there is no evil in the world, now if you'll excuse me I must be off, if you have any more questions to ask, this is your opportunity, Only one, Fine, go ahead, Why does the Lord want my son, Your son, in a manner of speaking, In the eyes of the world Jesus is my son, Why does the Lord want him, you ask, well there's an interesting question, but unfortunately I can give you no answer, for the moment the problem is between the two of them, and I don't believe Jesus knows any more than he has already told you. He told me he will have power and glory after death, Yes, I'm aware of that, But what will he have to do in life in order to merit these rewards the Lord has promised, Come now, you're being stupid, surely you don't believe that such a word exists in the eyes of the Lord or that what you presumptuously refer to as merit has any value or meaning, I can't imagine what you lot get into your heads when you're nothing but abject slaves of God's absolute will, I'll say no more for I am truly the servant of the Lord, and would have Him do with me as He will, but tell me one thing, after all these months, where am I to find my son, It is your duty to look for him just as he went in search of his lost sheep, In order to kill it, Don't worry, he won't kill you, but you will certainly kill him by not being present at the hour of his death, How do you know I won't die first, I am sufficiently close to the seat of power to know, and now I must bid you farewell, you've asked all the questions you wanted, except the one question you should have asked, but that's something which no longer concerns me, Explain, Explain it to yourself. And with these words the angel disappeared and Mary opened her eyes. All the children were fast asleep, the boys together in two groups of three, James, Joseph and Judas, the three older boys in one corner, in the other their younger brothers, Simon, Justus and Samuel, and lying beside Mary, Lisa on one side, Lydia on the other. Still troubled by the angel's words, Mary noticed to her alarm and dismay that Lisa was practically naked, her tunic in disarray and pulled up over her breasts, fast asleep with a smile on her face, the perspiration glistening on her

239

forehead and upper lip which appeared to be sore from kissing. Were Mary not certain that only an angel had entered, Lisa's appearance would have been enough to convince her that one of those incubuses who violate women in their sleep had been secretly having his wicked way with the poor girl while her mother was engaged in conversation. This probably happens all the time without our knowing, these angels go around in pairs at their leisure and while the one distracts attention by telling fairy-tales, the other carries out the wicked deed which, strictly speaking, is not all that wicked, and in all probability they will reverse their rôles next time so that the salutary meaning of the duality of flesh and spirit will not be lost either on the dreamer or the person dreamed about. Mary covered her daughter as best she could, pulling the tunic down to make Lisa look decent before rousing her and asking her in a whisper, What were you dreaming about. Taken by surprise, the girl had no time to invent a lie. She confessed that she was dreaming of an angel who had said nothing but simply looked at her with as gentle and sweet an expression as one could hope to find in Paradise, Did he touch you, asked Mary, and Lisa replied, Mother, no one touches with their eyes. Not altogether convinced, Mary said in an even lower whisper, I, too, dreamt of an angel, And did your angel speak or was he also silent, Lisa asked in all innocence, He confirmed that your brother Jesus was telling the truth when he said he had seen God, Oh, Mother, how wrong we were not to believe Jesus, who is so good and patient, no one could have blamed him had he taken back the money for my dowry. Now we must try to put things right, But we don't know where to find him, he has sent no news, oh if only we had asked the angel, after all, angels know everything, Of course, but the angel didn't offer to help, simply said it was our duty to look for your brother, But, Mother, if brother Jesus was truly with the Lord then our life is going to be different from now on, Different, perhaps, but for the worse, Why, If we don't believe in Jesus or in his word, how can you expect others to believe, we can't very well go through the streets and squares of Nazareth proclaiming Jesus has seen the Lord, Jesus has seen the Lord, unless we want people chasing us with stones, But if the Lord himself chose Jesus, then surely He would protect us, the rest of his family, Don't be too certain, we weren't around when Jesus was chosen and as far as the Lord is concerned there are neither fathers nor sons, remember Abraham, remember Isaac, Oh, Mother, how terrible, It would be wise, my child, to keep this matter to ourselves and say as little as possible, Then what shall we do, Tomorrow I'll send James and Joseph to look for Jesus, But where, since Galilee is so vast, and Samaria as well, if he went there, or to Judaea or Idumaea which is at the end of the world, Your brother has probably gone to sea, remember what he told us when he came, that he had been helping some fishermen, Isn't it more likely that he returned to the flock, Those days are over, How do you know, Try to get some sleep for it's getting late, Who knows, we might dream of our angels again, Perhaps, Whether Lisa's angel, having given its companion the slip, came to inhabit her dream once more, no one ever discovered, but the angel who brought those tidings, even if he had forgotten some detail, was unable to return because Mary's eyes remained open as she lay there in the semi-darkness, what she knew was more than enough, what she suspected filled her with apprehension.

Day broke, the mats were rolled up, and after summoning all her children before her, Mary explained that she had been thinking seriously about their recent treatment of Jesus, Starting with myself, as his mother, I think we should have been kinder and more under-standing, and I've come to the conclusion that it's only right that we should go and look for him and ask him to return home, for we believe in him and, God willing, will one day believe in what he told us. This was what Mary told them, unaware that she was repeating the same words used by Joseph, who was also present during that dramatic moment of rejection. Who knows, perhaps Jesus might still be here today if that discreet murmur, although we did point it out at the time for it was nothing more than a murmur, had been on everyone's lips. Mary kept quiet about the angel and the angel's words, and simply reminded them of the respect they owed their oldest brother. James dared not question his mother's change of heart although deep down he continued to doubt his brother's sanity unless perchance he had fallen under the spell of some dangerous trickster. Anticipating her reply, he asked, And who is to go and look for our brother Jesus, As the second oldest, you must go and Joseph will accompany you, for together you will travel more safely. Where should we start looking, By the Sea of Galilee, I'm sure you'll find him there, When do we leave, Jesus left months ago so there's no time to be lost. But the rains have started, Mother, and this is no time to be travelling, My son, the circumstances create the need, and when the need is great enough, then need creates the circumstances. Mary's children looked at her in surprise, unaccustomed to such eloquent maxims coming from their mother's lips, still too young to know that keeping company with angels can produce these and even more impressive results. Take Lisa, for example, who at this very moment is slowly nodding her head in a daze, the others suspecting nothing. Once the family discussion was over, James and Joseph took a good look at the sky to see if there was any chance of a dry day for their departure despite the recent bad weather. The sky must have noticed, for right over the Sea of Galilee it was turning a watery blue which promised an afternoon without rain. Having made their farewells discreetly indoors, since Mary felt the neighbours should know as little as possible, the two brothers finally set out on their journey, not along the road to Magdala, for there was no reason to believe Jesus had taken that direction, but by another route which would soon bring them to the new city of Tiberias. They went barefoot for with so much mud on the roads they could scarcely wear sandals and they kept them safely in their knapsacks until the weather improved. James had two good reasons for choosing the road to Tiberias. Firstly, because coming from the provinces he was curious to see the palaces and temples he had heard so much about and secondly, because he had been told that the city was more or less situated halfway up the coast on this side of the river. Since they would have to earn a living while searching, James hoped they might find work on some building-site in the city, despite what the devout Jews of Nazareth said about the place being unhealthy because of the polluted air and sulphurous waters nearby. They did not reach Tiberias that day because the promising signs in the sky came to nothing. Within an hour of their departure it started raining again and they were fortunate to come across a cave big enough to shelter them before the rain could turn into a deluge and sweep them away. They slept in safety, but no longer trusting in the weather. It took them some time to decide whether there was any hope of reaching Tiberias with their clothes more or less dry. As unskilled labourers, the only work they could find on the building-site was carting stones, but after a few days they had earned enough money to satisfy their modest needs, not that King Herod Antipas was generous to his workers. On their arrival in Tiberias they began enquiring if anyone had seen a certain Jesus of Nazareth, perhaps only passing through, he's our brother and looks more or less like this, but whether he's travelling alone or accompanied we're not sure. No one had seen him working there, so James and Joseph went round all the boathouses until they were sure no one had seen him. Clearly, if their brother had decided to rejoin the fishermen, he would not have wasted any time slaving on a building-site under some harsh foreman when the open sea was right there. Now that they had earned a little money, the next problem to resolve was whether the search along the river-bank, village by village, crew by crew, boat by boat, should be carried out to the north or south. James finally decided they should travel south where the road was flatter, while the northern route was much more uneven. The weather was stable, the cold bearable, the rain had passed and anyone with more experience of nature's cycle than these two youths would have recognized, just by sniffing the air and feeling the soil, the first tentative signs of spring. Ordained for some higher motive, this fraternal mission to find their brother was turning into an agreeable country outing, a pleasant holiday by the sea, and James and Joseph were almost in danger of forgetting why they had come here in the first place, when they unexpectedly ran into some fishermen who gave them news of Jesus, expressed in the strangest manner. One of the fishermen told them, Yes, we know him and when you find him don't forget to remind him we're waiting for his return as eagerly as if we were waiting for our daily bread. The two brothers were astounded and could scarcely believe these men were talking about Jesus, or could they have mistaken him for some other Jesus, Judging from your description, he's the same Jesus, but whether he came from Nazareth we cannot say for he never mentioned it. And why do you say you're waiting for his return as eagerly as if waiting for your daily bread, James asked them, Because whenever he was in the boat the fish swam straight into our nets, But our brother knows nothing about fishing, so he can't be the same Jesus, We never suggested your Jesus knows anything about fishing, but he only has to say, Cast your nets on this side, and no sooner are the nets lowered than they come up full, Then why is he no longer with you, Because he moves on after a few days, saying he must help other fishermen and that happens to be true, for he joined us on three occasions, always promising to return, And where is he now, We don't know, last time he went off was heading south, but he may possibly have gone north without our noticing, he comes and goes at will. James said to Joseph, let's go south, at least we know our brother is somewhere on this side of the water. It seemed straightforward but then they might miss him if Jesus happened to be out in the open sea on one of those miraculous fishing trips. We tend to overlook such details, but destiny is not what we imagine, we believe everything to be determined according to some principle or other, when in reality it is quite different. Note how certain encounters such as the one we have just described can only come about if the persons concerned happen to be in the same place at the same time which is not always easy, we need only pause for a moment to look up at a cloud in the sky, to listen to the song of a bird, to count the entrances and exits of an anthill, or, on the contrary, be so distracted that we neither look nor listen nor count, but go on our way, thus missing what seemed the perfect opportunity. Believe me, brother Joseph, destiny is the most difficult thing of all in this world, as you'll soon discover when you're my age. Forewarned, the two brothers kept a watchful eye, stopped along the way and waited to see if any boat was late in returning, several times they even retraced their steps in the hope of taking Jesus by surprise in some unexpected place. Until they finally reached the end of the sea. Passing over on to the other side of the River Jordan, they asked the first fishermen they met if they knew anything about Jesus. Naturally, the men had heard about his wondrous deeds but no one had seen him around these parts. James and Joseph retraced their steps and headed north, more observant this time, like fishermen dragging their nets in the hope of catching the King of fish. Whenever they spent the night on the road, they kept watch in turn lest Jesus should take advantage of the moonlight in order to steal from one place to another. Making enquiries as they went, they got as far as Tiberias, where they did not have to go searching for work since they still had some money left thanks to the generosity of the fishermen who supplied them with fish, prompting Joseph to ask on one occasion, James, has it occurred to you that the fish we are about to eat might have been caught by our brother, and James replied, That won't improve the taste, unkind words coming from a brother but justified when one considers James's frustration, God help him, as he wearily went on searching for a needle in a haystack.

They found Jesus an hour later, that is to say by our time, after leaving Tiberias. The first to spot him was Joseph who had keen eyesight and could see things from quite a distance. That's him, way over there, he called out. In fact there are two persons heading in this direction and one is a woman. No, says James, it can't be him. A young boy rarely contradicts an older brother, but Joseph is so overjoyed that he dispenses with the usual rules and conventions, I'm telling you, it's him, But I can see a woman there, Yes, a woman with a man, and that man is Jesus. Along the riverbank and across a stretch of flat terrain between two hills which sloped down virtually to the waterside, Jesus and Mary Magdalene could be seen approaching. James stopped and waited, and ordered Joseph to stay with him. The boy reluctantly obeyed, longing to run to his long-lost brother, to embrace him and throw his arms round his neck. James, however, was disturbed by the presence of that woman at his brother's side. Who was she, he asked himself, refusing to believe that his brother already had carnal knowledge of any woman, and the very idea seemed to create an enormous gulf between James and his older brother, as if Jesus, who boasted of having seen God, had now moved into a completely different realm, simply by having carnal knowledge of a woman. One reflection leads to another and one often gets there without noticing the connection between them. It is rather like crossing from one side of the river to the other by means of a covered bridge, we keep going without looking where we are going, we pass over a river we did not know existed, and James, too, began to think it was not right to remain standing there as if he were the eldest in the family and Jesus should come to greet him. No sooner did James stir than Joseph ran to Jesus with open arms and cries of joy, startling into flight a throng of birds which, concealed amongst the tall reeds, had been foraging for food in the marshes by the river. James began walking faster to prevent Joseph from passing on any messages which were his responsibility, and coming face to face with Jesus said to him, Thanks be to the Lord that we should find you, brother, whereupon Jesus replied, I am delighted to see both of you in such good health. Mary Magdalene, meanwhile, had lingered behind. Jesus asked, What brings you to these parts, and James suggested, Let's move over there where no one will overhear our conversation, We can talk here, replied Jesus, and if you're referring to the woman accompanying me, then let me assure you that whatever you have to say and I may wish to hear, can be said in her presence. The deep silence which ensued was like that of the sea and mountains put together, rather than the silence of four human beings confronting each other and summoning their courage. Jesus seemed older and his skin was tanned, but that feverish look had gone and the expression under his heavy, dark beard seemed composed and serene notwithstanding the tension aroused by this unexpected encounter. Who is that woman, asked James, Her name is Mary and she's with me, replied Jesus. Is she your wife, Well, yes and no, I don't understand, That doesn't surprise me, I must talk to you, Go ahead, I've brought a message from Mother, I'm listening, I'd prefer to tell you in private. You heard what I said, Mary Magdalene stepped forward, I can stay out of the way until you've finished your conversation, No, replied Jesus, you share all my thoughts, so it's only right that you should know what my Mother thinks of me, so that I don't have to repeat it to you later. James flushed with irritation and made as if to turn away, whilst giving Mary Magdalene black looks which betrayed mixed feelings of desire and resentment. Intervening, Joseph stretched out his hands to keep them apart, which was as much as he could do. James eventually calmed down and after a moment's thought remembered what he had to say, Mother sent us to find you and accompany you back home, for we believe in you, and with God's help, perhaps one day we'll believe in the things you told us, Is that all, Those were Mother's words, So, you yourselves will make no effort to believe in what I told you, and prefer to wait until the Lord helps you to change your mind, Whether we understand or not depends on the Lord, You're much mistaken, the Lord gave us legs so that we might walk and we walked, I've never heard of any man who waited for the Lord to say, Start walking, and it's the same with our mind, God gave us a mind to use according to our will and desire, I won't argue with you, Just as well, for you wouldn't win. What should I say to Mother, Tell her the message came too late, that Joseph spoke those same words in time but she paid no attention, and even if an angel of the Lord were to appear and convince her that everything I have said has been willed by the Lord, I have no intention of returning home, You're committing the sin of pride, A tree weeps when cut down, a dog howls when beaten, a man matures when offended. She's your mother and we are your brothers, Who are my mother and my brothers, my brothers and my mother are those who believed in my words the moment I spoke, my brothers and my mother are those fishermen who know that when I accompany them they will catch more fish than ever before, my mother and my brothers are those who do not have to wait for the hour of my death in order to take pity on my life, Have you no other message for Mother, That is all, but you will hear others speak of me, replied Jesus, then turning to Mary Magdalene, he said, Let's go, Mary, the boats are ready to leave, the shoals are gathering, time to reap this harvest. As they started walking away, James called out, Jesus, should I mention this woman to Mother, Tell her she's with me and her name is Mary, and the name echoed amidst the hills and over the sea. Crouching on the ground, young Joseph wept bitter tears.

When Jesus goes to sea with the fishermen, Mary Magdalene waits for him, usually seated on a rock at the water's edge or on some nearby hillock if there is one, from where she can easily follow the route they sail. Fishing is no longer a slow operation for there has never been so much fish in this sea, just like fishing with one's hand inside a bucket filled to the brim, but not for everyone, for if Jesus happens to go elsewhere then the bucket reverts to being almost empty, and hands and arms soon tire of casting net after net only to find the odd fish or two trapped in the mesh. In despair, the entire fishing community on the western side of the Sea of Galilee goes to ask Jesus, to implore Jesus, to order Jesus to help them and in some places they even received him with festivities and floral tributes as if it were Palm Sunday. But the bread of humanity being what it is, a mixture of envy and malice, with a little charity now and then, and the yeast of fear fermenting evil while suppressing good, one group of fishermen began quarrelling with another, one village with another, for they all wanted to lay claim to Jesus, leaving the others to provide for themselves as best they could. Whenever they started squabbling Jesus would withdraw into the desert and only return when the troublemakers repented and asked forgiveness for their rowdy behaviour while protesting their love and devotion. But what we shall never know is why the fishermen on the eastern side never sent any delegates over to this side in order to discuss the drafting of a fair treaty that would benefit all parties, except for the large number of Gentiles of different breeds and persuasions who are to be found in these parts. Under cover of darkness, those on the other bank might have sent a fleet with nets and pikes to kidnap Jesus, once more reducing those on the western side to a meagre existence after having got used to plentiful supplies of food.

But let us go back to the day when James and Joseph came to ask Jesus to give up this existence and return home despite his new-found prosperity since taking up fishing. By now the two brothers, James in a rage, Joseph in tears, are quickly making their way over hill and dale as they head back to Nazareth, where their mother continues to wonder whether the two sons who left will bring back a third, but she is doubtful. The homeward route taken by the two brothers, being near the spot on the coast where they had met Jesus, obliged them to pass through Magdala. James scarcely knew the town and Joseph not at all, but judging from appearances the place had little of interest to detain them there. So, after a brief rest, the two brothers resumed their journey. On passing the last of the houses before crossing the wilderness ahead, they saw on their left the bare walls of a house which had clearly been gutted by fire. The gate to the yard had been forced open but only partially destroyed and there was every indication that the fire had started inside the house. In such cases, every passer-by hopes that some treasure may have been left amongst the ashes and if he thinks there is no danger of a beam falling on his head, he cannot resist exploring further. Treading carefully, he pokes at the ashes with one foot hoping to see something shining there, a gold coin, an indestructible diamond, an emerald necklace. James and Joseph only entered out of curiosity, they are not so ingenuous as to imagine that rapacious neighbours have not been here already to loot the place, although the house is so small that any prized possessions would almost certainly have been removed by the owners, leaving only the walls which can soon be built elsewhere. The roof of the oven inside the house had caved in, the brick floor was broken and loose tiles trampled underfoot. There's nothing here, said James, let's go, but Joseph asked, What's that over there. It was a bedstead of sorts but the legs had been burnt and the whole frame was badly damaged, a phantom throne with bits of charred drapery still hanging there in tatters. It's a bed, said James, some people, such as great lords and wealthy merchants, actually sleep on these things, Mother also sleeps on one, argued Joseph, but there's no comparison, Well, this doesn't strike me as being a rich person's house, Appearances can be deceptive, James wisely reminded him. As they left, Joseph noticed that there was a distaff made of cane hanging on the outside of the yard gate, like those used for gathering figs and which no doubt had originally been much longer. What is this doing here, he asked, and without waiting for a reply, either from himself or from his brother, he removed the useless cane and took it with him, the souvenir of a fire, of a house razed to the ground, of people unknown. No one had seen them enter, no one saw them leave, they are simply two brothers returning home in soiled tunics and bearing sad tidings. One brother frustrated by the memory of Mary Magdalene, the other eagerly thinking of the fun he will have playing with the broken cane.

Seated on a rock and waiting for Jesus to return from fishing, Mary Magdalene is thinking about Mary of Nazareth. Until today, she simply thought of her as Jesus's mother, now she knows, after questioning him, that his mother is also called Mary, a coincidence of no great consequence when one considers the vast number of Marys on this earth and with so many more to come if the fashion persists, but we are inclined to believe that there is a greater sense of solidarity between those who share the same name, just as we believe that Joseph no longer thinks of himself as being that other Joseph's son but more as a brother, and this could be God's problem, no one else bears His name. These reflections may seem rather far-fetched for someone like Mary Magdalene but we have every reason to believe that she is perfectly capable of similar perceptions once her thoughts about the man she loves lead her to think of his mother. Mary Magdalene has never had a son of her own to love, but at long last she has known what it means to love a man, after having learned and practised the thousand and one deceptions of false love. She loves Jesus as a woman, but she also wants to love him like a mother, perhaps because she is not much younger than his real mother who sent a message asking her son to return home, only to be refused. Mary Magdalene wonders how Mary of Nazareth will feel when she receives his answer, but this is not the same as imagining how she herself would suffer were she to lose Jesus for she would be losing her man rather than her son. Oh Lord, punish me with both sorrows if necessary, murmured Mary Magdalene as she sat waiting for Jesus to return. And as the boat drew nearer and was pulled ashore, as the baskets laden with glistening fish were hauled in, as Jesus with his feet in the water helped the fishermen and laughed like a child at play, Mary Magdalene saw herself in the rôle of Mary of Nazareth, and rising to her feet she went down to the water's edge and waded in to greet Jesus. Kissing him on the shoulder, she whispered, My son. No one heard Jesus say, Mother, for, as we know, words coming from the heart are never spoken, they get caught in the throat and can only be read in one's eyes. Mary and Jesus were rewarded with a basket of fish and, as usual, they retired to the house where they were to spend the night, for they had no home of their own and went from boat to boat and from mat to mat. In the beginning, Jesus often remarked to Mary, This is no life for you, let's try and find a house of our own where I can join you whenever possible, but Mary insisted, I don't want to wait behind, I prefer to be with you. One day Jesus asked her if she had any relatives who might offer her shelter and she told him her brother Lazarus and sister Martha lived in the village of Bethany in Judaea, although she herself had left home when she turned to prostitution and to spare them any embarrassment she had moved further and further away until she ended up in Magdala. So your name should really be Mary of Bethany if that's where you were born, said Jesus, Yes, I was born in Bethany, but you found me in Magdala, so I prefer to think of myself as being from Magdala, People don't refer to me as Jesus of Bethlehem although I was born there, and I don't think of myself as being from Nazareth because people there do not want me and I certainly don't want them, perhaps like you I should say, I'm from Magdala, and for the same reason, Don't forget we destroyed our house, But not the memory, replied Jesus. No more was said about Mary returning to Bethany, this stretch of coast is their whole world and wheresoever Jesus may go, she will go with him.

How true that popular saying which reminds us that there is so much sorrow in this world, that misfortunes grow like weeds under our feet. And unless we are mistaken, such a saying could only have been invented by men, accustomed as they are to life's ups and downs, obstacles, setbacks and constant struggles. And the only people likely to question that saying are those who sail the seas for they know that even greater depths exist between their feet and the sea-bed, and, more often than not, unfathomable chasms. The misfortunes of seafarers, such as winds and gales, are sent from heaven, causing waves to swell, storms to break, sails to snap and fragile vessels to founder. And these fishermen and sailors truly perish between heaven and earth, a heaven hands cannot reach, depths feet never touch. The Sea of Galilee is nearly always as tranquil and smooth as any lake until the marine furies are unleashed and then it is each man for himself, although sadly some drown. But let us return to Jesus of Nazareth and recent worries which only go to show that the human heart is never content and doing one's duty does not bring peace of mind, as those who are easily satisfied would have us believe. One could say that thanks to the endless comings and goings of Jesus up and down the River Jordan, there is no longer any hardship, not even the occasional shortage all along the west bank, where not only fishermen have benefited, because the glut of fish has brought down prices and resulted in people getting more to eat. And while it is true that several attempts were made to keep prices high by the well-known corporative method of throwing part of the catch back into the sea, Jesus, on whom they ultimately depended for a successful catch, threatened to go elsewhere until those responsible for this abuse apologized and changed their ways, at least for the present. So everyone except Jesus has reason to feel happy. He is tired of the incessant toing and froing, the continuous embarking and disembarking, the same old routine, day in and day out, and since this power of making fish appear at will clearly comes from the Lord, why should he be condemned to this monotonous existence until that same Lord is ready to summon him as promised. Jesus is in no doubt that the Lord is with him, for the fish never fail to appear when he calls them, and this has inevitably led him to speculate whether the Lord might not be willing to concede him other powers for a time on the clear understanding that he puts them to good use. For as we have seen, Jesus, who has achieved so much already with nothing but intuition to guide him, should have no difficulty in meeting those conditions. There was one easy way of finding out, as easy as saying, Oh, and that was to try, and if it worked, God clearly approved and if it did not, God was showing His displeasure. The first problem to be solved was that of choice. Unable to consult the Lord directly, Jesus would have to risk it and choose between the possible powers which seemed to offer least resistance and would not be too obvious, yet not so discreet as to pass unnoticed

by those who would benefit, or by the world, for that would preju-
dice the glory of God which must prevail over all things. But Jesus
could not make up his mind, he was afraid God might ridicule and
humiliate him as He had done in the desert and might well do again,
for even now he shuddered at the thought of the embarrassment he
would have suffered if the nets had come back empty when he first
suggested, Cast your nets on this side. These matters worried him
so much that one night he dreamt someone was whispering in his
ear, Don't be afraid, remember God needs you, but when he woke
up he could not help wondering who had spoken, perhaps an angel,
one of the many who go around delivering messages from the Lord,
or even a demon, one of the many who do Satan's bidding. Lying
beside him, Mary Magdalene was fast asleep, so it clearly could not
have been her. This was how things stood when Jesus set out one
day, which seemed no different from any other, to perform the usual
miracle. The clouds were low in the sky and there were signs of
rain, but it takes more than rain to keep fishermen at home, used
as they are to all sorts of weather. On this particular day the boat
belonged to Simon and his brother Andrew, who had witnessed the
first miracle, accompanied by that of James and John, the sons of
Zebedee, for one can never tell whether the miracle will always
have the same effect and any boat which happens to be nearby can
always land some of the fish gathering there. The strong wind
carries them swiftly out to sea and, after lowering the sails, the
fishermen in both boats prepare their nets and wait for Jesus to tell
them where they should cast them. At this stage things start getting
difficult when a storm suddenly brews up without any warning,
apart from the overcast sky, and becomes so fierce that the waves
swell and rise, driven back and forth by the frenzied gale and those
fragile nutshells are buffeted out of control as the elements unleash
their wrath. The sorry plight of the defenceless creatures brought
shouts and lamentations from the people watching on the shore.
Wives, mothers, sisters, children, and the odd good-hearted mother-
in-law were gathered there and making such a din with their weeping and wailing that it must surely have been heard in heaven, Oh,
my poor husband, Oh, my beloved son, Oh, my dear brother, Oh,
my poor son-in-law, A curse on you, wretched sea, Holy Mother
of the Afflicted, help us, Protectress of the Voyager, come to our
aid, and all the children could do was to weep, but not all that

convincingly. Mary Magdalene was also there, murmuring, Jesus, Jesus, but she was not praying for him, for she knew the Lord was saving him for another occasion, and not likely to let him perish in any old storm at sea, with no more serious consequences than a few drowned men. She kept on repeating, Jesus, Jesus, as if the very sound of his name might rescue the fishermen who certainly looked close to meeting their fate. There in the boat, Jesus watched the despair and destruction all around him, the waves sweeping over the boats and flooding them inside, the masts breaking up and sending the sails flying through the air, the rain becoming a deluge capable of sinking one of the Emperor's own ships. Jesus watched, thinking to himself, It is not right that these men should die while I continue to live, besides, the Lord is almost certain to rebuke me, saying, You could have rescued those who were with you yet you made no attempt to save them, as if your father's crime were not enough. To be reminded of this particular episode was so painful that Jesus jumped to his feet and standing as firmly as if on solid ground he ordered the wind, Be quiet, and told the sea, Calm down, and no sooner had he spoken than the sea and wind abated, the clouds in the sky dispersed and the sun appeared in all its glory, ever a wondrous sight in the eyes of us poor mortals. It is impossible to describe the rejoicing in the boats, the kissing and embracing, the tears of joy ashore, those on this bank were puzzled that the storm should have died down so quickly, those over there, as if restored to life, could think of nothing except their lucky escape, and if some spontaneously exclaimed, Miracle, miracle, they seemed unaware that someone had to be responsible for its performance. A sudden silence fell over the waters, the other boats surrounded that of Simon and Andrew and all the fishermen looked at Jesus, too astonished to speak, for above the uproar of the storm they had heard him call out, Be quiet, Calm down, and there he was, Jesus, the man who had summoned fish from the sea and now forbidden the sea to deliver men to the fish. His eyes lowered, Jesus was sitting on the oarsman's bench, his expression conveying both triumph and disaster, as if on reaching a mountain peak he were already beginning his sad and inevitable descent. Forming a circle, the men waited for Jesus to speak. It was not enough to have tamed the wind and pacified the waters, he had to explain how a simple Galilean, a modest carpenter's son, could have achieved such a miracle when

God himself appeared to have abandoned them to death's cold embrace. Jesus rose to his feet and told them, What you have just witnessed was not my doing, the voice that quelled the storm was not mine but that of the Lord speaking through me, like the prophets, I am only the mouthpiece of the Lord. Simon, who was in the boat with him, said, Just as the Lord sent the storm, He could also have sent it away, but it was your will and your word which saved our lives when we believed them to be lost in the eyes of God, Believe me, it was God's doing, not mine. Whereupon John, the younger son of Zebedee, intervened, proving that he was not all that simple-minded, It may have been God's doing, for in Him resides all power and might, but He acted through you, so clearly it is God's will that we should know you, But you already know me, Only that you turned up from who knows where and that you have mysteriously filled our boats with fish, I am Jesus of Nazareth, the son of a carpenter who was crucified by the Romans, for a time I was a shepherd with the biggest flock of sheep and goats imaginable, and now, here I am with you, and perhaps I'll go on being a fisherman until the hour of my death. Andrew, the brother of Simon, said, You may rely on us to stay with you, for any man with your powers is condemned to solitude, a solitude heavier to bear than any millstone around your neck. Jesus said, Stay with me if that is what your heart asks, but tell no one what has passed here, for the time has not yet come for the Lord to reveal my fate, if, as John says, God wishes that you should know me. Then James, the older son of Zebedee, who, like his brother, was no simpleton either, said, Don't imagine people won't talk, just look at the crowd there on the shore, see how they're waiting to acclaim you, some so impatient that they're already pushing out their boats in order to come and join us, and even if we succeed in damping down their enthusiasm and persuading them to keep our secret, how can you be sure that God will not unexpectedly manifest Himself through you, however much you may dislike the idea. The living image of sadness and despair, Jesus hung his head and said, We are all in the hands of the Lord, You more than the rest of us, replied Simon, for He has chosen you, but we shall follow you, To the end, said John, Until you have no further need of us, said Andrew, For as long as possible, said James. The boats were fast approaching with much waving of arms and chanting of prayers, praising and thanking the Lord.

Resigned, Jesus told the others, Let's go, the wine is poured and we have to drink it. He did not seek out Mary Magdalene, he knew she was waiting for him ashore as always, that it would take more than a miracle to interrupt her constant vigil, and the very thought of her waiting there filled his heart with gratitude and peace. On disembarking, he fell into her arms and betrayed no surprise when Mary Magdalene, her cheeks pressed against his wet beard, whispered into his ear, You will inevitably lose the war, but win all the battles. Arm-in-arm and accompanied by friends, they greeted the cheering spectators who hailed Jesus like some victorious general. Arm-in-arm, Jesus and Mary climbed the steep path leading to Capernaum, the village overlooking the sea where Simon and Andrew lived and where they had been offered hospitality.

James was right when he warned Jesus that the episode of the storm would soon be on everyone's lips. Within a few days people were discussing nothing else for miles around. Although, strange to relate, given that the sea is not all that wide here, as we mentioned before, and can be seen from bank to bank if viewed from a height on a clear day, no one seems to have been aware of the storm in places such as Tiberias. So when someone arrived with the news that a stranger accompanying the fishermen of Capernaum has quelled the storm just by speaking to it, he was asked, What storm, leaving the messenger aghast. But there was no lack of witnesses to testify that there had indeed been a storm, not to mention the panic of those who had been involved directly or indirectly, and amongst the latter were some muleteers from Safed and Cana who chanced to be there in the course of their work. It was they who spread the news elsewhere, each man embroidering the details according to his fancy, but then the news did not reach everyone, and we know what happens to these stories, they lose conviction after a while and by the time the news reached Nazareth, no one was sure any longer if this was a genuine miracle or simply a happy coincidence between a word being tossed to the wind and a gale that was tired of blowing. A mother's heart, however, is never deceived and Mary only had to hear the dying echoes of this prodigy which people were already questioning, to know in her heart that her absent son was responsible. She grieved for the loss of that maternal authority which had led her to conceal the angel's apparition and revelations from Jesus, confident as she was that a simple message couched in a few reticent words would bring home the son who had left with his own heart grieving. And now that Lisa was married and living in Cana, Mary no longer had anyone in whom to confide her bitter sorrows. She could not turn to James, who had come back in a towering rage after his meeting with his brother. He spared Mary no details and gave a disparaging account of the woman with Jesus, She's old enough to be his mother and from the looks of her there's nothing she doesn't know about life, to put it mildly, not that James himself knows all that much about life, here in this remote village. So Mary unburdened herself to Joseph, the son who in name and appearance reminded her most of her late husband, but he gave her little comfort, Mother, we are paying for our mistake, and after being with Jesus I fear he'll never come back home, people say he calmed a storm and the fishermen themselves told us that he filled their boats with fish as if by magic. Then the angel was right, What angel, asked Joseph, and Mary told him everything that had happened, from the apparition of the beggar who had thrown luminous earth into the bowl to the appearance of the mysterious angel in her dream. They did not hold this conversation indoors, for with such a large family it was almost impossible to have any privacy. When these people wish to disclose any secrets they go into the desert where they might even meet God. Joseph and Mary were still deep in conversation when Joseph, looking over his mother's shoulder, saw a flock of sheep and goats with their shepherd pass over the distant hills. The flock did not appear to be very big, nor the shepherd very tall, so he watched without saying a word. And when his mother sighed, I shall never see Jesus again, he replied pensively, Who knows.

Joseph was right. About a year later Lisa sent a message to their mother inviting her on behalf of her parents-in-law to come to Cana for the wedding of her husband's younger sister, and she was to bring along as many of the children as she wanted, for they would all be most welcome. Despite this generous invitation Mary was reluctant to be a burden for there is nothing more tiresome than a widow with a horde of children, so she decided to take her current favourite Joseph and Lydia, who, like all girls of her age, adored parties and celebrations. Cana is not far from Nazareth, little more than an hour away if calculated by our time, and with gentle autumn already here, this promised to be a most agreeable outing, even had there been no wedding to look forward to. They set out at sunrise in order to arrive in Cana in time for Mary to give some assistance with the final preparations for festivities where the labour involved is in direct proportion to the pleasure and enjoyment of the guests. Lisa came to meet her mother and brother and sister and embraced them affectionately. She enquired about their health and well-being, they in turn asked her if she was well and happy, and since there was much work to be done they moved on quickly. Lisa and Mary went to the bridegroom's house, where the feast was traditionally held, in order to share the cooking with the other women of the family. Joseph and Lydia remained in the yard with the other children of the same age, the boys playing with the boys, the girls dancing with the girls, until it was time for the ceremony to begin. Then off they ran, boys and girls together, behind the men accompanying the bridegroom, his friends carrying the customary torches although it was a bright sunny morning, which only goes to show that a little extra light, even that of a torch, is not to be despised. Smiling neighbours came out to greet them, saving their blessings for the moment when the procession will return bringing the bride. Joseph and Lydia missed seeing the rest, but then they had already seen a marriage ceremony in their own family, the bridegroom knocking on the door and asking to see the bride, the latter appearing surrounded by her friends who carry simple little oil lamps which are more suited to women than great flaming torches, and then the bridegroom lifts the bride's veil and shouts with joy on finding such a treasure there as if he had not seen her thousands of times already during the last twelve months of courtship and gone to bed with her as often as he pleased. Joseph and Lydia missed these moments because Joseph, who happened to look down the street, suddenly caught sight of two men and a woman in the distance. On recognizing Jesus and the woman with him, he felt as if he were experiencing a curious sensation for the second time. He called out to his sister, Look, it's Jesus, and off they rushed to meet him, but suddenly Joseph stopped, he remembered his mother and the coldness with which his brother had received him there by the sea, not so much him, it is true, as the message he and James had been asked to deliver, and thinking to himself that he would eventually have to explain his behaviour to Jesus, he turned back. Before disappearing round the corner he took another look and felt so envious when he

259

saw his brother gather Lydia into his arms, like a feather in flight, and smother her with kisses, while the woman and the other man looked on approvingly. His eyes clouded with tears of frustration, Joseph ran and ran, entered the house, crossed the yard in leaps and bounds to avoid trampling the linen cloths and provisions set out on the ground and low tables, and called, Mother, Mother. Our own distinctive voice is our saving grace, otherwise mothers everywhere would be looking up only to see someone else's son. Mary simply had to look and she understood when Joseph said to her, Jesus is coming this way. The colour drained from her face, then she blushed, smiled, turned serious and pale once more, and these conflicting emotions brought her hand to her breast as if her heart were no longer beating and she had backed into a wall. Who is with him, she asked, for she was certain someone was accompanying him, A man and a woman, and Lydia who's still with them, replied Joseph, Is that the woman you saw before, Yes, Mother, but I don't know the man. Lisa joined them, curious, unaware that there was anything amiss, What's the matter, Mother, Your brother has arrived for the wedding, You mean to say Jesus is here in Cana, Yes, your brother Joseph has just seen him. Suppressing her excitement, Lisa could not stop smiling as she murmured to herself, My brother, and that quiet smile of hers betrayed the deepest satisfaction. Let's go and meet him, she said, You go, I'll stay here, her mother replied defensively and, turning to Joseph, she told him, Go with your sister. But Joseph still felt resentful that Lydia had been the first to be embraced by Jesus, and Lisa did not have the courage to go to him on her own, so there they remained, like three criminals awaiting sentence and unsure of the judge's clemency, if the words judge and clemency mean anything here.

Jesus appeared in the doorway carrying Lydia in his arms, and Mary Magdalene followed behind, but first to enter was Andrew, the other man in the group and related to the bridegroom as soon became apparent when he said to those who came smiling to welcome him, No, Simon couldn't come, and while some of those present were happily absorbed in this family reunion, others eyed each other over a chasm, asking themselves who would be first to set foot on that fragile, narrow bridge which, despite everything, still joined the one side to the other. We shall not say, as a poet once said, that children are the greatest joy in this world, but it is thanks to them that adults sometimes succeed in taking difficult steps without losing face, even if only to discover afterwards that they have not got very far. Lydia slipped from Jesus's arms and ran to her mother and, as in a puppet show, one move set off another, then another. Jesus went up to his mother and brother, greeting them in the sober, matter-of-fact tone of someone used to being with them every day and then passed on, leaving all of them dumb-founded. Mary Magdalene followed him and as she went past Mary of Nazareth, the two women, the one honest, the other disreputable, glanced at each other, not with hostility or contempt, but with an expression of mutual recognition, which only those familiar with the labyrinthine meanderings of the feminine heart can understand. The procession was drawing near, shouts and applause could be heard, the tremulous vibrations of tambourines, the scattered strains of gentle harps, the rhythm of the dances, the shrill sound of voices as everyone tried to speak at the same time, and seconds later guests were cramming into the yard, the bride and groom were almost swept in amidst cheering and clapping as they went before parents and parents-in-law to receive their blessings. Mary was also waiting there to give her blessing just as she had blessed her daughter Lisa, then as now without her husband or eldest son at her side to take their rightful place as head of the family. As they sat down to eat, Jesus was offered a special place, Andrew having discreetly warned his relatives that this was the man who filled empty nets with fish and calmed the storm, but Jesus refused the honour and chose to sit with the guests seated furthest away from the bridal party. Mary Magdalene served Jesus and no one questioned her presence there. Lisa, too, went to him several times to make sure he was all right and Jesus treated both women in exactly the same manner. Watching the comings and goings from the far side, his mother's eyes met those of Mary Magdalene. She beckoned her to a quiet corner of the yard and without further ado told her, Take care of my son for an angel warned me that great tribulations await him and I can do nothing for him, You may count on me to protect and defend him with my life if necessary, What is your name, I'm known as Mary Magdalene and I lived as a prostitute until I met your son. Mary said nothing, but began to see things more clearly as certain details came back to her, the coins, the guarded statements made by Jesus when she had asked where the money had come from, James's indignant account of his meeting with Jesus and offensive remarks about the woman accompanying his brother. Now she knew everything and turning to Mary Magdalene, assured her, You will always have my blessing and gratitude for all the good you have done my son, Jesus. Mary Magdalene leaned over and kissed her shoulder as a mark of respect but the other Mary threw her arms around her and held her tight, and there they remained for some moments, embracing each other in silence before returning to the kitchen where there was work waiting to be done.

The festivities continued, one dish after another was brought in from the kitchen, wine flowed from the pitchers, guests began singing and dancing, when suddenly the steward arrived to whisper in the ear of the parents of the bride and bridegroom, The wine is running out. They could not have been more alarmed to discover the roof was falling in. What are we going to do now, how can we face our guests and tell them there's no more wine, by tomorrow everyone in Cana will know of our shame, My poor daughter, sighed the bride's mother, how the people will mock her, saying that even the wine ran dry on her wedding day, what have we done to deserve this, and what a bad start to married life. At the tables the guests were draining their goblets, some anxiously looking round for someone to serve them more wine, when Mary, who had already entrusted her maternal duties and obligations to another woman, decided she would like to put Jesus's miraculous powers to the test before withdrawing into the silence of her own home, her mission on earth completed and ready to depart this world. She looked around for Mary Magdalene, saw her slowly close her eyelids and nod her assent. Wasting no time, she went up to Jesus and, confident that he would understand what she expected of him, she said, There is no wine. Jesus slowly turned to face his mother, looked at her as if she had spoken from afar and asked, Woman, what have I to do with you, shattering words which shocked and amazed those who overheard them, for no son treats the mother who brought him into the world in this manner. With the passing of time, those words would be rephrased and interpreted in different ways to make them sound less brutal. Some have even tried to refute them or completely change their meaning by insisting that what Jesus really said was, Why bother me with this, or, What has this got to do with me, or, Who told you to interfere, or, Why should we get involved, woman, or, Why can't you leave this to me, or, Tell me what you want and I'll see what can be done, or, You know perfectly well you can rely on me to do my best to please you. Mary bore the full brunt of those words, withstood Jesus's look of rejection and, placing her son in an awkward position, she ended her challenge by saying to the servants, Whatever he says, do it. Jesus watched his mother go off without saying a word or making any attempt to detain her, aware that the Lord was using her just as He had made use of the storm and the plight of the fishermen. Jesus raised his goblet which still contained some wine and, pointing to six stone water jars used for purification, ordered the servants, Fill them with water, whereupon they filled them to the brim and each jar held two to three measures. Bring them here, he told them, and they obeyed. Then into each jar Jesus poured a few drops of the wine in his goblet and ordered the servants, Take them to the steward. Unaware of where the jars had come from, the steward, after sampling the water which the small quantity of wine had barely coloured, summoned the groom and told him, Every man at the beginning serves good wine and when the guests have drunk their fill serves that which is less good, but you have kept the best wine until now. The bridegroom who had never before seen wine served in such jars and who knew, moreover, that the wine had run out, tasted it for himself and with an expression of false modesty confirmed the obvious by commenting on the excellent quality of this vintage nectar. Had it not been for the voice of the people, represented in this case by some servants who spread the news next day, this would have been a frustrated miracle, for the steward, if unaware of the transmutation, would have remained unaware, while the bridegroom would have been only too delighted to take the credit for another's achievement. No one expected Jesus to go around saying, I've performed such and such a miracle, Mary Magdalene who had been involved in the plan from the outset was unlikely to start boasting, He's worked a miracle, and his mother even less so, because this was something between Mary and her son and the rest was a bonus in every sense of the word, as any of the guests who had their goblets refilled will testify.

Mary of Nazareth and her son conversed no more. Without saying goodbye to anyone, Jesus and Mary Magdalene left that same afternoon and set off for Tiberias. Keeping out of sight, Joseph and

Lydia followed them to the outskirts of the village where they remained watching until the couple disappeared round the bend in the road.

Then the long wait began. The signs with which the Lord had manifested Himself so far in the person of Jesus had been little more than some clever witchcraft, spellbinding illusions, with a few quick words of abracadabra not unlike certain tricks performed with rather more finesse by oriental magicians, such as tossing a rope in mid-air and then climbing it without any visible signs of support either from a solid hook or the hand of some mysterious genie. In order to work these wonders, Jesus simply had to will them, but if anyone had asked him why he performed them, he would have been at a loss for any answer other than to say that he could scarcely have ignored the plight of fishermen left with empty nets, the terror inflicted by that raging storm, or the sudden lack of wine at the marriage-feast, for truly the hour had not yet come for the Lord to speak through his lips. Villagers dwelling on this side of Galilee were saying that a man from Nazareth was going round exercising powers which could only have come from God, and that he did not deny it, but in the absence of any motive, reason or justification for his mysterious appearance amongst them, they might as well take advantage of this sudden abundance and ask no questions. Naturally Simon and Andrew were not of the same mind nor the sons of Zebedee, but then they were his friends and feared for his life. Each morning when he woke up, Jesus asked himself in silence, Perhaps today, and sometimes he even asked the question aloud so that Mary Magdalene might hear him, but she would say nothing, just lie there sighing, then put her arms around him and kiss him on the forehead and eyes while he breathed in the sweet, tepid odour coming from her breasts. There were days such as this when he went back to sleep, others when he forgot the question and his anxiety and took refuge in Mary Magdalene's body as if entering a cocoon where he could only be reborn in some other form. Later he would go down to the sea where the fishermen were waiting for him, many of whom would never understand him and constantly ask him why he did not get himself a boat so that he might fish independently and keep the entire catch for himself. On certain occasions, when they were out at sea, and they happened to be taking a rest between catches, still necessary although the fishing had become as easy and casual as yawning, Jesus would have a sudden premonition and his heart would tremble, but rather than turn to heaven where, as we know, God resides, his eyes settled with obsessive yearning on the lake's calm surface, on those smooth waters which shone like the clearest complexion, as if waiting with desire and fear, to see rising from the depths what the fishermen referred to as our fish, and what Jesus probably thought of as the voice which is slow in coming. The day's fishing over, the boat returned laden, and Jesus, with lowered head, once more walked along the shore with Mary Magdalene following behind, as if looking for someone who might require his voluntary assistance as a look-out. And so the weeks and months passed, even years, the only visible signs of change being those at Tiberias where more buildings went up as the city prospered, otherwise things went on much as usual in this land which seems to perish with every winter and be reborn each spring, a false observation and crass deception on the part of the senses, for spring would have no impact were it not for the slumber of winter.

Jesus was now twenty-five years of age and the entire universe seemed to be suddenly awakening, and new signs began to appear, one after another, as if someone were anxiously trying to make up for lost time. To be precise, the first of these signs was not exactly a miracle, after all there was nothing so very remarkable about Simon's mother being afflicted by a mysterious fever and Jesus going to her bedside and placing his hand on her forehead, something we have all instinctively done at some time or other, without expecting to cure the patient by this simple and far from magical gesture. What no one expected, however, was that the fever should subside beneath Jesus's fingers like poisonous water being absorbed by the soil or that the old woman should get up immediately and say, somewhat irrelevantly, Anyone who befriends me, befriends my son-in-law, and then go about her household chores as if nothing had happened. This first sign was a private affair and took place indoors, but the second was more awkward because it brought Jesus into open conflict with the written and observed law, perhaps justifiably, bearing in mind normal human behaviour, since Jesus was living out of wedlock with Mary Magdalene, and she a former prostitute, so perhaps it was not surprising that on seeing an adulteress being stoned to death in conformity with the law of Moses, Jesus should have intervened and said, Stop, he that is without sin among you, let him cast the first stone at her, as if to say, Were I not living in concubinage and untainted by sinful deeds and thoughts, I would also join you in carrying out this punishment. Our Jesus was taking an enormous risk for it might have caused some of the more heartless and callous amongst them to turn a deaf ear to his rebuke and carry on throwing stones being themselves exempt from the law they were applying which was only meant for women. What appears to have escaped Jesus, perhaps from lack of experience, is that if we wait for sanctimonious judges to appear, who believe they alone have the moral right to condemn and punish, crime is likely to increase dramatically and sin will thrive, adulteresses will be on the loose, one minute with this man, the next with another, and adultery includes the thousand wicked vices which persuaded the Lord to send down fire and brimstone over the cities of Sodom and Gomorrah, reducing them to ashes. But the evil born with the world, and from which the world has learned everything it knows, dear brethren, is like that famous Phoenix no one has ever seen and which, even while appearing to perish in the flames, is reborn from an egg hatched from its own ashes. Good is fragile and delicate. Evil need only blow the hot breath of venial sin on to the face of purity for it to become scarred for evermore, for the stalk of the lily to break and the flower of the orange-blossom to wither. Jesus told the adulteress, Go, and sin no more, but deep down he had grave doubts.

Another notable event took place on the opposite side of the sea where Jesus decided he ought to go sometime rather than have it said that all his care and attention was being lavished on the western bank. So he summoned James and John and suggested, Let's explore the other side inhabited by the Gadarenes to see what fortune brings and on the way back we can do some fishing, so that we shall have something to show for our journey. The sons of Zebedee warmed to this idea and, after setting their boat on course, began to row, hoping that further ahead there would be a breeze to help them on their way. And their prayer was answered, but their elation soon turned to alarm when a storm brewed up which promised to be much more violent than the one they had experienced years ago, but Jesus chided the waters and the skies, Now then, what's going on here, as if scolding a naughty child, and the sea calmed down immediately and the wind went back to blowing at the right speed and in the right direction. All three disembarked, Jesus walking ahead, James and John following behind. They had never been to this region before and were surprised by everything they saw there, but the strangest and most disheartening sight of all on the road was the sudden appearance of a man, if one could use such a word to describe a filthy creature with matted beard and unkempt hair. The stench he gave off was as fetid as that of any tomb, and little wonder, for as they soon discovered that was where the possessed man took refuge whenever he managed to break the fetters and chains with which they had restrained him. Had he been simply demented, although it is well known that a madman's strength is twice as great when he goes into a rage, he could have been held merely by using twice as many fetters and chains. They had tried it once to no avail and repeated the experiment many times without result because the unclean spirit which possessed and ruled the man made a mockery of any attempts to imprison him. Day and night, the possessed man went bounding over the mountains, fleeing from himself and his own shadow, only to go back to hiding amongst the tombs and often inside them, from where he had to be dragged out by force to the terror of anyone who happened to be passing. And this was how Jesus first saw him, the guards in pursuit waving their arms at Jesus to get out of danger's way, but Jesus had come in search of adventure and was not going to miss this opportunity for anything. Although terrified by the madman's appearance, John and James did not abandon their friend, and so were the first to hear words no one would ever have expected anyone to utter because they criticized the Lord and His laws, as we are about to discover. The ferocious madman advanced with outstretched claws, baring fangs from which were hanging the remains of rotten flesh, causing Jesus's hair to stand on end with fright, when suddenly the possessed creature prostrates himself on the ground two paces away and cries out, What do you want from me, Jesus, son of the Almighty, I beseech you in the name of God to stop tormenting me. Now this was the first time in public, rather than in private dreams which prudence and scepticism caution us to doubt, that a voice had been raised, and a diabolical voice if ever there was one, proclaiming that Jesus of Nazareth was the son of God, something he himself had been unaware of until this moment, for during his conversation with God in the desert, the question of paternity had never been raised. I shall need you later, was all the Lord had said, and one could not even trust appearances, considering that his heavenly father had come before him in the guise of a cloud and column of smoke. The possessed man writhed at his feet, and a voice within finally revealed what had hitherto been suppressed, and at that moment, like someone who has just seen himself reflected in another, Jesus felt that he, too, was possessed and at the mercy of certain powers which might lead him who knows where but no doubt ultimately to the grave of graves. He asked the spirit, What is your name, and the spirit replied, Legion, for we are many. In commanding tones, Jesus said, Leave this man, unclean spirit. And no sooner had he spoken than a chorus of diabolical voices went up, some reedy and shrill, others deep and hoarse, some as gentle as that of any woman, others as harsh as the sound of a saw cutting through stone, some mocking and taunting, others pleading with the feigned humility of paupers, some arrogant, others whining, some prattling like children learning their first words, others crying out like ghosts and moaning in distress, but all pleading with Jesus to allow them to remain in these places with which they were familiar, one word from him would suffice to drive them out of the man's body, For pity's sake, the evil spirits begged him, do not expel us from here. And Jesus asked them, Tell me then, where do you want to go. Now as it happened a large herd of pigs was grazing on the slopes of the mountain nearby, and they implored Jesus, Allow us to enter the pigs. Jesus thought for a moment and decided it was the perfect solution. Those animals almost certainly belonged to Gentiles, since pig's meat which was considered unclean was forbidden to Jews. It never occurred to Jesus that by eating the pigs the Gentiles would also devour the demons inside them and become possessed, just as he failed to foresee the unfortunate events that were to follow, but in fact not even a son of God, who still had to get used to such elevated kinship, could have foreseen, as on a chessboard, all the consequences of a simple move or sudden decision. In great excitement, the evil spirits wagered bets and awaited Jesus's reply, and when he said, Yes, giving them permission to pass into the pigs, they cheered in triumph and eagerly inhabited the animals at one fell swoop. Either because of the unexpected shock or because the pigs were not accustomed to going about inhabited by demons, they suddenly went wild and threw themselves over the cliff, all two thousand of them, only to end up in the sea where they drowned. The wrath of the swineherds tending these innocent animals was indescribable. One minute the poor creatures had been grazing at their leisure, rooting amongst any soft soil they could find in search of roots and worms and pawing at the sparse tufts of grass on the parched surface, the next minute they were down below in the water, a pitiful sight, some already lifeless and floating, others almost senseless but making one last valiant effort to keep their ears above water for, as everyone knows, pigs cannot close their eardrums and once too much water gets in, the poor things drown. Enraged, the swineherds began throwing stones at Jesus and his companions and were already coming after them with the justified intention of demanding compensation, so much per head multiplied by two thousand, being easy enough to calculate. Yet not so easy to pay out. Fishermen rarely earn much money and lead a meagre existence, and Jesus could not even claim to be a fisherman. Nevertheless, the Nazarene decided to confront the irate swineherds, to explain to them that there is no greater evil in this world than the Devil and that compared with Satan two thousand pigs are neither here nor there and, besides, we are all condemned to suffer losses in this life, material or otherwise, So be patient, brethren, Jesus would urge them when they came face to face. But the last thing James and John wanted was another heated exchange with the swineherds. To all appearances, any such encounter would be far from amicable, and any show of friendship or goodwill on their part was unlikely to appease the wrath of these rough characters who seemed intent on revenge. Reluctantly, Jesus yielded to their arguments which sounded all the more persuasive as the stones fell closer and closer. They ran down the slope to the water's edge and jumped into their boat and, rowing at top speed, were soon out of danger. Swineherds, as a rule, did little fishing and if those in pursuit had any boats, they were nowhere in sight. Some pigs were lost, a soul was saved, the winner is God, said James. Jesus looked at him, his thoughts clearly on something else, something the two brothers staring at him were anxious to hear about and discuss, the strange revelation by the demons that Jesus was the son of God, but Jesus was gazing at the bank from where they had escaped. He was watching the sea, the pigs floating and rolling on the waves, two thousand innocent animals, and could feel the agitation rising within him and searching for an outlet until, no longer able to contain himself, he called out, The demons, where are the demons, and then sent up a roar of laughter directed at heaven, Listen to me, oh Lord, either You made a bad choice in this son who must carry out Your plans according to what those demons told me, or there is something missing amongst Your thousand and one powers otherwise You would be capable of defeating the Devil, What are you saying, asked John, terrified by this daring challenge, I'm saying that the demons who inhabited the possessed man are now free, for demons, as we know, don't die, my friends, not even God can kill them, and for all the good I did there, I might as well have cut the sea with a sword. On the other side a great crowd was descending on to the shore, some jumped into the water to rescue the pigs floating within reach, while others leapt into the boats and set off to retrieve any others they could find.

That same night, in the home of Simon and Andrew which was close to the Synagogue, the five friends gathered in secret to debate the extraordinary revelation by the demons that Jesus was the son of God. Baffled by these mysterious events, the protagonists of this adventure had agreed to postpone any further discussion until after dusk and the moment had now come to speak their minds. Jesus began by saying, One cannot trust the father of falsehood, clearly referring to the Devil. Andrew said, Truth and falsehood pass through the same lips without trace, the Devil does not cease to be the Devil just because he may have spoken the truth. Simon said, We soon realized that you are no ordinary man like the rest of us, first there were the fish we could never have caught without your help, then the storm which almost finished us off, then the water

271

you turned into wine, then the adulteress you saved from being stoned to death, and now these demons you've exorcised from someone possessed. Jesus said, I'm not the only one to have driven demons out of people, That's true, replied James, but you're the first person to whom they have ever submitted by addressing you as the son of Almighty God, Their submission didn't do much good, for in the end I was the one who suffered humiliation, That's not the point, interrupted John, for I was there and heard everything, why couldn't you have told us you are the son of God, But I'm not sure that I am the son of God, How can the Devil possibly know if you don't, A good question, but they alone can give you an answer, Who do you mean by they, I mean God, whose son the Devil claims I am, and the Devil who could only have been told by God. There was a sudden silence as if everyone there wished to give the powers invoked sufficient time to declare themselves, until finally Simon raised the crucial question, What is there between you and God. Jesus sighed, That's the question I've been hoping you might ask me since coming here, Who would ever have imagined that a son of God would choose to be a fisherman, I've already explained that I'm not even convinced I am the son of God, Well who are you then. Jesus covered his face with his hands, wondered where he might begin the confession they were asking of him, his life suddenly appearing to be that of someone else, and that was it, if the demons spoke the truth, then everything that had happened to him previously must have another meaning and some of those events were only now becoming clear in the light of this revelation. Jesus removed his hands from his face, looked at his friends one by one with a pleading expression, as if acknowledging that the trust he was asking of them was greater than any man could concede to another, then after a long pause, he told them, I've seen God. No one uttered a word but simply waited. Lowering his eyes, he continued, I met Him in the desert and He told me that when the hour came, He would give me glory and power in exchange for my life, but He never said that I was His son. Further silence. And how did God appear to you, asked James, Like a cloud, a column of smoke, You're sure it wasn't fire, No, not fire but smoke, and He said nothing else, Only that He would return at the right moment, What moment is that, I really don't know but probably He was referring to the moment when I must sacrifice my life, And what about this power and glory, when will these be granted, Who knows. More silence. Indoors the heat was stifling yet they were all shivering. Then Simon asked slowly, Are you the Messiah whom we should call the son of God because you will come to redeem God's people from bondage, Me, the Messiah, No more surprising than your being the son of the Lord, interrupted Andrew nervously, James said, Messiah or son of God, what I cannot understand is how the Devil came to know when even the Lord did not confide in you. John said pensively, I wonder what the secret relationship is between the Devil and God. Terrified of learning the truth, they eyed each other uneasily, and Simon asked Jesus, What are you going to do, and Jesus replied, The only thing I can do, wait for my hour to come.

That hour was fast approaching but before then Jesus would have two further opportunities to demonstrate his miraculous powers, although it might be better to draw a veil of silence over the second because it was a blunder on his part and resulted in the death of a fig tree as innocent of any evil as those pigs which the demons sent hurtling into the sea. However, the first of these two miracles fully deserved to be brought to the attention of the priests of Jerusalem so that it might later be engraved with gold lettering over the Temple door, for such a thing had never been witnessed before or indeed thereafter. Historians are at variance in trying to explain why so many different races should have gathered in that place, whose exact location, let it be said in passing, has also been the subject of much debate. Some historians claim it was nothing more than a traditional pilgrimage, the origins of which have long since been forgotten, others refute this explanation and insist the crowd had gathered there because of a rumour, later to be disproved, that an envoy had arrived from Rome to announce a reduction in taxes, and there are also some historians who, while refraining from making any hypotheses or offering any solutions to the problem, argue that only the simple-minded could believe in tax reductions or revised fiscal charges likely to benefit the tax-payer, and as for the pilgrimage of unknown origins, this could easily be verified if those who revelled in such fantasies were to take a little trouble and investigate the matter more thoroughly. What is beyond dispute, however, is that some four to five thousand men had gathered there, not counting the women and children, when it became clear that they had nothing to eat. How such cautious people, so used to travelling and never without a well-stocked knapsack even on the shortest journey, should have suddenly found themselves without as much as a crust of bread or scrap of meat, is something no one has ever been able to explain. But facts are facts, and the facts confirm that there were between twelve and fifteen thousand people, this time including women and children, who had gone without food for hours on end and who sooner or later must return to their homes at the risk of dying en route from sheer exhaustion unless fortunate enough to be rescued by some charitable passer-by. The children, who are always the first to complain in any crisis, were already growing impatient, some of them whimpering, Mother, I'm hungry, and the situation was fast threatening to get out of control. Jesus walked amongst the multitude with Mary Magdalene, accompanied by their friends, Simon, Andrew, James and John, who, since the episode of the pigs and its aftermath, went everywhere with Jesus, but unlike the rest of the crowd they had brought some bread and fish and so had come provided. However, to have set about eating in the presence of all those people would not only have shown the utmost selfishness on their part but also have put them at some risk for necessity has no law, and the most effective form of justice, as Cain taught us, is that we ourselves grab with both hands. Jesus did not imagine for a moment that he could be of any possible assistance to this vast multitude in dire need of food, but James and John, with the confidence of those who have actually witnessed certain wonders, went up to Jesus and told him, If you were able to drive demons from the man's body before they killed him, surely you can give these people the food they need in order to live, And how am I to do this, if we have no food other than the few provisions we brought for ourselves, As the son of God you must be able to do something. Jesus looked at Mary Magdalene who told him, There's no turning back now, and the expression on her face was one of compassion although Jesus could not be sure if it was meant for him or the famished multitude. Then, taking the six loaves they had brought with them, he broke each loaf in half and gave them to his companions, then he did the same thing with the six fish, keeping a loaf and a fish for himself. Then he said, follow me and do as I do. And we know what he did but shall never know how he managed it. Going from person to person, he divided and distributed bread and fish, each person receiving a whole fish

274

and a loaf. Mary Magdalene and his four friends did the same, and they passed through the crowd like a beneficent wind blowing over the harvest and raising the drooping ears of corn one by one, to the sound of rustling leaves as mouths chewed and offered thanks, It is the Messiah, said some, He's a magician, insisted others, yet it never dawned on anyone in the crowd to ask, Could this be the son of God. And to all of them Jesus said, Let those who have hearing listen, for unless you divide you will never multiply.

It was only right that Jesus should have taught this precept when he had the opportunity. But he had no right to observe that precept to the letter when inopportune, as in the case of the fig tree mentioned earlier. Jesus was walking along a country lane when he began to feel hungry, and on sighting in the distance a green fig tree, he went to see if he could find any fruit there, but on drawing closer he found nothing but leaves for it was too early for figs. Whereupon he said to the tree, No more fruit will grow on your branches, and at that very moment the fig tree dried up. Mary Magdalene who was accompanying him said, You must give to those in need, and ask nothing of those with nothing to give. Filled with remorse, Jesus tried to revive the fig tree, but it was quite dead.

A misty morning. The fisherman rises from his mat, looks at the white space through a chink in the door and says to his wife, I'm not taking the boat out today, in such a mist even the fish lose their way under the water. This is what he said and, using more or less the same words, all the other fishermen echoed his sentiments from one bank to another, puzzled by the rare phenomenon of mist at this time of the year. Only one man, who is not a fisherman by profession although he lives and works with fishermen, goes to the front door as if to confirm that this is the day he has been waiting for and, looking up at the dull sky, says to himself, I'm going out fishing. At his shoulder, Mary Magdalene asks, Must you go, and Jesus replied, I've waited a long time for this day to come, Won't you eat something, Eyes are fasting when they open in the morning. He embraced her and said, At last I shall know who I am and what is expected of me, then with surprising confidence, for he could not even see his own feet in the mist, he descended the slope to the water's edge, climbed into one of the boats moored there and began rowing out towards that invisible space in the middle of the sea. The noise of the oars scraping and hitting the sides of the boat, the disturbance and dispersal of water as it escaped, resounded over the entire surface and kept awake those fishermen whose anxious wives had told them, If you can't go out fishing, at least try to get some sleep. Restless and uneasy, the villagers stared at that impenetrable mist in the direction where the sea ought to be and waited, without knowing, for the noise of the oars to stop so that they might return to their homes and secure all their doors with keys, crossbars and padlocks, even though they knew that a simple puff of air would knock them down, if He who is yonder is whom they imagine Him to be and should decide to blow this way. The mist allows Jesus to pass, but his eyes can see no further than the tip of the oars and the stern with its simple plank which serves as a bench. The rest is a blank wall, at first dim and grey, then, as the boat approaches its destination, a diffused light turns the mist white and lustrous, and it quivers as if searching in vain for a sound amidst the silence. Moving into a wider circle of light, the boat comes to a halt, it has reached the centre of the lake. God is sitting on the bench at the stern.

Unlike the first time, He does not appear as a cloud or column of smoke which in this weather would get lost and merge with the mist. This time, He is a big man, elderly, with a great flowing beard spread over his chest, head uncovered, hair hanging loose, a broad and powerful face, fleshy lips, barely moving when He begins to speak. Dressed like a wealthy Jew, in a long, magenta tunic, under a blue mantle with sleeves and gold braiding, the thick sandals on his feet are clearly those of someone who walks a lot and whose habits are anything but sedentary. Once He has gone, we shall ask ourselves, What was His hair like, without being able to remember whether it was white, black or brown, judging by His age, the hair must have been white, but there are people whose hair takes a long time to turn white and He might be one of them. Jesus shipped the oars and rested them inside the boat as if preparing for a lengthy conversation and simply said, I'm here. Slowly and methodically, God arranged the folds of the mantle over His knees and added, Well, here we are. The tone of voice suggested that He might have been smiling but His lips hardly moved, only the long hairs of His moustache and beard were quivering like the vibrations of a bell. Jesus said, I've come to find out who I am and what I shall have to do henceforth in order to fulfil my part of the contract. God said, These are two questions, so let's take them one at a time, where would you like to start, With the first one, said Jesus, before asking for a second time, Who am I, Don't you know, God asked him, Well I thought I knew and believed myself to be my father's son, Which father do you mean, My father, the carpenter Joseph, son of Eli or was it Jacob for I'm no longer certain, You mean the carpenter Joseph whom they crucified, I didn't know there was any other, A

278

tragic mistake on the part of the Romans and that poor father died innocent having committed no crime. You said that father, does this mean there is another, I'm proud of you, I can see you're an intelligent lad and perceptive, There was no need for any intelligence on my part, I was told by the Devil. Are you in league with the Devil, No, I'm not in league with the Devil, it was the Devil who sought me out, And what did you hear from his lips, That I am Your son. Nodding His head slowly in agreement, God told him, Yes, you are My son, But how can a man be the son of God, If you're the son of God you are not a man, But I am a man, I breathe, I eat, I sleep and I love like a man, therefore I am a man and shall die as a man, In your case I wouldn't be too sure, What do You mean, That's the second question, but we have time, how did you answer the Devil when he said you were My son, I said nothing, I simply waited for the day when I should meet You, and drove Satan out of the possessed man he was tormenting, the man called himself Legion and said he was many, Where are they now, I have no idea, You said you exorcised those demons, Surely You know better than me that when demons are driven out of someone's body, nobody knows where they go, And what makes you think I'm familiar with the Devil's affairs, Being God, You must know everything, Up to a certain point, only up to a certain point, What point is that, The point where it starts to become interesting to pretend that I know nothing, At least You must know how I came to be Your son and for what reason, I can see you're getting somewhat more confident, not to say impatient, since I first met you, In those days I was a mere boy and rather shy, but I'm grown up now, And you're not afraid, No, Don't worry, you will be, fear always comes, even to a son of God, You mean to say you have others, What others, Sons, of course, No, I only needed one, And how did I come to be Your son, Didn't your mother tell you, Does my mother know, I sent an angel to explain things to her, and I thought she would have told you, And when was this angel with my mother, Let Me see, unless I'm mistaken it was after you left home for the second time and before you miraculously changed the water into wine at Cana, So, Mother knew and never said a word, when I told her I had seen You in the desert, she didn't believe me, but she must have realized I was telling the truth after the angel's appearance and yet she never confided in me, You know what women are like, after all you live with one, they have their little susceptibilities and scruples, What susceptibilities and scruples, Well, let Me explain, I mixed my seed with that of your father before you were conceived, it was the easiest solution and the least obvious, And since the seeds are mixed, how can You be sure that I am Your son, I agree that it's usually unwise to feel certain about anything, but I'm absolutely certain for there is some advantage in being God, And why did You want to have a son, Since I didn't have a son in heaven, I had to arrange one on earth, which is not all that original because even in religions with gods and goddesses, who could easily have given each other children, we have seen some of them descend upon earth, probably for a change, and at the same time benefit mankind with the creation of heroes and other wonders. And this son who I am, why did You want him, Needless to say, not for the sake of change, Why then, Because I needed someone to help Me here on earth, But surely being God, You don't need help, That is the second question.

In the silence that followed one could hear somewhere in the mist, without being able to determine from which direction, the noise of someone swimming this way, and judging from the puffing and panting, he was no great swimmer and fairly close to exhaustion. Jesus thought he saw God smiling and felt sure He was deliberately giving the swimmer time to appear within the circle clear of mist which had the boat at its centre. The swimmer unexpectedly surfaced on the starboard side when one might have expected him to arrive on the other side, a dark, ill-defined shape which, at first sight, Jesus mistook for a pig with its ears sticking out of the water, but after a few more strokes he realized it was a man or something with human form. God turned His head towards the swimmer, not out of mere curiosity but with genuine interest as if anxiously encouraging him to make one last effort, and this gesture, perhaps because it came from God, had an immediate effect, the final strokes were rapid and regular and it was hard to believe that this new arrival had covered all that distance from the shore. His hands grabbed the edge of the boat although his head was still half-submerged in the water and they were huge, powerful hands with strong nails, hands belonging to a body which like that of God must be tall, sturdy and advanced in years. The boat swayed under the impact, the swimmer's head emerged from the water, then his trunk, splashing water everywhere, then his legs, a Leviathan rising from the lower depths, and he turned out to be Pastor, reappearing after all these years. I've come to join you, he said, settling himself on the side of the boat equidistant between Jesus and God yet, strange to relate, this time the boat did not lean over to his side, as if the weight had gone from Pastor's body or he were levitating while appearing to be seated, I'm here to join you, he repeated, and hope I'm still in time to take part in the conversation, We've been chatting for some time but we still haven't come to the heart of the matter, replied God, and turning to Jesus He told him, This is the Devil whom we have just been discussing. Jesus looked from one to the other, and saw that without God's beard they could pass for twins, although the Devil looked younger and less wrinkled, but it must have been an optical illusion or mistake on Jesus's part. Jesus said, I know very well who he is, after all, I lived with him for four years when he was known as Pastor, and God replied, You had to live with someone, it couldn't be with Me, and you didn't wish to be with your family, so that only left the Devil. Did he come looking for me or did You send him, Frankly, neither one nor the other, let's say we agreed that this was the best solution, So that's why he sounded so certain when he spoke through the possessed man from Gadara and called me Your son, Precisely, Which means that both of you deceived me, As happens to all humans, You've already said that I'm not human, And I can confirm it, but you have been what might technically be described as incarnated, And now what do both of you want from me, I'm the one who wants something, not him. Both of you are here and I noticed that Pastor's sudden appearance came as no surprise, so You must have been expecting him, Not exactly, although in principle one should always count on the Devil, But if the problem You and I have to resolve only affects us, what is he doing here and why don't You send him away, One can dismiss the rabble in the Devil's service if they start being troublesome in word and deed, but not Satan himself, So he's here because this conversation also concerns him, My son, never forget what I'm about to tell you, everything that concerns God also concerns the Devil. Pastor, whom we shall sometimes refer to as such, rather than constantly be invoking the Enemy by name, heard their conversation without appearing to listen or be aware that they were discussing him, thus appearing to deny God's closing and all-important statement. However it soon became clear that his inattentiveness was mere pretence, because Jesus only had to say, Let's now turn to the second question, for Pastor to prick up his ears. But without uttering a single word.

God breathed in deeply, looked at the mist around Him and murmured in the hushed tones of someone who has just made an unexpected and curious discovery, It would never have occurred to Me, but this is just like being in the desert. He turned His eyes towards Jesus, paused awhile and then, like someone resigning himself to the inevitable, began speaking, Dissatisfaction, My son, has been put into the heart of men by the God who created them, I'm referring to Myself, of course, but this dissatisfaction which like all the other traits which I made in my image and likeness, I Myself pursued in My own heart and rather than diminish with time it has grown stronger, more pressing and insistent. God stopped for a moment to consider the effect of this preamble before going on to say, For the last four thousand and four years I have been the God of the Jews, a quarrelsome and difficult race by nature, but on the whole, I have got along fairly well with them because they now take Me seriously and are likely to go on doing so for the foreseeable future, So, You are satisfied, said Jesus, I am and I'm not, or rather, I would be were it not for this restless heart of mine which is forever telling Me, Well now, a fine destiny You've arranged after four thousand years of trials and tribulations which no amount of sacrifices on the altars will ever be able to recompense, for You continue to be the god of a tiny population which occupies a minute part of this world You created with everything that's in it, so tell Me, My son, if I can derive any satisfaction from this depressing sight which is constantly before My eyes, Never having created a world, I'm in no position to judge, replied Jesus, True, you cannot judge but you could help, Help in what way, To spread My word, to help Me become the god of more people, I don't understand, If you play your part, that is to say, the part I have reserved for you in My plan, I have every confidence that within the next six centuries or so, despite all the struggles and obstacles ahead of us, I shall pass from being God of the Jews to being God of those whom we shall call Catholics as in Greek, And what is this part You've reserved for me in Your plan, That of martyr, My son, that of victim, which is the best role of all for propagating any faith and stirring up fervour. God uttered the words martyr and victim as if His tongue were made of milk and honey, but Jesus suddenly felt a chill go through his limbs as if the mist had closed over him and the Devil looked at him with an enigmatic expression which combined scientific interest with grudging compassion. You promised me power and glory, stammered Jesus, still shivering with cold, And I intend to keep that promise, but remember our pact, you shall have them after death, What good will it do me to have power and glory when I'm dead, Well, you won't be dead in the absolute sense of the word, for as my son you'll be with Me, or in Me, I still haven't finally decided. In the sense You've just mentioned of my not being dead, That's right, for example, you'll be venerated in churches and on altars to such an extent that people will even forget that I came first as God, but no matter, abundance can be shared, what is in short supply should not. Jesus looked at Pastor, saw him smile and understood, I can now see why the Devil is here, if Your authority is to extend to more people in more places, his power will also spread, for Your limits are exactly the same as his, You're quite right, my son, and I'm delighted to see how perceptive you are for most people overlook the fact that the demons of one religion are powerless to act in another, just as any god, directly confronting another god would neither be able to vanquish him nor be vanquished by him. And my death, what will that be like, It is only fitting that a martyr's death should be painful and, if possible, ignominious, so that believers may be moved to greater fervour and devotion. Come to the point and tell me what kind of death I can expect, A painful and ignominious death on a cross, Like my father, You're forgetting I'm your father, Were I free to make a choice, I'd choose him despite that moment of infamy, You have been chosen and therefore have no say, I want to end our pact, to have nothing to do with You, I want to live like any other man, Empty words, My son, can't you see you're in my power and that all these sealed documents we refer to as agreements, pacts, treaties, contracts, alliances, and in which I figure, could be reduced to a single clause, and waste less paper and ink, a clause which would bluntly state that, Everything prescribed by the law of God is obligatory, even the exceptions, and since you, My son, are something of a notable exception, you, too, are as obligatory as the law and I who made it, But with Your power would it not be much simpler and ethically more honest for You to go out and conquer those other countries and races Yourself. Alas, I cannot, because it is forbidden by the binding agreement between the gods ever to interfere directly in any dispute, can you imagine me in a public square, surrounded by gentiles and pagans, trying to persuade them that their god is false and that I am their real God, this is not something one god does to another, and, besides, no god likes another god to come and do in his house what he is forbidden to do in theirs, So, You make use of humans instead, Yes, My son, man is a piece of wood that can be used for everything, from the moment he's born until the moment he dies, he's always ready to obey, send him there and he goes, tell him to halt and he stops, tell him to turn back and he retreats, whether in peace or in war, man, generally speaking, is the best thing that could have happened to the gods, And the wood from which I'm made, since I'm a man, what use will it be put to, since I'm Your son, You will be the spoon I shall dip into humanity and bring out laden with men who shall believe in the new god I intend to become, Laden with men You will devour, There's no need for Me to devour those who devour themselves.

Jesus lowered his oars into the water and said, Farewell, I'm off home, and you can both go back the way you came, you by swimming, and You by disappearing as mysteriously as You came. Neither God nor the Devil stirred, whereupon Jesus added ironically, Ah, so you prefer to go by boat, better still, I'll row you ashore myself so that everyone may see how alike God and the Devil are and how well they get on together. Jesus turned the boat to face the bank from where they had come and, rowing with vigorous strokes, penetrated the mist which was so thick that he could no longer see God nor so much as the Devil's face. Jesus felt alive and happy, and unusually energetic. From where he was sitting the prow of the boat was invisible but he could feel the boat rising with each stroke of the oars like the head of a horse in a race threatening to come apart from the rest of its body yet having to resign itself to pulling that weight to the last. Jesus rowed and rowed, they must be almost there and he wonders how people will react when he tells them, The one with the beard is God, the other is the Devil. Taking a backward glance at the coast, Jesus could make out a different light and announced. We're here, and rowed some more. Any second now he expected to feel the bottom of the boat softly gliding over the thick mud near the shore, the playful grazing of tiny, loose pebbles, but the prow of the boat which remained invisible was pointing out to the middle of the lake, and as for the light he had seen, it had become like that of the brilliant magic circle, the glowing snare from which Jesus thought he had escaped. Exhausted, his head fell forward, he crossed his arms over his knees, one wrist resting on the other, as if waiting to be bound, and he even forgot to retrieve the oars, convinced that any further move would be completely futile. He would not be the first to speak, he would not acknowledge defeat in a loud voice, nor ask to be forgiven for having disregarded God's will and mandate and indirectly prejudiced the interests of the Devil, the natural beneficiary of the subsequent rather than the secondary consequences of the exercise of the Lord's will and the effective realization of His plans. The silence following this frustrated act of defiance was short-lived. Sitting there on His bench, God arranged the folds of His tunic and the hood of His mantle and then with mock solemnity, like a judge about to pass formal sentence, He said, Let us start from the beginning and go back to the moment I revealed that you are in My power, for until you humbly and peacefully submit to this truth you will be wasting your time and mine, Let's start again then, agreed Jesus, but be warned, I refuse to work any more miracles and without miracles Your plans will come to nothing, a mere shower from heaven incapable of satisfying any real thirst, You would be right if it were in your power to work or not to work miracles, Don't I have the power, What an idea, I work miracles both great and small, naturally in your presence so that you may reap the benefits on my behalf, you're superstitious at heart and believe the miracle-worker has to be at the patient's bedside for the miracle to take place, but if I so wished, a man dying all alone with no one by his side, abandoned to utter loneliness without a doctor, nurse or beloved relative within reach or hearing, if I so wished, I tell you, that man would be saved and go on living as if nothing had happened to him, Then why not do it, Because he would imagine he'd been cured by the strength of his own merits and would start boasting, The likes of me could not possibly die, and with all the presumption there is already in this world I've created, I have no intention of encouraging any such nonsense, So all these miracles are Yours, All those you have worked and will work, for even supposing you were to persist in opposing My will, to go out into the world and deny that you are

285

the son of God, I should cause so many miracles to happen wherever you passed that you would be obliged to accept the gratitude of those thanking you, and thereby thanking Me. So, there's no way out, None whatsoever, and don't play the restive lamb that resists being taken to be sacrificed, becomes agitated and bleats in the most heart-rending manner, for your destiny is sealed, the sacrificial sword awaits you, Am I that lamb, You are the lamb of God, My son, which God himself will carry to the altar we are preparing here.

Jesus looked at Pastor, not so much for help as for a signal, for his understanding of the world must perforce be different, since Pastor is not nor ever has been man, god he has never been nor is ever likely to be, so perhaps a mere glance or raising of eyebrows might suggest some suitable reply which would allow Jesus to play for time and extricate himself, at least for a while, from the difficult situation in which he finds himself. But all Jesus reads in Pastor's eyes are the words he spoke to him when he banished him from the herd, You've learnt nothing, begone with you. Now Jesus realizes that to disobey God once is not enough, that he who refused to offer Him his sacrificial lamb must also refuse Him his sheep, that one cannot say, Yes, to God, and then say, No, as if Yes and No were one's left and right hands, and the only good work were that which is done with both hands. For notwithstanding His normal manifestations of power such as the universe and the stars, the lightning and thunder, voices and flames on top of mountains, God could not force you to slaughter the sheep and yet, out of ambition you killed the animal, and its blood could not be absorbed by all the soil in the desert, see how it has even reached us, that thread of crimson liquid which will follow in our tracks whenever we leave this place and pursue you and God and me. Jesus said to God, I shall declare before men that I am Your son, the only son God has, but I do not believe that even in these lands of Yours, this will be enough to enlarge Your kingdom as much as You would wish. At last you're speaking like a true son, now that you've given up these tiresome acts of rebellion which were beginning to anger Me, now that you've come round to My way of thinking without any prompting, amongst the many things one could say to men, whatever their race, colour, creed or philosophy, only one thing is common to all, only one, namely that none of these men, wise or ignorant, young or old, rich or poor, would dare to say, This has nothing to do with me, And what might that be, asked Jesus with undisguised interest, All men, replied God, as if imparting wisdom, whoever and wherever they may be and whatever they may do, are sinners, for sin, in a manner of speaking, is as inseparable from man as man from sin, man is like a coin, turn it over, and what you see there is sin, You haven't answered my question, Here is my answer, the only word no man can reject as having nothing to do with him, is Repentance, because to all men who have succumbed to temptation, had an evil thought, broken some rule, committed some serious or minor crime, spurned someone in need, neglected their duty, offended religion and its ministers, or turned away from God, to all such men you need only say, Repent, repent, repent, But is it really necessary to sacrifice Your own son's life for so little, surely all You had to do was to send some prophet, The time when people listened to prophets has passed, nowadays one needs to administer stronger medicine, to apply shock treatment in order to touch men's hearts and arouse their feelings, Such as a son of God hanging from a cross, Yes, why not, And what else am I supposed to say to these people, besides enjoining them to dubious repentance, if they get tired of hearing Your message and turn a deaf ear, Yes, I agree, it may not be enough to ask them to repent, you may have to use your imagination and don't make any excuses because I still have to admire the way in which you cunningly avoided sacrificing your lamb, That was easy enough, the animal had nothing to repent, A subtle reply but meaningless, although that, too, has its charm, people should be left worried and perplexed, be made to believe that if they don't understand, they are at fault, So, I'm to make up stories, Yes, stories, parables, moral tales, even if it means distorting Holy Law ever so slightly, don't let that bother you, the timid always admire daring liberties when taken by others, and I myself, while anything but timid, was impressed by the way you saved the adulteress from death, and that's saying a lot, for it was I who put justice into the commandments I handed down, It's a bad sign when You start allowing men to tamper with Your commandments, Only when it suits Me and proves to be useful, you must not forget what I told you about the law and its exceptions, for whatever I may will instantly becomes obligatory, You said, I shall die on the cross, That is My will. Jesus looked askance at Pastor who seemed to be absorbed as if he were contemplating some moment in the future and could not believe his eyes. Jesus dropped his arms and said, Then do with me as You will.

God was about to rejoice, to rise to His feet and embrace His beloved son when Jesus stopped him with a gesture and said, On one condition, But you know perfectly well you cannot lay down conditions, God replied angrily, Then let's call it a plea rather than a condition, the simple plea of a man sentenced to death, Tell me, You are God and, therefore, can only speak the truth when asked a question, and being God, You know the past, the present, what lies between them, and what the future will bring, That is so, I am time, truth and life, Then tell me, in the name of all You claim to be, what will the future bring after my death, what will the future bring which would otherwise not be there unless I had accepted to sacrifice myself because of your dissatisfaction, and this desire of Yours to reign wide and far. God responded angrily, as if trapped by His own words, and made a half-hearted attempt to shrug it off, Now then, son, the future is infinite and would take a long time to measure, How long have we been out here in the middle of the lake and surrounded by mist, asked Jesus, perhaps for a day, a month, a year, well then let's stay here for another year, month or day, allow the Devil to leave if he wants to, for in any case his share is guaranteed, and if the benefits are proportionate, as seems just, the more God prospers, the more the Devil will prosper, I'm staying, said Pastor, and these were the first words he spoke since revealing his identity, I'm staying, he said for a second time before adding, I myself can see certain things belonging to the future, but I'm not always certain if what I see there is true or false, that's to say, I can see my lies for what they are, in other words, my truths, but I don't know to what extent the truths of others are their lies. This tortuous outburst could have been rounded off nicely if Pastor had said something more about the future he envisaged, but he abruptly fell silent as if aware of having said far too much already. Jesus, who had not averted his eyes from God, said with a note of wistful irony, Why pretend to ignore what You know, You realized I would ask this question, and know very well You will tell me what I want to hear, so postpone no longer my time for dying, You began dying the moment you were born, True, but now I shall die all the sooner, God looked at Jesus with an expression which in a person we would have described as respectful, his whole manner became human, and, although the one thing did not appear to have anything to do with the other, we shall never know the deep links that exist between things and actions, the mist advanced towards the boat, surrounded it like an insurmountable wall in order to keep from the world God's words about the effects and consequences of the sacrifice of Jesus whom He claims as His son and that of Mary, but whose real father is Joseph, according to the unwritten law which commands us to believe only in what we see, although, as everyone knows, we humans do not always see things in the same way and this has undoubtedly helped to preserve the relative sanity of the species.

God said, There will be a Church which, as you are aware, means an assembly or gathering, a religious society which will be founded by you or in your name, which basically comes to the same thing, and this Church will spread far and wide throughout the world and be called catholic, because universal, although sadly this will not prevent discord and misunderstanding amongst those who will see you rather than Me, as their spiritual leader although this will only last for several thousand years, for I was here before you and I will continue to be here after you cease to be what you are and will be, Speak clearly, interrupted Jesus, It's impossible, said God, for human words are like shadows, and shadows are incapable of explaining light and between shadows and light there is the opaque body from which words are born. I asked You about the future, It's the future I'm talking about, What I want to know is how the men who come after me will live, Are you referring to your followers, Yes, will they be happier, Not in the true sense of the word, but they will have the hope of achieving happiness up there in heaven where I reign for all eternity, and where they may hope to live eternally with Me, Is that all, Surely it is no small thing to live with God, Small, great, or everything, we shall only discover after the Day of Final Judgement when You will judge men according to the good or evil they have done and until then You reside alone in heaven, My angels and archangels keep Me company, But You don't have any human beings there, True, and you must be crucified in order that they may come to Me, I want to know more, said Jesus vehemently, anxious to shut out the mental image of himself hanging from a cross, covered in blood and dead, What I'd like to know is how people will come to believe in me and follow me, don't try to tell me that anything I may say to them or those who come after me may say to them in my name will be enough, take the Gentiles and Romans, for example, who worship other gods, surely You don't expect me to believe they will give them up to worship me just like that, Not to worship you but Me, But You yourself said that You and I are one and the same, however, don't let's play with words, just answer my question, Whoever has faith will come to us, Just like that, as easily as You've just said, The other gods will resist, And You will fight them, of course, Don't be absurd, such things only occur on earth, heaven is eternal and peaceful, men fulfil their destiny wherever they may be, Let me get this straight, even though words are but shadows, men will die for You and for me, Men have always died for the gods, even for false and mendacious gods, Can the gods speak false, They can, And You are the one and only true god amongst them, Yes, the one and only true god, Yet You are unable to prevent men from dying for You when they should have been born to live for You on earth rather than in heaven where You have none of life's joys to offer them, Those joys, too, are deceptive for they originated with original sin, ask your friend, Pastor, he'll explain what happened, If there are any secrets You and the Devil do not share, I hope one of them is what I learned from him even though he insists I've learned nothing. There was silence, God and the Devil confronted each other for the first time, both giving the impression of being about to say something, but nothing happened. Jesus said, I'm waiting, For what, asked God, as if distracted, For You to tell me how much death and suffering Your victory over other gods will cost, how much suffering and death will be needed to justify the battles men will fight in Your name and mine, You insist on knowing, Yes, I do, Very well then, the assembly I mentioned will be founded, but in order to be truly solid, its foundations will be dug out in flesh, and the bases made from the cement of abnegation, tears, suffering, torment, every conceivable form of death known or as yet unrevealed, At long last, You're starting to make sense, carry on. Let's start with someone whom you know and love, the fisherman Simon, whom you will call Peter, like you, he will be crucified, but upside down, Andrew, too, will be crucified on a cross in the shape of an X, the son of Zebedee, known as James, will be beheaded, And what about John and Mary Magdalene, They will die of natural causes when their time comes, but you will make other friends, disciples and apostles like the others, who will not escape torture, friends such as Philip who will be tied to a cross and stoned to death, Bartholomew who will be skinned alive, Thomas who will be speared to death, Matthew, the details of whose death I no longer remember, another Simon who will be sawn in half, Judas who will be beaten to death, James stoned, Matthias beheaded with an axe, also Judas Iscariot, but as you will know better than me, spared death but strung from a fig tree by his own hands, Are all these men about to die because of You, asked Jesus, If you phrase the question in that way, the answer is Yes, they will die for My sake, And then what, Then, my son, as I've already told you, there will be an endless tale of iron and blood, of fire and ashes, an infinite sea of sorrow and tears, Tell me, I want to know everything. God sighed, and, in the monotonous tone of someone who preferred to suppress compassion and mercy, He began a litany in alphabetical order rather than offend any susceptibilities about order of precedence, Adalbert of Prague, put to death with a pikestaff with seven points, Adrian, hammered to death over an anvil, Afra of Augsburg, burnt at the stake, Agapitus of Praeneste, burnt at the stake hanging by his feet, Agnes of Rome, disembowelled, Agricola of Bologna, crucified and impaled on nails, Agueda of Sicily, stabbed six times, Alphege of Canterbury, beaten to death with the shinbone of an ox, Anastasia of Sirmium, burnt at the stake and her breasts cut off, Anastasius of Salona, strung up on the gallows and decapitated, Ansanus of Siena, his entrails ripped out, Antonius of Pamiers, drawn and quartered, Antony of Rivoli, stoned and burnt alive, Apollinaris of Ravenna, clubbed to death, Apollonia of Alexandria, burnt at the stake after her teeth have been knocked out, Augusta of Treviso, decapitated and burnt at the stake, Aurea of Ostia, drowned with a millstone round her neck, Aurea of Syria, bled to death by being forced on to a chair covered with nails, Auta, shot with arrows, Babylas of Antioch, decapitated, Barbara of Nicomedia, likewise, Barnabas of Cyprus, stoned and burnt at the stake, Beatrice of Rome, strangled, Benignus of Dijon, speared to death, Blandina of Lyons, gored by a savage bull, Blaise of Sebasta, thrown on to iron spikes, Callistus, put to death with a millstone round his neck, Cassian of Imola, stabbed with a dagger by his disciples, Castulus, buried alive, Catherine of Alexandria, decapitated, Cecilia of Rome, beheaded, Christina of Bolsena, tortured again and again with millstones, tongs, arrows and snakes, Clarus of Nastes, decapitated, Clarus of Vienne, likewise, Clement, drowned with an anchor fixed round his neck, Crispin and Crispinian of Soissons, both decapitated, Cucuphas of Barcelona, disembowelled, Cyprian of Carthage, beheaded, young Cyricus of Tarsus, killed by a judge who knocked his head against the stairs of the tribunal, and on reaching the end of the letter C, God said, from now it's all much the same with few variations apart from the odd refinement which would take forever to explain, so let's leave it at that, No, go on, said Jesus, so, reluctantly, God continued, abbreviating wherever possible, Donatus of Arezzo, decapitated, Eliphius of Rampillon, scalped, Emerita, burnt alive, Emilian of Trevi, decapitated, Emmeramus of Regensburg, tied to a ladder and put to death, Engratia of Saragossa, decapitated, Erasmus of Gaeta, also called Elmo, stretched on a windlass, Escubiculus, beheaded, Eskil of Sweden, stoned to death, Eulalia of Merida, decapitated, Euphemia of Chalcedon, put to the sword, Eutropius of Saintes, beheaded with an axe, Fabian, stabbed and spiked, Faith of Agen, beheaded, Felicity and her seven sons, beheaded with a sword, Felix and his brother Adauctus, likewise, Ferreolus of Besançon, decapitated, Fidelis of Sigmaringen, beaten to death with a spiked club, Firminus of Pamplona, beheaded, Flavia Domitilla, likewise, Fortunas of Evora, probably met the same fate, Fructoasus of Tarragon, burnt at the stake, Gaudentius of France, decapitated, Gelasius, likewise with more iron spikes, Gengolf of Burgundy, cuckolded and assassinated by his wife's lover, Gerard Sagreda of Budapest, speared to death, Gerean of Cologne, decapitated, the twins Gervase and Protase, likewise, Godleva and Ghistelles, strangled, Gratus of Aosta, decapitated, Hermenegild, clubbed to death, Hero, stabbed with a sword, Hippolytus, dragged to his death by a horse, Ignatius of Azevedo, murdered by the Calvinists who are not Catholics, Januarius of Naples, decapitated after being thrown to wild beasts and then thrown into a furnace, Joan of Arc, burnt at the stake, John de Britto, beheaded, John Fisher, decapitated, John of Nepomuk, drowned in the river Vltava, John of Prado, stabbed in the head, Julia of Corsica, whose breasts were cut off before she was crucified, Juliana of Nicomedia, decapitated, Justa and Ruffina of Seville, the former killed on the wheel, the latter strangled, Justina of Antioch, thrown into a cauldron of boiling tar and then beheaded, Justus and Pastor, not our Pastor but the one from Alcalá de Henares, decapitated, Kilian of Würzburg, decapitated, Lawrence, burnt on a grid, Léger of Autun, also decapitated after his eyes and tongue had been torn out, Leocadia of Toledo, thrown to her death from a high cliff, Livinus of Ghent, decapitated after his tongue had been torn out, Longinus, decapitated, Ludmila of Prague, strangled, Lucy of Syracuse, beheaded after having her eyes plucked out, Maginus of Tarragon, decapitated with a serrated scythe, Mamas of Cappodocia, disembowelled, Manuel, Sabel and Ismael, Manuel put to death with an iron nail embedded in each nipple and an iron rod driven through his head from ear to ear, all three of them beheaded, Margaret of Antioch, killed with a firebrand and an iron comb, Maria Goretti, strangled, Marius of Persia, put to the sword and his hands amputated, Martina of Rome, decapitated, the martyrs of Morocco, Berard of Carbio, Peter of Gimignano, Otto, Adjuto and Accursio, beheaded, those of Japan, all twenty-six crucified, speared and burnt alive, Maurice of Agaune, put to the sword, Meinrad of Einsiedeln, clubbed to death, Menas of Alexandria, also put to the sword, Mercurius of Cappadocia, decapitated, Nicasius of Rheims, likewise, Odilia of Huy, shot with arrows, Paneras, beheaded, Pantaleon of Nicomedia, likewise, Paphnutius, crucified, Patroclus of Troyes and Soest, likewise, Paul of Tarsus, to whom you will owe your first church, likewise, Pelagius, drawn and quartered, Peter of Rates, killed with a sword, Peter of Verona, his head slashed with a cutlass and a dagger driven into his chest, Perpetua and her slave Felicity of Carthage, both gored by a raging bull, Philomena, shot with arrows and anchored, Piaton of Tournai, scalped, Polycarp, stabbed and burnt alive, Prisca of Rome, devoured by lions, Processus and Martinian probably met the same fate, Quintinus, nails driven into his head and other parts of his body, Quirinus of Rouen, scalped, Quiteria of Coimbra, decapitated by her own father, Reine of Alise, put to the sword, Renaud of Dortmund, bludgeoned to death with a mason's mallet, Restituta of Naples, burnt at the stake, Roland, put to the sword, Romanus of Antioch, strangled to death after his tongue had been torn out, Are you still not satisfied, God asked Jesus who retorted, That's something You ought to be asking Yourself, carry on, So God continued, Sabinian of Sens, beheaded, Sabinus of Assisi, stoned to death, Saturninus of Toulouse, dragged to his death by a bull, Sebastian, pierced by arrows, Secundus of Asti, decapitated, Servatius of Tongres and Maastricht, killed by a blow to the head with a wooden clog, Severus of Barcelona, killed by having nails embedded in his head, Sidwell of Exeter, decapitated, Sigismund, King of Burgundy, thrown into a well, Stephen, stoned to death, Sixtus, decapitated, Symphorian of Autun, likewise, Taresius, stoned to death, Thecla of Iconium, mutilated and burnt alive, Theodore, burnt at the stake, Thomas Becket of Canterbury, a sword driven into his skull, Thomas More, beheaded, Thyrsus, sawn in half, Tiburtius, beheaded, Timothy of Ephesus, stoned to death, Torquatus and the Twenty-Seven, killed by General Muça at the gates of Guimarães, Tropez of Pisa, decapitated, Urbanus, Valeria of Limoges, and Valerian and Venantius of Camerino met the same fate, Victor, decapitated, Victor of Marseilles, beheaded, Victoria of Rome, put to death after having her tongue pulled out, Vincent of Saragossa, tortured to death with millstone, grid and spikes, Virgilius of Trent, beaten to death with a wooden clog, Vitalis of Ravenna, put to the sword, Wilgefortis, or Livrade, or Eutropia, the bearded virgin, crucified, and so on and so forth and all of them meeting similar fates. That's not good enough, said Jesus, to what others are You referring, Do you really have to know, I do, I'm referring to those who escaped martyrdom and died from natural causes after having suffered the torments of the world, the flesh and the devil, and who in order to overcome them had to mortify their bodies with fasting and prayer, there is even the amusing case of a certain John Schorn who spent so much time on his knees praying that he ended up with corns on his knees, of all places, and he's also reputed, and this will interest you, to have shut the devil inside a boot, ha, ha, ha, Me, in a boot, said Pastor scornfully, these are old wives' tales, any boot capable of holding me would have to be as vast as the world, and, besides, I'd like to see who would be capable of putting the boot on and taking it off afterwards, Perhaps only with fasting and prayer, suggested Jesus, whereupon God replied, They will also mortify the flesh with suffering and blood and grime, and innumerable other penances, with hair shirts and flagellation, there will even be some who scarcely ever wash and others who throw themselves on to brambles and roll in the snow to suppress carnal desires which are the work of Satan who sends these temptations with the intention of luring souls from the strait and narrow path which leads to heaven, visions of naked women, terrifying monsters, abominable creatures, lust and fear, weapons used by the Demon to torment the wretched existence of mankind, Is this true, Jesus asked Pastor, who replied, More or less, I simply took what God didn't want, the flesh with all its joys and sorrows, youth and senility, bloom and decay, but it isn't true that fear is one of my weapons, I don't recall having invented sin and punishment or the terror they inspire, Be quiet, God interrupted sharply, sin and the Devil are one and the same thing, What thing, asked Jesus, My absence, How do you explain Your absence, is it because You retreat or because mankind abandons You, I never retreat, never, Yet You allow men to abandon You, Whosoever abandons Me comes looking for Me, And when they cannot find You, I suppose You blame the Devil, No, he's not to blame, I'm to blame because I'm incapable of reaching out to those who seek Me, words uttered by God with a poignant and unexpected melancholy, as if He had suddenly discovered the limitations of His power. Jesus told Him, Go on, There are others, God continued slowly, who withdraw into the wilderness where they lead a solitary life in caves and grottoes and with nothing but animals for company, others who choose a monastic existence, others who climb to the top of high pillars and live there year in year out, others, His voice fell and died away, God was now contemplating an endless procession of people, thousands upon thousands of men and women throughout the world entering convents and monasteries, some rustic dwellings, many of them palatial buildings, There they will remain to serve you and Me from morning until night, with vigils and prayers, all with the same mission and destiny, to worship us and die with our names on their lips, they will use different names, be known as Augustinians, Benedictines, Capuchins, Carmelites, Carthusians, Cistercians, Dominicans, Franciscans, Gilbertines, Jesuits, Trinitarians, and there will be so many of them that I should dearly like to be able to exclaim, My God, why so many. At this point, the Devil said to Jesus, Note from what He has told us that there are two ways of losing one's life, either through martyrdom or by renunciation, it wasn't enough for all these people to have died when their time came, in one way or another they ran to meet their death, crucified, disembowelled, beheaded, burnt at the stake, stoned, drowned, drawn and quartered, skinned alive, speared, gored, buried alive, sawn in two, shot with arrows, mutilated, tortured, within or outside their cells, chapter-houses and cloisters, doing penance and mortifying the flesh God gave them without which they would have nowhere to rest their soul, these punishments were not invented by the Devil who is talking to you. Is that all, Jesus asked God, No, there are still the wars, and the massacres, No need to tell me about the massacres, I might even have died in one, and thinking it over, what a pity I didn't, for then I would have been spared the crucifixion awaiting me, It was I who led your other father to the place where he overheard the soldiers' conversation and therefore saved your life, You only saved my life in order to ordain my death at Your pleasure and convenience as if prepared to kill me twice, The end justifies the means, My son, From what You have told me so far I can well believe it, renunciation, cloisters, suffering, death, and now wars and massacres, but what wars are these, One war after another and everlasting, especially those waged against you and Me in the name of a god who has yet to appear, How can there possibly be a god who still has to appear, any true god can only have existed for ever and ever, I know it's difficult to understand or explain, but what I'm telling you will come to pass, a god will rise against us and our followers, entire nations, no, no, there are no words to describe the massacres, bloodshed and slaughter, try to imagine my altar in Jerusalem multiplied a thousandfold, replace the sacrificial animals with men, and even then you will have no idea what those crusades were like, Crusades, what are they and why do You refer to them in the past if they still have to take place, Remember, I am time and so for Me all that is about to happen has already happened, all that has happened goes on happening every day, Tell me more about these crusades, Well, My son, these parts where we now find ourselves, including Jerusalem, and other territories to the north and west, will be conquered by the followers of the god I mentioned who has been slow in coming, the followers of those on our side will do everything possible to expel them from the places you have travelled and I constantly frequent, You haven't done much to rid this place of the Romans, Don't distract me, I'm talking about the future, Carry on, then, Furthermore, you were born, lived and died here, But I'm not dead yet, That's irrelevant for, as I've just explained to you, as far as I'm concerned, for something to happen and have happened comes to the same thing, and please, stop interrupting otherwise I'll say no more, All right, I'll be quiet, Now then, future generations will refer to these parts as the Holy Places, because you were born, lived and died here, so it didn't seem fitting that the cradle of the religion you will represent should fall into the unworthy hands of infidels, this was sufficient reason to justify the invasions of those great armies from the west who for almost two hundred years tried to conquer and preserve for Christianity the cave where you were born and the hill where you will die, to mention only the most important landmarks, Are these armies the crusades, That's right, And did they conquer what they wanted, No, but they slaughtered many people, And what about the crusaders themselves, They lost just as many lives if not more, And all this bloodshed in our name, They will go into battle crying out, God wills it, And no doubt died crying out, God willed it, Such a nice way to end one's life, Once again, the sacrifice isn't worth it, In order to save one's soul, my son, the body must be sacrificed, I've heard You use much the same words before, and what about you, Pastor, what do you say about these amazing events which lie ahead, No one in his right mind can possibly suggest that the Devil was, is, or ever will be responsible for so much bloodshed and death, unless some villain brings up that wicked slander accusing me of having conceived the god who will oppose this one here, It strikes me that you are not to blame and should anyone hold you responsible you need only reply that if the Devil is false then he could never create a true god, Then who will create this hostile god, asked Pastor. Jesus was at a loss for an answer and God, who had been silent, remained silent, but a voice came down from the mist and said, Perhaps this God and the one yet to come are one and the same god, Jesus, God and the Devil pretended not to hear but could not help looking at each other in alarm, mutual fear is like this and readily unites enemies.

Time passed, the mist did not speak again and Jesus asked, now with the voice of someone who only expects an affirmative reply, Nothing more. God hesitated, and then, in a tired tone of voice, said, There is still the Inquisition, but if you don't mind, we'll discuss that at some other time, What is the Inquisition, The Inquisition is another long story, Tell me more, It's best you shouldn't know, But I insist, You will only suffer remorse today which belongs to the future, And You won't, God is God and suffers no remorse, Well, since I'm already bearing this burden of having to die for You, I can also withstand the remorse that ought to be Yours, I wanted to protect you, You've done nothing else since the day I was born, Like most children, you're ungrateful, Let's stop all this pretence and tell me about the Inquisition, Also known as the Tribunal of the Holy Office, the Inquisition is a necessary evil, we shall use this cruellest of instruments to combat the disease that will persistently infiltrate the body of your Church in the form of wicked heresies and their harmful consequences along with a number of physical and moral perversions, which if lumped together without regard for order or precedence will include Lutherans and Calvinists, Molinists and Judaizers, sodomites and sorcerers, some of these plagues belonging to the future, others which can be found in every age, And if the Inquisition is a necessary evil, as You claim, how will it go about eliminating these heresies, The Inquisition is a police force, a tribunal, and will, therefore, pursue, judge and sentence its enemies like any other tribunal or police force, Sentence them to what, To prison, exile, the stake, Did You say the stake, Yes, in days to come, thousands upon thousands of men and women will be burnt at the stake, You mentioned some of them earlier, They will be burnt alive because they have believed in you, others because they will doubt you. Isn't it permitted to doubt me, No, Yet we're allowed to question whether the Jupiter of the Romans is god, I am the one and only Lord God and you are My son, You say thousands will die, Hundreds of thousands, Hundreds of thousands of men and women will die and on earth there will be much sighing and weeping and cries of anguish, the smoke from charred corpses will blot out the sun, human flesh will sizzle over live coals, the stench will be nauseating, and all this will be my fault. You're not to blame, your cause exacts this suffering, Father, take from me this cup, My power and your glory demand that you should drink to the last drop, I don't want this glory, But I want that power. The mist began to lift and around the boat water could be seen, smooth, sombre water without so much as a ripple of wind or the tremor of a passing fin. Then the Devil interrupted, One has to be God to enjoy so much bloodshed.

The mist started advancing again, something else was about to happen, some revelation, some new sorrow or remorse. But it was Pastor who spoke, I've a proposal to make, he said, addressing God, and God, taken aback, replied, A proposal from you, and what proposal might that be, his tone was cynical and forbidding and would have reduced most people to silence, but then the Devil was an old acquaintance. Pastor remained silent as if searching for the right words before explaining, I've been listening carefully to all that has been said here in this boat and although I myself have caught glimpses of the light and darkness ahead, I never realized the light was coming from the burning stakes and the shadows from innumerable corpses, Does this bother you, It shouldn't really bother me since I'm the Devil and the Devil always profits from death, even more than You do, for it goes without saying that Hell is much more crowded than Heaven, Then why are you complaining, I'm not complaining, I'm making a proposal, Go ahead but be quick for I cannot be loitering here for all eternity, No one knows better than You that the Devil also has a heart, Yes, but you make poor use of it, Today I intend to use it by acknowledging and hoping that Your power will spread to the ends of the earth without any further need of so many deaths, and since You insist that anything which thwarts and denies You is the fruit of the Evil I represent and govern in this world, I propose that You should receive me into Your Heavenly Kingdom, my past offences redeemed by those I shall not commit in future, that You accept and preserve my obedience as in those happy days when I was one of Your chosen angels, Lucifer, You called me, the bearer of light, before my ambition to become Your equal consumed my soul and made me rebel against Your authority, And would you care to tell Me why I should pardon you and receive you into My Kingdom, Because if You were to do so and grant me that same pardon which one day You will promise so readily right and left, then Evil will cease at once, Your son will not have to die, and Your Kingdom will extend beyond the land of the Hebrews to embrace the entire world, whether known or yet to be discovered, Good will prevail everywhere and I shall sing amongst the lowliest of the angels who have remained faithful, more faithful than all of them now that I have repented, shall sing Your praises, all will end as if it had never been, all will start to become what it should always have been, I've always known you have a talent for confusing and losing souls, but I have never heard you make such a speech with such conviction and eloquence, you've almost won Me over, So You won't accept or pardon me, No, I neither accept nor pardon you, I much prefer you as you are and, were it possible, I'd prefer you to become even worse than you are, But why, Because the Good I represent cannot exist without the Evil you represent, it is inconceivable that any Good might exist without you, so much so that it defies imagination and, in short, if you were to come to an end, so would I, for Me to be Goodness, it is essential that you should continue to be Evil, unless the Devil lives like the Devil, God cannot live like God, the death of the one would mean the death of the other. Is that Your final word, My first and last, first, because that was the first time I said it, final because I have no intention of repeating it. Pastor shrugged his shoulders and addressed Jesus, Never let it be said the Devil didn't tempt Jesus one day, and getting to his feet, he was about to pass one leg over the side of the boat when he suddenly paused and said, In your knapsack there is something belonging to me. Jesus could not remember having brought the knapsack on to the boat, but, in fact, there it was, rolled up at his feet, What thing, he asked, and, on opening the knapsack found there was nothing inside apart from the old black bowl he had brought from Nazareth, That's it, that's it, replied the Devil picking up the bowl with both hands, One day this will be yours again, but you won't even know you have it. He tucked the bowl inside his shepherd's tunic of coarse cloth and lowered himself into the water. Without looking at God, he simply said, as if addressing an invisible audience, Farewell for evermore, since that is what He has ordained. Jesus followed him with his eyes as Pastor gradually moved off in the direction of the mist, he had forgotten to ask him what had possessed him to swim all the way here and back, Seen from afar, he once more looked like a pig with pointed ears and he was panting furiously, but anyone with a keen ear would have had no difficulty in noticing that there was also a note of fear there, not of drowning, what an idea, for the Devil, as we have just discovered, has no ending, but of having to exist forever. Pastor was already disappearing behind the broken fringe of the mist when God's voice suddenly rang out bidding an abrupt farewell, I shall send someone called John to help, but you will have to prove to him that you are who you say you are. Jesus looked round, but God was no longer there. Just then the mist lifted, vanished into thin air, leaving the sea clear and smooth from point to point between the mountains, there was no sign of the Devil in the water, no sign of God in the air.

On the bank from where he had come, Jesus, notwithstanding the distance, could see a large crowd with lots of tents pitched in the background, to all appearances a permanent settlement for people who did not live there and who, having nowhere to sleep, had organized themselves as best they could. Somewhat intrigued, but nothing more, Jesus lowered the oars into the water and guided his boat in that direction. On looking over his shoulder, he sighted boats being pushed into the water, and, on taking a closer look, saw Simon and Andrew, James and John inside them along with others whom he could not remember ever having seen before in these parts. Rowing hard, they soon caught up and came within speaking distance. Simon called out, Where have you been, obviously this was not what he wanted to know but he had to begin somewhere, Here at sea, replied Jesus, an answer as futile as the question, and communications really seemed to be getting off to a bad start in this new phase in the life of the son of God, Mary and Joseph. Within seconds Simon was clambering into Jesus's boat and the incomprehensible, impossible, and absurd was revealed. Do you know how long you've been out there in the middle of the sea in all that mist, while we tried in vain to launch our boats only to be pushed back by strong winds, asked Simon. All day, replied Jesus, before adding, all day and night, in an attempt to satisfy Simon's eager curiosity, Forty days, shouted Simon, then lowering his voice, he repeated, You've been out there forty days, and during all that time the mist never lifted as if hiding something from us, whatever were you doing out there, we haven't caught a single fish in these waters during the last forty days. Jesus passed one of the oars to Simon and both of them were rowing and conversing in harmony, shoulder to shoulder, moving at a steady pace ideal for exchanging confidences, and before any of the other boats could get closer, Jesus said, I've been with God and I know what the future holds for me, how long I shall live and the life that awaits me after this life, What is He like, I mean what does God look like, God does not appear in only one guise, He sometimes appears as a cloud, as a column of smoke, even turns up dressed like a wealthy Jew, one need only hear His voice once in order to know Him, What did He say to you, He told me I'm His Son, Did He confirm it, Yes, He confirmed it, So, the Devil was right when that episode with the pigs occurred, The Devil was also here in the boat and overheard

301

everything, he seems to know as much about me as God, and sometimes I think he knows even more than God, And where, Where what, Where were they, The Devil was on one side of the boat, right there between where you are and the bench near the stern where God was sitting, What did God say to you, That I am His son and I shall be crucified, If you're going to the mountains to fight on the rebel side we'll come with you, You will come with me, but not to the mountains, what matters is not to conquer Caesar with arms, but to make God triumph with words, With words alone, Also by giving good example, and by sacrificing our lives, if necessary, Are these your Father's words, Henceforth all my words will be His, and those who believe in Him will believe in me, for it is impossible to believe in the Father without believing in the Son, since the new path the Father has chosen for himself can only begin with me, His son, When you said we would come with you, to whom were you referring, First of all to you, then to Andrew, your brother, to the sons of Zebedee, James and John, which reminds me that God told me He would send someone called John to assist me, but he cannot be the same John, We don't need anyone else, after all, this isn't one of Herod's ceremonial processions, Others will come and perhaps some are already there awaiting God's sign, a sign God will manifest through me, so that those to whom He has not revealed himself may believe and follow me, What are you going to tell the people, That they must repent of their sins, and prepare themselves for God's new era which is about to dawn, an era in which His Flaming Sword will bend the necks of those who have rejected and vilified His Holy Word, At least, you must tell them you're the Son of God, I'll say my Father called me His son and that I have carried these words in my heart since the day I was born, and that God himself has now come to claim me as His son, one father does not make one forget the other, but the one giving orders today is God the Father, so let us obey Him, Then leave this to me, said Simon, suddenly dropping his oar and moving to the prow, and now within hearing distance, he called out in a loud voice, Hosannah, the Son of God approaches, he who has spent forty days at sea conversing with his Father and now returns to us so that we may repent and prepare ourselves. Don't mention that the Devil was also there, Jesus quickly warned him, fearful lest he should have great difficulty in explaining the situation if it became

302

public knowledge. Simon gave another cry, but louder this time, causing great excitement amongst the crowds gathered on the shore, before rushing back to his seat and telling Jesus, Leave the rowing to me, you go and stand on the prow, but say nothing, not a single word, until we get ashore. And so they arrived, Jesus standing on the boat's prow in his worn tunic and with his empty knapsack over his shoulder, his arms half raised as if he were about to greet someone or bestow his blessing but restrained by shyness or a lack of confidence in his own worth. Amongst those waiting, three men in particular were so impatient that they waded in until the water came up to their waist. On reaching the boat, they began pushing and pulling while one of them with his free hand tried to touch Jesus's tunic, not because he believed what Simon had said, but intrigued by the mystery of this man who had been out at sea for forty days as if searching for God in the desert and now returning from the cold depths of a mountain of mist, where he might or might not have seen God. Needless to say, people were speaking of nothing else in the vicinity and outlying villages and many of those gathered on the shore had come to see this meteorological phenomenon for themselves, and when they heard there was a man trapped in that mist, they muttered, Poor fellow. The boat glided to its destination as if carried on the wings of angels. Simon helped Jesus to step ashore, and visibly irritated, shook off the three men who had jumped into the water and thought themselves deserving of better treatment, Leave them alone, said Jesus, one day they will hear of my death and regret not having been there to bear my corpse, so let them accompany me while I'm still alive. Jesus climbed a knoll and asked his companions, Where is Mary, and no sooner had he asked than he saw her. It was as if the mere sound of her name had released her from some void or mist, one moment she was nowhere to be seen but the moment he uttered her name, she was there, I'm here, Jesus, Come here beside me, you, too, Simon and Andrew, and James and John, sons of Zebedee, for all of you trust and believe in me, trusted and believed in me when I was unable to confide that I'm the Son of God, this son who was sum-moned by God the Father and spent forty days with Him at sea before returning to tell you that the hour of the Lord has come, and that you must repent before the Devil arrives to gather the rotting ears of corn that may have fallen from the harvest God carries in His lap, for you are those rotting ears of corn if in sinning you have escaped from God's loving embrace. A murmur went through the crowd, passing over their heads like those tiny waves which had reappeared on the surface of the water, many of those present had, in fact, heard of the miracles performed elsewhere by this man standing there, some had seen them with their own eyes or even been the beneficiaries of these miracles, I ate that bread and fish, said one bystander, I drank that wine, said another, I was the neighbour of that adulteress, said a third, but however transcendent these wonders might be or seem, they were eclipsed by the sublime moment when Jesus was proclaimed the Son of God, and therefore, God himself, This wondrous revelation is as remote from those other miracles as the earth from the sky, and to the best of our knowledge, the distance between them has never been measured to this day. A voice rose from the crowd, Prove to us that you're the Son of God and I shall follow you, You would follow me forever if your heart were not locked away inside your breast, you ask for the proof your senses could have grasped, very well then, I'll give you proof that will satisfy your senses but be rejected by your mind until torn between mind and senses you'll have no alternative other than to come to me through your heart, Whatever that means, for I haven't understood a word, scoffed the man, What is your name, asked Jesus, Thomas, Come here, Thomas, accompany me to the water's edge, come and watch me make some birds with handfuls of clay, see how easy it is, I form the shape of the body and wings, model the head and beak, set in these tiny stones for the eyes, adjust the long feathers of the tail, balance the legs and claws, and once this is done I make eleven more, look here, one, two, three, four, five, six, seven, eight, nine, ten, eleven, twelve birds all made of mud, just think, we could even, if you like, give them names, this is Simon, this one James, this one Andrew, this one John, and this one, if you don't mind, will be called Thomas, as for the others let's wait until their names appear, names often get delayed en route and turn up later, and now watch me, I throw the net over the little birds to prevent them from escaping, for escape they will unless we're careful, Are you trying to tell me that if this net were to be lifted the birds would escape, Thomas asked in disbelief, Yes, if the net were lifted, the birds would certainly escape, Is this the proof you hoped would convince me, Yes and no, What do you mean, yes and no, The best proof, although it doesn't depend on me, would be for you not to lift the net and to believe that the birds would escape if you were to lift it, But birds made of clay cannot possibly escape, Try, even Adam, our first father, was made of clay and you're one of his descendants, It was God who gave Adam life, Doubt no more, Thomas, and lift the net, for I am the Son of God, Well if you say so, here goes, but I promise you these birds won't fly, and without further ado Thomas lifted the net and, once free, the birds took flight. Twittering with excitement, they circled twice above the astonished crowd before disappearing into space. Jesus said, Look, Thomas, your bird has gone, whereupon Thomas replied, No, Lord, I'm the bird, kneeling here at your feet.

Some of the men in the crowd surged forward, and several women behind them did the same. They drew near and gave their names, I am Philip, and Jesus saw stones and a cross, I am Bartholomew, and Jesus saw a flayed torso, I am Matthew, and Jesus saw his corpse amongst barbarians, I am Simon, and Jesus could see the saw that would sever his body, I am James, son of Alphaeus, and Jesus could see him being stoned to death, I am Judas Thaddaeus, and Jesus saw a club being raised over his head, I am Judas Iscariot, and Jesus took pity on him for he could see him hang himself from a fig tree. Then Jesus called the others and said, Now that we are all here, the hour has come. And turning to Simon, the brother of Andrew, he told him, Because we have another Simon with us, you Simon, will henceforth be known as Peter. Turning their backs on the sea, the men started walking, followed by the women, most of whose names we never learned, not that it matters, for most of them are called Mary and the rest will answer to that name, a man need only exclaim, Woman, or Mary, and they will look up and come to do his bidding.

Jesus and his disciples travelled from one village to the next and God spoke through Jesus, and here is what He said, Time has run full circle and the Kingdom of God is at hand, repent and have faith in this good news. On hearing this, the local inhabitants could find no difference between time running full circle and time coming to an end, and, therefore, believed the end of the world must be fast approaching which is where time is measured and consumed. They thanked God for having mercifully sent advance warning of their impending fate with someone who claimed to be His Son, which might well be true since he worked miracles wherever he passed, provided those seeking his help showed genuine faith and conviction, as in the case of the leper who pleaded, If you so choose, you can cleanse me, and Jesus, taking pity on the poor wretch covered in festering sores, laid his hand on him and commanded, It is my wish that you should be cleansed, and no sooner were these words spoken than the ulcers healed, his diseased body was restored to health and the leper from whom everyone had fled in horror was now free from any blemishes and looked perfectly fit and normal. Another remarkable cure was that of the paralytic. Such an enormous crowd had gathered round the door that the sick man had to be hoisted up on his bed, then lowered through an opening in the roof of the house where Jesus was staying, which probably belonged to Simon, also known as Peter. Moved by their deep faith, Jesus told the sick man, My Son, your sins are forgiven, but it so happened that some mistrusting scribes had turned up anxious to find some cause for complaint, always ready to quote from Holy Law, and when they heard what Jesus said, they lost no time in protesting, How dare you say such things, this is blasphemy, only God may pardon, whereupon Jesus asked, Is it easier to say to those sick of the palsy, Your sins are forgiven, than to say, Arise, take up your bed and walk, and without waiting for an answer he continued, But so that you may know that the Son of Man has power on earth to forgive sins, I say unto you, turning to the paralytic, Arise, take up your bed and go your way into your house, and with these words the man miraculously got to his feet, his strength suddenly restored after being immobile for so long, and taking up the bed, he lifted it on to his shoulders and off he went praising and thanking God.

Obviously, we do not all go around seeking miracles. In time we get used to our little aches and pains and learn to live with them, without ever thinking of importuning the divine powers. Sins, however, are a quite different matter, they get under our skin and torment us, unlike a crippled leg, a paralysed arm, or the ravages of leprosy, sins fester inwardly. So God knew what He was talking about when He told Jesus that every man has at least one sin, if not more, to repent. Now since this world is about to end and the Kingdom of God is at hand, rather than enter it with our body restored by miraculous means, it is much more important that we should be guided by our soul, purified by repentance and healed by forgiveness. Besides, if the paralytic from Capernaum spent much of his life on a bed, it was because he sinned, for, as we all know, sickness is the outcome of sin, therefore we may safely conclude that the essential requirement for good health, as for the immortality of our soul, and perhaps even our body, can only be the utmost purity, a complete absence of sin, either through passive and blessed ignorance or through active repudiation, both in thought and deed. Let no one think however that our Jesus journeyed through these lands squandering his power to heal and his authority to pardon sins granted him by the Lord himself. Not that he would not have liked to, obviously, for by inclination he would have preferred to become a universal panacea, rather than be obliged by God to announce the end of time and urge men to repent. And so that sinners should not lose too much time in meditation rather than face up to the difficult decision of confessing, I have sinned, the Lord put certain terrifying threats into Jesus's mouth which went as follows, In truth, I say to you that some of you who are present here will not experience death before seeing the Kingdom of God arrive with all its majesty. Just imagine the devastating effect those words must have had on the conscience of all those people who anxiously flocked from everywhere to follow Jesus in the hope that he would lead them directly to the new paradise the Lord would establish on earth and which would differ from Eden inasmuch as it would be enjoyed by many after atoning for Adam's sin, also known as original sin, by means of prayer, mortification and repentance. And since the majority of these trusting souls were from the working classes, artisans and road-diggers, fishermen and women of lowly condition, one day when God allowed him a little more freedom, Jesus ventured to improvise a little speech which left all who listened spellbound, and such tears of joy were shed there at the prospect of unexpected salvation, Blessed be you poor, Jesus told them, for yours is the kingdom of heaven, blessed are you that hunger now, for you shall be filled, blessed are you that weep now, for you shall laugh, but just then God became aware of what was happening and although too late to retract what Jesus had said, He forced him to speak other words which turned those tears of happiness into grim foreboding of the black future ahead, Blessed are you when men shall hate you, and when they shall separate you from their company, and shall reproach you and cast out your name as evil for the Son of Man's sake. When Jesus finished speaking it was as if his soul had fallen at his feet, for in that same instant he could see in his mind's eye the tragic vision of the torments and deaths God had foretold at sea. Numb with fear, the crowd watched Jesus sink to his knees and, prostrate, pray in silence. No one present could have imagined that he was begging their forgiveness, he, the Son of God, who gloried in being able to pardon others. That night, in the privacy of the tent he shared with Mary Magdalene, Jesus said, I am the shepherd who with the same crook leads to sacrifice both the innocent and the guilty, those redeemed and those lost, those born and those yet to be born, who will rid me of this remorse for I now see myself as I once saw my Father, who need only answer for twenty lives while I must answer for twenty thousand. Mary Magdalene wept with Jesus and tried to console him, It wasn't your doing, she sobbed, That makes it all the worse, he insisted, and as if she had known from the outset what we have only come to see and hear little by little, she said reassuringly, It is God who traces out the paths of destiny and decides who must follow them, He chose you so that you might open a path amidst paths on his behalf, but you will not tread that path nor build a temple, others will erect it over your blood and entrails, so you might as well accept the destiny God has chosen for you, for your every gesture has been determined, the words you must utter await you in those places you will visit, there you will find cripples to whom you will restore limbs, the blind to whom you will give sight, the deaf to whom you will give hearing, the dumb to whom you will give speech, the dead whom you will resurrect, But I have no power over death, You haven't tried, Of course I've tried, but the fig tree did not revive, Times have changed, you're obliged to want what God wills, but He cannot deny you what you may wish, That He should take from me this burden, that's all I ask, You're asking the impossible, Jesus, for the one thing God cannot do is not to love Himself, How do you know, Women see things differently, perhaps because our body is different, that must be it, yes, that must be the explanation.

One day, for the earth is much too big for the strength of one man, even when dealing with a place as tiny as Palestine, Jesus decided to send his disciples, in pairs, to announce the coming of God's Kingdom throughout the cities, towns and villages, and to teach and preach like him everywhere they went. And so finding himself alone with Mary Magdalene, for the other women had gone off with the men according to their respective tastes and preferences, it occurred to him that since they were travelling to Bethany which is situated near Jerusalem they might as well kill two birds with one stone, if you will pardon the expression, by visiting Mary's brother and sister. It was time they made their peace and the two brothers-in-law got to know each other and, once reunited, they could make the journey together to Jerusalem for Jesus had arranged a meeting with all his disciples in Bethany in three months' time. There is little to tell about the works of the twelve apostles in the lands of Israel, firstly, because, apart from certain details about their lives and the circumstances of their deaths, we have not been called upon to narrate their story, and secondly, because they had not been given any mandate other than to repeat, albeit each in his own way, the precepts and deeds of their master, which means they taught just like him, and carried out cures as best they could. What a pity Jesus had strictly forbidden them to follow the path of the

Gentiles or to enter any city of the Samaritans, because this surprising attitude of intolerance in someone so well-educated deprived them of the opportunity of reducing their future workload. For given God's explicit intention of extending his domain and influence, sooner or later His message would not only reach the Samaritans but, above all, the Gentiles, both here and elsewhere. Jesus had instructed his disciples to cure the sick and raise the dead, cleanse lepers and exorcize demons, but apart from the occasional vague reference there is no clear evidence that any such deeds were carried out, which only goes to show that God does not trust just anyone, however strongly recommended. Once they are reunited with Jesus, the twelve disciples will undoubtedly have something to tell him about the results of their sermons urging repentance but have little or nothing to report about any cures, apart from the expulsion of some fairly innocuous demons who do not need much persuading to pass from one soul to another. What they will certainly have to report, however, is that they themselves were often expelled or given a hostile reception on roads where there were no Gentiles and in cities uninhabited by Samaritans, with no consolation other than to shake the dust from their feet on leaving, as if it were the fault of the dust which is trodden by everyone without ever complaining. But Jesus had told them this was what they must do in similar situations as testimony against those who refused to listen, truly a regrettable and negative response, for this was the word of God himself which was being rejected, since Jesus had been most explicit when he told them, Don't worry about what you have to say, inspiration will come to you just when you need it. Now perhaps things cannot work like this, after all, and here as in other cases, soundness of doctrine, which must prevail, depends on the personal factor which is secondary, and this maxim, if you will forgive the presumption, makes good sense, so let us take advantage of it.

The perfume of freshly gathered roses hovered in the air, the roads were clean and pleasant as if angels were walking ahead sprinkling dew as they went before brushing them with laurel and myrtle. Jesus and Mary Magdalene travelled incognito, avoiding the caravanserai and other travellers on the road rather than run the risk of being recognized. Not that Jesus was evading his obligations, never easy under God's watchful eye, but it seemed that the Almighty himself had decided to grant Jesus some respite because no lepers came on to the road to beseech a cure, or possessed souls begging to be exorcized, and the villages they passed through were quietly rejoicing in the peace of the Lord, as if they had already made progress along the path of repentance by their own merits. The couple slept wherever they happened to be, seeking no comfort other than each other's lap, sometimes with only the sky for a roof, God's enormous eye, black but speckled with lights, lingering reflections left by glances raised to heaven by one generation after another, interrogating the silence and listening to the only answer silence ever gives. Later on, when she is alone in the world, Mary Magdalene will try to recall those days and nights, but she will find it increasingly difficult to preserve any memories of her moments of sorrow and bitterness as if trying to protect an island of love from the onslaught of a tempestuous sea and its monsters. That time is drawing near, but looking at the earth and sky, there are no visible signs yet of its approach, just as a bird flies across an open sky without noticing the swift falcon, its claws at the ready, drop like a stone. Singing as they walk along the road, Jesus and Mary Magdalene make an impression on other travellers who think to themselves, Such a happy pair, and for the moment nothing could be truer. And so they reached Jericho and from there, taking it easy because of the intense heat and lack of shade, they took two whole days to go up to Bethany. After all this time, Mary Magdalene wondered how her brother and sister would receive her, especially since she had left home to live as a prostitute, They may think I'm dead, she said, they may even want me dead, and Jesus tried to dissuade her from dwelling on such dark thoughts, Time heals everything, he assured her, forgetting that the wound inflicted by his own family was still raw and still bleeding. They entered Bethany, Mary half covering her face for fear any of the villagers might recognize her. Jesus gently rebuked her, Why are you hiding, your past life is now behind you and exists no more, I'm no longer the same person, it is true, but I am who I was and the person I am and the person I was are still bound together by shame, You are now who you are, and you're with me, Thanks be to God, but the day will come when He will take you from me. Dropping her mantle, Mary showed her face, but no one said, Look, there is Lazarus's sister, the one who went off to live as a prostitute.

This is the house, said Mary Magdalene, but she could not bring herself to knock or announce her arrival. Jesus gave the unlocked gate a gentle push and called out, Anyone at home, and a woman's voice responded, Who's calling, and with those words she appeared in the doorway. This was Martha, the twin sister of Mary, but now bearing scarcely any resemblance, for age had left its mark on Martha, or it could have been the hard life she had led, or purely a question of temperament and outlook. The first things she noticed were Jesus's eyes and expression as if a dark cloud had lifted all at once, leaving his face luminous and bright, then she saw her sister and became wary, her expression betraying her displeasure, Who is this man with her, she must have thought, or perhaps, How can he be with her, if he is what he seems, but if pressed to explain herself, Martha would have been unable to describe her first impression of Jesus. And this is probably why, instead of asking her sister, How are you, or, What are you doing here, all she could say was, Who is this man you've brought with you. Jesus smiled and his smile went straight to Martha's heart with the swiftness of an arrow and there it remained, her heart aching with inexplicable satisfaction, My name is Jesus of Nazareth, he told her, and I'm with your sister, the same words, mutatis mutandis as the Romans would say in Latin, as those he used when he took leave of his brother James by the sea, telling him, Her name is Mary Magdalene and she's with me. Pushing the door wide open, Martha said, Come in, make yourself at home, but it was not clear which of them she was addressing. Once inside the yard, Mary Magdalene took her sister by the arm and told her, I belong here as much as you do, and I belong to this man who does not belong to you, I've been frank with both of you, so do not flaunt your virtue or censure my wickedness, I came here in peace and in peace I wish to remain. Martha said, I'm prepared to receive you as my sister and I long for the day when I shall welcome you with affection but it's too soon, and she was about to continue when a sudden thought stopped her, she was not sure whether this man standing beside her sister knew about the life Mary had led or might still be leading, and somewhat confused she started blushing, momentarily hating the two of them and herself until Jesus finally spoke so that Martha might learn what she needed to know, for it is not all that difficult to guess what people are thinking, and he told her, God judges all of us and does so differently each day, according to what we are each day, now if God were to

313

judge you at this moment, Martha, don't imagine you'd be any different in his eyes from Mary, Explain that more clearly for I don't understand, There is no more to be said, but keep my words in your heart and repeat them to yourself whenever you look at your sister, Is she no longer, You mean am I no longer a whore, asked Mary Magdalene bluntly, despising her sister's reticence. Martha flinched, raised her hands to her face, No, no, I don't want to know, Jesus's words are quite enough, and unable to restrain herself she burst into tears. Mary went to her and embraced her, cradling her in her arms, while Martha kept saying between sobs, What a life, what a life, but one could not be certain whether she was talking about her own life or that of her sister. Where is Lazarus, asked Mary, In the synagogue, How is he these days, He still suffers from those bouts of choking, but otherwise his health is not too bad. She felt like adding resentfully that Mary had been slow in showing any concern, for during all these years of guilty absence, this prodigal sister, prodigal with both her time and body, Martha thought to herself with spiteful irony, had never bothered to keep in touch with her family or enquire after their sick brother whose health had always been precarious. Then turning to Jesus who was carefully observing the hostility between them from a discreet distance, Martha told him, Our brother copies out books in the synagogue which is as much as he can do in his poor state of health, and her tone, though not intentionally, was that of someone incapable of understanding how anyone could live without being constantly engaged in some worthwhile task from morning until night. What's ailing Lazarus, asked Jesus, Bouts of choking, as if his heart were about to stop beating, then he turns ever so pale until you'd think he was about to pass away. Martha paused before adding, He's younger than we are, she spoke without thinking, perhaps suddenly struck by Jesus's youthful appearance, and once again she felt perturbed, pangs of jealousy touched her heart, bringing words to her lips which sounded strange coming from Martha when Mary Magdalene, whose duty and privilege it was to say them, was standing there, You're tired, Martha said to Jesus, Sit down and let me bathe your feet. Shortly afterwards, when Mary found herself alone with Jesus, she remarked half-jokingly, It would seem that we two sisters were born to love you, and Jesus replied, Martha feels sad that she's had so little enjoyment out of life, That's not why she's sad, she's resentful because she thinks there is no justice left in heaven when a fallen woman gets the prize and virtuous women like her go unrewarded, God will reward her in other ways, Perhaps, but having made the world, God has no right to deprive women of any of the fruits of His creation, Such as carnal knowledge of men, Of course, just as you came to know woman and what more could you wish for, being as you are, the Son of God, He who lies with you is not the son of God but the son of Joseph, Frankly, ever since you came into my life I have never felt that I was lying with the son of a god, You mean of God, If only you weren't.

Martha entrusted a neighbour's little boy with a message for Lazarus, informing him that Mary had returned home, but only after much hesitation for she was anxious that no one should know that their disreputable sister was back in the village and that tongues should start wagging again after all this time. Martha asked herself how she would manage to face people on the street next day and, worse still, how she would find the courage to walk out with her sister. It would be difficult to ignore her neighbours and friends, and she dreaded having to say to them, This is my sister Mary, do you remember her, she's come back home, only to receive knowing looks and sly comments, Of course we remember, who doesn't remember Mary, let us hope these prosaic details will not shock our readers, because the story of God is not all divine. Martha was trying to suppress these uncharitable thoughts when Lazarus arrived and, embracing Mary, he simply said, Welcome home, sister, putting aside the sorrow of all those years of separation and silent anxiety, and since she felt it was up to her to put a brave face on things, Martha pointed to Jesus and told her brother, This is Jesus, our brother-in-law. The two men exchanged a friendly nod and then sat down at once to have a chat, while the women set about preparing a meal together as they had done so many times in the past. Now after they had eaten, Lazarus and Jesus went into the yard to enjoy the cool night air while the sisters remained indoors to resolve the important question of how they should arrange the sleeping mats, bearing in mind that they were now four instead of two. After gazing at length at the first stars to appear in the sky which was still clear, Jesus finally asked Lazarus, Do you suffer much pain, and Lazarus replied with surprising composure, Yes, I suffer all right, Your suffering will pass, said Jesus, No doubt, when I'm dead,

No, I mean almost immediately. I didn't know you were a physician, Brother, if I were a physician, I wouldn't be able to cure you, Nor will you be able to cure me, even if you're not, You're cured, Jesus murmured softly, taking him by the hand. And at that very moment Lazarus could feel the sickness drain from his body like murky water absorbed by the sun. His breathing suddenly became easier, his heartbeat stronger and, puzzled by what was happening, he asked nervously, What's going on, his voice turning hoarse with anxiety, Who are you, A physician I am not, smiled Jesus, In the name of God, tell me who you are, Don't take the name of God in vain, But what am I to make of this, Call Mary, she'll tell you. There was no need to call anyone. Attracted by the sudden raising of voices, Martha and Mary appeared in the doorway, afraid the two men might be quarrelling, but they saw at once they were mistaken, a blue light suffused the entire yard, that is to say the sky, and a visibly shaking Lazarus was pointing at Jesus, Who is this man, he asked, for he only had to touch me and say, You're cured and the sickness is gone. Martha went to comfort her brother, how could he possibly be cured if he was trembling from head to foot, but Lazarus pushed her away, saying, Mary, you brought him here, tell us who he is. Without stirring from the doorway, Mary Magdalene simply replied, He is Jesus of Nazareth, the Son of God. Now even though these parts have been favoured with prophetic revelations and apocalyptic signs since time immemorial, it would have been perfectly natural for Lazarus and Martha to express utter disbelief, because it is one thing for someone to acknowledge that he has suddenly been cured by miraculous means and quite another to be told that the man who touched your hand and cured you of sickness is no other than the Son of God himself. Faith and love, however, can achieve much, some even claim they do not have to go together in order to achieve everything, and as it happened Martha threw herself weeping into Jesus's arms, then, alarmed by her daring, slumped to the ground where she remained, her face completely transformed as she muttered to herself, I have washed your feet. Lazarus had not stirred, paralysed by fear, and we might even assume that if this sudden revelation did not kill him, it was because that timely act of love a moment before had given him a new heart. Smiling, Jesus went to embrace him and told him, Don't be surprised to find that the Son of God is a son of man, frankly, God had no one else to choose, just like the men who choose their women and the women who choose their men. These final words were intended for Mary Magdalene who would take them in good part, but Jesus forgot that they would only serve to aggravate Martha's distress and her desperate loneliness, this is the difference between God and His Son, God would do it on purpose, His Son out of carelessness, which is all too human. Never mind, today there is rejoicing in this household, and Martha can go back to suffering and sighing tomorrow, but there is one consolation she can be sure of, no one will dare to gossip about her sister's dissolute past in the streets, squares and market-places of Bethany once they learn, and Martha herself will make sure they are told that the man with Mary has cured Lazarus of his sickness without any recourse to potions or infusions of herbs. They were sitting at home enjoying each other's company, when Lazarus remarked, From time to time there have been rumours about a man from Galilee going round performing miracles, but it has never been suggested that he might be the Son of God, Some news travels faster than others, replied Jesus, Are you that man, You've said it, Then Jesus told his story from the beginning, but not quite everything, he did not mention Pastor, and said nothing about God except that He had appeared to him to announce, You're My Son. Were it not for those first rumours about remote miracles, now transformed into factual truths given the tangible evidence of this latest miracle, were it not for the power of faith, and for love and its powers, it would certainly have been extremely difficult for Jesus with a few laconic words, even though coming from God himself, to convince Lazarus and Martha that this man who would shortly be sharing a mat with their sister was made of divine spirit. For it was with flesh and blood that Jesus embraced this woman who had known so many men without fear of God. And let us forgive Martha the spiritual pride which led her to mutter, under the sheet pulled over her head so as not to see or hear, I deserve him more than she does.

Next day the news spread like wildfire, and people everywhere in Bethany praised and thanked the Lord and even those modest souls who were doubtful to begin with, believing the earth was too small to encompass these wonders, were forced to change their minds when confronted with the miraculously cured Lazarus, of whom it should never be said that he began selling good health to others, for he was so good-hearted that he would sooner have given it all away. People were already gathering round the door, curious to see with their own trustworthy eyes this miracle-worker whom they might even be allowed to touch as one last, definitive proof. Hoping to be cured, the sick and infirm also came in droves, some on foot, others carried in litters or on the backs of relatives, until the narrow street where Lazarus and his sister lived was completely blocked. On becoming aware of the situation, Jesus sent word that he would address the crowd in the main square of the village where they should make their way and he would join them shortly. But any man who is holding a bird securely in one hand is not going to be foolish enough to let it escape. So, understandably, either out of prudence or mistrust, no one would move from this vantage point and Jesus was obliged to show his face and leave the house like anyone else, without fanfare, pomp or ceremony, and without any tremors in heaven or on earth. Here I am, he said, trying to speak naturally, but assuming he succeeded, the words he spoke and coming from whom they came, were sufficient to force the inhabitants of an entire village to their knees to beg for mercy, Save us, cried some, Cure me, implored others. Jesus cured one man who, being mute, was unable to plead, and sent the others away because they did not have enough faith. He told them to come back some other day but first they must repent of their sins, because as we know, the Kingdom of God was at hand and time was about to end. Are you the Son of God, they asked him, and Jesus replied as enigmatically as ever, If I were not, God would strike you dumb rather than permit you to ask me such a question.

Jesus began his stay in Bethany with these remarkable deeds while waiting for the day to arrive when he would be reunited with his disciples who were journeying through distant lands. Needless to say, people were soon arriving from nearby towns and villages once it became known that the man who was performing miracles in the north was now in Bethany. There was no need for Jesus to leave Lazarus's house because everyone flocked there as though to a place of pilgrimage, but Jesus did not receive them, ordering them instead to gather on a hill outside the village where he would preach repentance and cure some of the sick. These events caused such excitement that the news quickly reached Jerusalem, making the crowds even bigger until Jesus began asking himself if he should remain there at the risk of provoking riots which are all too common when crowds get out of control. Humble folk were the first to come from Jerusalem in search of a cure, but it was not long before people from every social class began arriving, including a number of Pharisees and scribes who had refused to believe that anyone in his right mind would have the courage, one might almost say suicidal courage, openly to declare himself the Son of God. They returned to Jerusalem irritated and bewildered because Jesus never gave a definite reply when questioned, and if pressed about his parentage, insisted he was the Son of Man, and if, when referring to God, he happened to say Father, it was clear he thought of God as everyone's father and not just his. There remained, however, the troublesome question of these healing powers which Jesus had been exercising without any recourse to trickery or magic. All it required were a few simple words, Walk, Arise, Speak, See, Be cleansed, and a leper's skin would suddenly glow like dew tinged by the morning light when he touched it with his fingertips, mutes and stammerers became inebriated with words on regaining their speech, paralytics jumped out of bed and danced with joy until they dropped from sheer exhaustion, the blind could not believe that their eyes could see again, the lame ran to their hearts' content, and then teasingly pretended to be lame once more so that they could start running all over again. Repent, Jesus told them, Repent, and he asked nothing more of them. But the high priests of the Temple, who knew better than anyone of the upheavals and other historic disorders provoked in their time by various prophets and soothsayers, decided after pondering Jesus's sayings that there should be no more religious, social and political disturbances and that from now on they would pay close attention to everything the Galilean might do or say, so that whenever it became necessary, the evil foreseen would be uprooted and eliminated because, in the words of the High Priest, This man does not deceive me, the Son of Man is the Son of God. Jesus had not gone to sow seeds in Jerusalem, but here in Bethany he was shaping, honing and forging the scythe with which they would cut him down.

These extraordinary events were taking place when the disciples began to arrive at Bethany in pairs, two today, two tomorrow, perhaps even four if they had chanced to meet up en route. Apart from a few minor details, they all had the same story to tell about a man who had emerged from the desert and prophesied in the traditional manner, as if he were rolling stones with his voice and moving mountains with his arms, while foretelling the chastisement that awaited the people and the imminent arrival of the Messiah. The disciples never managed to see him because he was constantly on the move from one place to another according to the bits of information they gathered which, although generally consistent, was all at second hand, and they would have sought this prophet out for themselves, only the three months were nearly up and they were anxious not to miss their meeting. Jesus asked them if they knew the prophet's name and they told him it was John, which was the name of the man who was supposed to come and help Jesus according to God's words when He took His leave. So, he's here already, said Jesus, and his friends did not know what he meant by these words, except for Mary Magdalene, but then she knew everything. Jesus wanted to go and look for John who almost certainly must be searching for him, but of the twelve apostles, Thomas and Judas Iscariot had still not arrived, and since they might have more information, their delay was all the more frustrating. The waiting, however, was justified, because the late-comers had not only seen John but actually spoken to him. The others emerged from their tents, pitched outside Bethany, to hear what Thomas and Judas Iscariot had to relate and they sat in a circle in the yard of Lazarus's house, with Martha and Mary and the other women in attendance. Judas Iscariot and Thomas spoke in turn and they explained how John had been in the wilderness when he received the word of God, so he took himself off to the banks of the Jordan to baptize and preach penance for the remission of sins, but as the multitudes flocked to him to be baptized he chastised them with loud cries which startled everyone out of their wits, Oh generation of vipers, who has warned you to flee from the wrath to come, bring forth therefore fruits meet for repentance, and think not to say within yourselves, We have Abraham to our father, for I say unto you that God is able from these stones to raise up children unto Abraham, leaving you despised, and now the axe is laid unto the root of the trees, therefore every tree which brings not forth good fruit is hewn down and cast into the fire. Terror-stricken, the multitudes asked him, What must we do, and John replied, Let the man who has two tunics share them with him who has none, and he who has provisions do the same, and to the collectors of taxes he said, Make no demands other than those established by law, and do not think the law is just simply because you call it law, and to the soldiers who asked him, And what about us, what must we do, he replied, Use violence against no one, do not sentence anyone unjustly and content yourselves with your wages. At this point, Thomas, who had started this dialogue, fell silent, and Judas Iscariot, seizing the opportunity, took over. They then asked John if he was the Messiah, and he told them I indeed baptize you with water unto repentance, but he who comes after me is mightier than I, whose shoes I am not worthy to bear, he shall baptize you with the Holy Ghost and with fire, someone whose fan is in his hand, and he will thoroughly purge his floor, and gather his wheat into the granary, but he will burn up the chaff with unquenchable fire. Judas Iscariot said nothing more and everyone waited for Jesus to speak, but with one finger Jesus traced enigmatic lines on the ground and appeared to be waiting for one of the others to speak. Then Peter said, So you are the Messiah whose coming John prophesied, and Jesus still scribbling in the dust, replied, You said it, not I, God simply told me I am His Son, he paused for a moment, then ended by saying, I'm going off to look for John, We'll accompany you, said the son of Zebedee who was also called John, but Jesus slowly shook his head, I only need Thomas and Judas Iscariot because they've seen him, and turning to Judas, he asked, What does he look like, He's taller than you, answered Judas, and heavier, he has a long beard which looks as if it were made of bristles, and wears nothing except a garment of camel's hair and a leather girdle about his waist and people say that out there in the wilderness he feeds on locusts and wild honey. He sounds more like the Messiah than me, Jesus said, rising from the circle.

The three of them set out early next morning and, knowing that John never stayed more than a few days in the same place and that they would most probably find him baptizing on the banks of the Jordan, they went down from Bethany to a place called Bethabara, situated at the edge of the Dead Sea, with the intention of travelling up-river as far as the Sea of Galilee, and even further north to the headwaters if necessary. But when they left Bethany they never imagined their journey would be so short, for there in Bethabara itself they found John alone, as if he were expecting them. They caught their first glimpse of him from afar, a tiny figure of a man seated on the riverbank, surrounded by sombre mountains resembling skulls and valleys which looked like open scars, and stretching out on the right beneath the sun and white sky, the sinister Dead Sea, its awesome surface gleaming like molten copper. When they got within a slingshot, Jesus asked his companions, Is it him. Shading their eyes with one hand, the two disciples took a careful look and replied, Either it's him or his twin. Wait here until I return and don't try to get any closer, said Jesus, and without another word, he began making his descent towards the river. Thomas and Judas Iscariot sat down on the parched ground, watched Jesus move away, appearing and disappearing according to whether the terrain rose or fell, and then once he had reached the bank, they saw him walking towards John who had not stirred from the same spot during all this time. Let's hope we're not mistaken, said Thomas, We should have tried to get closer, retorted Judas Iscariot, but Jesus was certain the moment he saw him and had only asked for the sake of asking. Down below, John had risen to his feet and was looking at Jesus as he approached. What will they have to say to each other, asked Judas Iscariot, Perhaps Jesus will tell us, perhaps he won't, said Thomas. Now the two men way in the distance were confronting each other and speaking excitedly, judging from their gestures and the movements they were making with their crooks, and after a time, they walked down to the water's edge where they disappeared from sight behind the jutting embankment, but Judas and Thomas knew what was going on there for they, too, had been baptized by John after wading into the river until the water came up to their waists. Scooping up water in his cupped hands, John raised it to heaven and then pouring it over Jesus's head, recited the words, I baptize you with this water, may it nourish your fire. This accomplished, John and Jesus have come up from the river, retrieved their staffs, and are probably bidding each other farewell, they have embraced and John starts to walk along the riverbank in a northerly direction, while Jesus is coming this way. Thomas and Judas Iscariot stand there waiting for him, he arrives once more in silence, he passes and leads the way to Bethany. Feeling somewhat slighted, his disciples walk behind him, their curiosity unsatisfied until Thomas, unable to contain himself any longer and ignoring Judas's gesture to dissuade him, asked, Aren't you going to tell us what John had to say, When the time comes, replied Jesus, Did he tell you at least, that you're the Messiah, When the time comes, said Jesus a second time, and his disciples could not be sure if he was simply repeating what he had said before, or if he was telling them that it was not yet time for the Messiah to appear. Judas Iscariot opted for the second of these hypotheses when they despondently trailed behind, while Thomas, ever sceptical by nature, was of the opinion, and not without some irritation, that Jesus was repeating himself.

Only Mary Magdalene knew what happened that night and no one else, Little was said, Jesus confided, because no sooner had we greeted each other than John wanted to know if I was he who is to come or if we had to await another, And what did you tell him, I told him the blind receive their sight and the lame walk, the lepers are cleansed and the deaf hear, and the poor have the gospel preached to them, And what did he say, The Messiah won't need to do much so long as he does what's expected of him, Is that what he said, Yes, those were his very words, And what is expected of the Messiah, That's what I asked him, And what answer did he give you, He told me to find out for myself, And then what did he say, Nothing else, he took me to the river, baptized me and departed, What words did he use to baptize you, I baptize you with water, and may it nourish your fire. After this conversation with Mary Magdalene, Jesus never spoke for a whole week. He left Lazarus's house and went to join his disciples on the outskirts of Bethany where he set up a tent away from the others and spent the entire day there alone. Not even Mary Magdalene was allowed to enter the tent and Jesus only left it at night to go into the deserted mountains. Sometimes his disciples would secretly follow him, on the pretext that they only wanted to protect him from being attacked by wild beasts, which were, in fact, unknown in these parts. They discovered that Jesus would choose a comfortable spot and sit there staring, not at the sky, but straight ahead, as if waiting for someone to appear from the ominous shadows of the valleys or round the corner of some hill. There was moonlight, so anyone arriving would have been visible from afar, but no one came. At first light Jesus withdrew and returned to the camp. He ate very little of the food John and Judas Iscariot brought him in turn and made no attempt to return their greetings. On one occasion he even dismissed Peter brusquely when the latter asked if all was well and whether he had any orders to give. Peter had not completely misjudged this move, he had simply spoken too soon, that was all, because after eight days Jesus emerged from the tent in broad daylight, rejoined his disciples and ate with them, and, after he had finished, he told them, Tomorrow we shall go up to Jerusalem to the Temple, there you will do as I do because the time has come for the Son of God to know what use is being made of his Father's house and for the Messiah to begin to do what he must do. The disciples wanted to know more, but apart from telling them, You won't have to wait much longer before finding out, he would say nothing else. Now the disciples were not accustomed to being spoken to in this tone of voice nor to seeing him with such a severe expression on his face that he no longer looked like the gentle and tranquil Jesus with whom they were familiar, whom God led wherever He wished without his uttering a word of complaint. This change had clearly been brought about by the circumstances, as yet unknown, which had led him to separate himself from his disciples and to wander, as if possessed by the demons of night, over hill and dale in search of a word which is what one always looks for. Peter, however, as the oldest person there, thought it unfair that Jesus should order them to go up to Jerusalem just like that, as if they were mere scullions and only fit to fetch and carry, to go and come back without any further expla- nation. So he complained, We're prepared to recognize your auth- ority and obey you in word and deed, both as the Son of God and also as man, but it isn't right that you should treat us like irrespon- sible children or doddery old men, refusing to confide in us and simply giving orders without asking our opinion or allowing us to make our own decisions, Please forgive me, all of you, said Jesus, for I myself do not know what brings me to Jerusalem, all I've been told is that I must go and nothing more, you are not obliged to accompany me, Who told you that you must go to Jerusalem, Some voice in my head which tells me what I must and must not do, You're much changed since your meeting with John, Yes, that meet- ing made me realize it isn't enough to bring peace, one must also carry the sword, If the Kingdom of God is at hand, why carry a sword, asked Andrew, Because God did not reveal by which means His Kingdom will reach you, we've tried peace, now let us try the sword, and God will make His choice, but I repeat, you are not obliged to accompany me, You know very well we shall follow you wheresoever you may go, John told him, and Jesus replied, Don't swear to it, those of you who arrive there will find out.

Next morning when Jesus went to Lazarus's house, not so much to say goodbye as to reassure them that he was back living amongst his disciples after his mysterious retreat into the wilderness, Martha told him that her brother had left for the synagogue. Then Jesus and his disciples set off on the road to Jerusalem, Mary Magdalene and the other women accompanying them as far as the last houses of Bethany, where they stood waving, content to do so, although the men did not look back even once. The sky is clouded and threatening rain, perhaps this explains why there are so few people on the road, those with no urgent need to go to Jerusalem have decided to stay at home waiting for a sign from the heavens. The thirteen men advance along a road which is nearly always deserted, as thick, ashen clouds rumble above the mountains as if heaven and earth were finally about to come together forever more, the mould and moulded, male and female, concave and convex. By the time they reached the city gates, however, they found the usual crowd already gathered there and resigned themselves to a long wait before finally reaching the Temple. But things turned out differently. The appearance of the thirteen men, nearly all of them barefoot, with their great staffs, flowing beards and heavy, dark mantles over tunics which looked as if they had seen better days, caused the startled crowd to fall back and ask among themselves, Where can these men have come from, who's the one in front, and no one knew the answer until one bystander who had come down from Galilee said, He's Jesus of Nazareth who claims to be the Son of God and performs miracles, Where are they going, asked others, and since the only way of finding out was to follow them, many walked behind them so that by the time they reached the entrance to the Temple, they were no longer thirteen outside but a thousand, and there they remained waiting to see what might happen. Jesus walked on the side where there were moneychangers and said to his disciples, Here's what we've come to do, and with these words began overturning the tables, lashing and striking out at those who were buying and selling, causing such an uproar that his words would never have been heard except for the fact that his natural voice rang out in stentorian tones, railing, It is written that my house shall be called the house of prayer but you have made it a den of thieves, and he continued knocking over the tables and sending coins scattering everywhere which brought great joy to some two thousand people who rushed to gather this manna. The disciples followed Jesus's example and finally the tables of the dove-sellers were also thrown to the ground, and once released the birds flew over the Temple, circling wildly around the smoke from the altar in the distance, where they would not be burned for their saviour had come. The Temple guards rushed to the scene armed with batons to punish, capture or expel the rioters, only to find themselves up against thirteen formidable Galileans with staff in hand, who swept aside anyone who dared approach. Come on, come on, the lot of you, and feel God's might, they taunted, falling on the guards and destroying everything in sight before putting a torch to the tents. Soon a second column of smoke was spiralling into the air, and a voice cried out, Summon the Roman soldiers, but no one paid any attention, for happen what may, the Romans were forbidden by law to enter the Temple. More guards rushed to the scene, this time with sword and lance, and they were joined by the odd moneychanger or dove-seller, determined not to leave the protection of their property to strangers, so that little by little the guards gained the upper hand. And if this struggle were as pleasing to God as the crusades to come, He did not appear to be doing much to ensure victory for His own people. This was the situation when the High Priest appeared at the top of the stairs accompanied by all the other priests, Elders and scribes who could be summoned in haste, and in a voice powerful enough to match that of Jesus, he declared, Let him go this time, but if he ever shows his face here again we shall cut him down and discard him like those tares which threaten to choke the wheat during the time of harvest. Andrew said to Jesus who was fighting at his side, You weren't joking when you said you were bringing the sword rather than peace, now we know that staffs are as useless as swords, to which Jesus replied, Everything depends on who is brandishing the staff or wielding the sword, What are we going to do then, asked Andrew, Let's return to Bethany, answered Jesus, it's not swords we need but grit and determination. They retreated in orderly fashion with their staffs pointed at the jeering crowd who taunted them but went no further, and soon the disciples were safely out of Jerusalem and beating a hasty retreat, all of them exhausted, some even wounded.

On reaching Bethany, they noticed that neighbours who came to their doors looked at them with pity and sorrow, but the disciples thought it only natural, given the lamentable state in which they had returned from battle. However they soon discovered the real reason for the gloom on everyone's face when they turned into the street where Lazarus lived and realized that some tragedy had occurred. Jesus ran ahead of the others, entered the yard, and with mournful sighs the people gathered there stepped aside to allow him to pass. From within came the sound of weeping and lamentation, Oh, my beloved brother, Martha could be heard sobbing, Oh, my beloved brother, wailed the voice of Mary. Stretched out on the ground on a pallet, Lazarus appeared to be sleeping, only he was not asleep, he was dead. Nearly all his life he had suffered from a weak heart, then he was cured, as everyone in Bethany could testify, and now he was dead, at this moment as composed as if carved from marble, as intact as if he had already passed into eternity, but soon the first signs of putrefaction will begin to appear, causing those around the corpse to suffer even greater fear and anguish. As if strength had suddenly gone from his legs, Jesus fell to his knees, groaning and weeping, How did this happen, how did this happen, words that never fail to spring to our lips when confronted by something irremediable, enquiring of others how it happened, a desperate and futile attempt to postpone the awful moment when we must accept the truth, that is it, we want to know how it happened, as if we could replace death with life, exchange what has been with what might have been. From the depths of her despairing and bitter grief, Martha said to Jesus, Had you been here, my brother would not have died, but I know everything you ask of God He will grant you, just as He granted you sight for the blind, a cure for the lepers, speech for the mute, and all the other wonders which reside in your will and await your word. Jesus told her, Your brother will be raised from the dead, and Martha replied, I know he will come back to life on the Day of Resurrection. Jesus stood up and felt an infinite strength take possession of his soul, and in that supreme moment was convinced he could attempt and achieve everything, banish death from this corpse, fully restore it to life, give it speech, movement, laughter, even tears but not of sorrow, and truly claim, I am the resurrection and the life, he who believes in me, though he were dead, yet shall he live, and he asked Martha, Do you believe this, and she replied, Yes, I believe you are the Son of God who has to come into this world, and this being so, and with everything necessary disposed and arranged, such as strength and power and the will to use them, all Jesus has to do, looking at that body abandoned by its soul, is to stretch out his arms to it as if offering the path by which it must return, and say, Lazarus, Arise, and Lazarus will rise from the dead because it is the will of God, but at the very last moment Mary Magdalene placed a hand on Jesus's shoulder and said, No one has committed so many sins in life that they deserve to die twice, and dropping his arms, Jesus went outside to weep.

Like an icy gust of wind or numbing chill, the death of Lazarus suddenly extinguished the militant zeal John had aroused in Jesus's heart wherein, after a week of lengthy reflection and several brief moments of action, serving God and the people had become one and the same sentiment. After the first few days of mourning when the duties and habits of everyday life were gradually resumed, bringing momentary respite from unyielding sorrow, Peter and Andrew went to speak to Jesus. They questioned him about his plans, whether they should go and preach once more in the towns or return to Jerusalem for a fresh assault, because the disciples were already beginning to feel restless and anxious to be doing something. They complained, We didn't give up our possessions, our work and families just to sit around all day long. Jesus looked at them as if he were seeing them in a blur and listened as if trying to identify their voices amidst a chorus of discordant cries, and after a lengthy silence, told them they must be patient for a little longer, that he still had some thinking to do and could sense that something was about to happen which would decide their lives and deaths once and for all. He also assured them he would soon be joining them in the camp and both Peter and Andrew were puzzled that the two sisters were to remain alone when it still had to be decided what the men would do, You don't need to come back for our sake, said Peter, who had no way of knowing that Jesus was torn between two conflicting obligations, the first towards the men and women who had sacrificed and abandoned everything in order to follow him, and the second here in this house, towards these two sisters, similar yet opposed like the face and the mirror, a nagging conflict which distressed him deeply. The ghost of Lazarus was present and refused to go away. He was present in those harsh words spoken by Martha who could not forgive Mary for having prevented her own brother from being restored to life, nor forgive Jesus for refusing to use his God-given powers. Lazarus was also present in Mary's disconsolate tears who, by not subjecting her brother to a second death, would have to live forever with the remorse of not having freed him from this one. Like some enormous presence filling every nook and cranny, Lazarus was present in Jesus's troubled soul, the quadruple contradiction in which he found himself, whether to agree with what Mary had said but rebuke her for having said it, whether to condone Martha's plea but censure her for having made it. Jesus looked into his wretched soul and what he saw there were four wild horses pulling and tugging in four opposite directions, as if four ropes coiled round winches were slowly breaking every fibre in his soul, as if the hands of God and the Devil were divinely and diabolically amusing themselves and playing games with the remains. The afflicted and diseased turned up at the door of the house which had once belonged to Lazarus in the hope of being cured. Sometimes Martha would appear and resentfully drive them away, as if to say, There was no salvation for my brother so why should there be a cure for you, but sooner or later back they would come until they succeeded in reaching Jesus who cured them and sent them away without ever saying, Repent. To be cured was like being reborn without ever having died, for the newborn have no sins and therefore have no need to repent. But these acts of physical regeneration, if you will pardon my saying so, although most merciful, left a sour note and bitter after-taste in Jesus's heart, for they were nothing more than a postponement of inevitable decline, and he who has just left feeling healthy and content will be back tomorrow lamenting new woes without remedy. Jesus became so depressed that one day Martha told him, Don't you go dying on me for that would be like losing Lazarus all over again, and Mary Magdalene, whimpering beneath the sheet they share like a wounded animal hiding in the dark, tells Jesus, You need me now more than ever before but I cannot reach you if you lock yourself behind a door beyond human strength, and Jesus, who had answered Martha, saying, My death will embrace all the deaths of Lazarus who will go on dying without ever being restored to life, begged Mary, Even when you cannot enter, do not abandon me, stretch out your hand even though you may not see me, otherwise I shall forget life or it will forget me. A few days later Jesus went to join his disciples and Mary Magdalene went with him. I'll look at your shadow if you don't wish me to look at you, she told him and he replied, I wish to be wherever my shadow may be if that is where your eyes are. They loved each other and exchanged these amorous phrases not only because beautiful and true, if anything can possibly be both at the same time, but because they sensed that shadows were closing in and it was time they started getting used to the darkness of final absence despite being together.

Then news reached the camp that John the Baptist had been taken prisoner. Nothing more was known except that he had been arrested, Herod himself having ordered his imprisonment. Unable to think of any other reason for this decision, Jesus and his followers were inclined to believe Herod had been provoked by John's prophecies about the coming of the Messiah which he repeated everywhere between one baptism and another, He who comes after me shall baptize you with fire, and between one imprecation and another, Oh generation of vipers, who has warned you to flee from the wrath to come, Jesus then warned his disciples that they must be prepared for every manner of harassment and persecution, for since rumours had been rife for quite some time that they themselves were preaching the same message, it was only to be expected that Herod would come to the conclusion that two and two make four and pursue the carpenter's son who claimed to be the Son of God and his followers, the second and most powerful head of the dragon threatening to topple him from his throne. Bad news is certainly not preferable to no news, but it is understandable that it should be received with equanimity by those who, having waited and hoped for everything, have recently had to make do with nothing. They asked each other, and Jesus himself, what they should do, whether they should stand together and resist Herod's wickedness, disperse throughout the towns, or perhaps retreat into the wilderness where they could feed on wild honey and locusts, like John the Baptist before he left there for the greater glory of Jesus and, by the looks of it, to meet his own miserable fate. However, since there was no sign of Herod's troops arriving in Bethany to slaughter these other innocents, Jesus and his disciples were carefully considering the various alternatives, when several more reports arrived at once informing them that John had been beheaded and that his imprisonment and execution had nothing to do with the coming of the Messiah or the Kingdom of God. John had incurred Herod's wrath by speaking out against adultery of which the King himself was guilty, having married Herodias, his niece and sister-in-law, while her husband was still alive. The news of John's death brought tears to the eyes of men and women alike and the entire camp was plunged into mourning. No one there was convinced that he could have been sentenced to death for the reason given. Judas Iscariot whom, you may remember, John baptized, was beside himself with rage and swore that Herod's decision must have been influenced by some more serious motive which no longer appeared to exist or have any future importance. What is this, he asked the company gathered there, including the women, John announces the Messiah is coming to redeem people and they kill him for condemning an adulterous relationship and marriage between an uncle and niece, when concubinage and adultery have been common practice in this family since the time of the first Herod up to the present day. What is this, he railed, when God Himself ordered John to announce the coming of the Messiah, and I'm convinced it was God for the simple reason that nothing can happen without God willing it, so perhaps those of you who know more about God than I do can explain to me why He should wish His plans to go awry like this on earth, and before you try to tell me that God knows even if we don't, then let me tell you that I insist on knowing as much as God knows. A shiver of horror passed through all those listening, afraid that the wrath of God might descend on this insolent fellow and themselves for not punishing such blasphemy at once. Now since God was not present to give satisfaction to Judas Iscariot, the challenge could only be taken up by Jesus who was closest to the Supreme Being whose wisdom was being called into question. Had this been another religion and the circumstances different, perhaps things would have gone no further, except for this enigmatic smile from Jesus which, however faint and fleeting, betrayed mixed feelings of surprise, benevolence and curiosity, which might seem excessive were it not for the fact that the surprise was short-lived, the benevolence condescending and the curiosity somewhat jaded. The smile came and went, leaving behind a deathly pallor, a face which suddenly looked cadaverous, as if it had just glimpsed the living image of its own fate. In a languid voice almost without expression, Jesus finally said, Let the women withdraw, and Mary Magdalene was the first to rise to her feet. Then, after the silence had gradually formed a wall and roof to enclose them in the deepest cave on earth, Jesus said, Let John ask God why He allowed someone prophesying such fair tidings to die for so paltry a reason. He paused for a moment and Judas Iscariot was about to speak, when Jesus raised his hand to silence him before saying, I now realize it's my duty to tell you what I have learned from God unless He himself prevents me from doing so. Voices grew louder as the disciples began talking amongst themselves, nervous and afraid of what they were about to hear. Judas Iscariot was alone in maintaining that air of defiance with which he had opened the discussion. Jesus told them, I know my destiny and yours, I know the destiny of future generations, I'm aware of God's motives and designs, and we must debate these matters for they concern all of you and will concern you even more in days to come. Why, asked Peter, must we know what God has revealed to you, would it not be better to keep it to yourself. If He wished, God could silence me this very instant, Then surely God doesn't mind whether you remain silent or speak, it's just as meaningless, and if God has spoken through you, He will continue to speak through you even when you think you're opposing His will, as at present, Do you know, Peter, that I'm to be crucified, Yes, you told me, But I didn't tell you that you yourself, along with Andrew and Philip here, will also be crucified, that Bartholomew will be skinned alive, that Matthew will be butchered by barbarians, that they will behead James, the son of Zebedee, that the second James, the son of Alphaeus, will be stoned to death, that Thomas will be killed with a lance, that Judas Thaddaeus will have his skull crushed, that Simon will be sawn in half, these things you didn't know but I'm telling all of you now. These revelations were received in silence, there was no further reason for being afraid of the future, once revealed it was as if Jesus had finally told them, You will die, and they were to reply in chorus, So what, we know already. But John and Judas Iscariot had not heard what was to happen to them and they asked, What about us, and Jesus replied, You, John, will live to a ripe old age and die from natural causes, and as for you, Judas Iscariot, keep

333

away from fig trees because it won't be long before you hang yourself from one, So we shall die because of you, a voice asked, but no one ever identified the person who spoke, Because of God rather than me, answered Jesus, What does God want, after all, asked John, He wants a larger assembly than the one He has at present, He wants the entire world for Himself, But if God is Lord of the universe, how can the world belong to anyone but Him not just since yesterday or tomorrow, but since the beginning of time, asked Thomas, That I cannot tell you, replied Jesus, but if you've lived for so long with all these things in your heart, why only tell us now, Because Lazarus whom I cured, died, John the Baptist who prophesied my coming, was killed, and now death has come amongst us. All creatures have to die, said Peter, and men like all the rest. Many will die in future because of God and His holy will, If willed by God then it must be for some holy cause, They will die because they were neither born before nor after, Will they receive eternal life, asked Matthew, Yes, but the conditions should be less painful, If the Son of God said what he said, he has denied himself, protested Peter, You're mistaken, only the Son of God is permitted to say these things, and what is blasphemy on your lips is the word of God on mine, replied Jesus, You speak as if we had to choose between you and God, said Peter, You will always have to choose between God and God, and like you and all men, I'm in the middle. So what do you want us to do, Assist my death to protect the lives of future generations, But you cannot oppose God's will, No, but at least I can try, You are safe because you're the Son of God, but we shall lose our souls, No, if you decide to obey me, you will still be obeying God. The fringe of a red moon could be seen on the horizon of the remote wilderness. Speak, said Andrew, but Jesus waited until the entire moon, an enormous blood-red disc, had risen from the earth, and only then did he speak, telling them, The Son of God must die on the cross so that the will of the Father may be done, but if we were to replace him with an ordinary man, God would no longer be able to sacrifice His Son, Do you wish one of us to take your place, asked Peter, No, I myself will take the Son's place, For the love of God, explain yourself, An ordinary man, perhaps, but a man who was prepared to proclaim himself King of the Jews, to incite the people to depose Herod from his throne and expel the Romans from the land, and all I ask is that one of you go immediately to the Temple and say that I am this man and that if justice is swift perhaps God's justice will not have time to stay that of men, just as it did not stay the executioner's axe as he was about to behead John. Everyone was struck dumb but not for long, and soon there was an outcry of indignation, protest and disbelief. If you are the Son of God, then you must die as the son of God, a voice called out, Having eaten the bread you distributed, how could I now denounce you, wailed another, Surely someone destined to be King of the Universe won't wish to be King of the Jews, said one man, Death to anyone who dares to stir from here to denounce you, threatened another. At that moment the voice of Judas Iscariot rang out loud and clear above the din, I'll go if you like. The others grabbed him and were already drawing daggers from their tunics when Jesus ordered them, Leave him alone and do him no harm. He then rose and, embracing Judas, kissed him on both cheeks, Go, my hour is yours. Without saying a word, Judas Iscariot threw the hem of his mantle over one shoulder and, as if swallowed up by darkness, vanished into the night.

The Temple guards accompanied by Herod's soldiers came to arrest Jesus at first light. After surrounding the camp by stealth, a small detachment armed with swords and lances made a surprise attack, and the soldier in command called out, Where is this man who claims to be King of the Jews. He called a second time, Let the man who claims to be King of the Jews come forward, where-upon Jesus emerged from his tent accompanied by a tearful Mary Magdalene and he told them, I am King of the Jews. Going up to him, a soldier tied his hands while whispering in his ear, Although now my prisoner, were you to become my King, remember I was acting under orders from another, and should you ask me to arrest him I'll obey you as I'm now obeying him, and Jesus told him, A king does not arrest another king, a god does not kill another god, and that is why ordinary men were created so that arrests and killings might be left to them. They also tied a rope round Jesus's feet to prevent him from running away, and Jesus said to himself because convinced it was true, Too late, I've already taken flight. Just then Mary Magdalene let out a cry as if her heart were breaking and Jesus said, You will weep for me, and all you women will weep should such an hour befall these men or you yourselves, but know that for every tear you shed a thousand would be shed in future

335

were I not to die as is my will. And turning to the soldier in command, he asked of him, Release these men accompanying me for I am the King of the Jews, not they, and without further delay he stepped into the midst of the soldiers encircling him. The sun was up and hovering over the rooftops of Bethany when the multitude, with Jesus in front between two soldiers securing the ends of the rope tied round his wrists, began climbing the road to Jerusalem. Behind walked the disciples and their womenfolk, the men fuming, the women sobbing, but their tears and anger were to no avail, What are we to do, they asked themselves under their breath, should we turn on the soldiers and try to release Jesus, perhaps losing our lives in the struggle, or disperse before an order is also given for our arrest, and faced with this impossible dilemma they did nothing and continued trailing behind the retinue of soldiers from a distance. After a while, they saw that the procession had come to a halt and wondered if orders had been revoked for they were now untying the ropes round Jesus's hands and feet, but one would have to be naïve to imagine any such thing, and while some of them were simple souls, they were not so naïve. One knot, however, had come untied, that of Judas Iscariot's life, there on a fig tree at the side of the road where Jesus would pass. Dangling from a branch hung the disciple who had offered to carry out his master's last wish. The soldier leading the retinue ordered two soldiers to cut the cord and lower the corpse. He's still warm, observed one of the soldiers. Perhaps Judas Iscariot had been sitting on the branch of the fig tree with the noose already round his neck as he patiently waited for Jesus to appear in the distance before letting go of the branch, finally at peace with himself now that he had done his duty. Jesus drew near and the soldiers made no attempt to restrain him. He stood there, staring at Judas's face, twisted and deformed by sudden death. He's still warm, the soldier said a second time, and it occurred to Jesus that he might be able to do for Judas what he had failed to do for Lazarus, bring him back to life so that some other day in some other place he might have his own inevitable death, remote and obscure, instead of the haunting memory of betrayal. But, as we know, only the Son of God has the power to bring people back to life and not this King of the Jews who walks here, his spirit broken and his hands and feet bound. The soldier in command told his men, Leave the corpse there to be buried by the people of

Bethany unless the vultures devour it first, but check to see whether he is carrying any valuables. The soldiers searched but found nothing. Not a single coin, one of the soldiers confirmed, and little wonder, for the disciple in charge of the community's funds was Matthew who knew his job, having served as a tax-collector in the days when he was known as Levi. Didn't they pay him for his betrayal, asked Jesus, and Matthew who had overheard, replied, They wanted to, but he said he was in the habit of settling his accounts, and that's it, he won't be settling them any more. The procession advanced, while some of the disciples lingered behind staring pityingly at the corpse, but John said, Let's leave it here, he was not one of us, and the other Judas, also called Thaddaeus, hastened to correct him, Whether we like it or not, he will always be one of us, we may not know what to do with him, but he will go on being one of us. Let's move on, said Peter, this is no place for us, here at the feet of Judas Iscariot, You're right, replied Thomas, our place should be at Jesus's side, but it is empty.

They finally entered Jerusalem and Jesus was taken before the council of Elders, high priests and scribes. Delighted to see him there, the High Priest told him, I gave you fair warning but you refused to listen, your pride won't save you now and your lies will damn you, What lies, asked Jesus, First, that you are King of the Jews, But I am King of the Jews, And second, that you are the Son of God, Who told you that I claim to be the Son of God, Everyone says so, Pay no heed to them, I am King of the Jews, So you confess you're not the Son of God, How often do I have to tell you, I am King of the Jews, Be careful what you say, a lie like that is enough to have you sentenced, I stand by what I've said, Very well, you will appear before the Roman Prefect who is anxious to meet this man who wishes to depose him and wrest these territories from Caesar's power. From there, the soldiers escorted Jesus to Pilate's residence. The news had already spread that the man who claimed to be King of the Jews, who had thrashed the money-changers and set fire to their stalls, had been arrested and people rushed to see what a king looked like when led through the streets for all to see, his hands tied like a common thief, no matter whether he was a real king or simply an imposter. And, as always happens, since not everyone is alike in this world, there were some who took pity on Jesus, others who did not, some who said, Set the fellow free, he's

337

mad, while others believed that punishing a crime gives a warning to others, and there were as many of the latter as of the former. Mingling with the crowd the disciples felt somewhat disorientated. The women with them were easily recognized because of their tears, but one woman was not weeping, Mary Magdalene who grieved in silence.

There was no great distance between the house of the High Priest and the Prefect's palace, but Jesus thought he would never get there, not because of the intolerable hissing and jeering from the crowd expressing their disappointment with this sad figure of a king, but because anxious to keep his appointment with death, lest God should look this way and say, What's going on, are you backing out of our agreement. At the palace gates soldiers from Rome took charge of the prisoner, while Herod's soldiers and the Temple guards remained outside to await the verdict. Apart from a few priests no one was authorized to accompany Jesus within the palace. Seated on his throne, the Prefect, Pilate, for that was his name, looked at this man being led in, looking like a beggar, with a heavy beard and bare feet, his tunic soiled with stains both old and new, the latter of ripe fruits the gods had created to be eaten rather than to show hatred and leave a mark of ignominy. Standing before him, the prisoner waited, his head erect, his eyes looking into space and fixed on some proximate yet indefinable point between himself and the Prefect. Pilate only knew two kinds of culprit, those who lowered their eyes and those who stared in defiance, the former he despised, the latter always made him feel a little nervous, and he lost no time in passing sentence. But this man standing there seemed quite oblivious of his surroundings, and so self-assured that he might very well have been a royal personage, in fact and in law, who had been the victim of a lamentable misunderstanding and would soon have his crown, sceptre and mantle restored. Pilate finally decided that it might be more appropriate to include this prisoner in the second category and sentence him accordingly, so he began the interrogation without delay, What is your name, I'm called Jesus, son of Joseph and was born in Bethlehem of Judaea, but people know me as Jesus of Nazareth, having lived in Nazareth of Galilee. Who was your father, I've just told you, his name was Joseph. What was his trade, Carpenter, Then would you care to explain how a carpenter called Joseph came to father a king, Jesus,

338

If a king can beget sons who became carpenters, then why should a carpenter not father a son who became king. On hearing this, one of the priests intervened, Don't forget, Pilate, that this man also claims to be the Son of God, That isn't true, I simply claim to be the Son of Man, replied Jesus, but unconvinced, the priest continued, Don't let him deceive you, Pilate, in our religion the Son of Man and God are one and the same. Pilate made an indifferent gesture with his hand, If he were to go around proclaiming himself the son of Jupiter, bearing in mind that he would not be the first, then this case would be of some interest, but that he should or should not be the son of your god is a matter of no great importance, Then sentence him for claiming to be King of the Jews and we'll go away satisfied. It remains to be seen whether that would satisfy me, Pilate said sharply. Jesus patiently waited for their dialogue to end and the interrogation to begin. Who do you say you are, the Prefect asked Jesus, I am who I am, King of the Jews, And as King of the Jews what do you hope to gain, All that a king might expect, For example, to govern and protect his people, Protect them from what, From anything that may endanger them, Protect them from whom, From all who might oppose them, If I understand you rightly, you would defend against Rome, That is so, And in order to protect them, would you attack the Romans, There is no other way, And expel the Romans from these lands, One thing follows another, So, you're the enemy of Caesar, I am King of the Jews, Confess you're the enemy of Caesar, I am King of the Jews and refuse to say any more. The High Priest raised his hands to heaven in triumph, You see, Pilate, he confesses, and you cannot spare the life of someone who has publicly declared his enmity towards you and Caesar. Sighing with exasperation, Pilate rebuked the priest, Be quiet, then turning to Jesus, asked him, Have you anything more to say, Nothing, replied Jesus, Then I have no choice other than to sentence you, Do what you must, How would you prefer to die, I have already decided, How then, On the cross, Very well, you'll be crucified. Jesus's eyes sought out and finally confronted those of Pilate, Can I ask a favour, he asked, So long as it doesn't interfere with the sentence I've just passed, Would you put an inscription above my head saying who and what I am for all to see, Nothing else, Nothing else. Pilate beckoned a secretary who brought writing materials and in his own hand wrote, Jesus of Nazareth, King of the Jews. Roused from his complacency, the High Priest suddenly realized what was happening and protested, You mustn't write King of the Jews but Jesus of Nazareth who claimed to be King of the Jews. Feeling annoyed with himself, Pilate regretted not having dismissed the prisoner with a warning, for even the most wary of judges could see that this fellow was no threat to anyone let alone Caesar, and rounding on the High Priest, he told him dryly, Stop interfering, I have written what I have written. He signalled to the soldiers to remove the condemned man and requested water to wash his hands as was his wont after passing sentence.

They led Jesus away and took him to a hill known as Golgotha. Despite his strong constitution, his legs soon weakened under the weight of the cross and the centurion in command ordered a passer-by who had stopped to watch the procession to relieve the prisoner of his burden. The crowd continued to jeer and shout insults, but now and then someone would utter words of compassion. As for the disciples, they were walking around in a daze. A woman stopped Peter and challenged him, You were also with Jesus of Galilee, but he denied it, replying, I don't know what you're saying, and he tried to hide amidst the crowd only to meet the same woman a second time, and once more she asked him, Were you not with Jesus, and again Peter denied it with an oath, I do not know the man. And since three is the perfect number favoured by God, Peter was challenged a third time and for the third time cursed and swore, saying, I do not know the man. The women went up to Golgotha with Jesus, some on either side, and Mary Magdalene who keeps closest of all is not allowed to reach him because the soldiers push her away, just as they will make everyone keep their distance from the spot where three crosses have been erected, two already occupied by convicted men who yell and howl with pain, the third ready for occupation, standing tall and erect like a column supporting the heavens. Ordering Jesus to lie down, the soldiers extended his arms on the transom. As they hammered the first nail in, perforating the flesh of his wrist between two bones, sudden vertigo sent time into reverse, and Jesus felt the pain as his father had felt it before him, saw himself as he had seen him on the cross at Sepphoris. Then they drove a nail into his other wrist and he experienced that first tearing of stretched flesh as the soldiers started to hoist the transom in stages to the top of the cross, Jesus's entire weight suspended

340

from fragile bone, and it was almost a relief when they pushed his legs upwards and hammered another nail through his heels, now there is nothing more to be done except await death.

Jesus is slowly dying, dying, and life is ebbing from his body when suddenly the heavens overhead open wide and God appears in the same attire He wore in the boat, and His words resound throughout the earth, This is My beloved Son, in whom I am well pleased. Jesus then realized he had been brought here under false pretences, as the lamb is led to sacrifice and that his life had been planned for death since the very beginning. Remembering the river of blood and suffering that would flow from his side and flood the entire earth, he called out to the open sky where God could be seen smiling, Men, forgive Him, for He knows not what He has done. Then he began expiring in the midst of a dream. He found himself back in Nazareth and could see his father shrugging his shoulders and also smiling as he told him, Just as I cannot ask you all the questions, neither can you give me all the answers. There was still some life in him when he felt a sponge soaked in water and vinegar moisten his lips, and looking down he noticed a man walking away with a bucket and reed over his shoulder. But what he could not see lying on the ground was the black bowl into which his blood was dripping.

penguin.co.uk/vintage